Praise for

A ray of sunshine - a joyful book full of light and hope
Phillipa Ashley

If you're in need of a little lift, this feel-good book will make you warm and fuzzy all over *Fabulous*

Charming, cosy, candlelit romance all wrapped up in a gorgeous setting Veronica Henry

Brimming with seasonal secrets and festive feelgood - is Christmas even Christmas without Cathy Bramley?
Holly Hepburn

A gorgeously romantic comfort read Rachael Lucas

Filled with warmth and laughter Carole Matthews

A book full of warmth and kindness. I loved it
Sarah Morgan

A real treat. No-one does friendship better than Cathy
Karen Swan

Cathy Bramley is a British author of sixteen romance novels, and has sold almost two million copies worldwide. Her books have hit the UK best sellers' list and have been nominated for several awards including the British Book of the Year 2023.

Cathy has been a lover of stories since she was a small child and used to beg her mother to take her to the library every week for new books. Many of her passions have come and gone over the years, but her love for story, drama and romance will last a lifetime.

Cathy's favourite thing to do is to get comfy with a book in her lap, her dog, Pearl beside her and lose herself in a story. She loves the feel of a paperback, but is equally happy reading on a Kindle or iPad. She also listens to a lot of audiobooks, especially when driving. She reads a wide variety of novels, but there is a special place on her bookshelf for Marian Keyes, Maeve Binchy, Beth O'Leary and Emily Henry. Cathy didn't start writing until 2013, before that she ran a PR and Marketing agency for many years and loved hearing clients talk of how they started their businesses. Those stories must have stayed in her subconscious because she often writes about the sort of companies she used to work with. Her books are about people she would want to be friends with, characters her readers will cheer for. They are often about ordinary women doing extraordinary things.

Cathy has two grown up daughters and lives in a small village in countryside in the middle of England. Her house overlooks fields of barley in one direction and horses in the other, and the garden is full of fruit trees: damson; plum; pear and of course, Bramley apples!

You can keep up to date with Cathy Bramley's latest books on Instagram and X (formerly Twitter) as @CathyBramley and on Facebook as @ CathyBramleyAuthor

Cathy Bramley

A Merry Little Christmas

ORION

An Orion paperback

First published in Great Britain in 2024 by Orion Fiction,
an imprint of The Orion Publishing Group Ltd
Carmelite House, 50 Victoria Embankment,
London EC4Y 0DZ

An Hachette UK company

1 3 5 7 9 10 8 6 4 2

A CIP catalogue record for this book is
available from the British Library.

ISBN (Mass Market Paperback) 978 1 3987 1 3895
ISBN (eBook) 978 1 3987 1 3901

Typeset by Born Group
Printed and bound in Great Britain by Clays Ltd, Elcograf S.p.A.

www.orionbooks.co.uk

For Roger, for putting up with me when I was a stroppy teenager and for being the very best Grandad to the girls

Prologue

April

Nell held her phone, watching as the timer dragged its way towards zero; how could three short minutes feel like a lifetime? Perched on the edge of the bath with the door firmly closed, her heart was racing. Her gaze shifted to the pregnancy test in her other hand, turned face down so that she wouldn't look at the result until the three minutes were up.

Please, please, please be positive this time.

Oh, how she hoped that April would be the month when she'd cry happy tears instead of the other kind. She'd shout for Olek and the two of them would dance around the bathroom, eyes alight, talking over each other about how exciting it was, how wonderful it was going to be to have a child together. She'd show him how to work out her due date (even though she'd been keeping a mental note as to when the soonest she'd be a mum could be – January, currently) and they'd make an appointment with the doctor to have her pregnancy confirmed.

Officially, she and Olek had only just started trying for a baby. But, secretly, Nell had been a bit *que sera, sera* with her birth control tablets for a long time. She hadn't even told her best friend, Merry, which was unheard of, because she normally never kept anything from her.

Nor was it like her not to be honest with Olek. It hadn't been done with malicious intent, more that she'd had a niggling doubt about her abilities to conceive these days. At thirty-six, there had been so many times over the years when she'd been careless and could easily have got pregnant by accident but hadn't. Not since . . . She swiftly halted her thought processes and tucked that particular memory back into the dark corner of her mind where it had remained blissfully undisturbed for years.

Besides, she knew that Olek would have been happy even if she'd had a surprise pregnancy. He was already a devoted dad to sixteen-year-old Max and missed him when he was with his mother. And besides, Olek was happy when Nell was happy, and vice versa.

She and Olek had a wonderful marriage, she knew how lucky she was to be loved by him. And if she could be a mum, if they could have a child of their own to love, well, her life would be complete. But the months had ticked by without a pregnancy, confirming Nell's fears. She'd wanted to know what was going on with her body and the only way that was going to happen was to talk to Olek about it.

The timer on her phone was down to the last thirty seconds, but she still didn't peek, wanting to give the test the full three minutes to work. At least the delay in her pregnancy plans meant that by January, she'd have been a partner at Merry and Bright, Merry's candle business, for a whole year. So she wouldn't feel too bad about taking some maternity leave. Unless, of course, Merry got pregnant at the same time, that might be a bit tricky.

Nell's face softened into a smile. The two best friends, now business partners, were on the same motherhood journey and trying for a family. It would be crazy and chaotic if they both had babies next year, but what fun too. Their babies would be best friends from birth, she and Merry could do all the baby classes together and the bond between the two women would grow even stronger as they entered a new era at the same time.

The timer went off in Nell's hand, making her jump. With her heart in her mouth, she turned off the ringer, took a deep breath and flipped over the test stick.

Negative. Damn.

Of course it was. Just like every other month.

The disappointment was almost physical. A heavy curtain of sadness fell over her and she felt her shoulders start to shake.

'Darling?' Olek called, his Polish accent somehow imbuing that one word with extra love. He knocked softly on the bathroom door. 'Are you OK?'

Her heart twisted. He was so thoughtful, avoiding asking the burning question of whether the test was positive or not, merely asking how she was, instinctively putting her first, over his eagerness to know the outcome.

'Come in,' she replied. At least that was what she tried to say; her voice was strangled with sorrow.

Olek opened the door and knelt beside her, wrapping her in his love, his strong arms taking the place of words. Still clutching the negative test in her hand, she leaned into him and allowed the tears to fall.

'No baby,' she said, with a sad smile. 'Not this time.'

'Oh, sweetheart.' Olek kissed the tears from her cheeks and kissed her. 'Don't be sad. It's completely normal for it to take a few months and we've only just started trying.'

Except that they hadn't, thought Nell guiltily. She'd done the research; most couples conceived within a year. It had been longer than that. Plus, her age was starting to work against her.

She leaned her forehead against his. 'If I don't get pregnant next month, can we go and have some tests done to see if there's a problem?'

Olek pulled back from her, brushing her auburn curls off her face. 'How about waiting six months? Give it some time. And then I promise to do anything you ask.' He kissed her again. 'But I'm sure there won't be anything wrong.'

It wasn't as fast as she'd have liked, but it was a step forward. With every passing month, she became more convinced that she wasn't ever going to conceive. It was bad enough having a hunch, but how she'd be able to cope when a doctor confirmed that she was the problem, she had no idea.

'I hope you're right, my love.' She accepted a tissue from him and dried her eyes. 'I really do.'

★

Merry was itching to get a move on, but Cole, in true Cole fashion, was being extremely methodical.

'I bought three types,' he said, carefully unpacking the first from its box and smoothing the accompanying leaflet to remove the folds. 'This is my preferred starting point. Apparently, it's ninety-nine per cent accurate and has the best reviews on Google.'

'Trust you, Mr Belt and Braces. Just pass it to me and let me get on with it.' She took it out of her husband's hands and suppressed a giggle. She'd have just picked the cheapest, or the one which gave the quickest result. They had such a different approach to life; where Merry was always racing from one thing to another making snap decisions as she went, Cole was calm and considered, but despite their differences, as a couple, they just worked.

'I haven't read the instructions yet,' he complained. 'We need to do this properly, it's important.'

She looked at him now, an earnest frown on his handsome face, one hand ruffling his russet-brown hair distractedly, and felt a wave of love so strong that, for a second, she forgot why they were both squashed into the tiny bathroom at Holly Cottage.

'It is important.' She wriggled out of her jeans and sat down on the loo. 'But I'm dying for a wee, and everyone knows all you need to do is pee on the stick.'

He grinned at her. 'Never change, Mrs Robinson. I'm sure you're right.'

She gave him a prim look. 'Excuse me, Mr Robinson, can't a girl have a little privacy while she's indisposed?'

'You didn't give me a chance!' he blustered, turning away.

'Too late, my work here is done,' she said with a snort, holding up the stick. 'Ta-dah.'

'Now we wait.' He tore off some tissue paper for her to lay the pregnancy test onto, covered it over so they couldn't see the results window and set a timer on his watch for three minutes while she washed and dried her hands. 'Come here.'

He held his arm out to her, and she snuggled into him, resting her head under his chin, listening to the steady beat of his heart and wishing she was as calm.

Despite her laughter and impatience, deep down, Merry was a bag of nerves. She had wanted a baby for as long as she could remember. At school when other girls had been dreaming of going to university and having careers and travelling the world, her biggest wish was to start a family, a baby to love, her own flesh and blood to make up for growing up without a family. Last Christmas, she'd discovered that not only was her father alive, but that she had a half-sister, Emily, so she wasn't without family anymore. Even so, the chance to be a mother to her and Cole's child would be a dream come true.

Her childhood had been unconventional, to say the least. Her mum had been living rough before having her at seventeen, and while she had happy memories of being in their little bedsit, those memories had been overshadowed by her mum's suicide when Merry was only eleven. Her experience of a mother-child bond was sketchy at best. But Cole was a good dad to Freya and Harley. She could learn from him, couldn't she?

The timer on Cole's watch went off. He stopped the beeping and gave her a squeeze.

'Ready to find out?' he placed a soft kiss on her lips.

She nodded, swallowing the lump in her throat. 'Ready.'

He pushed aside the tissue paper and they both leaned forward to read the word which had appeared in the window.

'Pregnant!' they exclaimed together.

'I don't believe it,' Merry gasped.

Instinctively, she pressed a hand to her stomach. It would be months before anything was noticeable, but her baby – *their* baby – was already living and growing and moving around inside her. And then suddenly she was in the air as Cole picked her up and swung her around.

'You'd better believe it!' Cole cried triumphantly. 'Because we're having a baby! You clever, clever girl.'

Merry laughed at his exuberance, clinging on tightly around his neck. 'I think you might have had a part in it too.'

He set her down gently and kissed her. 'I did. And you've just made me the happiest man on the planet. I love you, darling, and I promise to be the husband and the dad that you and our baby deserve.'

'I know you will,' she replied, 'because you already are.'

A wave of emotion enveloped her and it was all she could do to stay on her feet. Excitement and gratitude, but something else too, a sense of peace that she'd been searching for her whole life.

She was married to the most wonderful man she could wish for, had two stepchildren she adored and now she was pregnant with a baby of her own. All she had ever wanted was within her grasp, and her future could not have looked rosier.

Chapter 1

Merry

Giant Christmas tree: check.

The market square festooned with fairy lights: check.

Wizzard singing that they wished it could be Christmas every day from speakers blasting out from the stage: check.

Standing in a crowd in the cold and dark with almost all of her loved ones, wearing a Christmas jumper: check.

Merry Robinson smiled to herself. It was official, it was the first of December and the countdown to the annual Christmas lights switch-on in her home town was about to begin.

'Are we ready to get this party started, Wetherley?' cried this year's celebrity a little too loudly into the microphone from the stage.

'Yes!' roared the crowd of excited residents, all of whom were wrapped in thick layers to combat the biting Derbyshire air. The night sky was clear, stars were out in their legions, and while incredibly pretty, it was bitterly cold. Merry was glad that Freya had insisted they all wear Christmas hats and jumpers. Her sister-in-law, Hester, and Hester's husband, Paul, had brought hot mulled wine to warm them up, but at almost eight months pregnant, Merry would be having an alcohol-free Christmas this year and had opted for the hot chocolate Olek had supplied.

As had Nell, who wasn't pregnant but wanted to be. Merry studied her best friend's face, noticing the dark circles under her eyes. Nell was almost evangelical in her determination not to let her own situation take the shine off Merry's pregnancy, and it broke Merry's heart to see it. If she could have one wish this Christmas it would be for Nell and Olek to conceive. Life could be very unfair sometimes.

'OK?' Merry asked Nell, tucking an arm through hers.

'A bit nervous,' Nell replied. 'We get our test results tomorrow.'

'I'll keep everything crossed for you,' she promised.

Nell glanced sideways at her husband. 'It's pretty obvious who's the one with the problem, seeing as he's already got a son, and I hate to be letting the side down. But at least once we know what we're dealing with, we can move forward and make a plan.'

'You don't know anything yet. But if anyone can work it out, it's you two,' said Merry. 'You've been such an inspirational couple to me since the day you met. You'll deal with this together, just like always.'

'Thank you, you're a good friend, and I hope so.' Nell chewed her lip nervously.

'I know so,' Merry said firmly.

'Who is that woman again?' Ten-year-old Freya tugged on her granddad's sleeve. 'I don't think she's a celebrity at all.'

She'd cut her hair on her birthday to mark reaching double digits. Gone were the plaits and the pink clothes. Now she wore her hair short, her jeans baggy and her boots chunky. Cole confessed to Merry that he missed his sunny little girl, but Merry was secretly impressed with this new confident young lady who wasn't afraid to try out a new look.

'Suzannah Merryweather,' Fred supplied, picking up his little dog, Otto, who'd started to tremble in the cold despite being dressed in a fleecy elf outfit. 'Presenter of a gardening TV show.'

Freya was unimpressed and went back to her hot chocolate.

'They should have asked you, Auntie Hester,' said Harley. At fourteen, he was already taller than Merry and liked to boast to Cole that it wouldn't be long before he outgrew his dad too. He'd agreed to wear one of his dad's Christmas jumpers but was keeping his coat zipped right up to the neck and the white furry pom-pom on the end of his Santa hat was just visible, peeping out of his coat pocket.

'I did it two years ago, darling, remember, when you were in Whistler?' Hester held out her mug to her husband Paul, who was topping up the mulled wine.

'Oh yeah, Dad sent us photos,' he replied with a grin.

Merry watched Harley while, presumably, the memories of his year in Canada ran through his head. He'd had a tough time readjusting to life in the UK, but now seemed to be thriving. A Saturday job working at Merry and Bright, a very sweet girlfriend and singing in a band with his mates all seemed to have helped him find his feet.

'And we've kept our Christmas plans low-key this year because of our trip to Australia,' added Paul.

'In two days!' Hester squeezed his arm excitedly.

Cole was envious of his sister and brother-in-law's month-long road trip around Australia. But it wasn't for Merry – barbecues on the beach didn't appeal; for her, Christmas was about traditions and home and being with her loved ones.

'You wore a red cape,' said Nell to Hester. 'And I completely fan-girled over you.'

Everyone started talking about their memories from previous Christmas lights switch-ons until Suzannah's voice rang out from the stage again.

'Ten, nine, eight . . .' she chanted, gesturing for everyone to join in with her.

And as she lifted her hands to hover dramatically over the big button, everyone did.

Everyone except Merry. From nowhere, a lump appeared in her throat, preventing any words from passing her lips as her emotions overwhelmed her. Christmas always did this to her. But this year, there were more factors at play: the baby would be here soon; they still didn't have a moving-in date for the new house; the busiest few weeks of the retail calendar were upon her; she was worried about her best friend's fertility problems; and she had swollen ankles and a husband approximately a thousand miles away.

'Three, two, one . . . Merry Christmas, everyone!' Suzannah cried, putting all her weight onto the button.

Instantly, the tall Norwegian spruce which towered over the square sparkled into colourful life, illuminating the giant star at the top and every single one of the glittering baubles hanging from the branches. At the same time, the Christmas decorations strung around the perimeter of the square came on and the people of Wetherley cheered and whistled.

'Wow!' Freya clapped her hands. 'That was magic. Everywhere is so beautiful.'

'Technically speaking, it's electricity,' her brother corrected her. 'Not magic.'

Freya stuck her tongue out and Merry hid her amusement. Harley loved to display his superior knowledge where his sister was concerned. 'I think Christmas lights are magical too, Freya.'

This event was always popular, signalling as it did the start of the festive season, and Merry wouldn't have skipped it for the world. Cole had been disappointed not to be there, and she was missing him very much. Hopefully, next year, the whole family would be here together, her half-sister Emily and Emily's boyfriend, Will, too.

Merry, having never known her father's name or whereabouts after her mother's suicide, had assumed that she didn't have any living relatives. When Emily had got in touch last year with her suspicions that they might possibly be related, Merry had been overjoyed. She'd gained a much-loved younger sister, whom she was now close to, despite Emily living in Jersey, and the father she had always wondered about. He suffered with dementia, which had worsened this year, but he was her sole source of information about her mother. Every so often, he'd come out with a tiny snippet about the young woman he'd been in love with and whom Merry had had so briefly in her life. And when he did, she felt as if she was discovering priceless treasure every time.

The thought of all being together warmed her. She slipped a hand inside her coat and felt her bump.

Less than seven weeks until you're due, little one. My life has changed so much in the last two years, and once you arrive, it'll change all over again. I hope . . . well, I hope I'm up to the job, that's all.

What sort of mother would she be? She wanted to be laid-back and fluster-free, but she had a sneaking suspicion that she might be the sort to be perpetually on the phone to the doctors' surgery, needing constant reassurance that all was well, holding her face to the baby's to check it was still breathing, fretting that she was making a bad job of it all.

She felt a tap on her arm and turned to see Fred beside her, looking concerned.

'OK, love?' he asked.

She blinked back any telltale tears and mustered up a smile for her beloved father-in-law.

'Absolutely fine!' She pulled her hand out from her coat and reached to stroke Otto's curly head. 'Wish Cole was here.'

'Hmm,' Fred grunted, 'so do I. He shouldn't be gadding about overseas, not with you in this condition.'

Merry suppressed her amusement. Fred's objection was mostly down to the fact that his partner, Astrid, was also 'gadding about' with Cole, in Germany. Astrid had recently inherited a *Bauernhof* – a small farmhouse with land attached – from a distant cousin of her father's. The letter from the Bavarian solicitor had come so completely out of the blue that Astrid had ignored it, assuming it to be a scam, but after two more had followed, she'd called the office and was told that she had an inheritance in her home town of Schongau, an hour south-west of Munich. It had taken a while for everything to be registered in Astrid's name and now that it was, she had absolutely no idea what she was going to do with it. Cole had suggested that they go over there together and he'd give her the benefit of his two decades of construction experience and help her decide.

'Cole's working, remember,' she pointed out. 'And Astrid's reason for going is valid too. Also, I'm not ill, I'm pregnant.'

'I don't know why she doesn't just sell it,' Fred grumbled to himself. 'Wetherley is her home now. Take the money and enjoy it, I say.'

Merry was inclined to agree. She was proud of Cole for offering to advise her oldest friend and mentor, but the timing couldn't be worse. His own building company was as busy as ever and he was project managing the renovation of their new house, which – as far as Merry was concerned – should be his top priority.

'Dad was always working when we were little,' said Harley. 'He said he regrets that now. So, don't worry, Merry, I think he'll be around more for this child.'

Merry marvelled at how mature he was these days. 'Good to know, but I'm not worried. He's already a great dad, you two are great kids.' She nudged him playfully. 'Most of the time.'

'I think it's a boy,' Freya said sagely. 'My teacher had a baby boy, and she was always grumpy too.'

Nell gave a snort. 'Out of the mouths of babes.'

'I'm not always grumpy, am I?' Merry asked, mildly offended.

'Not always. But you do this a lot.' Freya rolled her eyes comically and let out a huff of exasperation.

'And you swore at work on Saturday,' Harley said slyly under his breath.

Merry feigned a gasp. 'Only a tiny one, and in my defence, I was provoked.' A customer had entered the shop with three dogs, one of which had cocked its leg against the counter. Not the ideal aroma for a scented candle shop, and bending down to clean it up had not been the ideal job for Merry now that her body resembled a bowling ball.

Harley grinned. 'Your secret's safe with me. I might be looking for a pay rise soon, though. If you get my drift.'

'Cheeky,' Merry muttered. Not a bad idea actually; it was coming up to twelve months since he'd started working for them, and he was a big help. He'd be needed even more once the baby came, and she didn't want to lose him to a better-paid job. She made a mental note to chat to Nell about it; they made staffing decisions together.

'I thought Ray was coming this evening?' Hester said.

Merry winced. 'Dad's got a nasty cough. I popped round to see him in the home earlier. His carer and I agreed it wasn't a good idea for him to be out in the cold.'

'And you don't want to be exposed to any germs either,' Nell put in. 'The last thing you need is to catch something.'

'Quite,' she agreed. 'There's too much to do, I haven't got time to be ill.'

This time last year, she'd been planning their last-minute wedding. The year before that, she'd taken on the organisation of the town's Christmas celebrations. She'd hoped that this year would be quieter, but, if anything, life was even busier, especially now her sister was living in Jersey and Merry was the main contact for their father's care home. His dementia had worsened over the last couple of months; the last two times she'd seen him, he hadn't known who she was. If she thought about everything too much, she could literally feel her blood pressure spiking.

'I'm going to take some photos to send Dad,' said Harley, 'like he did for us when we were in Whistler.'

'FaceTime him!' said Freya excitedly, waving her mug of hot chocolate precariously. 'Then I can tell him about the magic lights.'

Harley pulled out his phone and the two of them bent over it while he called Cole.

'When are the property tycoons back in the country?' Hester asked.

'Two more sleeps,' Merry told her.

'Thank goodness,' Fred said wistfully. 'Otto misses Astrid like mad. He sits in her place on the sofa and whines all through the six-o'clock evening news.'

Merry, Nell and Hester exchanged looks. The dog wasn't the only one pining for Astrid. They might be in their seventies, but there was no mistaking how in love Fred and Astrid were. Love knew nothing about age, thought Merry; the colour of its flame may change over time, but its power to warm hearts never did.

'Hey, Dad,' Harley shouted, holding the phone high above his sister's reach. 'Thought you'd like to see the Christmas lights.'

Merry strained to see Cole, but the image of him on Harley's screen was too small from where she was standing. 'Hello, darling,' she called, waving a hand in case he could see her.

'Let me see him!' Freya jumped up to grab the phone. 'Dad, the tree's got a massive star on the top. Can we have one like that?'

'Just wait a minute,' Harley grumbled, blocking her with his arm.

Freya leapt up again and this time stumbled back into Merry, knocking into Merry. It didn't hurt, but all the same, Merry's arm flew to her stomach protectively.

'Careful, darling,' Hester chided. 'You need to be gentle with Merry now, especially her tummy.'

'Oh dear,' said Merry as a warm sensation soaked through her maternity jeans. 'You didn't hurt me, but I think you just spilled your hot chocolate on me.'

'Sorry about bumping you. But it wasn't my drink, I'd finished it all.' Freya looked round at her and giggled. 'Oops. It looks like you've wet yourself.'

'But you must have done . . .' Merry reached a hand to the top of her legs and froze. For a second, her mind went blank, until a shudder of dread ran through her. 'Oh no.'

Nell and Hester picked up on her reaction straight away.

'What's happened?' Nell asked, grabbing her arm.

'Could that be what I think it is?' Hester's eyes were wide.

Merry's heart thudded. 'I don't know. Possibly?'

'Dad!' Freya pulled Harley's arm towards her to get closer to his phone. 'Merry's weed!'

'Stop yanking me, you idiot,' Harley said with a scowl.

'At the risk of stating the obvious,' Fred cleared his throat, 'I think your waters may have broken, my dear.'

'I'm not even thirty-four weeks.' Merry could feel a sob forming in her throat. 'It's too early.'

'What's happening?' She heard Cole's alarmed voice in the distance. 'Merry?'

'Harley, may I?' Paul reached for the phone and Harley surrendered it straight away. 'Cole, looks as if you might need to come home, pronto, mate. We've got a situation here.'

Merry felt hot and panicky as everyone started talking at her, asking questions, making suggestions, and her head began to spin. She gripped Nell's hand tightly; Hester took her other arm as her knees went weak beneath her. Suddenly, Cole's face appeared in front of her as Paul held the phone out.

'Darling, I'll be there as soon as I can.' His brown eyes were huge with worry.

'I'm scared,' she whispered. 'I wish you were here.'

Why was this happening now? She hadn't had any contractions, no warning signs.

'I'm packing now, and I'll be on the first flight,' he promised.

'Me too,' Astrid piped up somewhere in the background.

'I love you,' said Cole.

'I love you too. Please hurry.' Merry's lip trembled before the screen went blank.

Olek put a hand on her back. 'I think we should take you to the hospital.'

'Agreed,' said Nell.

'We'll take the children back with us,' Hester offered. 'Come on, kids.'

'Oh crikey,' said Fred, shaking his head. 'I feel helpless.'

'Snap,' said Merry, tears trickling down her face. 'If the baby's coming, I don't suppose there's anything I can do about it.'

'Is this my fault?' Freya said in a small voice. 'Because I knocked into you?'

'No, darling, there's no need to worry, I promise,' Merry replied with as much conviction as she could muster.

'Let's go.' Nell's voice was firm. 'We need to get you to a doctor and see what's going on.'

Merry nodded, unable to speak for the second time this evening. This was not how she'd planned it. She wasn't ready to be a mother. Not tonight. Not yet.

Chapter 2

Merry

'PPROM?' Merry repeated the acronym back to the doctor who was standing beside her bed, jotting notes on her records.

'Preterm prelabour rupture of membranes,' the doctor explained, dropping the clipboard on the bed beside Merry's feet. 'It's the term we use when waters break before thirty-seven weeks of pregnancy and the mother hasn't gone into labour.'

It was 9 a.m. and she'd spent her first ever night in hospital. It had felt interminable. Thankfully, Nell had had a phone charger in her bag yesterday, so at least Merry had been able to catch up with the shop's social media activity and online orders while she'd been stuck on the ward all night.

Nell had also popped down to the hospital shop last night and picked up some emergency toiletries, while Olek had distracted Merry with stories of his son's birth, which apparently had been so swift that his first wife hadn't even had time for pain relief. She'd been glad when Nell had returned to save her from a detailed description of baby Max's first bowel movement. The couple had left once it had been established that there was no imminent danger of Merry giving birth, but despite being shattered, Merry had barely slept. Now all she wanted was to be told she could go home and have a bath and that there was absolutely nothing to worry about.

Judging by the serious expression on Dr Hill's face, that was looking unlikely.

Merry had had a few pains last night which she'd thought might be the start of her contractions, but they'd disappeared and the nurse who'd looked after her had been confident that all she'd felt were Braxton Hicks.

'Is that bad?' Merry asked the doctor, making a mental note to google it on her phone as soon as he'd gone.

'Not ideal and not without risks, but with conservative management, all should be well.'

She'd prefer something a bit more concrete than that, but before she had a chance to probe any further, Dr Hill attached a blood pressure cuff to her arm and indicated to her to stay quiet. He inflated it so much that she was almost at the point of complaint when he finally released the air, frowning as he listened to the whoosh of her blood through his stethoscope.

'*Should* be well?' she queried, once she deemed it safe to speak.

'As long as you look after yourself and don't do anything silly.'

'I'll cancel my ice-skating lessons immediately,' Merry replied.

The doctor looked sternly at her over his glasses. 'I assume that was a joke, but in my job, you get used to taking nothing for granted. Sex is off the menu too.'

Merry pressed her lips together to prevent herself from saying she'd been banking on that to kick-start labour. Someone in her antenatal class had said it had worked for her with her first baby. 'What does "conservative management" mean?'

He took the stethoscope from his ears. 'We watch and wait.'

Merry let out a breath. 'Good. I can do that. So I can go home?'

'Not yet.' He shook his head gravely. 'Your blood pressure is high. I'm going to keep you in for a day or so. I'd like to monitor you and, judging from the way you've refreshed your emails several times since I've been talking to you, I suspect you could do with forty-eight hours of complete rest.'

For a fleeting moment, the idea of lying down for two days with nothing to do except say yes to tea and toast, brought in bed to her like this morning, was very appealing. But there was no way she could agree to that; she had far too much else on her plate besides complimentary toast.

'I'm afraid that won't be possible,' she said, pulling herself upright.

The doctor raised his eyebrows. 'It is possible, and most certainly preferable to the alternative.'

'Thank you, yes, I can see her.' Cole's voice floated to her from the entrance of the ward.

Merry spotted him at the nurses' station and her heart squeezed with a mix of joy and relief at the sight of him. Thank goodness he was home.

'*Guten Tag*.' She waved sheepishly to him as he strode towards her bed.

'Good morning, Mrs Robinson, and good morning, doctor, please excuse me while I kiss my wife.'

He kissed her lips tenderly and stroked her cheek with the pad of his thumb. His hair was tousled, and he smelled of cold morning air and toothpaste, and Merry felt a rush of love for her handsome husband.

His eyes scanned hers and he touched a hand lightly to her baby bump. 'How are you? Are you very uncomfortable? Do you know what's going to happen next?'

'Fine, not too bad,' Merry replied, counting her responses with her fingers, 'and the doctor was just telling me that we don't need to do anything.'

Dr Hill reprised his stern look, but, thankfully, Cole missed it.

'I'm so sorry I wasn't with you last night,' he murmured. 'We were lucky to get the last two seats on this morning's flight. Dad came to the airport to collect Astrid, so I could come straight to the hospital.'

'It couldn't be helped, and Nell and Olek looked after me.'

Merry reached up to put her arms around his neck and he gave a soft groan as he enveloped her with a hug – a long hug which went on so long that she started to giggle.

'Sorry about my husband's protracted greeting,' she said, addressing the doctor when Cole finally released her. 'We haven't seen each other for five days.'

'No apology necessary,' the doctor said, smoothing his wiry moustache with his forefinger and thumb. 'The longer the hug, the better. If I could prescribe hugging on the NHS, I would. Your body is now releasing a hormone called oxytocin, which will help to lower your blood pressure.'

Cole frowned. 'Is her blood pressure too high?'

'It's nothing to worry about,' Merry answered hurriedly. 'I feel fine now. The baby isn't coming early, which was my big worry, and I'm really ready to go.'

'I know you are,' said the doctor. 'There's no better place than home, but I'm afraid you're going to have to put up with Hotel NHS for a bit longer.'

'Why, is there a problem?' Cole stiffened, gripping Merry's hand.

'Seriously, doctor, I'll be fine at home. I can watch and wait there.' As much as she was delighted about Cole's arrival, she would have preferred him not to hear what the doctor had to say so that she could cherry-pick what she wanted him to know. He was such a worrier.

'Watch and wait for what?' Cole asked, wide-eyed, proving her point.

'Just for baby Robinson to arrive,' she answered. 'No big deal.'

Dr Hill let out a barely audible sigh. 'Now that your waters have broken, you're at a greater risk, not only of infection, but also of going into labour. Have you got a busy week planned?'

'Um . . .' Merry chewed her lip, wondering how honest on a scale of one to ten she should be.

Cole laughed. 'My wife lives every day as if it's her last, she has a never-ending to-do list, which gets longer as the day progresses.'

'Cancel everything except the essentials for the next few weeks,' said Dr Hill. 'Doctor's orders.'

'Everything is essential.' Merry was full of indignation.

'Nothing is more important than the health of you and your baby,' the doctor replied. 'You have just over three weeks until your baby will be deemed full term, at which point you will be induced. I make that the . . .'

'Twenty-eighth of December,' Cole supplied.

'I'll have to be induced?' The thought that it would all happen to a timetable was quite disappointing.

'Wouldn't that be marvellous timing?' said the doctor. 'A birthday to celebrate in future in the boring bit between Christmas and New Year. The family will thank you for it.'

'Um.' Merry had been planning on spending those few days getting the nursery ready for the baby's arrival. She simply didn't have a spare moment before then. 'I suppose so.'

'Right then. I'll be back tomorrow morning. Don't do anything daft for the next twenty-four hours and, with any luck, I'll discuss discharging you in the afternoon.'

The doctor reattached the clipboard to the end of her bed and moved to the next patient.

'We've got four candle workshops this month,' Merry exhaled in frustration. 'We've got a festive shopping night on the thirteenth. Our free gift-wrapping service has just kicked in and the flat needs an overhaul in case we get any last-minute Airbnb bookings over Christmas. Plus, there is all our Christmas shopping to do.'

'Hmm.' Cole took her hand and kissed it.

'Are you listening?'

'Sort of, I'm also gazing adoringly into your eyes.'

'Cole!' Merry said, frustrated. 'This is a disaster.'

He smiled fondly. 'No it isn't. A disaster would have been if the baby had arrived early last night, partly because it would be premature, which might have brought its own problems, but also because I wouldn't have been there with you to see the birth of our child and for you to squeeze the living daylights out of my hand while you were in labour.'

'I suppose so,' she conceded. 'And at least now we've got a deadline to move into the new house by. We have to be settled by the twenty-eighth, so that when baby and I come out of hospital, we can go straight to the new house.'

He stared at her in disbelief. 'Darling, it can't be done. The doc just said you need to cancel as much as possible. We'll have Christmas at Holly Cottage like last year and postpone moving in until the end of January.'

'No, Cole.' Her heart began to race. 'The baby doesn't have its own bedroom at the cottage.'

'I know.' He smiled fondly. 'But newborn babies don't need a nursery. He or she could sleep in a drawer if necessary.'

'What?' Merry couldn't believe what she was hearing.

'We'd pull the drawer out of the chest, obviously. I mean, I'm sure there are rules about shutting babies in a chest of drawers,' he teased, clearly not picking up on her distress.

Merry's jaw tightened. 'This isn't funny. You promised me we'd be in before the baby came. We have to be in, I mean it. I'll sleep on the floor if I have to, but when I leave hospital with our new baby, I'm going straight to our forever home. And that's that.'

The smile slid from his face. 'I know you had your heart set on moving in before the baby arrived, but I'm sorry, it can't be done.'

'You've never known what it's like not to have a home. I have.' She pushed the bed sheets off her lap and swung her legs round, ready to stand up. 'All my life I've sworn to myself that when I have my own family, I'll do it differently. My baby is not going to sleep in a drawer. It's going to sleep in the beautiful cot we bought, which is currently still flat-packed and in its box in the hall, along with all the other equipment we haven't got room for.'

Merry didn't have many memories from her childhood, but she did know that her mum had been allocated emergency housing in a small studio flat after giving birth to her. Having a stable home and a family had been Merry's goal ever since she could remember. Her eyes swam with tears. Now, when her dream was so close, why was it slipping away from her? All she wanted was a welcoming home to bring her first child into, was that so much to ask?

'Darling.' Cole rested his hands on Merry's shoulders. 'You heard what the doctor said, you're in danger of going into labour if you're not careful. If you aren't going to be sensible, I'm afraid I will be. Leave everything to do with Christmas to me and delegate everything to do with Merry and Bright to Nell.'

Merry hesitated before nodding. As much as she loved and trusted Cole – and Nell, for that matter – when you'd been deserted by those who should have looked after you during childhood, it became very difficult to let down your guard later in life. Cole's upbringing had been the absolute opposite of Merry's: an idyllic childhood supported by two adoring parents. No wonder he didn't understand how important this house move was to her.

Merry's life was spinning out of control, and right now, she had never felt more vulnerable.

Chapter 3

Nell

'Help yourself to a drink from the machine,' said the receptionist, after checking her in.

There were distinct advantages in seeing a private doctor, Nell thought, as she sat down in a squishy leather armchair with a fresh cup of decaf coffee in her hand. Not that she didn't love the GP surgery in Wetherley where she'd been going for years, knew all the reception team and exactly which chair to avoid with its wobbly leg. They'd only gone private because she and Olek wouldn't be entitled to fertility investigation on the NHS until they'd been unsuccessful in conceiving for two years and Nell hadn't wanted to wait that long. Dr Bajek was Polish and Olek's family had known hers for years, and there was something comforting about embarking on such a personal journey with someone they had implicit trust in.

If the issue was on her side, she'd do anything the doctor suggested, she vowed: give up alcohol forever, do yoga every morning, cut out caffeine. Anything. She crossed her legs and pressed them together to stop them jiggling with nerves. She wouldn't get despondent, this was just the beginning. There'd probably be a magic fertility pill she could take to solve all the problems. Or IVF, if Olek agreed. She had money in the bank from the sale of her market stall last year; she'd gladly use all of it. She'd wanted to pay off a chunk of the mortgage with it at the time, but Olek had said she should keep it in case it didn't work out at Merry and Bright and she decided to set up another business. She'd loved him for the suggestion, but, in truth, she had no interest in that. Her focus on becoming a mother was pin-sharp at the moment, eclipsing any career aspirations. She didn't feel guilty about that; female empowerment should be about having the choice to do what felt right for you and not being obliged to fit a mould defined by someone else.

As she sipped her coffee, her phone pinged with a message. It would be Merry, she knew without even looking. There was a woman whose work/life balance needed a bit of tinkering with. What Merry could use was some rest, at least while she was in hospital. But, instead, her brain was working overtime. Nell read over her best friend's latest thought.

I thought we could have a little January sale after Christmas, what do you think? We could clear all the stock with festive names and make room for all the new-year stuff. If we've got any gift wrap left, we can sell that off at bargain prices too.

Nell had to admit, that was a good idea and sent her a reply.

Good thinking! Tell you what, I'll bring in a notebook and pen later and you can make a list of the things you think of, rather than text me with each idea.

Lol!! Am I getting on your nerves?

Noooooo – only slightly ;)

Sorry, I'm just itching to get out of here!

Merry was like a bottle of pop today. Nell understood; her friend was feeling like the birth of the baby was a ticking time bomb: one false move on her part and . . . boom, she'd go into labour. She sighed wistfully; if it was her, she'd want the baby to arrive as soon as possible so she could meet her child, hold her own baby in her arms and feel her heart melt with love. She was fairly sure that work would be the last thing on her mind.

It was hard not to feel envious of Merry, especially watching her stomach swell over the last few months, from the tiny bump you'd only notice if you were looking for it, to the almost comic spherical belly she had now. And it wasn't just her shape that had changed. While Nell had become more anxious and had lost weight along with her sparkle, Merry had bloomed and looked ever more adorable. It didn't seem fair. She flicked away her uncharitable thoughts; if anyone deserved a happy ending, it was Merry, and despite her own situation, Nell was thrilled that everything seemed to be finally falling into place for her best friend.

She finished her coffee and picked up her phone. Olek should be here by now. Their appointment was only ten minutes away, and they were always seen promptly.

She opened their WhatsApp chat and typed him a message.

Are you far away?

Sorry, darling. Still stuck at my last job. I was just about to message you. I don't think I'm going to make it. I'm gutted.

She groaned inwardly: not today of all days.

Please, darling, this is important.

Olek ran a successful business as a locksmith. Sometimes, a little too successful. He was in demand and worked long hours, many of which were at inconvenient times.

I know it is. Hold on, I'll go outside and call you.

She decided to do the same, and by the time she stepped out of the surgery, Olek had rung.

'I'm sorry, Nell. It has been crazy here,' he said. 'The customer is a woman with two small children. The ex-boyfriend smashed the lock on the door with a hammer because she wouldn't let him see the kids. By the time the police arrived, he'd put the hammer through all the downstairs windows.'

'Oh my word. Poor woman.'

'I know. I couldn't leave her, not until she feels safe.'

'Of course not, I understand, you did the right thing.'

He let out a breath of relief. 'Thank you for understanding. What sort of man would put his own children through that sort of trauma? How can he ever hope to have any sort of relationship with them after behaving that way? It is very sad, Nell. I am doing my best to show that not all men are animals.'

Nell felt a wave of tenderness for her big-hearted man. 'No one could ever mistake you for an animal, unless it was a big cuddly teddy bear.'

He laughed softly. 'Only where you are concerned. I can be tough if I have to.'

'I know.' Olek had had to be tough over the years. At fifteen years old, when he and his family had moved to the UK from Poland, he was thrust into a secondary school with only the barest grasp of the language. And later, when Yvonna, his wife of two years, announced that she didn't love him anymore and asked him to move out, Olek had behaved with dignity and done as his wife had asked. It had only been a matter of weeks before he'd discovered that his place in the marital bed had been taken over by his best friend, Viktor, with whom Yvonna had been conducting an affair for some time. Olek had been devastated by her betrayal but had made sure Max knew his father would always be there for him and that his parents' love for him hadn't changed even though their love for each other had.

Nell realised that Olek was still telling her about the job he was on and tuned in again.

'Her sister is here looking after them all, but the customer asked me to put new security bolts on the back door too. So I did that and now she's begging me not to leave until the glazers have been to mend the windows so that the house is secure again. I know it's not ideal, but could we rearrange today's appointment?'

'I don't want to rearrange.' Nell felt a flutter of panic. This appointment had been indelibly engraved in her brain for weeks. 'I didn't sleep last night, mulling over it all, working through the possible permutations and trying to decide what Plan B should be if the investigations uncover a problem. I need to know, Olek, it's eating me up.'

'Darling, whatever the results are,' he said gently, 'we can get through this together, you know.'

'I know, and I love you.' She felt her throat tighten with emotion as she returned to the waiting room, still with Olek on the line. She knew he meant what he said, but if the issue was on her side, as she predicted, she was going to be crushed with guilt. She didn't think she'd be able to get past that, however much he tried to support her.

'Mrs Dowmunt? Would you like to go through to the consulting room, please.'

'Too late to cancel now, I'm being called through,' said Nell. 'I'll only be able to get my results, but it's better than nothing.'

There were advantages of being alone, she reasoned. At least this way, he wouldn't see her crumble when the doctor delivered the news; she wouldn't have to put on a brave face and pretend that she was coping.

'Just an idea, but how about if I'm on the phone to you during the appointment?' Olek offered. 'I'm sure Dr Bajek won't mind; it's not as if she doesn't know us.'

Nell smiled. 'Good thinking, Batman. I knew I loved you for a reason. I'll suggest it and call you back.'

The doctor stood to shake Nell's hand and gestured for her to take one of the two velvet chairs on the other side of her white glossy desk.

'I'm afraid my husband has been held up,' said Nell, aware of the quaver in her voice.

This was it, the moment she'd been both desperate for and dreading in equal measure.

But at least you'll know for sure, said a little voice inside her head. *And then you can take action.*

'So it's just me today.'

'Ah,' said the doctor, looking down at the folder in front of her. 'That is regrettable.'

'I thought you could give me my results first,' Nell began, before outlining Olek's suggestion to get him on a call so he could listen in.

'You don't want him to hear your results?' the doctor queried.

Nell felt her face heat. 'No. I mean, not no, I will tell him, obviously, but . . . It might be easier if I hear that by myself.'

Dr Bajek frowned and Nell worried that she was going to object.

'Please put me out of my misery, doctor. It's me, isn't it? I'm the one with the fertility problem.'

Dr Bajek picked up a sheet of paper, scanned it and put it down again. Nell was so on edge that she thought her heart might burst out of her chest.

'Your results show nothing abnormal. In fact, quite the contrary, you are in excellent health and there is absolutely nothing to indicate any fertility issues at all.'

Nell stared at the doctor, processing the words. She had not expected that. 'Wow.' She sat back in the chair. *Nothing abnormal, nothing to indicate any fertility issues . . .* So it wasn't her. She was fine. Thank goodness. Thank goodness. She let out a shuddering sigh and covered her mouth, feeling light-headed with relief. 'Really? Are you sure?'

The doctor nodded.

'But, in that case, why am I not already pregnant?'

Dr Bajek looked at the notes. 'It says here that you've only been trying since Easter. That's not long at all. Why did you think that any issue would lie with you?'

Nell squirmed in her chair. 'Confidentially, I've been trying for a year, and I assumed the problem must be with me because, as you know, Olek already has a sixteen-year-old son, Max.'

The doctor's expression grew earnest, she looked down at her notes. For a split second, a look of something akin to anguish crossed the doctor's face before she regained her mask of professionalism. 'Hmm.'

So if the problem wasn't her, then it had to be Olek. Nell's chest tightened. 'Shall I call him?'

The doctor sucked in a breath. 'It's highly irregular, but if he consents to me delivering his results by telephone in front of you, I suppose I can make an exception.'

Nell called his number on speakerphone, and he answered immediately. There was a lot of shouting and crying in the background.

'Nell, it's chaos here, let me move away from the others.'

Once Olek had found a quieter spot and Dr Bajek was convinced he was content to continue, she picked up another sheet of paper.

'OK, Olek, the tests show that there is an issue with your sperm count. Unfortunately, it appears very unlikely that you could impregnate your wife naturally. I wonder, is there some sort of injury or trauma in your medical history?'

Trauma? Nell leaned forward in her chair. What did the doctor mean by that? If there was, it must have been a long time ago, because he'd never mentioned anything to her.

The sound of glass shattering echoed through the neat office and Dr Bajek flinched. 'This is not the right way to do things.' She shook her head at Nell, clearly regretting consenting to Nell's request.

'Sorry, doctor, I missed that, can you repeat it please?' said Olek.

Nell's fingers acted almost without her thinking about it. She tapped the screen, taking it off speakerphone, and pressed it to her ear. 'It's OK, Olek, it sounds like it's chaos where you are. We can do this another time. I'll see you at home, darling.' She ended the call, dropped the phone onto the desk and pressed her hands to her face. 'He didn't hear.'

'And you did.' The doctor regarded Nell so intensely that she felt heat rise to her face. 'That was most unfortunate and a significant breach of confidentiality on my part.'

'But the problem lies with him?' she asked, skating quickly over the doctor's point.

The doctor pressed her lips together; she looked like she'd rather be anywhere else in the world but here. Finally she spoke. 'It's certainly not you.'

'I see.' She'd assumed that she'd feel less badly about it if she wasn't the one with fertility problems. How naïve she'd been. This was as awful, if not worse. Her heart felt as heavy as a lead weight. 'And you mentioned trauma, what do you mean?'

Dr Bajek shook her head. 'I really can't discuss my patient without him being present.'

'I understand,' said Nell. 'I'll go home and talk to Olek, and take it from there.'

'Um. Right. Yes. Good idea, and there are always options. Sperm donors, et cetera. The important thing is that now we know what we're dealing with.'

What they were dealing with was the fact that her much-desired child was a long way from being born.

Nell's body was thrumming with sadness, a tidal wave of sorrow pushing her back out into reception. Somehow, she managed to pay the bill and find her way back to the car, her family plans in tatters.

Her dream to have a baby, to conceive naturally, to give birth to a child, their own biological child, had just turned into a nightmare. Nell prided herself on her positive outlook on life, but for once her inner sunshine had deserted her and her entire world had been eclipsed by this new information. Millions of other couples could have kids, so why couldn't they? Because Olek was infertile, that was why. And depending on what Dr Bajek meant by previous trauma, he might possibly have been infertile for a long, long time. Which led Nell to another awful thought: if Olek couldn't have ever had children, what did that mean for him and his son Max? Not only did today's results have repercussions for their future children, but they could have inadvertently uncovered a terrible, secret about Olek's relationship to his son. So what on earth was she going to tell Olek?

Chapter 4

Nell

The last thing Nell felt like doing was going back to work and facing customers in the shop this afternoon. She was sorely tempted to drive straight home from the clinic, dive under her duvet and sob until her tears ran dry. But with Merry in hospital, that wasn't an option; she couldn't let her down and leave the shop closed all afternoon. Which was why, half an hour after leaving Dr Bajek, still red-eyed from crying, she parked her car in the designated space behind Merry and Bright.

As she turned off the engine, she heard her phone ringing from the depths of her bag. She looked at the screen, Olek again. He'd left her a couple of messages already and she was feeling more and more guilty for not picking up. Her car wasn't sophisticated enough for her phone to connect to, so she never used it while driving. They were both respectful of each other's working day and under normal circumstances he wouldn't mind if she didn't phone him back straight away. But he'd be keen to know the fertility results after being cut off earlier. He deserved to know.

But know what exactly? She needed to think this through, work out what was best for everyone involved.

Whatever she told him, she thought morosely, there would be no Dowmunt baby. Not next year, and not the year after.

Nell pressed her hand to her flat stomach.

Her longing to be pregnant felt like a physical ache inside her now; she felt hollow and hopeless. How naïve she had been to assume that because she wanted to get pregnant, she would. That because Olek had already fathered one child, he could again. He'd be gutted, she knew, but mostly for her. His own desire to have a baby was nowhere near as strong as hers and she suspected that if she hadn't wanted to start a family, he'd have been happy to carry on as they were.

Tears of disappointment streamed down her face, and she gave herself up to her grief. For the baby she wouldn't have, for the family they wouldn't be, for all the holidays and birthdays and Christmases she'd fantasised about celebrating with her child. She was having to let go of so much that so many women took for granted, and it wasn't fair.

She cried for another few minutes, unable to stop the flow of her thoughts. She was entitled to this. Today, she'd let herself cry, but tomorrow, she'd do her best not to let her emotions rule her. Instead, she should look on the positive side and count her blessings. She had a lot to be grateful for. Olek was the love of her life, her soulmate, they rarely had a cross word, and even during the early days, when her snooty parents had made it clear that they didn't think Olek, a tradesman with Polish immigrant parents, was good enough for their only daughter, their love had only strengthened. She'd had Max in her life for years; he was a great kid and the two of them had a strong bond. From the very start, she'd tried to be a good friend to him, rather than parent him, and it had paid off. He was growing up fast, almost a man, and Nell felt privileged to have him in her life.

Yes, but he's not your own son . . . a little voice in her head reminded her.

Come on, Nell, pull yourself together.

She found a packet of tissues in the car, used one to dry her eyes and tucked the rest in her handbag. Then, climbing out and locking the car, she forced herself to open up the shop for the afternoon.

A few minutes later, the lights were on, soft Christmas music played in the background and the scent of the newly lit Winter Wonderland candles was beginning to fill the little shop.

Nell boiled the kettle to make a herbal tea before remembering that there was no need to restrict her caffeine levels now that she wouldn't be conceiving any time soon. She switched on the Nespresso machine and brewed herself an extra-strong cappuccino. If ever she deserved a decent coffee, it was now.

She'd had the first delicious sip and taken her phone out to compose a message to Olek when it rang in her hand. This time it was Merry.

Nell steeled herself before picking up. Merry was bound to ask how it had gone at the clinic and Nell wasn't ready to talk about it yet. But she couldn't avoid her call, not while the poor thing was in hospital. She took a fortifying breath and answered.

'Hello, you,' she said, forcing a smile into her voice. 'How are you feeling?'

'Fat and frustrated,' Merry said with a huff. 'I feel like a prisoner held against my will in here. I'd be fine at home; in fact, I'd be fine sitting quietly in the studio at Merry and Bright. It would be quieter and smell a million times nicer.'

'Nobody likes hospitals, but I'm sure the medical staff know what they're doing,' said Nell, mildly. 'You're in the best place for now.'

She flicked on the computer while she waited for Merry to give her whatever orders she'd phoned to impart.

'At least I've managed to do the online Christmas food shopping,' said Merry with a sigh. 'So that's something off my list. I mean, God knows where we'll be eating it, but I've got everything we need for Christmas lunch, down to the cranberry sauce and brandy butter. I'm absolutely determined to be in the new house by then, but Cole is dragging his heels. Oh yes, and did I tell you I've got a date for the baby to be induced? It'll be between Christmas and New Year, which means Cole and I will celebrate our first wedding anniversary without having a baby to look after. We'll be able to focus just on ourselves for once. Not sure how romantic it will be with me looking like a beached whale, but we'll think of something.'

Nell could feel her irritation rising. How could Merry witter on about the cranberry sauce before remembering that she had a date for when her baby would be arriving? Nell would have blurted that out first! And while she accepted that Merry had a lot going on right now, she hadn't even mentioned Nell's tests. Which, she admitted to herself, was a very contrary attitude, given that she didn't want to talk about it, but even so, Merry should have asked.

Before she could agree or otherwise with Merry, an email popped into the inbox from Airbnb.

'We've had a new enquiry about the flat,' said Nell, clicking on the message to read it. 'Oh bloody hell, arrival date on Monday for a stay of three weeks!' She scanned the rest of the message. 'And happy to work at Merry and Bright full-time.'

'That's handy. I don't suppose they know how to make candles, do they?'

As if Merry would let a stranger loose in her studio, thought Nell, bemused. 'We can but hope,' she replied diplomatically.

'The flat is clean and ready to go,' said Merry. 'But we should probably put Christmas decorations up. Oh and a tree! A real one, obviously. It'll look lovely.'

Nell snorted. 'By *we,* do you mean me?'

'Not out of choice,' Merry said spikily. 'You know I'd happily do it if I was allowed.'

'Easy, tiger,' she replied. 'And it's no problem, check-in time isn't until three in the afternoon, I can get it sorted on Monday morning. The booking is for just one person. Don't you think that's a bit odd; such a long stay at the last minute for one guest?'

'Who knows what goes on in other people's lives,' Merry replied. 'Perhaps it's someone who hates Christmas, or someone who's found themselves suddenly homeless, or chucked out by their partner, or recently bereaved and needs somewhere without any sad memories.'

'Let's hope it's someone who fancies a holiday in a lovely flat in our pretty town,' Nell said, noticing how even after all these years Merry's mind automatically reverted to her own worst fears. 'Anyway, leave it with me.'

Nell was secretly pleased to be able to take over the booking herself.

It had been her idea to list the apartment above the shop on Airbnb and she was proud of how successful it had been. She'd read about a scheme up north somewhere where holiday guests could work in a quaint bookshop by the sea and stay in the apartment above. Nell had had a feeling that a stay in the pretty Tudor town of Wetherley, plus the chance to learn how to make scented candles, would be just as popular and the duplex above Merry and Bright had been empty since Cole had moved in with Merry. It hadn't taken the two friends much time to convert it into a holiday let. Since then, they'd had an interesting assortment of visitors to stay and help out in the shop, and, with only a few exceptions (like the woman who was allergic to most essential oils and spent the entire week sneezing), the extra labour had come in very handy, and it had added variety to their working environment that both women enjoyed immensely.

'Thanks, I do appreciate it,' said her friend. 'I'm lucky to have you, Nell, and I am really sorry to be leaving you in the lurch.'

'Happy to help,' Nell said. 'And, actually, the timing is perfect. With you having to rest, I'll be super grateful for some help in the shop.'

'Hmm.' Merry didn't sound convinced.

Nell bit her tongue. Despite being only weeks away from becoming a mother, Merry was in denial about needing to take some maternity leave or recruit a member of staff to help out in the shop. She seemed to think that as the baby would be small and portable, she'd be able to come back to work almost immediately. But Nell wasn't going to tackle her about it now, she'd pick her moment, and at least with the arrival of the new Airbnb guest, she'd have immediate help.

'You look after yourself, and that baby. The sooner you behave and stop worrying the doctors, the sooner you'll be allowed out of your terrible prison.'

'Don't you start,' Merry grumbled. 'It's bad enough with the hospital staff and Cole telling me what to do. I don't have much choice other than to behave, do I? Speak to you later.'

She signed off abruptly, leaving Nell staring at the phone in surprise; Merry hadn't even asked about her and Olek's appointment. She was preoccupied with her baby, but even so, Nell couldn't help feeling hurt.

Still, looking on the bright side, at least she hadn't had to give her an edited version of the results.

She'd barely finished her coffee when the door opened and in came Sadie, the landlady from the Bristly Badger pub on the other side of the market square.

'Give me a good deal on a couple of candles, will you, love,' said Sadie, decanting a pile of pound coins from her pocket onto the counter. 'One of my barmaids is leaving and the customers had a whip-round last night. There's thirty quid here.'

Nell picked out two bestsellers, added a couple of little freebies and gift-wrapped them while Sadie leaned on the counter.

'No Merry?' Sadie craned her head through the doorway leading to the studio where Merry was usually to be found. 'Not had the baby, has she?'

'The doctor persuaded her to put her feet up for once,' Nell replied vaguely. Telling Sadie anything interesting was akin to publishing it in the *Wetherley Gazette*.

'Doctors.' Sadie pulled a disparaging face. 'Always so flippin' cautious. When I went into labour with our Jack, I finished my shift and locked up before going into hospital. And I was back by lunchtime the next day to open up.'

Nell resisted raising her eyebrows. If she'd had a baby, she'd want to relish those first few hours – and days and weeks – with her little one, to fall in love and create that precious bond. Why would anyone want to prioritise work at such a special time? And now she might not ever experience it . . .

She felt her eyes begin to tear up and gave herself a shake. 'Please don't share that story with Merry, she's already causing enough trouble on the antenatal ward.'

Sadie's eyes widened. 'So she's in hospital, is she? I'm sorry to hear that.'

Nell cursed herself for letting it slip. 'Only for the day. Nothing to worry about.' Hopefully.

She held the door open for Sadie and ushered her out before she gave away anything else, then forced herself to send a message to Olek.

Sorry I haven't returned your call. It's been all go at Merry and Bright. I'll see you at home for a proper chat later. Love you xxx

Look forward to it! Max has invited himself round, says he's got something to tell us. He's asked if we can have *pierogi* for dinner, so I'll cook. Love you too xxx

Nell squeezed her eyes tightly shut for a second. On any normal occasion, she'd love to see her stepson, but tonight she'd assumed they'd be talking about this afternoon's revelations. They couldn't do that if Max was there. Although maybe fate was lending a hand and giving her some extra time to process what had happened. And she did love the little Polish dumplings called *pierogi* which Olek had been taught to make by his grandmother when he'd still lived in Poland, so every cloud . . .

There was a steady stream of customers for the rest of the afternoon and Nell was grateful for the distraction. Her forte was sales – a skill honed in her previous career as a stallholder on the market just across the street. Nell's Nuts had been an institution for almost a decade before she'd sold it last Christmas to a couple who'd since renamed it The Nut Hut. She'd had enough of working alone and outdoors, and when Merry had offered her a partnership in Merry and Bright, she didn't hesitate to accept.

For almost one year, she and Merry had worked alongside each other in perfect harmony: Nell taking over the retail side and Merry focusing on production. Harley helped out on Saturdays and Max had worked for them during the long summer holidays. Cole's dad, Fred, had officially retired, but couldn't resist popping in now and then for an hour or so, to 'keep his hand in' as he liked to call it. With the addition of some of the Airbnb guests, the two women had so far managed without taking on any other staff.

Now it was closing time and for the first time in her life, Nell was dragging out the last few jobs in order to postpone going home. She finally flipped the sign from open to closed and as she was about to lock the door, Cole appeared on the other side of it.

She stood back and let him in.

'Glad I caught you.' He kissed her cheek, his skin rough against hers. He held out his arms to show her the two bulging bags he'd brought with him. 'Merry asked me to drop in these Christmas decorations urgently. She said you'll know what they're for?'

Nell narrowly avoided rolling her eyes. Despite saying she would leave Nell to dress the Airbnb for Christmas, Merry clearly hadn't been able to resist getting involved. And had roped poor Cole in unnecessarily too. He had dark circles under his eyes and that, coupled with the several-day-old stubble along his jaw, told Nell all she needed to know about how worried he was about Merry.

'I do,' she said, opting to keep her opinions to herself, since voicing them wouldn't help Cole. 'Thank you, you're a lifesaver. Are you going back to the hospital now?'

'Oh yes.' He shook his head fondly. 'She's given me a list of stuff to take in. She's going to write all the Christmas cards, order curtains for the new house and embroider the kids' names on some new Christmas stockings she's bought.'

Nell laughed. 'And this is her idea of complete rest?'

'Tell me about it.' He set the bags down and rubbed his forehead wearily. 'Please can you visit her tomorrow and make her see sense? She's refusing to listen to me. She's still adamant that we'll be moving house before Christmas.'

'Merry is a "can-do" person,' Nell reminded him. 'Always has been. And she hates accepting help. For her, it's a sign of weakness.'

Cole nodded. 'I've learned that about her. I've tried to tell her that helping her makes me happy, but she can't see it.'

'Life made her tough out of necessity; she learned to be self-reliant when her mum died,' she told him. 'For her, the hardest thing in the world is to relinquish control.'

'But she and I are a team now, and I don't want to control anything, I just want to make life easier for her.' Cole looked bewildered and Nell's heart went out to him.

'I know you do and, deep down, she loves you for it.' She smiled, remembering how Cole had come to see her for her advice before he proposed to Merry. He was such a gallant and thoughtful man and she'd been so happy for her friend when the two of them had got together. 'And I hear you. She and I are a team at Merry and Bright, but trying to get her to hand stuff over to me is like prising a bone off a dog.'

'With sharp teeth.'

'And a killer gleam in its eye.'

They both laughed.

'Look, I'll see what I can do. I'll pop in and visit her in the morning,' Nell promised, 'and try to at least get her to agree to scale back events in the shop.'

'If you could also manage her expectations about the house move, I'd be very grateful,' Cole sighed. 'If we'd have had one of my new builds, we'd have been in months ago, but Merry was holding out for the perfect home.'

Nell grinned. 'And you found it.'

'We found one that fitted her bill,' he argued, 'but my idea of perfect does not include rising damp, dodgy electrics, gurgling plumbing and a roof which has tiles sledging off it at the slightest sign of a breeze.'

'I'll do my best,' Nell said without a huge amount of conviction.

Merry had fallen in love at first sight with the old Victorian house on the outskirts of Wetherley. 'You can tell it's a happy home,' she'd said dreamily. 'There's a patch of peeling wallpaper in the study and when I tore it, there were layers and layers of old paper underneath. Just think of all the happy times that house has seen, all the families who've lived in it, the Christmases, the summers . . .'

Cole had commented that all he could see was the hours ahead of him stripping off all that wallpaper. But for Merry, the house represented a proper home, a place to put down roots and finally settle down. And it was that sense of security and belonging that Nell knew was more important to Merry than anything else.

'Thanks, I appreciate it. OK, I'll leave you to it. And is everything all right with you? Sorry, I should have asked. I'm just so . . .' He waved his hands around his head. 'Taken up with the baby, I can't think straight.'

Nell conjured up a smile. Cole knew nothing about her own pregnancy woes. She'd made Merry swear not to say anything to anyone about their attendance at the fertility clinic until they had good news to share. 'All fine, thanks. And try to get some rest yourself, you look terrible.'

He laughed and kissed her cheek again. 'That's what I like about you, Nell. Your unwavering dedication to telling the truth.'

Her smile slipped a little; was that all about to change? Could she bring herself to tell Olek the truth? It was time to go home and face the music.

Chapter 5

Nell

Olek's and Max's laughter was just about audible over the sound of singing coming from the kitchen when Nell got home. Max had got into music over the last year and liked to educate his dad about his new favourite bands whenever he came over. Olek's musical taste hadn't changed since Kim Wilde was in the charts, and it always made Nell smile to see him gamely feigning appreciation of his son's obscure indie bands.

She paused in front of the mirror in the hallway and looked at her reflection. She rarely wore make-up, so at least she didn't have smudged mascara. But there were telltale signs of her mood in the puffiness around her eyes and set of her mouth. She considered running upstairs and trying to do some damage limitation with foundation and blusher, but it was too late; the volume of the music went down, and Olek's broad figure filled the open kitchen doorway.

'Here's my girl.' He crossed the hall in a few strides and folded her into his arms, kissing her warmly. And then, tilting her chin up towards him, said softly, 'I haven't been able to stop thinking about you. Are you OK?'

'I'm fine.' Nell felt her pulse speed up; what was she going to tell him? She still hadn't decided. She leaned her forehead against his chest. 'Shall we talk later?'

'Of course,' he murmured, giving her a squeeze.

'Hey, Nell!' Max called from the kitchen. 'Dad, let me tell her.'

'Hey, sunshine, tell me what?' She raised her eyebrows.

Olek glanced over his shoulder at his son and grinned. 'Don't worry, I'm not going to steal your thunder.'

Olek's English was word-perfect, and yet despite being here for over half of his life, he had still retained his Polish accent, which Nell had found very sexy when they first met, and still did.

They joined Max in the kitchen and Olek returned to making the dough for the *pierogi* while Max fetched them all drinks. He took three cans of Diet Coke out of the fridge. Olek opened his, but Nell shook her head.

'I fancy a glass of wine tonight,' she said, pulling a bottle from the wine rack. 'A nice full-bodied Malbec, I think.'

Olek did a double take and said nothing, but she knew what he was thinking. They'd both cut down on their alcohol consumption, and didn't drink at all during the week, to optimise their chances of having a healthy baby. Nell's choice of drink was as clear a signal as any that something significant had happened at the clinic.

'So, come on,' she said, taking a seat at the table. 'The suspense is killing me, Max.'

Her stepson set his can down and stretched his arms above his head nonchalantly. 'Nah, it's nothing,' he teased.

Olek turned the ball of dough out onto the work surface and began to knead it. 'It's not nothing at all. I'm so proud of you, son.'

Max grinned. 'Thanks, Dad. But let's not get ahead of ourselves just yet. There's a long way to go.'

'Ahem!' Nell swigged her wine and the alcohol hit the back of her throat. This was good; naughty but nice. She was going to have another after this, she could already tell. 'Come on!'

'A scout came to watch the Wetherley Lions play on Saturday,' said Max, unable to keep the joy from his face. 'I've been spotted.'

'OK, go on.' She gave him an enquiring look, willing him to continue; it sounded good, but she didn't know enough about football to understand what this meant. Although the sight of Olek's puffed-out chest was a bit of a clue.

'He was scouting for Derby County!' Max continued. 'And he'd come especially to see me play.'

'Can you believe that, Nell?' Olek marvelled. 'A professional scout came to see my boy.'

'I scored as well, Dad. From a free kick.'

Father and son high-fived each other and Nell's heart melted to see the excitement bubbling out of them both.

Max had been football-mad since he was little. His bedroom at their house was a shrine to his beloved Liverpool Football Club. Even when they'd upgraded his bed from a single to a double this year, he'd asked if he could still have the official LFC bed linen. He played for his school side, but also played for the local team. He'd confided in Nell once that his dream was to be a professional footballer but that he didn't think he was good enough. He was like his father in that respect; adorably humble and never one to shout about his talents. Fortunately, it seemed that someone might have noticed them anyway.

Olek wasn't a huge football fan, but just like with Max's music, he took an interest in it because it was important to his son. He went to as many Wetherley Lions matches as he could and took Max to see Liverpool for the odd game too.

'After the match, the scout asked for my contact details. Our manager gave him the landline number. He phoned tonight when I got in from school. Viktor answered and thought it was a scam at first.'

Nell quickly glanced at Olek and saw the twitch in his jaw. How he'd have loved to have been the one to receive that call from Derby County instead of his replacement. He caught her eye and smiled sheepishly. *I love you*, she mouthed across the kitchen.

Both of them listened as Max delivered the rest of the story in garbled half-sentences; Nell sipping her wine and Olek shaking his head in wonderment. Max would be starting a three-week trial at Derby County immediately.

'And listen to the best bit. My final trial will be a friendly match against—' Max paused for effect. 'Liverpool! Which means I'll get to play at Anfield. *The actual* Anfield pitch. I can't believe it. It's . . . like a dream.' He punched the air, his face turning red with a mix of pride and disbelief.

Olek abandoned his dough, grabbed his son around his shoulders, and the pair of them leapt up and down. They were so alike in many ways. Max had the same shock of blond hair, the same vivid blue eyes as Olek. But their build was totally different. Where Olek was broad and muscular, Max was slim and wiry. Nell had always put it down to Max's age, thinking that he had time to fill out as he got older. She hated the fact that she now found herself scrutinising every feature, looking for evidence that Max might not be Olek's. However, there was no mistaking how much the pair loved each other. And that was what really mattered.

'But it's not a dream, boy, it's real because you've earned this, and you've got the talent.'

'You two look like you're on the pitch celebrating already.' Nell laughed and pushed her way in between them to give Max a hug. 'Well done, Max, I'm so proud of you.'

Olek was right; he deserved every bit of his success. He put football above everything, would rather go training than go out with his friends, and Nell was thrilled for him that his sacrifice was paying off.

'This is just the start,' said Olek, taking his son's shoulders. 'You could go all the way to the top.'

Max exhaled and his eyes sparkled. 'Imagine if I get to play at Wembley one day. Would you come and watch me?'

'Just you try to stop me.' Olek's voice cracked with emotion. 'I'll be the proudest dad in the stadium.'

Max's frow furrowed. 'I could still play for England, even though I've got Polish parents, can't I?'

Nell was starting to think that Olek needed to step in and manage Max's expectations at this point, but he simply threw his arms out.

'Of course you can. You're a British citizen. And you have the added bonus of dual citizenship, you lucky lad!' Olek extracted himself from the hug and turned away.

Nell noticed him surreptitiously wiping his eyes. How glad she was, she thought, that the consultant was interrupted before she managed to tell him the truth. Otherwise, the sweet joy of this evening might never have happened. Olek might have been as tormented by 'what if' as she was.

'Right.' Olek blinked and turned back to his dinner preparation. 'We'll eat in half an hour. And, Max, if you're not already too important to help, you can start grating the cheese.'

'On it,' Max replied, sliding over to the fridge to remove the cheese.

Nell looked at them, drinking in the bond that they shared. She'd never have that with a child, she mused, and felt herself on the verge of tears.

'I'm going to have a bath,' she announced, topping up her glass again. The wine was already starting to make her woozy.

'OK, darling,' Olek said warily.

She hadn't drunk this much since they'd been at Merry and Cole's barbecue earlier this summer. She felt his stare on her back as she left the kitchen and escaped to the sanctuary of the bathroom to avoid further conversation.

'Nell? Are you asleep?'

It was ten o'clock and she was in bed with the lights off, feeling buzzy from the wine and almost asleep. Almost.

After a long candlelit bath, and as soon as she'd eaten her *pierogi*, she'd left the boys in the kitchen, still talking football, and watched an episode of *Married At First Sight*, knowing that neither of them would come within twenty paces of the living room while that was on television. Then, while Olek had driven Max home, she'd gone up to bed, intending to be asleep before he returned.

But she hadn't been able to sleep, and now he was back. He'd tiptoed around, using the bathroom and getting undressed, taking care not to disturb her.

It would be so easy for her to fake deep breathing; to put off the difficult conversation she knew was coming until tomorrow. But that would only mean that she'd wake up with a feeling of dread, and besides, it wasn't fair to keep Olek in the dark any longer.

'I'm awake,' she whispered.

He climbed into bed beside her, lying on his back and reaching for her so that he could scoop her into his side. 'Come here, darling.'

She shuffled nearer, wrapping one leg over his until they were as close as possible. At once, she felt the press of tears at her eyes, the constriction in her throat. She loved this man so much, why could it not have worked out for them? Why was life not treating them fairly?

'I'm so pleased for Max,' she whispered, avoiding the subject for as long as possible.

'Mmm.' Even in that one word, Nell could sense Olek's joy. 'Me too. Your child's success is even sweeter than your own.'

'It must be.' Nell let out a breath; this was so hard. So incredibly hard.

'Sometimes it's easy to take for granted the effect that the next generation has on our lives and then something like this happens and you realise that whatever we have to go through for them is worth it.'

'Like when you and Yvonna divorced, you mean?'

'Yeah. She didn't always make it easy for me to see Max, not at the beginning.'

'I know, darling.' Nell tightened her arms around him. It didn't matter how many times she heard this story, it always made her love Olek more. He was such a wonderful father to Max, which was why today's results were all the more difficult to process.

'Then, of course, Viktor quickly became the man Max had the most contact with. I had to work hard to keep a father-son bond, when sometimes it felt like the easiest thing to do would be to let it go, start again.'

'And now you have an . . .' Her voice stuttered, and she blinked back tears. 'An unbreakable bond with him. I'm so proud of you for that.'

'Thank you, that means a lot, and, darling, it's partly down to you that I've been able to keep playing an active role in his life, you always include Max in everything we do. I love you for that.' He paused for a moment. 'I don't want you to think that Max would always be my favourite child. I've got plenty of love to go round. You and I could have any number of kids and I'd love them all the same.'

Nell felt a sob form in her throat. 'I know you would.'

'Do you want to talk about today?' he murmured. 'You don't have to, if you don't want.'

She squeezed her eyes tightly shut. This was it. Whatever she said now, she'd have to stick with. There'd be no going back.

If Olek found out that he was infertile, he'd want more details from Dr Bajek. And more details would inevitably include the fact that he might never have been able to father a child. Could it really be true, might Olek not be Max's father? She remembered Olek and Max dancing in the kitchen earlier, Olek's love for his son on display. She hated the thought of lying to him. But she hated the thought of doing anything to damage the father-son bond even more. Surely it would be better to lie to him than break his heart? She had never felt so conflicted in her life. It was an impossible situation, she concluded, but this time, the truth wouldn't work. It just wouldn't. She was going to have to lie to her husband.

'I can't have our baby, Olek,' she blurted out. 'I'm so sorry.'

'So the test results—'

'Proved that I'm a faulty model,' she butted in.

'Oh, darling.' His eyes found hers in the darkness and the pain in them almost undid her. 'Don't apologise, please, there's no need.'

'So if you want more children, you're going to have to swap me for one with fully working parts.'

'Nell!' He pulled away from her, a look of disbelief in his face. 'We've always been in this together, no fault, no blame. And no more talk of swapping you for another model. I can't think of anything worse.'

'Well, that's a relief.' She made a noise somewhere between a laugh and a sob.

'Did the doctor give you any more details; was she able to pinpoint any particular issue?'

Nell could hear both of their heartbeats, his slow and strong, hers racing as panic flooded her body. What could she say to that? 'It all got a bit technical, and I was so distraught, it was difficult to take in. Something to do with my ovaries.'

Lying to him was even worse than she could have imagined, and with every sentence, she was stepping further and further away from the truth. This morning when she'd got up, she'd been sure that whatever happened at the clinic, they'd find a path through it together. Now she was going to be on her own. Had she made a mistake, was it too late to put it right? She felt awful, and so, so exhausted.

Olek held her while she cried. She thought he was crying too, but she couldn't be sure.

'I'm so sad,' she whispered, once she'd finally found her voice again.

'I'm sad too for you, *for us*. Darling, there are lots of ways to be a family, perhaps there are other options for us? We can explore every avenue, if that's what you'd like; this doesn't have to be the end. We'll make another appointment to see the doctor.'

A hot flash of dread ran through her. He was right, there were alternatives to natural conception, but they couldn't access those without him finding out the truth. It was going to be tricky enough keeping their medical reports from him.

'Can we leave it for now,' she said, thinking on her feet. 'I think I need to process this first before we do anything else.'

'Of course. Nothing matters more to me than making you happy. You already make my world complete, Nell. And you always will. I love you.' He kissed her deeply and she tried to respond with the same passion, but it didn't feel right, and she broke away from him. She had lied to her husband now; the die was cast and she couldn't take it back. She had never felt so uncomfortable with her own actions in her life.

'I'm glad,' she replied. 'And I love you too.'

But did her world feel complete in the same way? She couldn't honestly say that it did. Not anymore.

Chapter 6

Merry

'Your personal chauffeur has arrived, *Madame*,' said Cole, pushing a wheelchair into the ward the following day.

'I'm not getting in that,' Merry exclaimed in horror. 'I'm pregnant, not an invalid.'

He brought it to a halt beside her bed and gave her a kiss. 'Humour me, *ma cherie*, it's miles to the car. Also, it will be quicker this way. I've left the kids in the car, and I've got twenty minutes tops before war breaks out.'

This afternoon had dragged. She'd hoped to be out of here just after lunch, but they'd wanted to check her blood pressure and the baby's heartbeat one last time before she was released. She'd finally called him to collect her at four o'clock; an hour had gone by since then. She'd been packed, dressed and lying on her bed desperate to leave for ages.

'I can walk fast,' Merry argued, which anyone with a brain cell could see was a lie. She'd waddled before her waters had broken; now she'd developed a habit of walking with her legs pinched together as if sheer willpower would keep the baby from making a bid for freedom. She'd never felt more ungainly in her life.

'You *are* getting in that.' Nurse Liz, who'd spent two days with Merry and knew that only a firm manner would do, took Merry's arm and helped her into the chair. 'We'd very much like you to leave the premises without further incident, if it's all the same to you.'

'Thank you, Liz,' said Cole with obvious relief.

Merry had to bite her tongue to stop herself from getting snappy with him. She was fine! All this fuss was beginning to get on her nerves. OK, she did feel light-headed standing up after being in bed for so long, but all the more reason to get up and moving again. Still, she was on her way home and that was the main thing. At long last, life could start getting back to normal.

'Thank you for looking after me.' Merry was so delighted to be finally let out of the ward that she was tempted to give her nurse a hug. 'See you on the twenty-eighth.'

'Remember: essential jobs only,' Liz wagged her finger, 'or we'll be seeing you a lot sooner than that.'

'I'll make sure she gets plenty of rest,' Cole promised, wrangling Merry's laptop bag off her.

'I can manage that,' Merry retorted. 'It's not even heavy.'

'On second thoughts,' Cole said with a wry smile, 'can you keep her in for a bit longer please?'

'Oi.' Merry shoved her husband's arm playfully. 'Don't give her any ideas.'

'Good luck,' said the nurse, to Cole. 'You're going to need it. And, Merry, just for the next few weeks, take every offer of help going. You've got a legitimate reason to be lazy and let everyone run around after you. Make the most of it.'

Merry forced a smile. No thank you. The thought of having to rely on other people to do things for her was not a happy one. Far quicker to do it herself. She'd be careful though; she wasn't stupid. And she really didn't want the baby to come any earlier than her induction date.

'I must ring Springwood House and see how Dad is,'

she said with a pang of guilt once they were in the lift and on their way down to the ground floor of the hospital. 'I've been so preoccupied with my waters breaking that I've completely neglected him.'

'Ray's no better, but he's no worse either,' Cole told her. 'I called and checked.'

She craned over her shoulder to smile at him. 'That was kind of you, thank you.'

'The manager said he's been seen by a doctor and given the all-clear, so nothing much to report, but he's very tired and needs lots of rest.'

Merry nodded. 'Best thing for him.'

'And for you,' Cole pointed out.

'Yeah, yeah, yeah.' She was quiet for a moment as she mentally ran through her to-do list. 'Gosh, I haven't even told Emily that he's ill.'

'It's OK, I've spoken to her. So she knows about Ray. And you.'

'Cole!' She gritted her teeth. 'Now she'll be worried. I was trying to avoid that.'

'For future reference,' he said smoothly, 'if I'm ever admitted into hospital, please let my family know rather than keep it to yourself. They love me and would feel hurt if they later found out I'd been ill and they hadn't been given the chance to look after me.'

'Darling, of course I'd tell them,' Merry replied, hurt that he'd even suggest such a thing.

'Indeed.' He cleared his throat pointedly.

'Oh. Yes, I see what you mean,' she said contritely. 'I'm sorry. I just don't want to be a nuisance.'

He squeezed her shoulder. 'You could never be that.' He paused. 'Unless, of course, you decide to ignore the doctor's advice and end up back in here again.'

The lift doors opened, and Cole steered her out towards the main exit.

'Emily asked if you'd send her a message tonight and let her know how you're feeling.'

'I will, I promise.'

A blast of cold air hit her as the automatic doors opened. It was refreshing after the stifling heat and stuffiness of the ward and Merry inhaled contentedly.

'I am so glad to be out of there. Now I can get cracking on everything that needs to be finished off before the baby comes.'

'Whoah.' The wheelchair stopped abruptly, and Cole squatted down in front of her, taking her hand. 'Merry, we could easily be coming out of hospital as parents of a newborn baby, and—'

She shuddered. 'I know!'

Cole looked at her quizzically. 'Did you just shudder? Darling, what's going on?'

'Yes, but I don't mean . . .' Her face flooded with heat, and she felt flustered all of a sudden. What had she meant? 'Obviously I'm looking forward to the baby coming.'

He waited, still clearly unsure what was on her mind.

'But we wouldn't want it to be here yet, would we?' she continued. January, when the baby was actually due, would have been perfect. But certainly not before Christmas, not when everything was still up in the air.

His face softened and he kissed her hand. 'No, of course not. Much safer for the baby to arrive when it's full-term, without possible health risks.'

'Exactly.' Merry looked down at her lap feeling bad that she hadn't said that herself.

'We'd better get back to the car,' he said, starting to push the wheelchair again. 'The kids will be getting anxious.'

Ten minutes later, Cole had returned the wheelchair

to the hospital and was loading her things into the boot of the car while Freya and Harley gave her a gentle hug.

'Dad said the baby could come at any moment,' said Harley, glancing nervously at her bump.

'In theory,' Merry told him. 'But I think it's comfy where it is for now. Here, feel this.'

Harley offered up his hand and Merry placed it on her side, where the baby's heel was quite easy to detect.

'Yuk. Does that hurt?' he said, recoiling.

She laughed at the look on his face. 'Not really.'

Freya had a feel too. 'It's moving, like it's dancing about. A girl! Maybe we're going to have a sister, Harley!'

'Oh goodie, another one,' he replied flatly, making Merry smile.

'Boys can dance,' said Merry. 'And at the Christmas lights switch-on, you thought I was having a boy, remember?'

Freya flung her arms around her. 'I'm so sorry about knocking into you. I cried when I got home because I thought it was my fault that you had to go to hospital.'

'Oh, sweetpea.' Merry kissed her head, shifting a little so Freya wasn't pressing quite so hard on her stomach. 'It wasn't your fault, I promise.'

She blew out a breath. 'Phew.'

'But Mum did say you had to be gentle with her,' Harley pointed out and hopped into the front seat before his sister could get there.

'Harley!' Freya tugged his arm. 'It's my turn.'

'Oi, you two, stop fighting, and, Merry, why aren't you in the car!' said Cole.

'We've been feeling the baby,' Freya told him. 'It's moving.'

His eyes widened. 'Really? Is everything OK?'

'Yes, Cole, please stop fussing,' Merry said, wishing he'd just relax.

She clambered into the back seat where she could stretch out beside Freya.

'Has the water definitely stopped leaking out now?' Freya eyed her dubiously, squashing herself up beside the opposite door just in case.

'I hope so.'

'But from now on, Merry has to be super careful to make sure the baby stays safe,' Cole told his daughter. 'We don't want her or the baby getting ill.'

It wasn't the actual words, but more the tone, which made her hackles rise, as if somehow it was her fault that her waters had broken in the first place.

'I've been *super careful* ever since I found out I was expecting our baby,' she said in a clipped voice. 'And I have no intention of doing anything to jeopardise that now.'

Cole laughed softly as he started the car and drove up to the car park barrier. 'Apart from organising four Christmas candle-making workshops to run while you're eight months pregnant and packing the house up ready to move and—'

Merry let out a noise which could only be described as a deep growl. 'It's my livelihood, and I'm packing because you promised we'd be in before the baby came, remember? And I don't see you slowing down, Mr Fly Off to Germany at the Drop of a Hat.'

Harley whistled under his breath. 'She's got a point, Dad.'

'Ha,' Merry folded her arms, realising as she did so that she was being very immature.

'But I'm not the one carrying the baby, am I?' Cole caught her eye in the rear-view mirror and gave her a knowing look.

'And don't I know it!' she retorted, turning away.

'Let's talk about this when we get home,' he said nervously.

They never argued, ever, but if they did need to talk about something sensitive, they'd avoid doing it in front of the children, all too aware that anything they said might get repeated to Lydia, Cole's ex-wife.

'Uh-oh,' said Freya. 'She's turning into Momzilla. That's like Bridezilla, but for mums.'

Harley spluttered with laughter and out of the corner of her eye, she saw Cole was trying to smother a smile too.

Merry focused on the traffic as they whizzed through the dark streets back towards Wetherley. She hated feeling out of sorts like this. She was ashamed of herself for her outburst, particularly in front of the kids. She hated being helpless and breathless and being blamed for her waters breaking early. She hated feeling like she should apologise for everything. And, worst of all, having these thoughts was confirming her darkest fears about herself. She knew nothing about motherhood, why would she? While other girls had watched and learned from their mums from an early age, she'd been shunted from house to house, children's home to children's home, after her own mother hadn't loved her enough to stay alive.

Merry was going to make a terrible mother; she just knew it. How could she be anything else?

Chapter 7

Nell

Nell was in the flat above the shop, putting milk and butter in the fridge and arranging mince pies, cinnamon cookies, tea, coffee and a bottle of wine in the wicker welcome hamper for the imminent arrival of their Airbnb guest.

Merry and Bright was usually quiet on Mondays. But while customers might have been few and far between, the online weekend orders had kept Nell working non-stop all day.

The brand had developed quite a following online thanks to Merry's slot on a popular TV shopping channel for over a year. The show had gone off air now, but demand for Merry's hand-poured candles continued to burn brightly.

And this morning not only had she had the usual backlog of orders to deal with, but a particularly time-consuming one of twenty gift-wrapped candle bundles for a corporate Christmas order. Now it was two o'clock and she'd only just finished stocking the log basket, stringing twinkly lights along the banister and decorating the Christmas tree Merry had had delivered from the Christmas tree man on the market.

Even Merry couldn't find fault with the festiveness of the flat, Nell thought, standing on a chair to tie a bunch of mistletoe to the light fitting in the hall.

She raced back downstairs, unlocking the shop door again to let in customers while she prepared her lunch of soup left over from yesterday's supper with two slices of her mother-in-law's rye bread.

She was blowing on her soup when Merry called.

'Nell. I'm really sorry,' said Merry in a small voice. 'You and Olek had your appointment at the fertility clinic last week, and I completely forgot to ask you about it. I'm a terrible friend.'

Nell painted on her biggest smile before replying. 'No! Darling girl, you're not at all; you've had far bigger things to deal with.'

This was her new skill, to sound happy even though her heart was still aching. She'd done as she'd promised; the day after getting the results, she'd tried to be positive. She'd spent Saturday practically gurning at customers in the shop. On Sunday, she and Olek had visited her parents, where she'd given an Oscar-worthy performance, smiling broadly at her father's in-depth story about missing funds at the golf club and nodding happily while her mother tried on dress after dress in readiness for their Christmas Caribbean cruise.

'So how did it go?' Merry asked.

Nell hesitated. Merry knew her inside out; in some ways, better than Olek did. She yearned to tell her best friend the truth, confide how complicated everything had become and ask for her advice. But could she risk it getting back to Olek? All it would take would be one slip of the tongue and her carefully constructed lie would crash around her ears. No, the safest, if not her preferred, thing to do was to tell Merry exactly what she'd told Olek.

'To misquote Taylor Swift, it's me, I'm the problem.' She managed to muster up a half-laugh, even though it wasn't in the least bit funny. Thank goodness they were having this conversation over the phone; at least Merry only had Nell's voice to go on and not her body language.

For a moment, Merry was silent and Nell could only imagine the anguish on her best friend's face.

'Ah, Nellie,' Merry said finally, her voice thick with emotion. 'I'm so sorry.'

'Yeah. Me too.' *Your results show that there's absolutely nothing wrong* . . . Nell blinked away her dangerous thoughts.

'And I'm even more sorry that we're only having this conversation now,' Merry continued. 'I want to give you a big hug.'

'I need one,' she replied. 'Although I'm a bit scared of touching you at the moment in case the baby pops out.'

'Don't you start,' Merry grumbled. 'Cole offered to go and sleep in the kids' bedroom for that reason.'

'He's just looking after you,' Nell reminded her. 'You'd like it even less if he didn't show how much he cared.'

'Don't change the subject,' her friend chided. 'This is important. I know you've always suspected you'd be the one who couldn't conceive. Did you get any details? What is the actual issue? Is it fixable?'

'Um . . .' Nell hadn't worked out what she was going to tell people yet. Not that Merry was 'people', she was her best friend and would naturally expect all the details. 'Actually, it's hard to talk at the moment, do you mind? I'm still cut up about it.'

'Of course, of course. Gosh.' Merry tutted as the news sank in. 'So not fair, is it? I mean, me getting pregnant in the first month of trying and you . . .'

'Yes, thanks for pointing that out.' Nell gritted her teeth before remembering she was supposed to hold on to that smile.

'Oh God, sorry, I'm saying all the wrong things.' Merry groaned. 'It's just that I'm feeling . . . Nothing. Forget I said anything.'

Happily, thought Nell. It had been hard enough watching Merry's bump grow over the last few months without being envious, while she still had hope that she'd be pregnant herself soon. How she was going to cope when she met Merry's baby for the first time, she had no idea. She was looking forward to it, of course, but there would be a bittersweet twinge there too.

'If you really don't want to discuss it, shall we talk about something else?' Merry suggested.

'Yes, let's,' Nell said gratefully. 'The first Christmas candle workshop. We've had one cancellation but two new bookings. So we're fully booked.'

'Oh that's a shame,' Merry sighed. 'I was hoping for a small group, it would make it easier for me to manage.'

'You?' Nell squawked. 'You can't possibly run it.'

'The doctor said I could do the essentials,' Merry said defiantly. 'This is my business, therefore it's essential.'

'It's our business,' said Nell gently. 'We're partners, remember? And the whole point of you bringing me in to the company last year was so that we could be a team and I could support you, rather than you having to cope with everything alone.'

'True,' said Merry. 'But you do sales, I make the candles.'

'Usually, yes,' she pointed out. 'However, we can both do everything, like when you and Cole went to visit Emily in the summer and we had a run on Home candles and I had to make more.'

'Teaching other people to make candles is a whole other skill set. I'd say you're only at beginner's level yourself.'

That was a bit harsh in Nell's opinion, but she kept quiet, determined not to rile Merry. The last thing she wanted was for her to insist on coming in to run it; Cole would go bananas.

'I'm less experienced than you, of course, but I helped you pull this beginners workshop together; I know the schedule and you tested it out on me. I'll be fine.' In fact, the more she thought about running the workshop herself, the more anxious she became. There'd be eight loose cannons in a small space, plus herself. She wasn't completely sure she'd be able to cope.

'It's the first workshop and I wanted to be there,' Merry said.

'It's not ideal, but I can manage,' Nell reassured her.

'Hmm.'

'Thanks for your vote of confidence,' Nell said, feeling her nostrils twitch with annoyance. 'I'm doing my best here.'

'I know, it's just . . .' Merry paused. 'I guess Merry and Bright was my baby.'

'Of course it was, and obviously still is if you don't trust me. And rub it in, why don't you?' Nell's temper fizzed over, and she could no longer contain it. 'They're all your babies, aren't they? Whereas I get none. No baby at all.'

'Nell, that's not what—'

She had heard enough; the pressure of keeping everything in was too much for her. With a flash of anger, she stabbed at the 'end call' button and sent her phone skidding across the counter, then sank down onto the floor on her knees and burst into tears.

She must have been crying louder than she realised because she didn't hear the shop bell ring and jumped at the sound of a male voice hovering above her.

'Um. Hello, is this a bad time?'

Nell looked up to see a very attractive man with kind grey eyes, dark hair and a salt-and-pepper beard peering over the counter at her. He was slim and well-dressed and despite the presence of several scented candles in the shop, she was able to pick out the spicy aroma of his aftershave.

She scrubbed her tears away, bounced to her feet and reprised her earlier smile. 'Not at all! How can I help?'

He gave her a sceptical look before extending his hand.

'I'm Woody,' he said. 'I'm your last-minute Airbnb guest.'

'Oh!' Nell's eyes widened. She raked a hand through her curls and straightened her apron. 'Oh, how lovely. Welcome to Merry and Bright, I'm Nell.'

The door opened again and in came a tall, muscular man dressed in jogging bottoms and a hoodie, his hair tightly cropped and an earring glinting in one ear. He slid a large suitcase inside the door and Woody dashed over.

'Thank you, I can manage from here,' Woody insisted.

'You don't need to do this, you know,' the other man murmured, touching Woody's shoulder.

Woody sighed. 'I do. Spencer, I do.'

'You've made your point, love. Let's go home. We can sort this out.'

'By which you mean that you'll persuade me to do things your way.' Woody shook his head. 'Sorry, but I've made my mind up.'

The two men fell silent and rested their foreheads together. Nell realised she was staring and forced herself to turn away; she'd never seen such a good-looking male couple.

'I love you,' said Spencer with a sigh.

'I love you, and I'm going to miss you a lot.'

There were a few seconds of quiet, during which Nell assumed the couple were kissing. Then they said their goodbyes and the shop door closed with a tinkle of the bell.

'Oh gawwwd,' Woody murmured under his breath, watching Spencer out of the window. 'What have I done?'

He turned as Nell's phone beeped with an alert. It was Merry trying to call her back. She stuffed her phone in her pocket to deal with later.

'Sorry about that display,' he said, pressing his palms to his face. 'What must you think of me?'

The poor man looked on the verge of tears.

'I think that you're a man in desperate need of a glass of wine,' she replied, striding past him to flip the sign on the door to closed and turning the key.

'Oh gosh.' Woody managed a wobbly smile. 'Nell, darling, you and I are going to be the best of friends, I just know it.'

'Follow me,' she said, leading the way upstairs to the flat.

Woody didn't know just how fortuitous his pronouncement was, because after that last conversation with Merry, she might just be in need of a new best friend.

Chapter 8

Merry

'You're going to be amazed by how much the house has changed since you last visited.'

Merry gripped the door handle of the car as Astrid rounded the bend without slowing down. It was a good job her midwife, Pip, hadn't had prior knowledge of Astrid's skills behind the wheel when giving her blessing for this afternoon's jaunt.

The two women were on their way to visit the new Robinson family home. Strictly speaking, Merry was supposed to be resting, but she'd reasoned with the midwife that as the new house would soon be their home, she ought to be allowed to go, as long as she didn't do anything dangerous.

Astrid, her former art teacher and the closest thing she'd had to a mother figure, was dramatic in every aspect of her life: from her velvet cloaks in every hue, and the many bracelets which jingled on each wrist, to driving with one hand on the wheel and the other painting pictures in the air as she talked. Normally, Astrid's driving style didn't worry Merry, but now that she had to hold the seat belt away from her stomach, she was forced to keep her feet braced against the sides of the footwell to stop herself bouncing about.

'I'm not so sure, *Schatz*.' Astrid's eyes twinkled with mischief. 'You have been a little ball of energy since you first came into my art class as a teenager and wanted to learn to draw. When you put your mind to something, you have a way of making it happen.'

'I'm doing my best to chivvy the house renovation along so that we can bring the new baby home from hospital to this address,' said Merry determinedly. 'Being induced on the twenty-eighth does make it tricky, I admit.'

'If anyone can do it, it's you,' Astrid said. 'I know I say this often, but I am so proud of the woman you have become, *mein Liebling*. You have had to work hard for everything you have, I am looking forward to seeing the progress in your new home.'

'Thank you, Astrid, you say lovely things.' Merry felt herself glow with pride.

At a time when she felt as if she was doing everything wrong: upsetting Nell, arguing with Cole, and feeling guilty for her waters breaking, it felt good to be praised for once.

They turned into Oakwood Lane and Merry's spirits started to lift as they always did. It was a quiet residential street, leafy in the summer, but strung with elegant Christmas lights now. It had an eclectic mix of homes, from smaller terraced houses at the top, a short run of incongruous seventies-built bungalows in the middle and finally a delightful row of Victorian detached properties which, on one side of the road, backed onto hedgerows and green fields.

It was one of these, Meadow View, which Merry had come across in the summer when the previous inhabitant moved into Springwood House where her dad lived.

She and Cole had had their offer accepted before the house had even been officially photographed by the estate agent.

Astrid pulled up onto the drive and Merry let out a happy sigh. Sometimes she felt like pinching herself that her name was on the deeds for this beautiful house. For a girl who'd grown up with virtually nothing to her name, it seemed almost impossible that she was now a homeowner.

Before she had a chance to get out of the car, she heard her phone ring. She looked at the screen: Springwood House. Her stomach plummeted: *Please let it not be bad news . . .*

'Merry Robinson speaking,' she said tentatively.

It was one of his carers. 'Your dad isn't feeling well, and he wanted a quick word, Merry. Can I put him on?'

'Oh dear, thank you, of course.' She looked at Astrid, who nodded encouragingly.

There was a series of muffled noises, and then he was on the line.

'The car's gone, love. Looked out this morning and it wasn't there. The keys have gone, too.'

According to Emily, he hadn't owned a car for several years. But, despite that, the theft of it was one of his recurring worries. The sisters had learned to simply go along with it, rather than correct him; he'd forget about it soon enough.

Merry's heart stuttered, his voice was frail and croaky. 'It's OK, Dad, don't worry. The car has gone to be mended, that's all. It'll be back later.'

'Oh. I didn't remember. Thank you, silly me . . .' He broke off then and had a coughing fit. She wasn't sure he even heard her when she promised to come in and see him soon. The carer came back on the line and ended the call.

That cough sounded nasty. Merry chewed her lip. She really wanted to go and see him, give him some reassurance, but with her own health in jeopardy, even she could see that it wasn't wise.

'Come on,' said Astrid, patting her knee. 'Show me this home of yours.'

'Home sweet home,' Merry said, giving herself a shake. She gazed up at the front bedroom which would soon have her, Cole and the new baby sleeping in it. 'Or it will be before long.'

'It is a nice feeling,' Astrid agreed, wistfully, 'to find somewhere you belong.'

'Apart from mine and Mum's little flat where I spent the first few years of my life, I've never experienced home in the true sense. But maybe I will here.'

Astrid reached for her hand and gave it a squeeze. 'You know, you have already put down roots in Wetherley and established yourself among a community in which people care for you. You don't need a house to achieve those things.'

'I know that. As soon as I fell in love with Cole, I felt as if I'd come home. But I want more for this baby,' she said, glancing down at her bump. 'This house will be its sanctuary. A place to feel safe and to always know love. I want this house to be a constant in my child's life, somewhere he or she knows they can always return to, always be welcome.'

'You want your baby to have what you didn't,' Astrid summed it up perfectly. 'That's natural.'

'A forever home,' Merry murmured under her breath, her eyes roaming over Meadow View, so named because of the vista across the fields at the rear. 'I can't imagine ever wanting to leave.'

'Can I tell you something?' Astrid lowered her voice.

'Of course,' said Merry.

'It's about Germany.' She gripped Merry's hand with her other one so that Merry's fingers were sandwiched between hers.

Long artistic fingers, Merry had always thought. Though Astrid had retired from teaching two decades ago, she still loved to be creative and always had oil paint under her fingernails. How often had Astrid held her hands to comfort her over the years, she wondered? From the days of art classes when Merry had to call her Miss Beckermann, through her early years of living independently after the care system had spat her out into the world at eighteen. And through the many ups and downs of life ever since. Astrid had always been there for her.

'I made my home in England forty years ago. And for the last thirty of those, I don't think I've thought about ever living in Germany again.'

'But now?' Merry's heart began to pound. She wasn't thinking of leaving, was she? Astrid had been a touchstone of advice and support and love for so long. Merry couldn't contemplate not having her in her life.

'I'm conflicted.' Astrid shook her head, her gaze drifted and Merry sensed that her thoughts were hundreds of miles away in the forests of Bavaria.

'Before receiving this inheritance, I felt as if I had nothing to link me to my home country. My family is all gone. But now a strange thing has happened.' She tapped a hand on her chest. 'It feels as if home is calling me.'

'And?' Merry prompted. 'Are you thinking of answering that call?'

Her old friend sighed. 'I'm torn. Fred would not want to live in Germany. His home is here, and his family of course.'

'I can only imagine what it feels like for your heart to yearn for a particular place. I hope that one day I'll feel that way about this house, once I have raised a family here. I guess you have to decide whether it's more important for your home to be with the people you love or in the place that you feel connected to.'

Astrid smiled weakly. 'A lot to think about, and thank goodness I have your husband to give me his peas of wisdom.'

'I think you mean pearls,' Merry smiled.

'*Genau*. Exactly. So,' she said, nodding to the house. 'Enough of me, today is about you and your home.'

Merry made a mental note to bring this subject up again. Of course, Astrid should move back to Germany if that was what she truly wanted. There was something lovely about returning back to your roots; the full circle of life, she supposed. But after forty years? Surely it was better to stay here, where she already had a full life, surrounded by people who loved her? And, selfishly, Merry wanted Astrid to have the role of grandmother that nobody else could come close to fulfilling.

'It has such a nice face, don't you think?' Merry said, drinking in her new home.

It was a substantial symmetrical house built from yellow stone, twin-fronted with bay windows flanking the porch. Above, three slender Gothic arches formed the bedroom windows either side and a smaller version sat directly over the front entrance. The pitch of the roof was steep, hiding wonderful attic space which Merry intended to use to create a grown-up room for Harley. There were four chimneys in total, one on each corner, all with slightly different brickwork, which always made her think of Mary Poppins for some reason, and her favourite feature was the run of lacy white wooden fascia boards which finished off the perimeter of the roofline like bunting.

'A lovely welcoming face,' Astrid agreed, turning off the engine.

'I knew you would understand.' Merry smiled at her. 'Cole can't see a face at all. He sees bricks which are difficult to match, mortar which needs repointing and roof tiles which have slipped.'

'And that is why you two make a good team.' Astrid leaned behind her seat to collect her bag. 'Now, you sit there until I open your door, the ground is icy, and I do not want to have to scrape you up off the ground.'

Merry decided to do as she was told for once. She'd agreed with Cole that she wouldn't go into Merry and Bright today, and she had promised that she wouldn't drive anywhere on her own. But as long as she was careful, she didn't see what harm a trip to the new house would do, especially if she was accompanied by Astrid.

'We're so close to being ready to move in. One last big push and . . .' She held on to her friend's arm and took a couple of steps towards the house when she realised something was missing and frowned. 'Oh. There are no vans here.'

'Lunch break, perhaps?' Astrid suggested.

'They usually bring food with them and eat here.'

Once inside, it was clear that none of the workmen had been there all day. There were no tools left out, no obvious work in progress.

Merry went from room to room downstairs, taking in the exposed brickwork on the internal walls where the plaster had been stripped off. 'I don't understand,' she murmured. 'These should all have been plastered by now.'

Upstairs, Astrid was shouting down to her about the incredible light and how she would be able to see both sunsets and sunrises from up there.

But Merry wasn't listening, she was calling Cole.

'Darling, I'm at Meadow View and there is no one on site,' she said without preamble.

'What are you doing at the house?' Cole exclaimed. 'There are trip hazards everywhere, Merry. Please go home.'

'I'm fine. Astrid is with me,' she said defiantly.

'What did the midwife say?'

Pip had paid her a house visit this morning after hearing about her trip to the hospital and had made Merry promise to call her night or day if anything untoward were to happen between now and her induction date.

'Baby's heartbeat fine, blood pressure stable, temperature normal, so nothing to worry about, I promise. Cole, there is not a plasterer in sight. I thought I should let you know.'

'I already knew. The plasterers aren't there because I cancelled them for this week.'

'What?' She was horrified. 'Why would you do that? It's three weeks until Christmas. You said we needed to leave it as long as possible to decorate after plastering to give it time to dry out.'

'We do,' Cole replied. 'But the walls can't be plastered until the first fix of the electrics has been done.'

'Oh.' Merry was confused. How had the schedule slipped so far without her knowing about it? 'So why hasn't that been done?'

'Well, um, long story.'

She could almost hear him squirming from across town. 'I'm listening.'

'Because they had to do another job.'

'That is not on,' she fumed. 'Call them up and tell them they're in breach of contract. We'll fire them and get someone else.'

'Darling,' Cole cleared his throat. 'You've done a fantastic job designing the kitchen, the bathroom layout and selecting colour schemes for the bedrooms.'

'Except that none of that can be finished off yet,' she countered. 'Because the walls aren't plastered.'

'I know, I know. But the building work is my area, please leave it to me to sort.'

She looked around her kitchen; there were wires protruding from the walls and ceiling, pipes in place in preparation for the sink to go in, drains for the dishwasher . . . it was a building site, there were no other words for it. Her plan to be in before the baby came felt like a pipe dream.

'I have left it to you,' she argued, her hand rubbing her bump automatically. 'Until now. But we're running out of time. One of us needs to get shirty with them, and if you won't, I will. A heavily pregnant woman is a very scary prospect.'

'I know, believe me. OK, fine!' She heard him draw in a breath. 'We can't fire them because the other job they are on is for me. I've got a client desperate to be in for . . . in for . . .' His voice petered out as presumably he realised the massive hole he'd dug for himself. 'Christmas.'

She was so angry that for a few seconds she couldn't speak. 'You deliberately took them off our job to make someone's Christmas moving-in plans a reality? I don't believe it. Cole, what were you thinking?'

'Merry—'

She didn't wait to hear his excuse, she cut the call and stared at the dead phone. He'd made her a promise and now he'd broken it. She felt completely let down. And this was why no one, not even her darling husband, could be relied on – no one but herself.

Chapter 9

Nell

'I've only ever made one candle and that was from a kit,' Woody confessed, after Nell had told him about the upcoming workshop. 'And I would probably have had to pay someone to take it off my hands, rather than sell it.'

Nell giggled. 'At least you're honest.'

They were at either end of the sofa in the flat upstairs. But with the Christmas tree aglow, the flames from the fire and the twinkle of lights along the mantelpiece, they could see each other well enough. Nell should be thinking about going home, but she was warm and cosy and didn't want to. Not yet.

'But, in my favour, I am a professional event organiser so what I lack in expertise, I can make up for in pizzazz.' He did a little shoulder shimmy. 'Your students will be raving about their experience to all and sundry. Repeat bookings virtually guaranteed.'

'In that case,' she said, tearing into the bag of crisps from the welcome hamper, 'what could possibly go wrong?'

They'd already drunk the wine from it, and they'd made headway with the bottle of Fleurie that Woody had brought with him. She was feeling an awful lot more cheerful since chatting to him.

'Quite,' said Woody, taking a neat sip from his glass. 'Plus, it's only a small group. I'm used to handling events for several hundred people. Christmas, as you can imagine, is normally mayhem.'

'I'm surprised you were able to take time off then.'

She was very curious to know what had brought him here, especially after overhearing that conversation with his husband, Spencer. It was obvious that something major was going on, but rather than pry, Nell was letting him unfurl his story in his own time.

He pulled a cushion onto his lap and hugged it. 'Long story, but I quit my perfect job recently because . . . well, because I had plans for the new year, which would have involved me being at home for a while. The plans have changed, and I tried to get my job back, but my boss had already replaced me, so . . .' He shrugged. 'I'm footloose and fancy-free, and at your service for as long as you need me. There were lots of Airbnbs available, but I saw the opportunity to work in Merry and Bright and knew instantly that this was the one for me.'

'I'll drink to that.' Nell chinked her glass against his and thought how serendipitous it was that he'd arrived just when she needed not only some help in the shop, but a friend too.

They both took a slurp and made an exaggerated 'Ahhh' noise, making each other laugh.

Nell's phone rang and she flushed with shame when she saw it was Merry. She should have called her back after putting the phone down on her. What must she be thinking? This was a time to pull together, not have silly arguments. Merry needed her more than ever right now.

'Excuse me a sec, I need to take this,' she said to Woody, scrambling to her feet.

'Take your time,' he replied. 'I'll put some music on.'

'Hey, Merry, I'm sorry about earlier,' Nell moved to the window overlooking the market square below. It was dark now, but the Christmas lights lit up the square and surrounding shops, the tall Christmas tree sparkling magnificently in the centre, giving the town a magical glow.

'Yeah, I know, we got cut off,' Merry replied, 'No worries. I was going to call you back, but then Astrid arrived, and we went to the new house.'

Nell breathed a sigh of relief; Merry hadn't even realised that she had hung up on her. At least that saved her an awkward apology. 'It's been busy here too. Woody arrived. Our Airbnb guest. We've been having a glass of wine while I show him around.'

She blinked to clear her vision, noticing that she was quite tipsy. She couldn't drive home. Maybe she'd stay on Woody's sofa. He was fun and easy to be around, and she hadn't told him any lies, which meant no matter how drunk she got, she wouldn't be able to spill any beans. By contrast, she was finding it hard to be around Olek at the moment, which was so very sad.

She watched Woody trying to pair his phone to the Bluetooth speaker and giggled. It had been ages since she'd had a dance and she suddenly really wanted to. She'd definitely stay. Olek was fetching Max from football training, so he wasn't at home anyway.

'Oh, are you drinking again?' Merry asked.

It may have been innocently meant, but Nell was extra sensitive at the moment and easy to rile.

'Yes, why not?' she said, keeping her voice light. 'No reason not to now, is there?'

'You lucky thing. I'd kill for a glass of wine right now.'

Nell bit her lip. 'I'd hardly call it lucky. I'd rather be pregnant, given the choice.'

'No. Sorry. Of course.' Merry sounded very meek. 'Oh please don't be cross, Nell, I'm so fed up with everything.

And now I've had another row with Cole. Anyway, I was just ringing back about the candle-making workshop.'

'If you're going to give me another lecture about me not being up to the job, don't. Cancel it or don't cancel it. Up to you.'

'I was going to say that of course you can run it; it makes perfect sense,' said Merry, sounding hurt. 'I'm very grateful to you for stepping in.'

'Thanks,' Nell was mollified and regretting jumping to conclusions. 'I won't let you down.'

'We haven't got a lot of choice really, other than cancel.'

The phrase 'damning with faint praise' sprang to mind, but Nell knew what she meant. 'If we cancel at short notice, people might be too annoyed to rebook, and we don't want that.'

'Absolutely,' Merry agreed. 'I've worked so hard to build this business, I mean, we have, that I'd hate to damage our reputation. So I've had a brilliant idea; I can join you via Zoom. You can set up your laptop in the corner of the studio and I'll be there virtually to help you, give you some guidance if you get stuck. Answer tricky questions, that sort of thing.'

Nell's jaw fell open. She could just imagine Merry butting in every few seconds with helpful suggestions. She meant well, but it would undermine Nell's meagre confidence to have her friend there in the background. 'That's very kind of you, but I don't think that will work, Merry. Far better if—'

'Oh hell,' Merry interrupted. 'I'm sorry, Nell, but Dad's care home is trying to get through. I've already spoken to him once today and he wasn't well. I'll catch up with you soon. Thanks for being understanding about the Zoom, I think it'll be brilliant.'

'Brilliant?' Nell muttered once the line had gone dead. 'That's not quite the word I'd use. But I guess we'll soon find out.'

Chapter 10

Merry

In a small flat, on the ground floor of Springwood House, Ray Meadows lay motionless under a sheet and blanket, except for the shallow rise and fall of his chest, his breath fluttery and faint. Occasionally, he'd have a coughing fit and the rattling sound of his lungs made his daughters, Merry and Emily, exchange worried looks. They sat either side of his bed, each holding a hand. Gail, the manager of the dementia residential home, stood by the door, having a whispered conversation with his carer. Merry's heart ached just looking at him. His skin had taken on a grey pallor, his cheeks were sunken and his jawline unshaven.

'I'm so glad you're here, Em,' Merry told her. 'Thanks for coming so quickly. It's lovely for me, and I'm sure Dad appreciates it too.'

Since Merry had received the call the day before to inform her that Ray's health had deteriorated, he'd been moved from his one-bedroomed flat with a view of the gardens into this one, which was geared up to make it easier for staff to care for him. Dominating the space was a hospital bed which could be raised and lowered, with bars on each side to stop him rolling out. Other than a kettle and mini fridge to keep milk in, there weren't any cooking facilities. It wasn't safe to give him access to anything more complicated than that anymore.

'Of course.' Emily dismissed her thanks. 'I was primed to fly over when I heard you were in hospital, but you wouldn't let me.'

Emily had grown up only a stone's throw from Merry; they often marvelled at how much of their lives had been like sliding doors. There'd been so many occasions and places where they may have been close to each other and not known who the other was. Earlier this year, Emily and her boyfriend, Will, had decided to start a new life on Jersey, helped by Emily's best friend, Izzy, who'd been trying to get her to move over for years. Merry was glad for her, but sad to have lost the spontaneous 'fancy a coffee?' moments that the two of them had enjoyed.

'I'm very grateful.' Merry smiled. 'But there was nothing you could have done, and I'd much rather have you to stay once the baby arrives.'

'I could have done both!' Emily shot her a stern look. 'I wanted to help, even if it's just to cook dinner or fold laundry. So next time, let me.'

'Noted,' she replied, meekly. Her sister meant well, but Merry knew how she liked things to be done. Sometimes it was easier to do it yourself than watch someone do it not to your liking.

'And just you try to stop me coming when my niece or nephew makes their entrance,' Emily added. 'You'll be desperate to get rid of me.'

'Not going to happen. I'd have loved an aunt when I was little,' said Merry, 'or any relative at all, come to that. I'm going to make sure my kids get plenty of Auntie Emily time.'

'Good.' Her sister's eyes shone and Merry smiled too.

A year on from discovering the other existed, neither of them could quite believe how fortunate they were to have the sibling they'd always longed for. The fact that they got on like a house on fire sometimes made their relationship feel too good to be true.

Before they had met, Emily had been totally responsible for looking after Ray, but ever since, Merry had tried to ease Emily's burden and make sure she knew she wasn't alone. When Emily had moved away, Merry had become the first point of contact for the care home. But this was the first time that Ray had been properly ill, and Merry was relieved Emily was on hand if his condition worsened.

Since receiving the call from Gail yesterday, Merry had spent as much time here as she could. A fact that had not gone down well with Cole.

'There are always coughs and colds and viruses going round in that place,' he'd pointed out, not unreasonably, when she'd called to tell him she planned to visit her dad immediately.

They'd ended up having harsh words with each other. She felt emotional just thinking about it, especially as they hadn't even dealt with their previous row about the workmen being pulled off Meadow View. Gail's message had made her dad's condition sound so serious that she hadn't stopped to consider the consequences and had driven herself over to the home immediately.

'He's my dad, Cole, I can't not visit him when he's alone and ill,' she'd argued. 'That's cruel.'

'How about I go, and you stay in the car park outside? I can FaceTime you so you can say hello? That way, at least you won't pick up any germs. You heard what the doctor said, you're susceptible to infection now that you don't have the amniotic fluid to protect the baby.'

'Dad's got flu, Cole,' she'd said curtly. 'I hardly think that's going to be a danger to my vagina. And don't think

I've forgotten about the workmen situation at Meadow View, I haven't. But right now, Dad has to take priority.'

'Of course he does. I'm just looking out for you and our baby, darling.' Cole had looked so sad that she'd almost relented. But her streak of independence was too wide to back down. There had still been a slight frosty atmosphere between them this morning and Merry felt wretched about it.

Now, looking at her dad so poorly, she felt justified. He hadn't been awake yesterday when she came, and so far today he hadn't woken up either. What if he didn't wake up ever again? She frowned at herself for being morbid, but the truth was that if anything happened to him and she hadn't been in to see him, she'd always have to live with that guilt.

'You look amazing,' said Emily. 'Like a woman in a Renaissance painting – all softness and curves and radiant skin.'

'Thanks.' Merry forced herself to concentrate on her sister and pretended to pout. 'I think we should FaceTime every morning so that you can boost my ego like that.'

'Gladly,' Emily said with a grin. 'Seriously, I was so worried about you last week.'

'You look great too.' Merry changed the subject. She wished everyone would please stop worrying, she was perfectly capable of looking after herself. 'Brimming with health and vitality, and how can you still have a tan in December?'

Her sister pressed her free hand to her face. 'It's probably windburn. My skin is like leather these days. I'm outside every day, on the beach mostly. Will has got his first bookings for next spring. I've been getting the beach shack ready while he has been completing all his safety courses and instructor training.'

Will and Emily's love story was so cute. He'd been the occupational therapist here at the home when Emily met him, and part of the team looking after Ray. Within weeks, they'd fallen head over heels in love with each other and he'd moved into her cottage. As a mad-keen surfer, his dream had always been to open a surf school with a not-for-profit element offering tuition to disadvantaged kids. His own upbringing hadn't been easy, and he'd seen first-hand how developing a passion for surfing could boost self-confidence. Merry couldn't wish for a lovelier man for her sister.

'And what about you? Your fashion business?'

Emily looked down at her hands. 'It's in the planning stage.'

She had been working in a senior school this time last year, as the PA to the head teacher. She'd taken the job on largely because the hours had afforded her plenty of time to look after their father. But her true passion was for buying vintage clothes, upgrading them with her own fashion twist and selling them on. Merry had encouraged Emily to follow her dream and try to make a living from doing what she loved.

'What's to plan?' Merry smelled a rat; Emily wasn't meeting her eye. 'You've got suitcases full of vintage finds ready to go.'

She knew that because she'd helped Emily to pack up her little cottage in the spring. Cases, trunks, boxes . . . stuffed full of beautiful things, many of which Emily had added her own creative touches to.

Emily looked shifty. 'I have, but we've been putting all our time into Will's surf school. It's far more involved than mine; it makes sense to get that up and running first.'

'You said that about Izzy's business when you first arrived in Jersey.'

Izzy had a busy holiday cottage business and Emily had been employed to help her renovate a new property when she'd first arrived on the island.

'I always wanted a pushy big sister.' Emily gave Merry a sideways look.

'Oh very funny. It's just . . .' Merry chewed her lip, torn between wanting to just enjoy being together and feeling like it was her duty to give her younger sister a pep talk. 'When it was just you looking after Dad, you had to do everything, and I know you put your own life on hold. Now you don't have to.'

'And now I've got you to share the load and I'm really grateful.' Emily reached across their sleeping father's legs and squeezed Merry's hand. 'But I feel guilty that I've abandoned you, especially now.'

'You can stop with guilt-tripping yourself right now, lady.' Merry gave her a stern look. 'If it wasn't for you tracking me down, I wouldn't have had my dad and my sister at my wedding last Christmas Eve.'

An image popped into Merry's head. She and Cole emerging from the registry office and into a sparkling white snowy scene, all their loved ones around them, throwing confetti and wishing them well. She'd felt more surrounded by love in that moment than ever before. It had been a wonderful occasion, made even more magical because she'd never imagined for a second that she'd have real family at her wedding. Emily had made that possible.

'Merry, I'm miles away and completely useless and you're about to drop and not supposed to be doing anything at all.'

'Who said that?' Merry frowned. 'Don't answer that: Cole.'

'You'd be disappointed in him if he didn't show he cared about you and the baby.'

She harrumphed. If he cared that much, she thought, crossly, he'd get on with finishing Meadow View, so his baby had a home to move into. She kept that to herself, because every time she mentioned moving house, everyone leapt on her and said that waiting until the new year was more sensible. She didn't care about sensible; she cared about wanting to finally feel at home.

'You've neatly deflected my question,' she said instead. 'So when does Emily's new venture get a look-in?'

'There's no rush,' Emily protested. 'I'm enjoying helping Will set up his business. I can't teach surfing, obviously – although I'm actually getting quite good now with Will's help. But I can do the rest. If I was off doing my own thing, it wouldn't be the same. This way, if I need to, I can manage the business in his absence. I'm enjoying living in the moment. One thing at a time. At some point, we're going to sort out a room at the cottage for me to spread out and start trading. Maybe in the spring.'

Merry shook her head, bemused. 'You look blissfully happy, and that's all that matters. I couldn't do it. I'd be champing at the bit to get started on my own thing.'

She remembered back to the early days of running Merry and Bright, how she'd worked late into the night at the kitchen table coming up with the perfect combination of essential oils to create exactly the right scent for each type of candle. She'd leapt at every opportunity to grow her business, developing bespoke products and even overcoming her nerves to appear on TV as Hester's guest. She was proud of what she'd achieved.

As far as Cole was concerned, his money was their money, and they were both open with how much the other brought into the family. But Cole was also of the opinion that if Merry didn't want to work, he would be perfectly content to look after her. She knew how fortunate she was to be in that position, but the thought of being reliant on someone else for money brought her out in goosebumps. As long as she could work, she would.

'Sorry about that, ladies,' said Gail, rejoining them. 'I was getting an update from the carer who was with your father last night. He had a restless night, and his temperature was spiking. We gave him some medication and it's come down a little, but we'll need to keep an eye on him and let the doctors' surgery know if he deteriorates.' She hesitated, appearing to consider her next words with care. 'Flu can be dangerous for dementia patients, but as Ray's relatively young, I have every faith he'll get through this.'

Emily's eyes widened. 'Dangerous? What do you mean?'

Merry reached for her hand across the bed. She'd made the mistake of googling 'flu and dementia' last night, only to find that for dementia patients, flu could be very serious and, in some cases, fatal. She wished she didn't know herself, and hadn't planned on mentioning it to Emily.

Gail's expression softened. 'For a person whose auto-immune system is already weak, it can be hard to fight off the illness, which can lead to more serious problems.'

'Oh.' Emily's face was a mask of horror. 'Oh gosh.'

'But we're not there yet, and may not be at all,' Merry countered. Everyone already had enough to worry about, what was the point of heaping more on unnecessarily? 'Isn't that right?'

Gail nodded. 'For now, you're giving him what he needs, which is your presence – that will be his best medicine.'

Imagine if she'd gone into labour at the Christmas lights switch-on when her waters broke? There was no way she'd have been able to sit at her father's bedside and risk taking flu home to the baby. She pressed a light hand on her stomach. *Stay there, little one, just for a while longer.* A feeling of panic rushed up inside her; there was so much to think about, so much to do.

'Can I open a window?' Merry begged, fanning her face with a scarf to calm herself.

'You may not,' Emily intervened quickly, pressing her sister's shoulder to ensure she stayed seated. 'I'll do it.'

Gail winced. 'Just a crack please, ladies, we try to maintain a steady temperature. I'll leave you alone with your father. There's a pull cord above Ray's bed if you need anything.'

Emily struggled to open the sash window. Just as well she'd not attempted it herself, thought Merry; despite her habitual 'can-do' attitude and refusal to ask for help, she knew she had to be careful physically. She hadn't told another soul, but her stomach ached as if she'd been overdoing her sit-ups today, and she'd vowed to be sensible.

As if she'd read her mind, Emily slid a stool underneath her feet.

'There we are, Madam,' said her sister. 'Let me know if I can do anything else to enhance your comfort.'

'A glass of champagne would be nice,' Merry replied, making herself more comfortable. 'In my dreams.'

'Hmm.' Emily inspected the refreshments on offer. 'I can do lemon barley water or black tea without milk.'

'Maybe later, thanks.'

'Dad taught me how to make tea,' Emily mused. 'He used to be so pedantic about it. The water had to be scalding hot, poured the second the kettle boiled. The teabag had to be stirred for at least three minutes. Next, add the sugar, and finally a splash of milk. By the time I moved him in here, he'd forgotten how he liked it. He'd even forgotten how to make it.'

Merry wished she'd known Ray before he'd started to lose his memory. She loved hearing Emily's childhood stories. Occasionally, she'd feel a tweak of sadness that she hadn't had a father figure in her own life while growing up, but Ray hadn't been perfect, and she was mature enough now not to view other people's lives through rose-tinted glasses.

Ray moaned softly and the sisters stared at each other and then him.

'I think he's waking up!' Merry felt giddy with relief. 'Thank goodness.'

'He squeezed my hand!' Emily whispered.

Ray's mouth started moving.

'What is he saying?' Merry leaned as close as her bump would allow.

'Something about his girl?' Emily guessed.

'It's OK, Dad. We're here,' Merry said. 'Both your girls, Emily and Merry.'

He lifted his head up and Merry was struck by how much weight he had lost even in the past couple of weeks. The collar of his pyjama shirt swamped his neck; he looked tiny against the pillow. She'd planned to buy him some new ones for Christmas, but perhaps she should buy them now and bring them in.

'Don't try to sit up, save your energy,' Emily soothed, taking his hand again. She looked at Merry and shook her head. 'He's changed so much in the month since I was last here, I feel terrible.'

Ray nodded and lay back down. 'Is that you, Tina?'

'I'm Tina's daughter, Dad, Emily. Merry is here too,' Emily told him.

His voice was barely audible and Merry filled a beaker of water from the jug by his bedside and popped a straw in it.

‘Let me,’ said Emily, taking it from her.

Merry was happy to let her, stretching forward was uncomfortable.

Sometimes, Ray called her Sam, her mum’s name. It was a bittersweet moment. It saddened her to think that he didn’t recognise her, but when he spoke of Sam with such love, sometimes even recalling things they’d done or said, she treasured the fleeting glimpses into her parents’ relationship, always aware that she may never hear that story again.

Ray sipped the water and coughed. Water trickled out of the corner of his mouth and Emily grabbed a tissue to dry his face. ‘Lift up,’ he rasped, making an upward motion with his hand.

Merry fumbled down the side of the mattress for the bed remote-control button. She raised up the bed so that he could see them both and a slow smile appeared on his face.

‘Look at you two, pretty as pictures.’

‘And Merry’s having a baby soon, Dad, remember?’ Emily prompted him.

‘I can see that. She’ll be a great mum,’ Ray mumbled. ‘Bloody great.’

Merry felt her chest heave. How could he know? How could this man, who’d barely got any grasp on who he was, let alone his grown-up daughters, identify her worst fears?

‘Too right she will,’ Emily boasted.

‘Why do you say that?’ Merry demanded. ‘How do you know I will?’

‘You’re kind, lass,’ Ray’s voice was croaky and shook on every word. ‘Just like your mum. She put you first, every time. Even got rid of me because she didn’t think I’d be good for you.’

Merry shook her head. ‘She abandoned me. Left me to be put into care.’

'No.' He closed his eyes again. 'I know Sammy; she saved you, even though she couldn't save herself.'

'But I don't know how to be a mother, Dad.'

'Pah.' He rolled his head to the side. 'Nobody knows what they're doing. I've seen you with your husband's kids. You know how to love other people. That's all you need. You can do it, I know you can.'

'And it's not long now until the baby comes,' Emily told him. 'Are you looking forward to meeting your first grandchild?'

'Course I am.' Ray's voice was only a whisper and after a few moments his breathing slowed.

Merry had tears in her eyes. Her dad couldn't have said anything more perfect.

Suddenly, his eyes flew open, making the sisters jump.

'Is it Monday?' he muttered. 'We have chops on Monday. Mum's gone to the butchers.'

Merry and Emily shared a sad smile as they watched their dad slip out of lucidity and into sleep.

'He's gone again,' Emily sighed.

'As long as he keeps coming back,' Merry replied, patting his hand. It was icy cold, so she tucked it inside the covers. 'I want him to meet this baby. I want a picture of them together, so I can say, look, this is you and your granddad. Does that sound mad?'

'No,' Emily said softly. 'It sounds like something a loving mum would say to her child.'

Merry wasn't so sure. A loving mum would be following doctor's orders and not wishing she was running a candle-making workshop rather than staying at home to take care of her soon-to-be-born baby.

Chapter 11

Nell

The day of the first candle-making workshop had arrived and Nell was a bag of nerves and regrets. She wasn't sleeping well at the moment, which didn't help. There was so much whirling around in her head and lying beside Olek listening to his deep, easy breaths only increased her anxiety. The closer the hands of the shop's clock crept towards the 2 p.m. start time, the more she began to doubt herself.

What had she been thinking? She wasn't anywhere near experienced enough in the art of making candles to impart knowledge to others. Merry made it look so easy; she could judge when the molten wax was ready to pour into the glass jars just by looking at it and her candles were perfectly flat on top, while Nell's invariably developed more craters than the dark side of the moon.

She paced up and down the shop, debating whether to call everyone booked onto this afternoon's session and make up some excuse. She could tell them the wax melter was broken, or she'd come down with a vomiting bug in the last half-hour . . . They'd have to refund everyone's money, but the way she was feeling right now, she'd gladly do that from her own pocket.

From the other side of the closed studio door, the sound of a Michael Bublé Christmas song blared out and, a second later, Woody started singing along in falsetto.

She erupted into laughter, and the music went off.

'I heard that,' he yelled. 'Just testing my technology. Two ticks and I'll be ready for the grand reveal. You are going to die!'

Imminent death notwithstanding, her new friend's enthusiasm must have been contagious because Nell gave herself some stern words.

Come on, Nell. You can do this. Woody will be there to gee up the participants. And, more importantly, Merry will be on hand via Zoom to pick up on any major errors. What's the worst that could happen?

Thank goodness for Woody, that was all she could say.

He'd been an absolute diamond since his arrival, he'd already made himself at home both in the flat and at Merry and Bright.

Nell was particularly talented at listening to customers' requirements and selecting the most appropriate product, regularly managing to unintentionally upsell to them. She was also pretty hot on keeping an eye on stock levels and shelf replenishment, if she did say so herself. Woody talked far too much to every customer and Nell had had to have a word with him about throwing in freebies when he got on particularly well with someone. And then there was that unfortunate incident of setting fire to the sleeve of his own jumper with a lit candle. But, on the plus side, he was the fastest and neatest gift wrapper she'd ever met, while simultaneously getting customers to add their details to the mailing list, following Merry and Bright on social media and, his masterstroke, persuading them to take a selfie with their purchases, post it on Instagram and tag them.

'Okey-dokey, Nell, close your eyes, I'm opening the door,' Woody shouted.

'My eyes are shut!' she replied.

For the last two hours, she'd been banned from the studio while he worked his magic. He'd told her to trust him, which, even though she hardly knew him, she did.

The door opened and, at once, the scent of Christmas trees hit her. Woody took her hand and led her in.

'You may open your eyes,' he said. 'Ta-dah!'

'Oh my goodness!' She turned in a full circle, taking it all in.

'Careful, the floor might be a little bit slippery,' he said with a wince. 'I dropped a bottle of essential oil near the sink.'

'Noted,' said Nell, adding 'scrub floor' to her job list. 'But I forgive you, because this room is incredible.'

The studio had been totally transformed from a neat and clinical production area to what could only be described as a wintry scene from Narnia. Snow-sprayed branches, garlands of holly, spruce and ivy, strings of lights . . . everywhere Nell looked, there were touches of Woody's genius. The work table had a big bunch of mistletoe suspended above it and had been set with eight workstations, each with a small tote bag on which Woody had written the participants' names in glitter pens. A festive floral and candle centrepiece gave the finishing touch to the space.

Woody clasped his hands together under his chin. 'You like?'

'I *love*!' Nell nodded. 'You've worked wonders. It's obvious you're an expert at this sort of thing.'

'Thank you,' he said with a bow. 'I'm honoured.'

He gestured towards the wax melter, where Nell had previously set out the essential oils for the attendees to make the lemon, lime and rosemary candle, which Merry had selected because it was her first-ever product. Those oils had been replaced with different ones.

'I've had a little swap around,' Woody admitted. 'I know you advertised making one of the original products. But as it's Christmas, it's got to be Mistletoe Kiss.'

Nell chewed her lip. 'Merry isn't going to like it, but that is a really good point.'

'I've made a romantic Christmas playlist too,' he said, touching the keypad on the laptop.

'Christmas Lights' by Coldplay struck up and Nell was instantly transported to New York, where Olek had taken her on a romantic autumn break, and they'd come across Coldplay rehearsing in Central Park.

'I love this song.' Her heart fluttered momentarily for her husband.

Olek had tried repeatedly to get her to open up about the fertility tests and she had found herself getting short-tempered with him purely to get him to change the subject. She conjured up his hurt expression and felt a wave of indecision. Had she done the right thing by deceiving him? They didn't have any secrets from each other – at least not during their relationship. There was one thing she hadn't told him which had happened before she'd met him. She'd contemplated talking about it on several occasions but had never found the right words or the right moment. And after a while they had reached a point when it was too late to reveal anything significant from their previous lives. Now she was glad of her omission.

'Wakey-wakey.' Woody waved a hand in front of her face. 'Our guinea pigs – I mean, attendees – will be here any minute. You look like you need a double espresso to pep you up.'

She blinked at him, dragging her thoughts back to the moment. 'I do. I really do.'

'Coming right up.'

He was a live wire and just what she needed, but every so often, she caught a glimpse of pain in his eyes. He was hiding something, but as she was equally as secretive, she couldn't very well challenge him about it, could she?

The next hour flew by and before Nell knew it, her guests had arrived and were all set up in the studio and Merry had joined them on Zoom.

'I'm Merry, founder of Merry and Bright. Thanks so much for coming to our first Christmas Candle Workshop. And, as you can see, I'm sitting with my feet up, doing precisely nothing, other than sipping hot chocolate.' Merry raised her mug before resting it back on her bump. 'But I do have a built-in shelf these days, which is very handy.'

Merry being present only via a screen had been accepted without complaint by the workshop participants, who were all women. As was the fact that Nell was their substitute tutor. They consisted of a group of three friends celebrating a fortieth birthday, a mum and her two daughters and two elderly sisters who declared themselves Christmas addicts who couldn't resist a festive craft session. All of them had gathered around the laptop in a semicircle, while Nell stood to the side. Woody had cleared away coffee cups and gingerbread biscuits with which the ladies had been welcomed and was now manning the shop.

'Make the most of it,' said one of the women. 'My little girl is six months old. I don't think I've had chance to sit with my feet up since the day she arrived; not alone, at least.'

'I'll be coming back to work soon after this one makes an appearance,' said Merry, 'so I probably won't have much time to put my feet up anyway.'

Nell frowned. Merry would be popping in of course, but coming back to work, surely not too soon? She was on the verge of challenging her friend about it but then remembered they had a studio full of visitors to entertain.

'Thanks, Merry,' said Nell, deciding to take ownership of the session. 'OK, let's get cracking. Before we start melting the wax, we need to prepare our glass containers.'

'Hold on a minute, Nell.' Merry leaned forward and gave an awkward laugh. 'I've just spotted the essential oils you've got out; they're not the right ones.'

'Change of plan,' she intervened quickly. 'Woody and I have gone for a wintry theme and realised the best candles to make today are Mistletoe Kisses. You're all happy with that, ladies?'

There was a round of nodding and assent.

'I was going to buy some of those anyway,' someone said, 'so even better.'

Merry picked up her phone and typed something. Nell's phone pinged. She read Merry's message and bit her lip. She'd anticipated this.

Nell, what are you doing? I picked the lemon candle for a reason.

I know, but Woody has done such an amazing job decorating the studio. It was his idea to make Christmas candles. It makes sense, I think, and it's no biggie.

Hopefully Merry would be fine with that, she thought, dropping her phone in her apron pocket. Anyway, it was too late, they couldn't change things now. She glanced at her notes; the first job was to preheat the glue gun.

She flicked the switch and moved to the second.

'Ladies, help yourself to cotton wicks from the box on the table. We're going to glue the wicks to the base of the jars to keep them secure when we pour the wax.'

In her pocket, her phone vibrated again. Nell ignored it.

'Nell?' Merry called from the laptop. 'Sorry to interrupt but I've messaged you.'

Nell didn't look at the laptop because someone asked a question.

'Can you use different sorts of wick?' asked one of the elderly sisters. 'They were dipped in wax in my youth.'

'Absolutely,' Nell nodded. 'We like to be as sustainable as possible, hence the cotton, but you can—'

Merry cleared her throat. 'Sorry, Nell. Can you just look at your phone?'

'Excuse me, one second,' she smiled an apology at the old lady.

It has NOTHING to do with Woody!! I wanted you to make the Lemon candles.

I'm a partner in this business. Treat me like one. I repeat this is NO BIGGIE!

Nell turned her phone onto flight mode. Merry could reply all she wanted now, but Nell wasn't going to read the messages.

'Actually, ladies,' Merry piped up from the laptop, her voice an octave higher than usual, 'I'm going to pop in and say hi myself. See you in twenty minutes. My sister can drive me.'

Nell positioned herself in front of the screen, blocking everyone else's view. 'Oh no you don't, Merry Robinson.

That baby is counting on you to relax and take care of yourself. That's your priority right now.'

Merry's face was like thunder. 'I am sick and tired of being told—'

Nell gently closed the laptop and turned back to the group. 'Oh dear, it looks like we've lost her. Never mind, where was I? Oh yes, wicks . . .'

Chapter 12

Merry

'No way. I don't believe it.' Merry stared at the black screen for a few seconds, waiting for Nell and the studio to reappear, but nothing happened. 'Nell just cut me off.'

She checked her Wi-Fi connection, just in case she was doing Nell a disservice. But there was nothing wrong with it. Of course there wasn't. Nell had deliberately ended the Zoom call after having preached to her first about her priorities. How dare she? How bloody dare she?

Emily brought them both grilled cheese sandwiches, set Merry's down on the table and bit into her own. 'Never mind, eat this instead.'

Merry gave her sister a look of apology. 'I can't, Em, I've got to get in to work. Can you drive me to the shop, please?'

After visiting their father, they had come back to Holly Cottage. Emily was going to stay in the kids' room for a couple of nights, at the end of which, hopefully, Ray would be over the worst. Merry had decided to do the Zoom from the living room. Emily had lit a fire; the lamps were on and, as usual, a selection of branded candles were burning cheerily around the room, layering the fragrance to suit Merry's mood. At least that had been the plan. She'd been feeling cosy and comfortable before speaking to Nell. Now, if she'd had a cat, it would be in danger of being metaphorically kicked.

'Is that wise?' Emily said in a rhetorical sort of way. 'Budge up.'

Merry, who was sitting in the centre of the sofa, leaving little room either side of her, stuck her hand up. 'If you help me up, you can have my space.'

'Not until your face has reverted from beetroot to its normal English rose pink,' said Emily. 'You don't want your blood pressure to skyrocket again. Not on my watch. Now, give me some room, fatty.'

Emily attempted to make herself spherical by inflating her cheeks, sticking her belly out and holding her arms out to the sides.

'Rude.' Merry conceded a giggle. Despite her frustration with Nell, it was incredibly nice to have a bit of sibling teasing in her life these days after believing that she was an only child. 'Fine, then.'

She shifted over and Emily squeezed in beside her.

'What have you got your knickers in a twist about?' Emily took another bite of her sandwich.

'We've got eight people on our first candle-making course. We had a deal that it only went ahead if I was virtually supervising, because Nell doesn't really have the skills to make candles, let alone to teach. The students hadn't even started, and she cut me off. She's out of order.' So much for her staying at home and taking it easy, Merry could almost feel her veins thrumming with stress.

'But is she *really* out of order?' Emily dipped the corner of her sandwich into mayonnaise.

Merry gave her a sideways look. 'What's that supposed to mean?'

'From what I overheard, you might have been a bit bossy.'

‘Don’t fall into the “bossy trap”, Em,’ she warned, crossly. ‘Women get called bossy while men are admired for being assertive.’

‘OK, unfairly critical, then.’ Emily passed her sister her plate and gestured for her to start eating. ‘Does that work better for you? Or how about you were being a control freak?’

‘Seriously?’ Merry fumed. ‘I’m the face of the company, I’m the Merry in Merry and Bright. I just want to make sure things go well, that’s all.’

She took a giant bite of her grilled cheese sandwich. Emily had added a layer of pickles and mustard as per her request and it was off-the-scale delicious. It was going to give her heartburn, but the way she was feeling, she didn’t care. All she could think about was the fact that the baby would arrive very soon and, for a little while at least, she was going to have to leave Nell in charge of the business, and that thought scared her. A lot. Merry and Bright was the first thing she’d had that had been all hers. And the thing was, she’d brought Nell in as partner, exactly for this reason, so that she’d be able to share responsibility, but, in practice, it was harder to relinquish control than she imagined.

As if reading her mind, Emily nudged Merry’s shoulder with her own. ‘Look. It was a brilliant idea to bring Nell into the business. The two of you know each other inside out, you can spend hours and hours together without getting fed up with each other’s company. Maybe Nell won’t do things exactly the same as you would. But she deserves your trust. You needed to let go of the reins just a touch, and guess what, there she is picking up the slack. You’re lucky she hasn’t got kids or isn’t pregnant too. Imagine if you both needed time off together!’.

Merry squeezed her eyes shut as her anger seeped away, to be replaced by shame. Emily might not have any idea that Nell and Olek were having a fertility investigation, but Merry did and she should have been a lot more sensitive and grateful. If Merry hadn't been told to rest, she'd have suggested that Nell take some time off and go away for a few days with Olek so that they could have time to process what they were going through together. She was a terrible person, a terrible business partner, and even worse, a thoughtless friend.

'Oh God, you're right. Thanks, Em,' she said in a small voice. 'I didn't handle that well at all.'

She cringed, remembering that she'd referred to Merry and Bright as her baby the other day when speaking to Nell. No wonder Nell was annoyed with her.

'And from what you told me earlier,' Emily went on, 'Woody and Nell sound like they have the shop well under control. I think it's a brilliant idea, offering Airbnb guests the choice of working in the shop. Rental income and free labour: win-win.'

That had been Nell's idea too.

Merry chewed on her sandwich, aware of a niggle of jealousy. 'Woody does look fun, especially given how *not* fun I'm being at the moment.'

'Stop beating yourself up,' Emily chided. 'You've had a serious health scare, this is the first time you're having a baby, being snappy is allowed.'

'Pregnancy is no fun at all,' she said, feeling grumpy and cumbersome and suspecting Nell was relieved that she wasn't in the shop this week. 'I thought it would be all antenatal clubs and lunches and decaf coffee dates with other pregnant mums, going to baby showers and buying adorable tiny clothes.'

'And it isn't?' Emily looked bemused.

Merry shook her head. 'It's all don't do this or that, make sure you do this or the other. I'm not used to following rules. And my body's not my own; I haven't seen my nether regions for weeks. I was going to go to the salon for a tidy-up before the baby came, now I can't because of possible infection. I can only wear slippers or boots because of my fat ankles, and I need a wee all the time, usually just after I've got comfortable in bed, which, by the way, takes ages.

'Haven't you made friends with any of the mums-to-be from your antenatal group?' Emily asked.

Merry wrinkled her nose. 'A couple of them have been out together outside of the group, but it was over a lunch-time, and I was working. So, no.'

She and Cole had attended most of the sessions held by their local antenatal group. Merry had been quite looking forward to it, even though Cole had been through it all before, having already had two children. But, once there, Merry had felt inadequate, as if there was something she lacked in order to fit in. It was only after a couple of sessions that it dawned on her that the other women were so much more at ease with imminent motherhood, they just seemed part of a club that she didn't belong to, one in which their mothers had already passed on all the knowledge they needed. Whereas the closer her due date got, the more out of her depth she felt, but she was too embarrassed to tell anyone.

'And you didn't ask Nell to hold the fort while you went?'

'No, because . . . I didn't really want to go,' Merry's voice petered out sheepishly. She picked up her grilled cheese sandwich and took a big bite. 'This is delicious by the way.'

'And have you ever been to a baby shower?'

Merry winced. 'No, the ones I've watched online have been like the cheesiest pastel-coloured, themed parties I've ever seen, made worse by being alcohol-free.'

'Right, that's it.' Emily took the sandwich out of Merry's hand and dropped it on her plate. 'Leave that. We're going out.'

'Really? So you will take me to Merry and Bright?' Merry's heart leapt; she'd apologise to Nell, and she wouldn't stay too long, just long enough to reassure herself that it was all going well.

Her sister rolled her eyes. 'No, because as we've just agreed, you're going to trust Nell to run the workshop by herself. We're going to do something from the list you just mentioned. You'll love it.'

Emily was right, of course, Nell deserved to be left alone. And the thought of doing something baby-related with her sister was very appealing.

'Thank you. Sounds great.' She couldn't remember the last time she did something spontaneous, except for her waters breaking at the Christmas lights switch-on. It felt naughty and a lot like her old self. 'But why can't I finish my food?'

'Because as well as doing something baby-related, I thought we could go for tea and cake.'

Merry shoved the sandwich in her mouth. 'I'm almost eight months pregnant and constantly starving. I can quite literally have my cake and eat it.'

'Very good,' Emily said with a smirk.

'Yeah,' Merry grinned, 'I can still be fun, can't I? And do things on the spur of the moment. Let's go, go, go.'

She pushed herself gingerly to the edge of the chair and peered down at her feet. She didn't think she could reach them, or get up, and before they went anywhere, she was going to have to go to the loo.

Maybe not quite spur of the moment . . .

Chapter 13

Nell

'Thanks for the lift.' Nell unclipped her seat belt, leaned over to the driver's side of Olek's van and kissed his cheek.

They were outside Olek's parents' house in Bakewell. His parents had lived in it since they'd first arrived in the UK from Poland when Olek was a teenager. His old bedroom was now Max's room when he came to stay, which was less frequent now that football had begun to dominate every hour outside of school.

'You're welcome. Hey.' As she turned away, Olek cupped a hand to her face, preventing her from pulling back. He touched his lips so softly to hers that his kiss was barely there, almost as if he wasn't sure whether he was welcome. 'I love you, you know, Mrs Dowmunt.'

Although it was dark, Mr and Mrs Dowmunt Senior had so many multicoloured Christmas lights on the front of the house that the concern on his face was illuminated in shades of orange, red and green.

That was her doing, she'd made him question the equilibrium of their relationship. She knew that her behaviour had changed since getting their test results; where once she'd have always chosen the spot on the sofa beside him, where she could loop her arms around his waist and cuddle into his chest, now she sat on the far end, resting her feet in his lap. She kept conversation topics general instead of talking about what was really in her heart, and, when possible, she'd take the seat beside him at the dinner table rather than opposite to avoid the questioning look in his eye. And the awful thing was that she knew that all these little things were clues to him that something was wrong; he was bound to associate them with her sadness about not being able to conceive. When, in fact, at the heart of everything was her love for him and her desire to protect him from the truth.

'I love you too, darling, very much,' she replied.

She breathed in the familiar scent of him and willed herself not to cry. Her lovely, lovely man. She was a storm of emotion at the moment. Angry one minute and desperately sad the next. And her mood swings weren't only saved for Olek. Fancy slamming the laptop down on Merry! She couldn't remember them ever falling out like that before and she was ashamed to have done so now when Merry had so much going on.

'Best news I've heard all day.' Olek released her. 'Listen, I've been thinking we should let my parents know about our fertility issues.'

Nell blinked at him, heart in her mouth. 'Why? I thought we were going to stay quiet until we had some proper news.'

'Darling, we have had proper news, it's just not what we wanted to hear.' He chewed the inside of his lip. 'And sometimes honesty is the best policy.'

She felt herself flush; she'd always thought the same. Right up until she decided that being honest with Olek about his test results might do more harm than good. 'Sometimes it is. But at other times, it isn't.'

He narrowed his eyes teasingly. 'Now you've got me worried about what's causing that guilty look. When is honesty not the best policy in Nell's world?'

Oh God. This conversation was getting more and more difficult. She picked up her bag from the footwell and prepared to leave the van. 'Well, in this case, we haven't mentioned anything to your parents about trying for a baby before now. Once we tell them – your mum especially – they'll want weekly updates, and Irena will have lots of "helpful" suggestions. I love your mum, but this is private.'

He took her hand and laced his fingers through hers. 'My mother does have a habit of poking her nose in. She's asked me in the past whether you and I would have children and I know she's dropped hints to you before. I'm wondering whether if we told her that things weren't straightforward that she'd perhaps be a bit more sensitive around the subject.'

Nell nodded slowly, seeing his point. 'Can I think about it? I'm not ready to talk about it with anyone.'

He held her gaze. 'And that seems to include me.'

She felt her throat constrict. 'It's not that . . .' She couldn't get the words out. 'I'm still coming to terms with it myself, that's all.'

'OK,' he said sadly. 'I think we should make another appointment with Dr Bajek. I feel bad about not being there at the last one.'

Nell's stomach lurched and it took all her willpower not to jump out of the van and put an end to this conversation. The last thing she wanted was to see Dr Bajek again. 'It wasn't your fault.'

Olek touched her leg. 'Maybe not, but if I'd known . . . Well, I wish I'd never accepted that emergency job, I regret it now. I should have been with you. I know you're finding it hard to talk about, but I wish I understood more. I know how important this is to you.'

His wording made her breath catch. 'But not important to you?'

This time, she held his gaze.

'Nell!' He looked wounded. 'Nothing would make me happier than for us to have a child together. Nothing. You're such an important person in Max's life and he thinks the world of you. But having stepchildren is not the same as your own flesh and blood. Sometimes when I look at Max, I could burst with love and pride, just knowing that I'm his father. I'd love for you to experience that feeling; you'll be a wonderful mother.'

His use of the future tense, and his certainty that it would happen one day, brought a lump to her throat, as did his expression of love for Max.

'Thank you, my love, for saying such nice things, but . . .' She shook her head, struggling to find the right words. 'It's not to be.'

He brought her fingers to his lips, kissing them before speaking again. 'Nell, if there's a chance that we could get pregnant somehow, wouldn't you want to look into it?'

Oh, Olek, not if you aren't the father.

'Surely, Dr Bajek has some advice for next steps?' he pressed her.

'Maybe,' she said, swallowing.

'Then we will explore every avenue,' he promised solemnly. 'Shall I call the clinic?'

Her heart twisted; it really did sound like he was as keen on having a baby as she was, which made it even worse that he was the one who couldn't. 'Can we leave it just now? Get Christmas out of the way and talk about it in the new year. I don't want to be thinking about *not* being pregnant when it's all Merry can talk about. It's not her fault, but fate can be cruel sometimes.'

'It can,' he murmured, 'I'm sorry. And yes, let's wait a while. Just say the word, I'll be guided by you.'

‘Thank you.’ She nodded her agreement, wondering how long she’d be able to string this out before he brought up the subject again.

‘And talking of time,’ Olek winced. ‘I’d better get going. It’s Max’s first game with Derby and I don’t know who’s more nervous, him or me.’

Nell took in his piercing blue eyes glinting with excitement in the light of the street lamp. The same sparkle which had drawn her to him all those years ago when they’d first met. She kissed him again, this time wrapping her arms around his neck to pull him in close.

‘You’re a wonderful father, Olek. Never forget that.’

‘Thank you, I do my best,’ he replied.

There was a thump on the glass of Olek’s window and both of them flinched. His mum, Irena, beamed at them and gestured for them to get out of the car.

‘Kissing outside my house like two kids!’ she cried, once Nell had got out.

Olek wound down his window. ‘I can’t stop, Mama, I’m on my way to see Max.’

‘What sort of son doesn’t have time for his mother,’ she chided, reaching into the van and kissing both of his cheeks. ‘One minute, that’s all it will take. Your dad has messed up the TV and can’t get his programme.’

‘Again?’ Olek grumbled but nevertheless did as he was told.

‘Nell!’ Irena Dowmunt grabbed hold of her face and squashed it to her own as soon as they were both inside the hall. ‘My *kochanie*. Gienek? Nell and Olek are here.’

‘Hello, Mama,’ Nell replied, submitting to Irena’s exuberant greeting.

She was used to it now, but in the early days of dating Olek, this show of affection had come as a massive shock to Nell. Her own mother had air kissing down to a fine art, making an extravagant 'MWAH' sound whilst gingerly holding onto Nell's shoulders with her fingertips. In other words, all show and very little warmth. Being welcomed into the bosom, quite literally, of Olek's family had been a revelation. As soon as Olek had proposed to her, Irena had insisted she be known as Mama. By contrast, Nell's parents had made it clear that Olek should address them as Mr and Mrs Thornberry until Nell finally put her foot down at her and Olek's fifth wedding anniversary party.

Her father-in-law, Gienek, popped his head out from the kitchen with a mug in his hand. 'Just in time, I've made tea. Anyone want one? Olek, look at the TV for me, son, I don't know what's wrong with it, but I haven't touched it.'

'It's a mystery, Tata,' Olek said, hugging his old man gently to avoid spilling the tea. 'I can't stop long enough for a drink, I'm afraid.'

He disappeared into the living room to sort out the TV, while Irena held her hands out to take Nell's coat. 'Or we can open the Christmas sherry? Unless you're not drinking at the moment?'

Her in-laws looked at her: Gienek with nothing but polite interest, Irena with a keen eye. Women missed nothing, thought Nell, and they knew the signs. The last couple of times she and Olek had been to visit for Sunday lunch, she had been the designated driver to hide her real reason for not drinking. Tonight, Irena would see Olek drive off from her front-room window. If Nell refused a sherry this evening, it would be ringing all sorts of hopeful alarm bells. She wondered if Olek was listening.

'Sherry please, as we're wrapping presents,' she replied lightly. 'Let's get into the Christmas spirit.'

Irena's hesitation was so brief it was almost imperceptible. 'Sherry it is! Come on through to my Christmas room and we can start.'

'Christmas *room*?' Nell said bemused, as Irena opened the door off the hallway into what used to be Gienek's study.

'Holy moly!' Nell laughed. 'I thought I was organised by having one shelf in a cupboard reserved for birthday and Christmas.'

'Where Christmas is concerned,' said Irena, 'less is less and more is more. It's the only time I can spoil my family without getting told off.'

Her husband's old desk was strewn with wrapping paper, ribbons, sticky tape and several pairs of scissors; the carpet was virtually invisible due to all the carrier bags and cardboard boxes.

'Max only wants money,' Nell said, eyeing up the stack of bags. 'Shame really, I used to love buying him toys.'

'Money.' Irena shook her head, dismayed. 'How can you get excited opening money at Christmas?'

Max spent every other Christmas with Nell and Olek, and it was always a much noisier, fun day when he was with them. The festivities would begin on Christmas Eve: Olek's parents would host a traditional Polish dinner of many courses which went on until almost midnight. After which, one Christmas present each would be exchanged. If Irena and Gienek had their way, all the presents would be opened that night, as they'd done in Poland growing up. But Nell and Olek liked Max to come down in the morning and find a pile of presents under the tree and a stuffed stocking hanging at the end of the fireplace.

'Who are these all for?' Nell marvelled.

Olek was their only son and Max, therefore, their only grandchild. They had family in Poland still, but there were enough gifts here to fill Santa's sleigh.

'Let me think.' Irena listed off the children's ward at the local hospital, parcels for the worst hit war-torn countries, a family new to the area whose children were sleeping on airbeds, the homeless shelter who'd asked for thermal socks and gloves. 'And I have bought a few bits for Merry's baby.' Irena picked up a bag and pulled out a pale blue soft rabbit, a pastel striped velour onesie and a tiny hat with bear ears on it. 'Nothing much until we know if it is a little girl or a little boy.'

A little girl or a little boy.

How simple. How wonderful. And how bloody beyond Nell's reach.

'Oh, Irena, they're beautiful. Merry will be so touched.'

They should be for my baby, thought Nell, feeling her heart clench with sorrow. *I want a pile of presents under the Christmas tree for Baby Dowmunt.*

She felt like sobbing and pressed a hand to her stomach. She thought of all the months when she'd been sure that, this time, she felt different, that she had a suspicion that she might be pregnant; each time her period was even a day late, she'd be filled with euphoria and hope. But month after month her hopes had come to nothing. And now she knew why.

And the worst thing about it was that a part of Nell believed that this was karma, that she was only getting what she deserved.

Irena poured them both a generous measure of sherry and the two of them settled down on the carpet, each with a pile of presents to wrap.

Irena sat back on her heels to sip her sherry. 'You know, you can tell me to mind my own business.'

'Can I?' Nell prickled, sensing that Irena was about to broach the obvious subject. 'Good.'

It was a topic her own mother had no qualms about bringing up and each time it resulted in harsh words, Nell saying things she regretted and her mother acting hurt. She willed Irena not to go there.

'But,' Irena continued, 'I did think that once Merry settled down and started a family, you would want to do the same.'

'We are best friends, and have shared a lot over the years,' Nell agreed stiffly, 'but I draw the line at co-ordinating family plans.'

'Of course. But you do have a plan?' Irena leaned in eagerly, eyes bright.

'I . . . I . . .' She swallowed, she would like so much to confide in this woman who'd shown her nothing but love and kindness since the day Olek had introduced them. 'I can't say.'

Irena scanned her face. 'It is OK, it is none of my business. But don't be surprised if you lose Merry for a while once the baby comes. She will still love you just as much, but new parents become very wrapped up in their babies. The responsibility of another life, the lack of sleep, the worry that you don't know what you're doing. Being afraid to carry the baby around all the time in case you get into bad habits, being scared to put it down in case it wakes up. Maybe she'll be the sort of mother who takes to it easily, but many aren't. I think I cried every day for three months after Olek arrived.'

Nell's shoulders slumped. Being a new parent sounded perfect to her. Absolutely perfect. 'I'm going to try to make sure that doesn't happen.'

Irena patted her leg. 'You are a good friend. Like sisters. My boy would have loved more children with his first wife, you know.'

'Would he?' Nell had not known that. 'And did they try?'

Irena sniffed disapprovingly. 'She wasn't interested. Now we know why. It wouldn't surprise me if Yvonna started cheating on my son with that stupid oaf Viktor soon after Max was born. He was always hanging around.'

'They do still seem happy together.' Nell had learned that diplomacy was the best policy when the subject of Olek's first wife came up at family gatherings. She had met the couple many times over the years and didn't understand how Yvonna could prefer Viktor to Olek, but then you couldn't choose who you loved, could you?

'Still.' Irena raised her glass and chinked it against Nell's. 'I suppose we have to thank Viktor for one thing.'

'Being a good stepfather to Max?'

'No,' she shook her head vehemently. 'Max doesn't need another man in his life, not when he has a real father. I meant you, *kochanie*. If that woman hadn't gone off with Viktor, then we could not have had you in our lives, and you are very precious to Gienek and me. You are not flesh and blood, but we love you just as much as Olek and Max.'

'And I love you too, Mama.' Nell blinked back tears. Irena had welcomed her so warmly into the family, and knew how lucky she was to have her.

The door opened and Olek's head appeared around it. 'I've fixed the TV. And now I must really rush, or I'll be late to watch Max.'

Irena didn't appear to hear the second sentence. 'You are a good son. I was just talking about Yvonna. You would have liked more children, but she said no.'

Olek came into the room with a reluctant sigh.

'That was a long time ago, Mama, I don't think Nell needs to have my first marriage raked up.'

'Of course, of course.' Irena took another generous sip of sherry. 'I'm just saying. You always wanted more than one child, that's all. And your father and I wouldn't say no to more grandchildren.'

'And maybe Nell and I will have them one day, and that's our business,' he said sternly. 'But, in the meantime, you have Max. And now I am definitely going.'

He stopped to kiss Nell's head, squeezed his mum's shoulder and left the room.

'He is right.' Irena made an effort to smile. 'We have Max, we are very lucky. And if more grandchildren come along, we will love them just as much.'

'You have such a big heart, Mama. Any child will be lucky to have you as their *babcia*,' said Nell just as a terrible thought came to her. So far, she'd thought of Olek's infertility only in terms of the effect it would have on her husband. But it was just as devastating for Irena and Gienek too.

Her hands started shaking and she had to set down her glass for fear of spilling her drink. She sat on them before Irena noticed and prayed her face hadn't gone white.

If it turned out that Max wasn't Olek's son, then he wasn't their grandson either. That boy was the light of their lives, it would kill them to find out that he might not be their flesh and blood. The enormity of the responsibility she had heaped onto her own shoulders suddenly weighed impossibly heavy.

'Hey, hey.' Irena's face crumpled with concern. 'Shush, it is OK, it is OK, you can tell me anything, or tell me nothing, up to you.'

Suddenly, the wall of emotion that had built up was in danger of crumbling and the urge to talk to her mother-in-law became inevitable.

'Oh Mama . . .' Nell tried in vain to hold back her tears. 'Oh, Mama. I would like a baby, but I can't.'

'Can't? What is can't?' Irena looked bewildered.

'There's something wrong with me and I can't have children naturally.'

'Does Olek know?' She pressed a hand to her mouth in shock.

Nell nodded. 'We both went for tests.'

'Of course he knows. I'm sorry. I know that you would never deceive him, would you?'

If only Nell was able to promise that she'd never lie to him, if only she could give Irena the reassurance she was seeking now, her bright eyes roaming Nell's face. But, of course, she couldn't. She'd already deceived him and every day the repercussions of her actions grew worse and worse.

'Life doesn't always deliver what we want, does it?' she said instead.

'*Ojej*,' Irena tutted, rocking Nell from side to side in her arms. 'You poor, poor girl. I am so sorry, I had no idea.'

That was certainly true, thought Nell. Nobody did, and she had no one she could confide in either.

She wished she'd never had those tests, she wished she didn't know what she did. She hated the seed of doubt that had planted itself and taken root in her brain about Max. She'd never understood before how ignorance could be bliss, but now she'd give anything, anything at all, to be as in the dark about Max's possible parentage as the rest of his family was.

Chapter 14

Merry

'As I say, that's my top-line valuation, Mrs Robinson. I'll firm it up and send everything in writing, of course.' Steve Mann, estate agent from Home and Castle, handed her a glossy brochure. 'Here's a summary of our comprehensive services, both for rental and property sales.'

'Thank you, and thanks for dropping in at short notice.' Merry tucked the brochure underneath a pile of magazines on the table next to the sofa. She'd read that later when Cole wasn't around.

'No problem. Although it's a shame your husband wasn't available.' He zipped up his portfolio case and snapped the lid in place on his pen. 'We generally like to see couples together, just in case one half is planning on selling from under the other's nose.'

He laughed heartily and Merry shifted in her seat.

'He'll be sorry to have missed you,' she said, not meeting his eye.

She had every intention of telling Cole about this appointment, just as soon as she'd got all the details in front of her. She wanted to be able to answer the questions she knew he'd have. He liked facts and figures, whereas Merry was more into hunches, feelings and spontaneous decisions. She liked to think that that was why they got on so well: yin and yang in marriage form. It wasn't as if she was being completely deceitful; they'd have to do something with Holly Cottage once they'd moved out. She was simply making herself useful while she was sitting around doing nothing. Moving things on.

'Anything else you want to ask before I leave you to it?' He reached for the last *Lebkuchen* gingerbread cookie and bit into it. It was one of Astrid's recipes, which she and Emily had had a go at this morning. They weren't as chewy as Astrid's and her icing was thicker, but making them had kept her occupied for a while and, more importantly, had distracted her from the fact that Nell hadn't returned any of her messages since the incident on Zoom the other day. Emily had taken the rest with her for afternoon tea with an ex-colleague.

Merry had hoped to be back at work by now and able to go in and smooth over things with her oldest friend, but Pip had prescribed another forty-eight hours' rest. She'd argued that she was fine, but her midwife had joked that at least she was getting used to losing her freedom – a taste of what was to come once baby arrived. Merry had not found that funny at all.

Steve was awaiting her response. Did she have any questions . . .?

Merry looked around the living room at Holly Cottage and felt a wave of nostalgia; she'd been here a little over two years and had nothing but fond memories. Her life had changed beyond compare in that time. She'd been heartbroken and single when she'd moved in, trying to get her small candle-making business off the ground to make ends meet. She'd done that and more, turning it into a successful brand with a shop on the high street and a thriving online presence. But even more important, she'd met and married Cole and their lives had become one here in her tiny home. Even though things were a little tense between them now, she wouldn't change a thing.

'I don't think so,' she said finally, 'but I hope that whoever moves in here next takes good care of it and loves it as much as we have.'

'Home and Castle can't guarantee that, I'm afraid.' Steve put his coat on and wrapped a Burberry scarf around his neck. 'But I can promise we'll find either good-quality tenants or a buyer with solid financial credentials. You'll have no problem selling or renting a character cottage like this, I assure you. Do you have any idea which way you'll swing?'

'We want to keep our options open at this stage,' said Merry, ushering the estate agent into the hallway and opening the front door. Cole was unlikely to be home for another hour, but it would be Sod's Law if today he arrived home early.

That last thought was still fresh in her mind when she spotted Cole's van in the distance heading their way.

'Quite right. And I hope that you'll choose Home and Castle to help you do so.' Steve pumped her hand; he had soft hands, almost feminine. Give her the rough, calloused, strong hands of a builder any day. The sound of Cole's van made him look up. 'Good luck with the baby. Is that your husband, by any chance? I could wait.'

'Yes, possibly, but it looks like he's on a call and he could be a while. You'd better hurry, I think it's about to rain.'

She almost shoved the poor man outside, who glanced up at the clear sky looking very puzzled. She waved at Cole, who was in fact on a call, and went inside to manufacture an identity for the man who'd just left.

It was another couple of minutes before he let himself in and found her in the kitchen clearing away their mugs and the biscuit plate.

He dropped a kiss on her cheek and wrapped an arm around her waist. 'Was that Steve Mann the estate agent I just saw?'

'Um . . . yes. You know him?' Her heart sank. Of course he bloody did. Cole probably knew everyone involved in residential property in a fifteen-mile radius. 'It was. He just popped in on the off chance.'

'Merry.' Cole gave her a look which was part bemused and part stern. 'Please don't ever take up poker, you'll lose everything we own. Besides, I've known Steve a long time, he doesn't make house calls unless he can smell a fee.'

She sighed in resignation. 'Fine. You got me. I thought I'd make some initial enquiries, to move things along a bit.'

'I love how resourceful you are,' he said carefully, 'and you're right, we do need to think about the future of Holly Cottage.'

She sensed a 'but' and jumped in quickly. 'Exactly. Make a decision and move on.'

'What did Steve say?' he asked.

'That he could find a tenant or a buyer quickly.'

Cole shook his head. 'Standard Steve. He likes clients to think that his is the only estate agency which can deliver the goods.'

'So what do you think: sell or let?' Merry had planned on having this conversation later, snuggled up in front of the fire rather than leaning up against the kitchen sink, but it was what it was.

He pondered before answering. 'The last time I rented it out, I found the most gorgeous tenant. So gorgeous in fact that I married her, and we're expecting our first baby any day.'

'Hopefully not *any day*,' she put in.

'But,' he continued, 'we're in the lucky position of being able to leave this place vacant for the time being while we get ourselves sorted. There's no need to rush. Estate agents can wait. Let's just do one thing at a time, hey?'

Merry frowned. Why did they have to wait? Why do something next week, or next month, when she could do it today?

'Says he,' she muttered.

He frowned. 'Meaning?'

'Seriously?' she said crossly. 'Here's a question for you. Is Meadow View your priority?'

She stepped back from him and folded her arms, which wasn't as easy as it once had been thanks to her bump.

Cole cleared his throat. 'Yes, but—'

'But,' she interrupted, 'there's a project *so* urgent that you moved our electricians on to it, thus putting *our* home behind schedule. I know I'm not the builder in the family, but that doesn't look like priorities to me.'

'Not this again.' He picked up the kettle, shook it and switched it on.

'Again?' she bristled with indignation. 'We haven't even talked about it yet.'

'True, but only because you've been worried about your dad. And then you had that candle workshop on your mind. It's not as if I've been avoiding it. And it's sorted now. The electricians will be there on Friday, Monday at the latest. Problem solved.'

'Problem which you created.'

'Technically speaking—' he began.

'Stop. I'm not interested in the technical.' Merry held up her hand. 'I'm interested in fact. And the fact is that I want to be out of this house and into Meadow View before the baby arrives.'

'I know, but it's looking increasingly unlikely.' Cole was doing his low, soothingly reassuring voice, which normally had the effect of making her insides melt. But today all she wanted to do was yell at him. 'Far better to plan it properly, stay stress-free and be in for January.'

'No, Cole, wrong answer.' Frustratingly, she felt tears prick at the back of her eyes. 'You promised. We took that pregnancy test eight months ago, and you swore that you'd get us moved in. You're moving the goalposts. And I'm moving them back.'

The two of them stared at each other. Merry's heart was thumping, and she was itching to press her hand to her chest to calm her heartbeat, but she daren't in case Cole asked if she was OK. And she didn't think she could stomach one more enquiry about her health, especially not now, as she wasn't OK, not at all.

'Merry, can I . . .' Cole took a step towards her, but before he could finish his sentence, there was a ring on the doorbell.

'Saved by the bell,' Merry said grimly as Cole went to see who it was.

The door opened and she heard him greet Fred and Astrid. There was a scamper of paws on the tiles and Otto appeared wearing a tartan coat, he jumped up for some fuss.

Merry squatted down to scratch the little dog under his chin where he liked it. This was going to be awkward; now she and Cole were going to have to pretend they weren't in the middle of a row.

'Come in,' she heard Cole say. 'Merry and I were just . . . Go on through, we're in the kitchen.'

'And the kettle is already on,' said Fred, rubbing his hands together. 'We must have a sixth sense. Any tea going?'

'I'll make you one,' said Merry, reaching for the tea caddy.

'*I'll* make tea,' Cole countered.

'You look like a blooming rose.' Astrid kissed Merry's cheek, forced her to take a seat and placed a wicker basket on the kitchen table. She was wearing a magnificent emerald cape with a tartan lining.

'If you mean prickly and red in the face,' Merry muttered. 'That sounds about right.'

'It is a compliment, *mein Schatz*,' Astrid chided. 'You should take them gracefully; they get scarcer as you get older.'

She gave Fred a side eye.

'May I say, Astrid,' he said immediately, 'you look ravishing in that coat thingy, and match Otto perfectly.'

Astrid inclined her head at her partner. 'Thank you, *mein Bärchen*. Although, next time, I'd prefer not to be compared to the dog.' Despite her dark mood, Merry let out a giggle. 'Now,' Astrid continued, 'I've brought soup, a goulash and a chicken and leek pie. And some little *Stollen* bites because I know you love those.'

'So do I,' Fred grumbled, unbuttoning his heavy overcoat and handing it to his son. 'But you didn't make any for me.'

'I am making a large one just for you.' Astrid patted his cheek, making him blush.

The romance between them put Merry and Cole to shame; she couldn't even look at her husband at the moment without feeling cross.

'It's lovely of you to bring food for us,' she said, giving her old friend a hug. 'But you needn't. I'm not an invalid, and even if I was, Cole can cook.'

Astrid flapped a hand. '*Mein Schatz*, I know that, but this is my way of showing you that I care.'

'Thank you,' Merry replied, dangerously close to tears. 'I'm touched, really.'

'It all smells amazing,' said Cole, lifting the lid on the goulash. 'Shall I put this one in the freezer for now, Merry?'

'Why not?' she said, unable to keep the edge out of her voice. 'I was trying to keep the freezer contents to a minimum as I thought we'd be moving soon, but I guess it doesn't matter now.'

Fred looked between Cole and Merry and frowned. 'Is this a bad time? We can leave the food parcel with you and be on our way.'

'Well . . .' Merry began. That was exactly what she wanted; she and Cole needed to finish this conversation and get rid of the tension that crackled between them.

'It's not a bad time, Dad. There's no need for you to go.' Cole put a hand on his father's shoulder. 'We were discussing our moving date, that's all. It makes sense to stay here until January and things are a bit less busy.'

Astrid caught Merry's eye and pulled a face. 'I know you wanted to be in before Christmas, but that does make sense.'

Fred pulled out a chair and sat down heavily. 'Rubbish. By January, you'll have a new baby and a second trip to Germany coming up. I'd move heaven and earth to get in now, if I were you, son.'

'What?' Merry stiffened and glared at Cole, who squirmed. 'A second trip?'

'Thanks, Dad,' he muttered through gritted teeth.

'Oops.' Fred winced. 'Have I put my size tens in it?'

'So,' Merry fumed, 'you're off to Germany, leaving me at home with the baby? When were you going to tell me?'

'This afternoon,' he said darkly. 'Which was why I came home early. So imagine my surprise when I walked in to find you getting the house valued behind my back.'

Astrid's head was swivelling between everyone. 'This is my fault. I'm sorry. Merry, don't blame Cole, he is doing this to help me.'

She loved Astrid dearly, but this was between her and Cole. She fixed her husband in her gaze. 'You're making it sound more underhand than it is. I was doing it for us.'

'No, you were doing it because, for some reason, you don't think I have the best interests of my family at heart anymore. And you feel compelled to take matters into your own hands.'

'And disappearing off to Germany just after your new baby has been born demonstrates otherwise?' She was so angry that she could feel a pulse throbbing in her neck. 'You'd better just hope that your trip doesn't coincide with my trip to Jersey to see Emily, because you'll be looking after the baby while I'm away.'

She tilted her chin defiantly and folded her arms. The full effect of her arm folding was diluted thanks to having to balance her forearms on her bump, but still. He got the message.

'You can't go away without the baby!' Cole looked horrified.

'But apparently you can,' she retorted. 'It seems to me that motherhood has a whole different set of rules to fatherhood. I'm not sure I like it.'

'Too late for that now.' Cole's face was as dark as a rain cloud.

'And don't I know it.' Merry pushed herself up from the chair, stormed out of the room and slammed the door behind her. 'Don't I just bloody know it.'

She stomped upstairs, determined not to cry. This pregnancy was not going to plan at all. She'd had enough of today, she was going to bed and shutting everyone out. Including Cole.

Chapter 15

Nell

It was still dark outside when Nell arrived in Wetherley to open up for the day, but the square was already coming to life. The stallholders in the market joking and calling to each other from the backs of vans or from underneath their tarpaulin covers, clipping Christmas lights and menus and price lists in place for the day. It was a thriving and lively market, a place to find everything, from flowers to food, fabric to footwear, community and camaraderie.

She glanced briefly at the successor to Nell's Nuts and waved just in case they saw her. It had been a year since she had sold the business; occasionally she missed life as a market trader, but she rarely missed working alone. It had been lonely running a business by herself, and then there were the sub-zero mornings, or, even worse, the wet ones, and finding someone to mind the stall while she went to the loo or to fetch lunch. Working at Merry and Bright was a cushy number by comparison. Inside all day, hot drinks and loos on hand and, of course, the biggest draw, the chance to work with her best friend.

Olek had thought she might miss being her own boss; he said he could never work for anyone else again. Until recently, it hadn't bothered her. Now, she had her doubts. Merry might have made Nell an equal partner, but since she'd been forced to stay at home and not come to work, it was obvious that Merry still considered herself in charge.

Nell took out the shop keys as she approached the door, considering for the first time since joining Merry and Bright whether her future here might not be so bright after all.

To her surprise, she found the door unlocked, the lights on and the candles behind the counter lit. 'Hello?'

'In the studio!' Merry shouted back.

Nell followed the smell of fresh coffee into the studio and found Merry sitting at the workbench arranging pastries onto a plate.

'Morning, this is a nice surprise.' She hovered by the door and gave Merry an awkward smile, not sure what to say. They had never fallen out before, this was new territory. Over the last few days, Merry had really wound her up, but she hadn't exactly covered herself in glory either. She thought about the unanswered messages on her phone and felt ashamed of herself. No matter what had happened between them, Merry was her closest and oldest friend, and going through her first pregnancy. Nell should have cut her some slack.

'Is it a nice surprise? I hope so.' Merry chewed her lip. In red corduroy dungarees and Birkenstocks without socks and her toenails painted in silver glitter, she looked great. Under normal circumstances, Nell would snort with laughter and tell her she looked like one of Santa's elves – a particularly spherical one. For the first time in almost two decades, she didn't dare make fun of her. Merry picked up the plate. 'Peace offering, and I've made fresh coffee too. Decaf. For both of us.'

'Thank you.' Nell was mainlining caffeine to combat the effects of her insomnia at the moment, but Merry didn't know that and she appreciated the thought. 'And you've got pecan ones too.'

'Because they're your favourite, and . . .' Merry's face crumpled. 'Nell, will you forgive me? I've been a control freak and a nit-picker and a terribly impatient patient and I'm sorry. I couldn't have managed without you; I *don't want* to manage without you. And, on top of all that, I've been so caught up with myself that I haven't been a good friend to you at all.'

Nell opened her arms wordlessly and her best friend stepped into them. Then they both laughed because Merry's bump prevented them from getting close to each other.

'Excuse my baby,' said Merry with a soft laugh. 'I need to develop a different hugging technique for the next couple of weeks.'

They shuffled sideways away from each other until Nell managed to get her arms around Merry's shoulders.

'I need to ask for forgiveness too,' she said. 'I shouldn't have shut down that Zoom call. I lost my temper, and I was rude to you.'

'I deserved it.' Merry grinned at her. 'And I bet the workshop went really well after that, didn't it?'

'Really well.' Nell released her and poured them both a coffee. 'I was so nervous, but Woody helped, and if I have to run one again, I'll be much more confident.'

'I'm dying to meet him.' Merry added sugar to her mug and stirred it messily, dropping the spoon down on the counter.

Nell wiped up after her, as she'd been doing for the length of their friendship, and picked the pecan and maple twist, just as Merry had known she would.

'And I can't wait to introduce you. He's looking forward to meeting you too. He . . .' Nell broke off before saying that he'd saved her life by helping her out, not wanting to make Merry feel even worse about her absence. She also skipped the part where Woody had dropped three glass candle jars and when Fred had popped in with Otto to see how she was doing, they'd had to shoo them out before Otto got glass splinters in his paws. She watched as Merry tore off a piece of cinnamon swirl and dunked it in her coffee. 'I've never seen you do that before.'

Merry folded the pastry into her mouth. 'Mmmm, I do anything I want now and blame it on pregnancy. It's very liberating.'

Nell felt her heart skip. 'It must be.'

Merry's face fell. 'Nell, I—'

Nell knew exactly where this conversation was headed next and pre-empted it. 'By the way, I love those dungarees. You look like a jolly Santa who's eaten all the mince pies.'

'I know, look.' She pulled a red Santa hat out of her bag and jammed it on over her blonde hair. 'Tell me I'm not the sexiest woman you've ever seen.'

'You're not,' she replied. 'But I love you.'

'I love you too.' Merry gave a muffled sob. 'And I'm not crying, you're crying.'

The two women hugged again.

'You're right, I am. But so are you. Let's not argue again, I can't cope.'

'Me neither. Cole and I are arguing quite enough as it is, I need someone on my side.'

'You and Cole?' Nell took in Merry's forlorn expression. 'I thought you were still in the honeymoon period.'

'I'm afraid so.' She dunked another piece of pastry. 'Luckily, Emily is here to act as referee. Goodness knows what's going to happen when she leaves in a couple of days. I've even asked her to stay on a bit longer, but Izzy's husband is turning forty and Emily promised to help with the party.'

'Merry?' Nell exclaimed. 'What's going on? This isn't a time for you to start rowing.'

'I don't want to talk about it.' She rubbed a tired hand over her face. 'Anyway. I've been thinking about the shop.'

Nell narrowed her eyes, torn between wanting to probe her about her relationship and needing to know what she meant. 'Oh?'

'Mondays are quiet.' Merry popped the last of her pastry in her mouth and chewed. 'Online orders keep us busy, but the shop itself? Dead as a dodo except for the lunch-time moochers.'

'You are so right,' Nell agreed. 'In fact, I wanted to suggest we don't—'

'Open on Mondays?' Merry put in.

'Yes, we could trial closing.'

'At least for January.'

'And see how it goes.'

'Precisely.'

They both exhaled with relief and shared a smile.

Nell felt a weight lift from her shoulders; she'd been worrying for nothing about working with Merry, it was all going to work out fine. 'We're on the same page again.'

'Feels good, doesn't it?' Merry's eyes sparkled.

'Right.' Nell eyed up the remaining pastries. She shouldn't really, but today felt like a day for celebrating. She cut one in two and put half on Merry's plate. 'So, on that note, our festive shopping evening is next week. Discuss.'

'I have had an idea about that . . .' Merry began.

'Course you have,' Nell laughed. 'Go on.'

It was to be the first time they'd had an after-hours event. As well as gift wrapping and special offers and candle-making demos, there'd be Christmas refreshments and Harley had persuaded some of the kids from his school choir to perform a few festive tunes to add to the ambiance.

'Assuming this baby doesn't have other ideas, I'm planning on being here, so . . .'

Over the last of the pastry and a top-up of coffee, the two of them planned out how they would split the evening, each of them taking over responsibility for separate areas, and, as a special occasion, draft in Fred to help in the studio and, if he was willing, Woody to handle the gift wrapping.

'Brilliant,' Merry beamed. 'And now that's sorted, I guess I should start replenishing all the stock you've sold while I've been gone.'

The door opened, signalling the arrival of customers. Nell left Merry preparing the wax melter for making a batch of new candles and for the next hour, they busied themselves in their own part of the shop, as they'd been doing successfully for the last year.

Nell was packing an online order when Merry came to join her on the shop floor, while she waited for a batch of wax to cool.

'I hesitate to tell you this,' said Nell, tucking tissue paper into a gift box. 'But we are almost out of Home scented candles.'

'Give me an hour to finish the Winter Wonderland,' said Merry, stifling a yawn, 'and I'll be on it.'

Nell had already seen her rub her back as if she was easing the pain. She should be thinking about going home, not working for longer.

'Why don't you leave it for today?' she suggested. 'But we should probably talk about what's going to happen when the baby comes.'

Merry pulled a face. 'Cole keeps saying the same. I've been in denial about it. And I suppose I thought a solution would present itself. Most things usually have a habit of working out in the end.'

Nell shook her head fondly. If she had been the one about to head off on maternity leave, she'd have had a plan in place by now. She'd have worked out when she'd realistically want to return to work and, with Merry's agreement, she'd have already started the recruitment process for her temporary replacement. Everyone would know where they stood and could plan accordingly.

'You've lived your life making spur-of-the-moment decisions and acting spontaneously, it's part of what makes you such a fun person to be around. But I'm not sure you can run a business that way, not if you want it to stay successful,' she said, her tone tempered with diplomacy.

Merry sat on the stool behind the counter. 'I'd hoped to get ahead with production, so we'd have plenty to see us through for at least January. But now I'm behind. Fred might come in and help, especially as Astrid is preoccupied with her German project. And I thought I could do the accounts and stuff from home, when the baby naps.'

Nell adored Fred, and she knew Merry was reluctant to take on unknowns, but they needed a more formal arrangement if the shop was going to operate efficiently. 'Or . . .' She took a deep breath. 'We employ someone.'

Merry opened her mouth to argue and closed it again. 'I know you're right, but . . . ughhh.'

'I get it,' Nell said. 'You're worried no one will do as good a job as you.'

'It's not that . . .' Merry began until Nell started to smirk. 'OK, it is that, but it will be hard to monitor the quality if I'm at home with a baby.'

'Then let's get someone to work in the shop; retail skills are easily transferable if we get the right person. Meanwhile,

I can be your apprentice. Monday can be our training day if we're closed. The baby can come into work, and we can make candles together. We can take it in turns to change nappies and rock the baby to sleep while we work. It'll be fun.'

'It might work, and I'd like to bring the baby in with me, but . . .' Merry hesitated, and gave Nell a thoughtful look. 'Can I ask you a personal question? About the baby?'

'Fire away.' Nell steeled herself; she'd succeeded in avoiding in-depth conversation about her baby woes so far. But it was inevitable that Merry would ask.

'Me having a baby, bringing it in to work, and you . . .' Merry rubbed her stomach just at that moment, a slight look of discomfort crossing her face.

'And me and Olek not being able to conceive. Yes?' Nell's words came out sharper than intended and Merry flinched.

'I was going to say and you spending so much time with us. But will it upset you, being around us?'

Us. Mum and baby. Nell's chest felt tight, and she willed herself not to cry. But how could she tell her best friend that even though she was delighted for her, it was going to be a daily reminder of her own childless state. 'Of course not, you're my best friend, and this baby will practically be my nibling. That's a word, by the way.'

Merry let out a rush of breath. 'Thank goodness. I've been worried about that. I'm so glad. And, of course, you'll practically be its aunt, because you and I have been as close as sisters for years.'

Nell felt a wave of guilt that Merry had been worried. 'No matter what happens, I'll always be there for you.'

Merry was quiet for a moment. 'And you and Olek . . . I feel as if we haven't really talked about your family plans since you had your test results. You don't have to tell me if you don't want to, but . . .'

'I don't want to, thank you,' said Nell quickly. 'Other than to say there are no plans at the moment. End of story.'

'OK.' Merry looked taken aback and Nell relented.

'Olek and I have decided to just keep it between ourselves,' she said as lightly as she could manage. 'It's a very private thing and, well, it's not up for public debate.'

Merry's smile slipped. 'Am I classed as public?'

'No, no, sorry,' Nell said, feeling flustered. 'Of course you aren't. I'm still looking for the right words to express my . . . disappointment.'

Merry reached for her hand. 'But you and Olek are definitely talking about it?'

She nodded. 'Oh yes,' she said, forcing a smile. 'All the time. You know us.'

'Good. Because he's the one person you should be able to say anything to.'

'Absolutely.' No one was more keenly aware of that than Nell. She heard Woody descending the stairs and breathed an inward sigh of relief that the conversation could now move on. 'Prepare yourself, I think Woody has completed his morning ablutions.'

Merry glanced at the time on her phone. 'Lucky him. I've been awake for four hours.'

'I forgot to mention that he's not a morning person,' Nell told her. 'He greets the day very slowly with matcha tea, meditation and the lengthiest self-care routine imaginable. And the number of products in his bathroom . . . I didn't know there were so many different types of serum.'

'Good morning, angel,' Woody began. 'I'm up with the lark this morning, because I need to pop home and do a few chores while Spencer is out. He's missing my cooking and I'm going to make him a pie as a surprise. But I'll be back at one.' He spotted Merry leaning against the wall in the studio and pressed a hand to his chest. 'Merry, we meet properly at last.'

'I've heard nothing but glowing things about you,' she said, leaning forward to shake his hand. 'Thank you for all your help in the shop so far.'

Woody took hold of both of her hands. 'Oh, look at you,' he exclaimed in a shaky voice. 'Oh my goodness.'

'Is everything all right?' Merry asked, slightly bemused.

He released her hands and nodded. 'I knew you were pregnant of course, Nell told me.' Woody fumbled in his pocket and brought out a tissue. 'But I wasn't prepared . . . I'm so sorry, please excuse me. Lovely to meet you. I'll see you later.' He touched Nell's arm on his way to the door and the two women heard a sniffle as he let himself out of the shop and into the winter's morning.

'Gosh, I think I've made him cry, do you know why that could be?' Merry asked.

Nell stared after him, watching him disappear into the crowds in the market. Poor Woody, the sight of Merry's baby bump really seemed to upset him. 'No idea, I'm as in the dark as you are.'

Woody had hinted at plans for next year that had gone awry. Could they perhaps be family-related? Maybe she wasn't the only one who had unfulfilled dreams of being a parent. Her mind leapt several steps ahead, imagining him and Spencer having debates about whether to have children or not. Perhaps Woody was for and Spencer against? This might explain why the two men were living apart now, even though they clearly loved each other deeply. Could it be that she and Woody had a lot more in common than she'd thought? She decided to make it her mission to find out, let him know she understood, and maybe . . . A dangerous notion entered her head: maybe Woody could be an impartial person for her to confide in, because the weight of the secret she was keeping from Olek was getting too big for one person to carry.

Chapter 16

Merry

Merry entered the lounge at Springwood House, followed by Emily, who was pushing Ray in the wheelchair. Her back was aching after working at the shop yesterday and she was having serious regrets about the angora jumper she was wearing; the temperature in the home was virtually tropical and Merry could feel the steam rising from her warm body. Today was one of those days when she felt more beached whale than blooming, and she could have really done without accompanying Emily. But Emily was heading to the airport straight from here and Gail had wanted to see them both together about Ray's health before she left.

The lounge, like the rest of the building, was exuberantly decked out in all its festive finery: a plump Christmas tree sparkling with glittery baubles in the bay window, chains of tinsel decorations looping lattice-like across the ceiling, fairy lights around windows and sprigs of holly and mistletoe tucked into the top of every mirror and picture frame. It was tea time, which meant that the lounge was full. Irrespective of the varying states of the residents' memories, almost all of them knew that tea and cake wasn't something to be missed. After a year of being a visitor, Merry knew many of them, although circumstances meant they didn't always remember her.

'I'll put your chair here near the fire, Dad,' said Emily, rubbing his arm affectionately. 'Unless you'd rather sit at the table near Bernard?'

Ray was recovered from flu and having one of his better days. He'd been sitting up in bed when they'd arrived and talking about getting dressed and leaving his room. Everyone agreed that the change of scene might do him good, but his legs were weak from lying down for so long and the carers suggested he hitch a ride to the communal part of the home in a wheelchair.

'Sofa please. Sod Bernard.' Ray tried to get out of his chair, but his arms didn't have the strength to pull himself up. He gave in to a coughing fit and sank back resignedly.

Merry and Emily exchanged worried glances. His lungs sounded very congested.

'Poor Bernard!' Merry said, waving to her dad's friend. He had a female visitor with him, and they were playing Scrabble; Bernard would spend all day playing Scrabble if he could find an opponent.

'Who are all this lot then?' Ray gestured around the room vaguely. 'What are they doing in my house?'

'Same as you, Dad,' Emily told him. 'Waiting for a slice of lemon drizzle and a hot drink.'

'Over here by me, dear,' called Lavinia, who had a soft spot for Ray. 'We can watch the television together like the old days. I'll even let you choose the programme.'

'Is Mary Berry on?' Ray asked.

'Yes. Probably.' Lavinia pressed at the remote control repeatedly. 'Possibly not. Damn it.'

'Oh, Lavinia, you're incorrigible. He doesn't want to watch TV,' her friend, Maude piped up, from the middle of a sofa so enormous and soft that she was swamped by the cushions. 'Sit here, Ray, loads more room, and we can have a nice chat.'

'Look at that, Dad, the ladies are arguing over you,' Emily teased.

'I met Mary Berry once.' Ray allowed Emily and one of the carers to help him onto the same sofa as Maude. 'She'd lost her car keys. I had to give her a lift in my van.'

Merry smirked at her sister. This was a well-worn story. If Ray were to be believed, Michael Caine, Barbara Streisand and Joey from *Friends* had all, at one time or another, had lifts in Ray's van. It was obviously sad how confused he was, but knowing her own father's little foibles and being able to share them with her sister still felt like a dream. She didn't think she'd stop marvelling at how precious these two people were, and how lucky she was to finally have a family to be a part of.

Once they'd got him settled with a mug of tea and a small piece of cake, Merry found a seat away from the fire where it was slightly cooler, while Emily went to speak to Bernard and fetch them both glasses of water.

'How's the Scrabble king?' Merry asked, gulping her cold water when Emily returned.

'Missing Will,' said Emily. 'Says that his friend Hilary isn't a patch on him at games, which went down very well, as you can imagine. I've said Will plans to visit him next time he's here.'

Will had been Bernard's occupational therapist this time last year, as well as his Scrabble partner, and had even on one occasion cut his toenails for him. No wonder he was missed.

'You must be looking forward to seeing him too,' Merry said.

'He's meeting me at the airport, and I can't wait to see him.' She chewed her lip. 'But I'm worried about leaving Dad in case anything happens. He's so frail, and that cough is still awful. If it was anybody else's birthday party, I'd make my excuses, but I really don't want to let Izzy down, she's been so good to me, and she wants her husband to have a fantastic fortieth.'

They both looked over to where Ray was sitting, now sandwiched between Lavinia and Maude. He'd already dropped off to sleep and the two women were tussling over a blanket they were trying to tuck over his knees.

Secretly, Merry was worried too. There'd been times over the last few weeks when she'd felt as if he'd checked out of life altogether. She'd been to see him, only for him to simply sit in his chair listlessly, staring out of the window at nothing. She'd hated those visits, mentally willing him back to lucidity, hoping that he'd at least recognise who she was and talk to her.

'Try not to fret too much. He's in the best place,' she reassured her sister. 'Gail is on the ball, and I'm here.'

Emily gave her a stern look. 'With more than enough on your plate already. Promise you'll call me if you're worried about anything at all.'

'Promise.' Merry's voice shook.

Emily meant anything concerning Ray, but Merry had a whole other list of things which were keeping her awake at night. Like how to be a role model to a small person, about how to cope with a baby when Cole was away, when they were going to move into the new house and how the baby was doing since her waters had broken, was it still thriving? If she stopped to think about everything that she was worried about, she'd dissolve into tears.

Emily glanced at her phone as a text came through. 'That's my taxi.'

Merry felt herself gripped with dread. Despite the circumstances, it had been a relief to share the stress of Ray's fading health and generally just lovely spending time with her sister. 'I'm going to miss you. And thank you again for taking me shopping for baby clothes. I'll always treasure the things we found.'

Emily's surprise trip on the afternoon of the candle -making workshop had been to their favourite vintage shop in Bakewell, where Merry had found her wedding dress last year. They'd sifted through baskets of baby clothes and found the most exquisite lace christening gown, three hand-crocheted cardigans and a delicate patchwork quilt with baby animals all over it.

'I probably loved it more than you did, and I'll be back as soon as this baby comes,' Emily promised. 'If not before.'

'You'd better be,' Merry said wanly, as Emily got up and helped her to her feet.

'You are OK, aren't you?' Emily studied her sister's face.

Merry hesitated, wondering whether she could tell her the truth.

Not really, I wanted a baby more than anything, but I don't know if I can do it. Being a mother feels so daunting, and now I realise just how much I'll have to give up.

'Of course,' she said instead, deciding against it. 'Just got a bowling ball pressing down on my bladder, but apart from that, happy as a clam.'

'Ouch,' Emily giggled. 'No wonder you look tense. I'd better say goodbye to Dad and go.'

She gave Merry a hug. 'Love you.'

The baby chose that moment to start its afternoon aerobics and Merry took Emily's hand and guided it to the right spot.

'And I love you too, little one,' said Emily. 'Please be good for your mum.'

'More to the point,' Merry murmured, 'will I be good for the baby?'

Emily couldn't have heard the note of anxiety in Merry's voice because she called her a loon, gave her one last kiss and ran to say goodbye to Ray before dashing to get in her taxi.

Ten minutes later, Merry was in the ladies' bathroom feeling perilously close to tears. She was probably just tired. She should go home and have a rest, then perhaps this morose mood would pass. This time last year, she'd been planning her wedding and had really wished her mum could have been there to help her. Now, her first child was on its way and Merry was missing her mum even more fiercely than ever. She would love to have someone to reassure her that she was going to make a fantastic mother, that just because Sam hadn't felt capable of looking after her daughter, it didn't mean that Merry didn't have what it took to be a good mum to her own baby.

She'd tried to explain to Cole how inadequate she felt, but instead of really listening to her underlying worries, he'd told her how Lydia had been just the same when she was expecting Harley and how every new parent wishes babies came with a manual and that everyone muddles through in the end. How his first wife coped wasn't what Merry wanted to hear and didn't help in the least.

She half regretted not confiding in Emily while she had the chance, but there'd been a slight danger of Emily feeling the need to warn Cole about Merry's worries. That was the last thing she wanted. Nell was the one she really wanted to confess to, but that wasn't an option, not now that Nell and Olek were having fertility problems. How could she admit to being scared about her impending role as a mother when poor Nell was desperate to be in her position? It would be cruel. And that was weird, Merry mused, that Nell didn't want to talk about it; they'd always talked about everything in the past.

Her phone buzzed with a text message, and she took it from her bag to read. It was from Cole and her heart squeezed with a rush of anxiety, followed by a burst of sadness at how quickly and how low their relationship had sunk. She took a paper towel from the stack and dried her hands before reading it.

> Darling girl, I'm sorry we argued, and I'm sorry we haven't made up before now. I'm sorry I didn't tell you straight away about going to Germany. Originally, Astrid planned to go before the due date mid-Jan and I'd agreed to go, but obviously everything has changed now. TBH, Astrid is pushing me into this, she's extremely keen, and Dad's worried she's going to go back to Germany without him. Families, eh!
>
> But I've let Astrid know I won't be going, and she understands.
>
> I'm sorry Meadow View isn't ready yet, but I give you my word I'm throwing all my best men at it to speed it up. We'll be in as soon as humanly possibly, I promise. I'm cooking your favourite tonight, and we can snuggle up by the fire and watch a film, I promise I won't say a word if you make me watch *The Grinch* again. I love you xxx

'Oh Cole,' Merry murmured. She didn't deserve him; he was too gorgeous, kind and thoughtful. This baby was the luckiest child in the world – alongside Freya and Harley – to have him as its daddy. If only – if only she could say the same about its mother.

Her eyes pricked with tears and for once, instead of blinking them away, she let them fall.

She was mopping her eyes a few minutes later when the door opened and Bernard's elderly Scrabble partner walked in. She was a no-nonsense, steely-haired woman in an olive-green jumper and tweed trousers, the sort you knew would always have a clean handkerchief and would calmly see off a burglar with a few sharp words.

'Oh dear,' she said, spotting Merry's tears. 'I can either look the other way and save you the discomfort of having to explain yourself . . .'

'Or?' Merry asked with a sniff.

'Or you can unburden yourself to a stranger,' she said, briskly. 'Easier than telling someone with skin in the game, I always think. I'm Hilary by the way. Ex-colleague of Bernard, and apparently one of his few friends. Hardly surprising given how rude he is to me.'

She locked herself into a cubicle and Merry twisted her damp tissue between her fingers, debating whether to make a run for it or take the opportunity for a non-subjective ear.

'I'm Merry Robinson,' she began in faltering tones. 'I'm Ray's daughter. My baby is due very soon.'

'Yes, well, I might not be an expert in these matters, but that much I'd gleaned for myself,' said Hilary.

No wonder she got on so well with Bernard; neither of them took any prisoners and it appeared that Hilary had no time for sentimentality. Opening up to her might actually be just what Merry needed.

'Yes, sorry for stating the obvious. It's my first baby.'

'Ah. Big change then.' The older woman flushed the loo, opened the door and joined Merry at the sink.

'Huge,' Merry agreed. 'I grew up in care and haven't had the benefit of a loving home like my husband has.'

'My dear,' Hilary frowned, 'I'm so very sorry to hear that. I worked on the periphery of the social care system myself as an archivist for many years, as did Bernard, as a matter of fact. We have a robust system for looked-after children in this country, but, as you rightly say, nothing compares to the family home environment.'

'Exactly. All I wanted growing up was to feel as if I fit in, but I never quite did. Right from my first ever stay with foster parents when my mum needed a break from looking after me. The other kids didn't have another home elsewhere like I did. It felt like it was my fault that I was there, as if I was so badly behaved that my own mum couldn't cope. But then, when it was time to go home, it didn't feel right there either.'

'So your mum was around when you were being fostered?' Hilary shook water droplets off her hands and held them under the dryer.

Merry nodded. 'At first. She took her own life when I was eleven.'

Hilary tutted. 'Gosh, that's tough.'

'My experience of family life was gleaned from TV, or enviously glimpsed from the lens of my friends' experiences. Neither felt real to me. We were a family of two, until we were a family of one, which isn't a family at all. I have memories of her laughing and dancing in our flat, but are they real or imagined? Is that simply what I wanted our life together to have been? And if it was real, why didn't she love her child enough to stay alive? She didn't have a clue where I would be sent, or who would end up raising me. When she gave up on life, she gave up on me.'

'Now, now,' Hilary soothed. 'Perhaps your mum was in a difficult situation that you weren't aware of as a child. In my work, I came across heartbreaking stories, dire circumstances and some awful cases of pure bad luck. Of course, there were examples of bad people who should never have been allowed to have children in their care. But, in my experience, the majority of parents loved their children, and often their reasons to give up a child came from a place of love. Maybe she loved you too much to want to keep you.'

Merry let that sink in for a moment. Could her mum have been motivated by love after all? It was a heartening notion. 'Thank you, that's reassuring.'

'And you didn't have other family?' Hilary asked.

'She was estranged from them and there was no one else at that time. I don't even know for sure if Ray is my father, although he's adamant he is, and my half-sister Emily and I have decided that that's enough. I didn't even have anything of hers as a keepsake until my wedding day when Dad gave me the ring he'd proposed to her with. She turned him down, so it was never really hers, but it's the best I've got. It's only a small thing, but I wish she could have shared her thoughts with me, left me a note. People write suicide notes, don't they? Maybe it wouldn't have helped, it would have made no sense to me as a child, but now . . . I'd have loved a window into her world. A chance to understand and know her, woman to woman. She used to write me letters when I was with foster parents; it has always felt wrong that she didn't leave me one final letter.'

Hilary winced. 'That's a shame. You know, perhaps she did, and it got mislaid. Things got filed or stored away for safekeeping for when the child was older. But the system wasn't fail-safe and occasionally items got misplaced or misfiled. It has improved now thanks to digitalisation. In fact, that was one of my jobs in the 1990s; to handle the transition from paper to computer records. It used to drive me mad when I came across documents which weren't in their correct file.'

Hilary disappeared into her memories for a moment.

'Maybe that's how I should view it,' said Merry, 'that Mum did leave me a letter but that it went missing.'

'It's not an entirely preposterous supposition.' Hilary frowned. 'What was her name?'

'Sam, Sammy Shaw,' Merry supplied. 'She called me "M", which is ironic because I call my sister Emily "Em".'

'M,' Hilary murmured. 'M, hmmm. Gosh, that does . . .' She cleared her throat. 'I'm sorry, dear, your story has brought back some memories and I feel a little unsteady.'

'Are you all right?' Merry asked, concerned. 'I'm so sorry. I've completely overshared with an almost stranger.'

'Not at all, and don't apologise.' Hilary blinked as if clearing her vision. 'I'd better get back to Bernard before he works out the Scrabble points for "search party"!'

'Of course, sorry to have kept you. I'll say goodbye to Dad and head home. Lovely meeting you.'

'You too, dear, you too. You sent me on quite a trip down memory lane.'

'Thank you for listening to me.'

Hilary took both of Merry's hands in hers. 'I know I don't look like it, but I'm an old hippy at heart and a big believer in fate. I think we were meant to meet.'

'Me too,' she agreed. 'Just when I needed someone to confide in, there you were.'

'I don't have children, so feel free to take my advice with a pinch of salt, but I would wager that you have a much wider support network to help with baby than your mother did, so try not to worry about the things that might go wrong, focus on the things you're looking forward to.'

Merry nodded. 'You're right of course. I'll try.'

They walked to the door together, both trying to open it for the other. Hilary won.

'Just remember to ask for help occasionally,' Hilary said gently. 'People aren't mind readers.'

Merry walked back into the lounge pondering Hilary's advice. She could admit to struggling now and again, she supposed.. It was time to start trusting the people who loved her, the people who in turn would trust her to help them out when they needed it. After all, how did the saying go . . . it takes a village to raise a child? Merry shuddered. The very thought of having an entire herd of people getting involved was enough to give her sleepless nights; it was effectively how she had been raised in the care system. Nope, this baby was going to be raised by its mother; the opinions of the rest of the village would not be required, thank you very much.

Chapter 17

Merry

Merry was in her element. She was enjoying being back at Merry and Bright for the Wetherley Festive Shopping event so much that she hardly noticed the dull ache in her back or that her shoes pinched her swollen feet.

The entire event had organised by the festive committee to bring business into the town centre in the run-up to Christmas between the official lights switch-on and the annual Christmas Eve gathering. Most of the shops around the market square were taking part.

'It's great to see you smile, Merry, you look like your old self,' Fred boomed to make himself heard over the Christmas music. He sipped his second mulled wine. 'I was a bit worried about you when Astrid and I popped round the other day.'

'I am happy tonight,' she replied. 'When I'm at work, I feel like my old self too. This is my turf, Fred, I know what I'm doing when I'm here. It's everywhere else I feel out of my depth at the moment.'

It was now six-thirty, half an hour past the shop's usual closing time and the till hadn't stopped ringing. Max and Harley were manning the counter between them; meanwhile, Woody's gift-wrapping service was doing a roaring trade. Nell was taking the time to greet each customer and serving small paper cups of mulled wine or hot ginger and lemon tea. Merry and Fred were in the studio giving demonstrations on how to blend essential oils to create the perfect fragrance, in between making their Rose and Frankincense candles, which smelled amazing.

The shop looked, smelled and felt like Christmas. This was Merry's happy place, which was why she found it so difficult to commit to a period of maternity leave. Maybe she'd feel different when they were in the new house and she'd have chance to put down proper roots for the first time. But, for now, the business was her priority, and this was where she felt compelled to devote her energies.

'That doesn't sound like you?' Fred put down his cup, primed to concentrate on what she was about to tell him.

'I just mean with becoming a mum, you know, and the house move and everything,' she said vaguely. No need to go into detail with her father-in-law about her worries about Ray. He hadn't got out of bed since Emily had left he'd lost his appetite and had been very confused and distressed yesterday when she'd popped in. She missed Emily dreadfully and wished she was still here to share the visiting with her.

Fred's wiry eyebrows knitted tighter momentarily. 'Not doing too much, are you? I hope that son of mine is making himself useful.'

'He is.' She'd taken Hilary's advice about accepting help, or at least delegating the jobs she didn't mind not doing. 'He's now in charge of the cooking and he's forging ahead with the house renovation.'

The electricians were making good progress, which gave her renewed hope that the Robinsons weren't too far away from moving in. She had been a bit alarmed when she'd heard her husband having a heated discussion with the kitchen fitters on the phone earlier this evening but didn't get involved. She couldn't risk getting into an argument moments before leaving to come to the shop. Not when he'd been worried about her working tonight.

'Glad to hear it.' Fred turned to greet a customer who was hovering near the door to the studio. 'Hello, dear, would you like to see some candles being poured?'

'Christmas Time' by The Darkness came belting through the speaker. Merry tweaked the volume up; she loved this one.

She was singing along to the chorus so enthusiastically that it took her a moment to notice that Nell was standing beside her, hands on hips. Her cheeks were pink, and tendrils of her auburn hair had escaped from her bun. She'd looked too pale recently, perhaps things were starting to improve. Now the news had settled, Nell would feel able to tell her more about the fertility stuff. Merry wanted to ask, but Nell had closed down so completely last time she'd tried to discuss it that Merry was wary of upsetting her. Now she examined Nell's expression properly, Merry wondered if the colour in her complexion might be down to being cross about something.

'Everything OK?' she asked warily.

'I'm sorry, Merry, but this music just isn't conducive to shopping,' she whispered in her ear so as not to alert the woman who was examining the wax melter with Fred. 'Two men just walked in and walked straight out again.'

'They obviously have no taste.' Merry wiggled in her chair to the music. 'This is a great song. They aren't our target customer anyway.'

'Everyone's our target customer when it comes to buying gifts for others.' Nell pinched her lips together crossly, looking so un-Nell like that Merry was quite taken aback. 'People are out tonight with Christmas presents on their mind. If they don't buy from us, they'll buy elsewhere. It's as simple as that.'

'Yes, I do know how Christmas shopping works,' Merry replied. 'I was enjoying the music, that's all; I didn't realise it was impinging on business.' Merry took the top off a bottle of essential oil and inhaled before passing it to a woman who was hovering nearby. 'Smell this. Bergamot is in our Mistletoe Kiss candle; gives it a citrusy kick. It took me ages to get the aroma just right.'

'Pardon?' The woman strained to hear over the music and Merry had to repeat her words.

'See what I mean?' Nell squeezed past Merry to the speaker in the corner and turned the volume down a touch.

'That's better,' the woman said, relieved. She sniffed the bergamot oil. 'Mmm, I'll take one of those candles for the babysitter.'

Merry directed her to the display of Mistletoe Kisses and returned to Nell. 'You see, another satisfied customer.'

'This music would be perfect for a party, but—'

'That's because I did make it for a party.' Merry's eyes twinkled at the memory. 'A party you came to and complimented me on the music. But this year, this is as close to dancing at a party as I'm going to get. Thanks to the baby, plus the lack of amniotic fluid we now have between us, all I'm allowed to do is shuffle about from chair to chair. In my head, I'm leaping about like a loon.'

'I remember that party.' Nell smiled reluctantly. 'It was fun. But this is not shop-event music.'

A few days before Christmas last year, Merry and Cole had had a party, giving Merry the opportunity to introduce Emily to all her friends. They had all danced their socks off.

'I'm happy with it.' Merry shrugged. 'It puts people in a good mood to be able to sing along as they're browsing.

Anyway, we agreed to split responsibilities and I'm in charge of the playlist.'

'You are the stubbornest woman on the planet.' Nell threw her hands up. 'As you say, you're in charge of the music. I'll get back to my own responsibilities.'

Merry's heart sank as Nell stomped back into the shop. One minute they were OK, the next they were at loggerheads. What was happening to them? They never used to row about anything.

Merry watched from the studio as Nell went to open the door for some new arrivals, and in burst Astrid and Irena in a whirl of shopping bags, woolly hats and unrestrained laughter.

'No prizes for guessing who that is,' Fred chuckled, catching Merry's eye over a customer's bent head. He was allowing two friends to have a go at gluing down some wicks inside glass candle holders.

'I'll go and say hello. By the look of them, they may have had a drink already,' Merry added, noticing Irena clutch onto Nell's shoulder for support. Both of them looked a bit flushed. 'Still, nice to see them getting on so well.'

Unlike her and Nell, she thought sadly as she went through to the shop. Astrid and Irena had got to know each other at Merry and Cole's wedding last year. It was yet another bond between Nell and Merry, making them feel more like family than simply friends.

'*Liebling*!' Astrid swooped on Merry, kissing both her cheeks. 'What an excellent turnout. You and Nell must be so pleased.'

'We are,' Merry said, looking to Nell for her agreement.

Nell cupped a hand to her ear innocently. 'Sorry? I didn't catch that.'

'The music is a little loud,' Woody said, putting his hands gently over his ears. 'I'm going to turn it down a tad.'

'Party poopers, one and all,' Merry declared resignedly.

Irena grabbed hold of Max, smothering her grandson with kisses. 'And how is my football star?' she said, pinching his cheek.

Max dutifully endured the attention and mumbled his response, while Harley sniggered at his plight.

Merry greeted Irena with a hug. 'Glad you could make it. Are you shopping or browsing?'

'Drinking, mostly, at a guess,' said Max, miming knocking back shots.

'Sadie was serving beef and sauerkraut canapés at the Bristly Badger,' said Astrid, glassy-eyed. '*Lecker.*'

'We ate them with vodka.' Irena hiccoughed. 'Very more and moreish.'

Their German and Polish accents respectively were thicker than usual as they were tipsy and they looked like a comedy double act: Astrid tall and willowy in her habitual cape, and Irena short and plump in a chunky sheepskin duffel coat.

'Here you go, ladies.' Woody handed them both some mulled wine. 'This should go down a treat.'

'*Prost*!' Astrid bashed her paper cup against Irena's. 'Here's to avoiding mumps.'

'Mumps?' Merry took an instinctive step back. 'Should I be worried?'

'Since when has mumps been a major concern at the retirement home?' Nell asked, bemused.

'Yes, several of our residents have mumps,' Astrid said between sips. 'Cheeks like fat rodents. There has been an outbreak of cases at the nursery and, of course, some of us have spent much time there recently. Poor *kinder.*'

The social team at the Rosewood retirement village had teamed up with the Wetherley preschool nursery for some joint Christmas activities. Fred and Astrid and their friends had been having a whale of a time talking to the littlies about what Christmas was like in the olden days, making stained-glass window decorations from sweet wrappers and teaching them some of their favourite carols.

A woman holding hands with her small son glanced up worriedly. 'Mumps can be nasty. Especially for boys.'

Max and Harley gave each other a wary look.

'Why specifically boys?' Nell asked.

'It's rare but . . .' She cupped a hand over her mouth and whispered behind it, eyeing up Harley and Max nervously, 'I've heard it can make you infertile.'

'Really?' Woody leaned in closer. 'How?'

'Orchitis. Look it up if you dare.' She mimed holding a large round object and turned to her son. 'Come on, darling, let's get you home.'

'Aren't most kids vaccinated against it these days?' Merry asked.

'Nell?' Max gave her a pleading look. 'I should leave too. I don't want to catch mumps.'

'Me neither.' Harley touched his hand to his face uneasily. 'I already feel a bit hot.'

'I think you'll have been vaccinated against mumps. You too, Harley,' said Nell, distractedly. 'But why don't you call your mum to find out, Max, put your mind at rest.'

'Are you sure? Because if I get mumps and can't play football, I won't be happy,' Max warned.

'It is nasty.' Irena sucked in a breath while shaking her head solemnly. 'Olek had mumps when he was about your age, Max. He was very poorly.'

'Olek had mumps?' Nell exclaimed with such alacrity that Irena flinched. 'I didn't know that.'

'Gosh, how traumatic!' said Merry. She had no idea if she'd been vaccinated or not. And did vaccines work forever anyway?

'Olek did not have the vaccine.' Irena grimaced. 'I felt very bad about that. It was around the time we moved from Poland. We did not register with a doctor in the UK straight away and, somehow, I never got around to getting him jabbed. His balls swelled up like beetroot.' She hooted with laughter. 'His father kept making jokes about beetroot soup, poor boy.'

'Poor Olek,' said Merry. 'I think I'll get my baby vaccinated against everything. I know there's a risk, but . . .'

Out of the corner of her eye, she saw the colour drain from Nell's previously pink face.

'Traumatic, long-standing trauma,' she murmured under her breath.

'Nell?' Merry asked, concerned. 'What are you saying?'

But Nell didn't appear to be listening. She put down her tray of mulled wine and walked straight out of the shop and into the street, as if she was in a trance. Merry was bewildered. What on earth was wrong with her?

Chapter 18

Nell

A blast of wintry air hit Nell as she stumbled outside. But she was impervious to the cold. She walked a few paces into the marketplace and over to the far side of the Christmas tree, away from the glare of the Merry and Bright windows.

Olek had had mumps. Mumps could cause infertility. And Olek was infertile. The worry in the back of Nell's brain that had been circling ever since that distressing day at the clinic was now front and centre. It could not be a coincidence, it simply couldn't. An image of Dr Bajek questioning Olek about past trauma flashed into her mind. The doctor had obviously been trying to establish the cause of his infertility. Now a chance conversation in the shop had revealed the answer.

Orchitis. That was what that woman had called it. Nell googled it on her phone and winced at a picture of severely swollen testicles. Poor Olek having to deal with that as a teenager. She scanned the text until her eyes rested on the words, 'male infertility'. A rare complication, apparently, but not unheard of. If Olek had suffered as badly as Irena suggested, this could well be the cause of his problem.

Nell pressed the phone to her chest and squeezed her eyes tightly shut. Her darling man. He was the absolute best father a man could be to a child and yet, if this was true, the chances of him having fathered Max really were very slim. She recalled the things he'd said outside his parents' house the other night, about being prouder of your children's accomplishments than your own. She couldn't take that away from him by telling him her fears. She wouldn't.

For the first time since she'd misled Olek about the results, she felt grateful for her decision. He must never find out. He must never even have an inkling that Max might not be his. He and Max shared the same colouring, even if build-wise they were chalk and cheese. But unless you were looking for differences, you'd never suspect a thing. More importantly, neither would Olek.

She blotted the tears which had gathered in her eyes and blew out a breath. She could do this. She could be strong for Olek and make sure he never, ever found out. She and he might never have biological children of their own, but at least Olek would always have Max. Yes, she was being dishonest by not passing on her theory, but faced with the knowledge that if she did she'd damage their relationship permanently, she'd live with that dishonesty.

'Nell?' she heard Max call. 'Nell, are you out here?'

'Yes! Coming!' She injected a positive tone to her voice, sniffed back any remaining tears and hurried back towards the shop. Max was standing in the doorway directly underneath the bunch of mistletoe which Merry hung up every year. Nell resisted an impulse to gather him to her and give him a big hug. Thank goodness he was oblivious to everything that was going on in her head. 'What's up?'

Her stepson frowned. 'Mum can't come and fetch me. She's already drunk a bottle of wine with Viktor.'

'No problem.' Nell opened the door and gestured for him to go in ahead of her. 'I can take you home.'

Now, ideally, she thought. She was emotionally exhausted. But she'd stay until the end; she wouldn't desert Merry, no matter how much her friend's music was annoying her.

'Cool.' Max gave her a bashful smile. 'Thanks, Nell. You're the best. You and Dad.'

Her stomach plummeted towards the floor; she was so lucky to have this wonderful, trusting young man in her life. Even if he wasn't Olek's son, as far as she was concerned it didn't change how she felt about him. 'Max?'

He turned towards her, and she gave him a tight hug.

'You're the best too.'

'Weirdo,' he said with a grin.

She followed him back inside. The shop was even busier than before. Harley had a queue of customers at the till, Woody was gift-wrapping as fast as he could, and Fred had come through from the studio to chat to Astrid. For the next ten minutes, Nell threw herself into sales mode, talking to customers and advising shoppers on which aroma would suit whom on their Christmas gift list.

'Oh God,' Woody muttered, pressing a hand to his chest. 'You are kidding me. Who brings a pet shopping with them?'

Two girls had come into the shop, one of whom had a pet carrier which she wore as a backpack. There were mesh panels on all sides and the beak of a bright yellow budgie was poking through a tiny gap in the back panel.

'You big wuss,' Nell snorted. 'It's not going to get you.'

Woody shuddered. 'I hate birds. Like real full-on phobia. It's the wings and the way they flap at you. I'm staying in the studio until the coast's clear.'

'The rest of the choir has arrived,' said Harley, brightening as the door opened and a group of excited kids piled in. 'We'll sing for thirty minutes and then I'm going to leave too. Granddad, are you still OK to give us a lift?'

Fred clapped a hand over his mouth. 'I forgot all about it. And I've drunk too much mulled wine now. I'm sorry, lad.'

Harley groaned. 'You're supposed to be dropping me and my mates off at Nando's. That was partly how I got them to agree to sing tonight.'

Fred put a hand on his shoulder. 'Book a taxi for you and your friends, I'll pay for it.'

'Or I can take you?' Nell offered. 'I'm giving Max a lift, so it's no bother.'

'Thanks, Nell. But a taxi would be cool, please Granddad,' he mumbled and sloped off to join his friends.

'Pastry-enclosed Christmas nibbles!' Woody announced, returning with two trays of food.

'That's a lot of pastry,' Merry frowned, appearing from the studio with some Winter Wonderland candles to replenish the shelves. 'What about people who don't like it or who are gluten-free?'

On any other night, Nell would have laughed it off, but tonight, she was feeling too sensitive. 'I've catered for all dietary needs,' she said, bristling. 'I've got vegan and gluten-free mince pies. I just haven't put them out.'

Astrid and Irena bit into sausage rolls and a shower of pastry crumbs fluttered to the ground.

'*Ojej*!' said Irena.

'*Entschuldigung*!' said Astrid at the same time. '*Aber also lecker*!'

'I rest my case,' said Merry through gritted teeth. 'Now I'll have to vacuum the floor before I leave.'

'Or,' said Nell, crossly, 'as I am also a partner in this business, maybe I'll do it.'

'You've literally just said you'll take Max home,' said Merry, a little smugly for Nell's liking. 'So you won't be able to.'

'I'm amazed you heard that over the volume of this music,' Nell retorted.

'Oh, Nell, please!' She rolled her eyes. 'Change the record. The music is fine, it's Christmas music.'

'Mince pies and sausage rolls are fine, it's Christmas food,' she shot back, folding her arms.

She glared at Merry and Merry glared back. It was so childish that Nell almost cracked up with laughter, but the thought hit her suddenly that her best friend would be holding her own baby in her arms in a matter of weeks but that she herself, unless she did something extremely drastic, never would. So, instead of laughing, she tensed her jaw and tried not to notice the look of hurt in Merry's eye.

The awkward moment was broken by a scream and someone shouting, 'Oh no!'

The budgie had set itself free from its pet carrier and was flying around the store was darting from display to display.

Nell ran to the door to make sure that the bird couldn't escape if someone opened it. 'Harley, please can you turn the music off so we can hear ourselves think.'

'Like that makes any sense,' Harley grinned, clearly enjoying the drama. 'But OK.'

'I'm so sorry!' cried the girl who owned the bird. She took a handful of bird seed out of her pocket and threw it onto the floor.

'Marvellous,' muttered Merry. 'And no doubt it'll poo everywhere as well.'

'Birds like me,' Astrid boasted. 'I think I can get it to land on me, get ready to catch it.' She held out her arm and began whistling. The budgie landed momentarily on Astrid's head. She yelped and batted at her hair. 'Get off me.'

The kids from the choir joined in, leaping into the air, climbing on the shelf units and grasping at thin air as the bird evaded them.

'Here, birdy birdy,' cooed Irena, holding out the last of her sausage roll.

Merry sighed. 'I don't believe this. Will someone please catch it.'

'Yes!' Woody shrieked from his crouched position behind the counter. 'Seriously, guys, I'm freaking out here. If that bird touches me, I won't be responsible for my actions.'

The music went off and Harley returned with a broom.

The owner started to cry. 'Please don't hurt it, it was my granny's and she's just died.'

She had big green eyes peeping out from under her woolly hat and deep dimples in her cheeks.

Max puffed his chest out. 'Don't worry, we'll catch the damn thing. What's it called?'

'Chump,' sniffed the girl.

Everyone started calling to it. 'Chump? Chump? Come down, Chump! Here, Chump!'

'This is turning into a farce,' Nell muttered. 'Please tell me I'm dreaming.'

'Can anyone see it?' Max asked, searching the room.

'There!' Merry pointed up to a display by the window. 'I think it disappeared behind a candle on the top shelf.' Before anyone could stop her, she'd grabbed the stepladder and had climbed up to the top step. 'I can see it. Come here, Chump!'

'Hells bells, Merry Robinson,' Nell gasped. What was she thinking? 'Get down immediately.'

'I will,' Merry panted. 'Just as soon as Chump is safely in the palm of my hand.'

'I don't think a pregnant woman should be the one coming to the rescue of your budgie,' Irena wagged a finger at the bird owner.

'Quite,' said Fred, positioning himself at the base of the stepladder. 'Merry, come down immediately. That's a direct order.'

'For the millionth time,' said Merry through gritted teeth, straining to push candles on the top shelf to one side, 'I'm a fit, active woman, not a bloody invalid.'

'Your phone is ringing inside your bag, Merry!' Woody shouted. He was still behind the counter.

'Answer it please,' she said breathlessly. 'I'm nearly there . . . Come on, bird.'

The top of Woody's head popped over the counter. 'It's Cole.'

Nell marched over to the stepladder and tapped Merry's leg. She was furious with her friend. To take a risk like this over a budgie. 'No, get down now!' she yelled at her. 'There's a shop full of people here, all of whom are more suitable candidates than you to be catching a wayward budgie.'

'Bear with, Cole,' said Woody cheerily. 'Merry's just up a ladder at the moment, trying to catch a bird.'

'Nooo!' Merry yelled. 'Don't tell him that!'

Nell couldn't hear Cole's words, but she did hear the explosion of sound.

'Oh dear.' Woody thrust the phone away from his ear to avoid being deafened. 'He doesn't sound happy.'

Merry's foot slipped on the step, and she yelped as she clung on to regain her balance. There was a collective gasp among the crowd.

'*Vorsicht*!' Astrid clasped a hand to her chest.

'For heaven's sake. Look at you,' Nell hissed, hoping the rest of the shop wouldn't hear.

'It is a bit foolish,' Astrid agreed, joining Fred at the bottom of the stepladder.

'You are the most selfish person I've ever met,' Nell continued. 'I'd give anything to be in your position, and I don't mean up a ladder behaving like an absolute idiot, but a mother-to-be, literally days away from having your own baby. One you've created with your husband. You have no idea how lucky you are and how hurtful it is for me to see you being so careless. And I can't stand by and watch you risk the baby's life like this, so get down now or, I swear I will never, ever speak to you again.'

'The baby, the baby, the BLOODY baby!' Merry cried. 'I'm sick of hearing about the baby. What about me? Where am I in all of this? Nobody ever worries about me and what I'm feeling.'

'What? That's not fair and it's not true either.' Nell's lip trembled; how could she say that? Nell had done nothing but love and care for Merry for almost twenty years. She felt a tight band around her chest. Merry had crossed a line and Nell had had enough. She drew herself up tall. 'You know what? That's me done. You think you can do everything by yourself, so on you go, prove it. I quit. I am resigning immediately.'

As the shop fell totally silent, the budgie swooped down to its owner, who tucked it securely back into its carrier.

Merry's head whipped around, and she stared at Nell open-mouthed. 'Seriously?'

Before Nell had a chance to reply, Woody cleared his throat. 'Sorry to interrupt, Merry, but Cole says your dad's care home has tried calling you. You need to get over there immediately. Apparently, it's urgent. Very urgent.'

'Oh my God, Dad!' Merry's feet stumbled down the steps in her haste to get off the ladder.

'*Mein Gott*!, Astrid yelped. 'Be careful, *Liebling*!'

Nell put a hand out to steady her. 'I'm so sorry.'

But Merry didn't even acknowledge her. Instead, she grabbed the phone from Woody, scooped up her handbag and fetched her coat from the studio.

'Merry, ' she called after her,' let me drive you.'

Merry shook her head without even looking in Nell's direction. 'Leave me alone.'

Poor Merry. What had she done? How could she have turned on her best friend like that at a time like this? Nell just hoped she'd find a way to make it up to her before it was too late.

Chapter 19

Merry

Merry made it to her father's bedside at Springwood House as fast as she could, where manager, Gail, and Peter, one of his carers, were waiting for her. Ray was lying propped up, his gaunt face and thin neck dwarfed by a stack of pillows. His skin was translucent, as if all the blood had drained from him, and his breathing wheezy and faint. Merry was shocked by how much he'd deteriorated in only a couple of days; she wished with all her heart that Emily was still here. But he was breathing, thank goodness, and while he could still breathe, she had hope that he'd recover.

'Dad!' She took his hand in hers. 'It's me, Merry.'

She was breathless from rushing, shaky with fear and wanted more than anything to sink into a chair and close her eyes.

'I'll give you some privacy.' Peter's expression was grave. He patted her arm before leaving the room.

'Thanks for coming so quickly, Merry.' Gail put an arm around her shoulders, her voice gently deferential.

'Of course,' she replied, scarcely able to drag her eyes away from her dad. 'How is he?'

Gail let out a deep breath. 'I think you need to prepare yourself for the worst.'

Merry blinked at her. 'But he seemed to have stabilised, and then Emily went home and now she won't . . .' she choked on a sob.

'I know, and she mustn't blame herself,' Gail soothed. 'These things are impossible to predict. But in your father's case, I don't think he has long.'

Merry brushed a tear from her face. 'Emily will be so upset if she doesn't get the opportunity to say goodbye.'

She had rung her sister from the car on the way over, but the call had gone straight to voicemail. Merry hadn't left a message, not wanting to worry her. Now she wondered if she'd done the right thing. She'd call again as soon as she had the chance.

'The important thing to remember is that he's comfortable,' Gail reassured her. 'He's not in pain, and now that you're here, he's got a loved one with him.'

'He has.' She stroked his hand with her thumb. 'I love you, Dad. So does Emily.'

'You're shivering.' Gail touched her arm.

'Not with cold.' In actual fact, she felt clammy and hot. 'It's been quite a day already, and now this.'

Understatement of the century. So far this evening, she'd alienated everyone she'd come into contact with. She had so many apologies to make. She released Ray's hand and peeled off her coat, hanging it on the back of a chair, and took out her phone. There was a missed call from Cole but nothing from Emily. She'd leave Cole for now; she was bound to be in trouble after her outburst from atop the ladder. Justifiably so, she acknowledged with a shudder, but she had enough on her plate. Right now, her priority was Ray.

Gail patted her arm. 'Oh love, let me get you a nice soothing drink. We need to be looking after you as well as your father.'

'That would be lovely.' Merry swallowed the lump in her throat; the older woman's kindness was almost too much to bear.

When Gail had left the room, Merry moved her chair as close as she could to the bed and stretched out her legs to get comfortable. She'd try calling Emily again in a second, but for now, she wanted to spend a few minutes alone with the man she'd only had in her life for the last twelve months, imprinting his features into her memory.

'Remember my wedding, Dad?' She took his hand again; it was cool and dry and unresponsive to her touch. 'When you gave me Mum's ring? That was such a special moment. I don't think anything you could have done would have topped that, it made me so happy to have something of hers, especially on my wedding day.'

On her little finger, next to her wedding and engagement rings, was the silver wishbone ring she'd worn every day since then.

She smiled, recalling the moment of panic and Emily's mortification during the wedding service when Ray had escaped from his seat and approached them at the front of the room just as the registrar had asked the congregation if anyone had any objections to their marriage. Emily had dashed up to retrieve him, and for a split second, Cole had thought his future father-in-law was going to object. But, instead, the most magical thing had happened; he'd produced this little ring. He'd proposed to Sam with it once upon a time, he'd told Merry, but she'd turned him down, and now the ring was hers.

'I'll treasure it forever, Dad,' she promised now. 'It'll always remind me of you and her and that you loved each other once.'

The door to Ray's room opened again and in came Gail carrying a tray.

'Here you are,' she said, setting it down. 'I've brought you herbal tea and a couple of mince pies too. I remember being permanently starving when I was pregnant.'

Merry's eyes blurred with tears at the sight of the mince pies as she recalled her words to Nell. *That's a lot of pastry*.

There had been no need to say that, no need to say *anything*. She'd turned into a control freak, she thought miserably; she was doing it with Nell, and she'd even been doing it at home with Cole, trying to micro-manage every aspect of her life, not letting other people in. She'd had trust issues as a teenager; that was understandable given her upbringing, but it was no excuse now. If she couldn't even let her best friend select refreshments for an in-store event, then she was no sort of friend at all. It was so nit-picky, so unlike her. She didn't know herself at the moment.

No wonder Nell had resigned. And now Merry would be left to run Merry and Bright on her own. Oh God, Merry groaned under her breath; it didn't even bear thinking about.

'Are you all right?' Gail's voice jolted her from her thoughts. 'Can I call anyone for you?'

She shook her head. 'I'll be fine. Thank you for the drink, just what I need.'

She wouldn't eat the mince pies; she had no appetite, but the tea was very welcome. She took a sip and watched Gail put on some latex gloves and pick up a tiny sponge, which she dipped in water and touched to Ray's lips. 'Let's wet your whistle too, shall we?'

Ray twisted his head away and Merry's heart lurched; it was the first movement he'd made since she'd arrived. 'Hello, Dad. Do you think he can hear me?' she asked Gail.

'We're never really sure, but possibly,' she replied, removing her gloves and dropping them in the waste bin. 'He may recognise your voice even if he doesn't understand what you're saying. My advice is to take this moment as much for yourself as for Ray, say what you need to say.'

Merry nodded and bit her lip. 'Is it OK to be alone with him for a few minutes?'

'Of course,' said Gail, with a sympathetic smile.

Once she had gone, Merry set down her mug and reached for Ray's hand again. She felt stiff all over and every bone in her body ached. She'd been a fool to do so much today, and as for her attempt to rescue that budgie by climbing a ladder, that had been beyond ridiculous. She forced herself to put all of that out of her head and take Gail's advice. If this was the last chance she'd ever have to talk to her dad, she'd regret it later if she'd spent her time worrying about things she couldn't change.

'I hope this isn't our last conversation, Dad,' she began hesitantly. 'But if it is, I want you to know that I really love you and having you in my life this last year has been the most unexpected gift. I'll always wonder what might have happened to Mum if you and she had got together properly after I was born. Maybe she'd have felt able to cope if you'd have been around. Who knows; there are all sorts of reasons why people take their own life. What I am sure of is that I'm really grateful that you had another daughter. You gave me a little sister. I love her so much, Dad, and even though she doesn't live close by anymore, we have such a special bond already. I miss her, so you must miss her terribly.'

She paused to study her dad's features for movement. Underneath his eyelids, she thought she saw his eyeballs flicker from side to side. He could hear her; she was sure of it.

'I'm sorry it's me here and not Emily,' she said. 'You have so many more memories with her than me. But the few you and I have made together have been all the sweeter for their scarcity. Having real relatives has been the icing on top of a spectacular couple of years.'

The baby chose that moment to wake up and do its exercises. Merry had to lean back and stretch out. Sometimes she felt like a pinball machine, with the baby like a little ball, pinging from one side of her to another.

'My baby will be born soon, Dad,' she told him. 'I hope you'll get to meet your grandchild, I hope I make you the proudest granddad in the world, but . . .' She couldn't bring herself to say, 'if you don't'. Instead, she stood up and pressed his hand to the fabric of her dress, guiding his palm as the baby continued to push and shove against her. 'Can you feel those little knees and elbows? Oh gosh,' she sniffed. 'I so wish the baby was already here, so I could put him or her in your arms for a cuddle.'

Her phone started to ring, making her jump, and she quickly laid Ray's hand down on the covers to answer it.

The sight of Emily's name on the screen made her breath hitch. She was dreading this moment. Delivering news like this had to be the worst job in the world.

'Sorry, sorry!' Her sister sounded full of energy and bounce. 'I was down at the beach hut, and I didn't have my phone with me. What's up?'

'Um . . .' Merry swallowed and tried to talk, but the ball of sadness in her throat was too big, and the words wouldn't come out.

'Oh my God,' whispered Emily. 'Is it Dad?'

'Yes,' Merry managed to say with a croak in her voice. 'He's very weak, Gail has told me he might not have long. I'm here with him now.'

'Oh please, no.' Emily let out a moan. 'I knew I shouldn't have left you, I'm so cross with myself. I'm sorry you're having to deal with this on your own, with all that you've got going on too. Listen, hold tight and I'll come straight over. I'll rush, I won't even bother to pack. I'll call you when I know what flight I'm—'

'Em, listen,' Merry jumped in. 'I don't think there's time.'

There was silence on the other end of the line.

'What? But . . .' Emily swallowed a sob. 'You mean . . .'

'From what Gail has said, we're quite near the end.' Merry turned away from her dad, not wanting him to hear, just in case he understood.

'So I might never see him again?' Her sister's voice sounded strangled with sadness. 'Poor Dad, poor you. What can I do?'

Merry shook her head, wishing she had the answers and not wanting to reply that there was nothing she could do.

'Can you switch this to video call, so I can see him?' Emily suggested.

'Good idea.' Merry let out a sigh of relief. 'Gail has said he might recognise our voices, so let's talk.'

She swapped the call to FaceTime and turned her body so that the camera could get both of them in. 'Dad, Emily is here now too,' she said while Emily settled herself on the sofa.

'Hi, Dad, sorry I can't be there,' said Emily, in a trembly voice. 'But I'm sending you my love from Jersey.'

'We're both going to keep you company for a while.' Merry took his hand in hers; his fingers had turned as cold as ice. 'Let's make you comfortable,' she said, tucking his other arm under the covers.

'What should we talk about?' Emily whispered.

'Special memories of him? Happy times?' she suggested. 'I haven't got many, apart from this year, but I'm so glad I got to hear some of your stories about your family, Dad, and how you always had pork chops—'

'On Mondays!' Emily finished for her, and they both laughed.

'I do remember you coming round to read stories to me,' Merry told him, 'and I remember you and my mum dancing around our tiny bedsit to Fleetwood Mac. I was only young, and my memories are vague, but I know we were all happy.'

'The day I brought you to Springwood House to meet Dad for the first time, we danced to Fleetwood Mac too, remember?'

Merry nodded. 'That was one of the happiest days of my life.'

'And mine,' Emily replied after a pause.

'I know this is a sad occasion,' Merry continued, 'but I'm so grateful to you for finding me, finding us really, our family.'

'Hey, Dad, remember when Peter found that you'd thrown all the sofa cushions from the lounge into the skip outside,' said Emily with a giggle.

'Or what about the time you took Lavinia some flowers to her room?' Merry laughed. 'Wearing only your pyjama jacket.'

'Oh yes,' Emily added. 'And instead of a bunch of flowers, it was a plant you'd pulled up from the garden and trailed soil all through the corridors and up the stairs.'

'Still, Lavinia was pleased,' said Merry with a snort. 'But Maude was so jealous that she didn't talk to her for a week.'

Emily giggled. 'I've just remembered something funny. Dad, do you remember the face-painting we did?'

Merry watched Ray's expression for changes, but there didn't seem to be a response. 'Tell me the story.'

'When I was six, I had a set of face paints and wanted to look like a pirate. Dad spent ages doing my face and I looked brilliant. I then asked to do his. He bravely agreed, but all I managed for him was scribbled panda eyes, white blotches on his cheeks and black stripes on his chin. I'm sure he was horrified, but he said he loved it, and I was so pleased. Later, he took me with him to the fish and chip shop; I'd washed my face paint off, but Dad had forgotten about his. He wondered why everyone was laughing at him until he saw his reflection in the glass of the warming cabinets.'

'Oh no!' Merry laughed, imagining Freya doing the same thing to Cole. 'What did he say?'

'That was the lovely thing,' said Emily, drying her eyes. 'He could have been embarrassed or cross, but he told everyone that his daughter had painted his face to look like a pirate and wasn't she a superb artist. Lots of people congratulated me and I felt so proud. Good old Dad.'

'Yeah,' Merry agreed, 'good old Dad.' She looked at Ray, his fingers were clenching and unclenching and whereas his face had looked peaceful before, now his features were scrunched up. 'Dad? Are you OK?'

'What's happening?' Emily said, squinting at the screen.

'He looks really uncomfortable.' Merry felt herself go cold with fear. 'I don't like this. Maybe the painkillers have worn off.'

Ray's head thrashed from side to side.

'It's OK, Dad,' said Merry, trying to sound calm.

'Pull the emergency red cord behind the bed,' Emily demanded. 'Get someone in there.'

'Good idea.' Merry pushed herself off the chair and tugged on the cord. 'Come on, come on, come on.'

Ray's arms went rigid, fingers splayed, and his face was contorted. The soft wheezy breathing had changed to a harsher choking sound. Merry had never felt so afraid and out of her depth in her life.

'Help!' she yelled. 'Someone help!'

'It's OK, Dad, we're getting help, hang on in there,' Emily pleaded.

'Where is everyone?' Merry cried. 'Why hasn't someone come to help?'

'Merry!' Emily gasped. 'He looks as if he's trying to say something.'

Merry leaned over him as best she could and put her ear close to his mouth. 'What is it, Dad?'

But Ray didn't speak. Instead, he made a gurgling sound as if there was fluid in his throat. He gave one, two, three more ragged attempts at breathing, and then his face went slack as the last vestige of life ebbed out of him.

Merry patted his cheek. 'Wake up, come on, Dad, don't leave us.'

She stared at him in vain, hoping to see a sign of life, but there was nothing. And she knew, she simply knew, he was gone.

She was aware that Emily was crying and needed comforting, but in that moment, she gave herself up to her own sadness, her own loss and the unfairness of finding her father only to lose him again so soon.

The door opened softly and in filed the team from Springwood House to take over. Merry rested her forehead on the edge of her dad's bed, still holding tightly to his hand, and cried and cried and cried until finally she felt the warm embrace of a familiar shape.

'Come here, darling,' said her husband in a whisper.

'Cole!' she sobbed. 'He's gone. My dad has gone.'

'I know, baby, I know.' He took her in his arms and kissed her cheek. 'I'm here and I love you, it's OK.'

Merry let herself sink into him, taking comfort from his strength, his love and the steadfast beat of his heart.

She heard him send his love to Emily and let her know he'd collect her from the airport while she clung to him and wept.

She cried for the man she'd hardly known and for the baby who'd never know its grandfather and, unexpectedly, for the mother she missed now as keenly as she ever had done as a child. Because, when all was said and done, she realised, family and loved ones and feeling a part of something bigger than yourself was what life was all about. And her family would never be the same again.

Chapter 20

Nell

Nell drove Max back home on autopilot; grateful for once that her stepson was engrossed in his phone and didn't want to chat. She couldn't get the image of Merry out of her head. Not the one where she shouted from the ladder about no one caring about her, but the look of terror on her face when she received the instruction to get to her dad's residential home immediately. As far as Nell was concerned, that had been the wake-up call for both of them. It had pressed reset on the situation. They were best friends and had been for over two decades, and Nell wanted to be there for Merry in her hour of need. Nothing else mattered. Merry's dad was clearly in a serious condition; whatever else was going on could wait.

Nell wished she had been firmer with Merry and insisted on driving her to Springwood House. Merry had been in no fit state to drive herself, but she was incredibly stubborn. Once she'd made up her mind, there'd be no changing it.

After Merry had gone, people had started speaking again. Someone had put the music back on, at a lower volume, Nell had been pleased to hear. Harley had watched anxiously, waiting for instruction; the two girls with the budgie had escaped into the night, along with several other customers, while Woody had done his best to regain the earlier mood by chatting to the remaining shoppers and topping up cups of mulled wine. Irena had stepped in to give Nell a hug and by the time she had extricated herself from her mother-in-law's bosom and mopped her eyes, she was exhausted.

'Not my call, darling, obviously,' Woody had slid an arm around her shoulders. 'But if I were you, I'd call it a night. What do you say?'

Nell had leaned her head on his shoulder, her eyes prickling with tears again, and nodded. 'You're an angel, you know that, Woody. I don't know what I'd have done without you.'

He'd planted a swift kiss on her head. 'You'd have managed, my love, like we all do. Come on, let's call last orders on the mulled wine, as if we were a pub. I've always wanted to do that.'

'Nell?' From the passenger seat, Max's voice penetrated her thoughts. 'We're here, you're about to drive past.'

'Sorry, love.' Nell pulled the car to a stop outside Max's house, and he jumped straight out.

'Thanks for the lift,' he called, slamming the door, as Yvonna appeared on the drive in her winter coat and slippers. 'Hey, Mum.'

He gave his mum a lightning-fast kiss on her cheek and ran inside. Nell felt a rush of adrenaline at the sight of Yvonna.

What secrets did this woman hold? Nell wondered, as she prepared to turn the car around and drive away. What lies had she been keeping all these years? If mumps had made Olek infertile all his adult life, as Nell suspected, then Yvonna must have been having an affair as far back as when Max was conceived – years before Olek had found out about it. Not only had she cheated on Olek, but she'd allowed him to believe that Max was his, let him support the boy financially all this time after they'd separated, but, more important than that, she'd sat back and watched her ex-husband form an unshakeable bond with a child who wasn't his.

Nell gripped the steering wheel, angry on Olek's behalf. Should she tackle Yvonna on it? Hint that she'd found out the truth? She hesitated for a second, her foot hovering over the brakes. No, she wouldn't, she decided. It was late in the evening, she'd had a stressful day already, and she still needed to check up on Merry to see how her father was.

She nodded at Yvonna out of politeness and selected first gear, but the other woman raised a hand to stop her from driving away.

Nell bit back a groan and lowered her window to Yvonna to talk to her.

'Thanks for bringing him home. I owe you one.' Yvonna was shivering. She was only wearing a strappy vest underneath her coat, and she pulled the lapels together for warmth. 'I had one of those days at work and the bottle of Malbec in the kitchen was calling to me. Before I knew it, I'd had two glasses and didn't dare drive.'

'And Viktor didn't fancy picking him up either?' Nell couldn't resist asking.

As his stepfather, naturally he wasn't going to be as dedicated to Max as Olek or Yvonna, but in all the years she'd known Viktor, he'd only ever shown an interest in Max when there was something to boast about. He'd already asked for free tickets to the Derby v Liverpool match on Christmas Eve. Max only had two and he'd promised them to Olek and Yvonna's dad, who'd been supporting Max's football career since he was small. Viktor had apparently sulked for two days.

'Viktor?' Yvonna chuckled. 'No, he's had *three* glasses.'

Fair enough, thought Nell. It was Christmas, a time when lots of people were drinking more than usual. Plus, Yvonna had known either she or Olek would step in and bring her son home, as usual, but Nell couldn't help finding the other woman's casual attitude to Max reckless. If she had a child . . . She brought herself up short, she had to stop this sort of thinking, this criticism of parents who, in her mind, fell somehow short of her own standards. After all, what did she know, what would she *ever* know, about the true day-in, day-out responsibilities of parenthood?

'Are you listening?' Yvonna's sharp voice brought her back to the moment.

'Sorry?' Nell replied with a start. 'I missed that.'

Yvonna smirked. 'If I didn't know you were such a saint, I'd think you'd been drinking. You're away with the fairies. I said, did it go well? Your little shopping evening?'

The hairs on the back of Nell's neck prickled. Yvonna was pressing all her buttons tonight; the sooner she could drive off, the better.

'Yes! Great, thanks for asking!' she said with such enthusiasm that Yvonna's eyebrows shot up in surprise.

If only she knew that it had been Nell's worst experience at work ever: she'd had a slanging match with her pregnant best friend, had to shut the shop early and in a fit of pique had resigned and was now jobless.

'A busy night then.' Yvonna hugged herself against the cold. 'I'm surprised Olek didn't offer to drive you. You two are usually joined at the hip.'

Nell gritted her teeth; the back-handed compliments were coming in thick and fast tonight.

'He had an emergency call-out to fit new locks after a break-in. Poor family had all their Christmas presents stolen from under the tree. He is having to secure all doors and windows before he can leave.'

Yvonna pursed her lips. 'I used to hate his long hours, especially when my friends were all going out with their husbands, and I was sitting at home watching TV alone.'

Except when she was having an affair with Olek's friend, thought Nell.

'Well, have a nice evening tonight with Viktor,' she said, preparing to wrap up the conversation.

'I will, Viktor is always here. The good thing about being a baker is that he finishes early; he is always home in the evenings, ready for an early night.'

'So no going out with this husband either then,' Nell pointed out slyly.

'Not anymore, we're past that now,' said Yvonna with a sniff. 'Back in the early days, we were party animals.'

'That must have been a challenge when Max was so young.' Poor Max, Nell thought, imagining him as a little boy, bewildered by the replacement of his quiet, mild-mannered father with Viktor, the jolly baker.

Two pink spots appeared on the other woman's face. 'I meant while Max was with Olek. One of the best benefits of splitting up from a good dad is that you've always got a willing babysitter.'

The nerve of the woman, thought Nell indignantly. She seemed proud of the fact that by splitting from her husband, she'd got such a good babysitter for Max.

Olek had caught them red-handed, and Yvonna had never admitted how long their affair had been going on. But Nell wanted to know. Because if Viktor was around at the time Max was conceived, then the chances were that they were father and son.

She really wanted to find out. Yvonna had just said she owed her one, but this was a biggie. On the other hand, when else would she get an opportunity like this, just the two of them?

'Yvonna, can I ask . . .' She hesitated, watching as Yvonna leaned in, her gaze intense. What the hell was she thinking? Of course she couldn't ask. 'No, no, it's nothing, forget it.'

Nell gave the other woman a tight smile and retreated into her car.

'What? Go on, you can't leave it there,' Yvonna probed. 'I'll be thinking about it all night. I hate mysteries.'

Nell wavered. Her heart was knocking against her ribs. This was not one of her best ideas. And what if it got back to Olek?

'Nell.' Yvonna folded her arms. 'Out with it, what do you want to know?'

'OK, hold on.' Nell couldn't do this sitting down with the other woman looming over her. She got out and faced Yvonna directly, eyeball to eyeball. 'You said you owed me one.'

Yvonna's eyes narrowed. 'It was a figure of speech, but carry on.'

The night air was freezing, and their breath swirled mistily in front of their faces. Nell didn't like conflict, she was the good-natured one. Olek sometimes joked that he couldn't have married two more different woman.

'This must never reach Olek.' She looked back at the house to check that no one was in earshot.

'Well, well, well.' Yvonna smirked. 'I'd never have had you down as someone to keep secrets from your husband. But yeah, sure, if you want.'

You don't know the half of it, thought Nell. The list of lies she'd told him was getting longer by the day.

'Olek and I had some tests.' This was a dangerous game she was playing; she licked her dry lips. 'At a fertility clinic.'

Yvonna's gaze intensified. 'Oh? You're having problems? Sorry to hear that. Although, at Olek's age, I'd be surprised he wants to go through the baby years again; I certainly wouldn't.'

'Unfortunately, we might not be. It turns out that he can't . . .' She licked her dry lips. 'Look, the thing is, I wondered if . . . Oh God.' Nell pressed her hands to her face. 'What am I doing?'

'No idea,' Yvonna scoffed. 'But I'm freezing out here, so spit it out, or let me go in and get on with the rest of my evening.'

The audacity of the woman. She'd had an uninterrupted evening so far, thanks to Nell, who'd come out of her way to drop off Max and still had to go back to the shop to finish tidying up. Nell felt her anger bubble up and spill over.

'OK, fine. Is Max . . . I mean, was there any doubt that Olek . . .?' she blurted. Even as her words came spilling out, regrets started to smother them. 'Actually, forget I said that. Please. Ignore me. It's been a long and stressful day and I'm tired.'

The colour drained from Yvonna's face, and her eyes were wide with shock. 'Are you insinuating that Olek might not be Max's dad?' Yvonna drew herself up ramrod straight and tilted her chin at Nell.

'I didn't say that. I didn't finish my sentence.' Nell stared at her, but Yvonna could scarcely meet her eye, guilt etched into every line on her face. 'Interesting that you assumed that was what I was going to say.'

'How dare you?' Yvonna seethed. 'How bloody dare you? What happened before you came on the scene has absolutely nothing to do with you. 'You're right,' said Nell.

'It's none of my business, but it is Olek's.' 'I'd like you to leave now.' Yvonna glared at her. 'Go on, get out of here.'

Wow. What was that saying about the lady protesting too much? Nell mused.

'Fine. I'm going.' Nell opened the car door and threw herself into the driving seat. The hem of her coat was hanging over the doorsill, and she quickly whipped it into the car as Yvonna bent over her.

'I think this conversation is best kept between us, don't you?' Yvonna said, archly. 'If you ever mention this again, I'll be going straight to Olek and commiserating with him on his infertility. He'd be very surprised to find out who was gossiping about him behind his back, would't he?'

'You wouldn't do that.' Nell felt sick at the thought of Olek hearing anything of the sort from Yvonna.

Yvonna simply gave her a smug smile.

She was hiding something, it was obvious. Not that it made the situation any better for Nell and Olek. In fact, having her worst suspicions confirmed made it much, much worse. Now not only had Nell lied to her husband, but she was withholding information about the most important person in Olek's life: his beloved son.

Chapter 21

Nell

Twenty minutes after leaving Yvonna, Nell had made it back to Merry and Bright.

'What a day. Thank goodness you're still here,' she said to Woody, stifling a yawn. She dropped her bag and car keys on the counter and tugged off her coat. 'Is there any of that mulled wine left?'

'Yes, loads,' said Woody, turning off the vacuum cleaner and taking her coat from her. 'I almost threw it away and then couldn't bring myself to do it. I've had two glasses while I was clearing up.'

'Good.' Nell picked up a handful of nuts from a bowl and crunched on them. 'I'm going to get drunk.'

The drive from Yvonna's had passed in a blur. The constant low-level anxiety was nothing new after the rubbish couple of weeks she'd had, but tonight everything had ramped up tenfold and her mind was in a whirl.

What had possessed her to even consider asking Yvonna if Olek really was Max's father? As if she was likely to admit otherwise after all this time. And now she'd laid herself open to all sorts of trouble. If Olek ever found out that she'd been asking his ex-wife probing questions, it was all bound to come out. Olek being infertile would be difficult enough to accept, given Nell had told him she was the one with the issue, but to discover that he hadn't fathered Max either and she'd kept it from him, he'd . . . well, she didn't know how he'd react, and she'd rather not find out, ever.

Woody lifted the lid of the slow cooker which was keeping the mulled wine warm. A delicious smell of orange, cinnamon and nutmeg wafted out. He poured her a large mugful. 'Just checking you're not driving home?'

Good question. Nell sank onto a stool and took a long sip, her eyes widening as the alcohol hit the back of her throat. That felt good.

The shop's Christmas lights still twinkled, the smell of a myriad of scented candles lingered, and Woody had changed the music to soothing carols, and for the first time in several hours, Nell could feel her heart rate returning to normal. The thought of going back out into the cold again didn't appeal at all. And right now she was scared that if she looked into Olek's lovely trusting eyes, she'd blurt out her truths, lies and suspicions.

She shook her head. 'I don't want to go home. I might just stay here. Oh, I keep forgetting you're a paying Airbnb guest. Sorry. Of course I'll go home, I'll get a taxi.'

'Don't be silly,' he said, pouring some for himself. 'I can make the bed up on the sofa for you. Anyway, it'll be fun to have a guest, it gets a little lonely here at night.'

'That settles it, but *I'll* make the sofa bed up,' she insisted.

He laughed. 'You haven't even had a drink yet, let's play it by ear.'

'Such an odd expression that,' Nell mused.

He gave her a curious look. 'I just mean that we'll see how we go, no need to follow a plan.'

'I know that, but playing something from memory without the music in front of you to follow is amazing. It implies you can get by without putting a foot wrong, or without playing the wrong tune. All I ever do is put my foot in it and play bum notes.'

'O-*K*.' Woody gave her a wary look. 'That's a bit deep. Oh don't cry!'

'Ignore me, it's just been a hell of a day. This tastes better than it did before,' she added, sniffing her mug.

'Ah. I should have warned you that I've added a glug of something your mother-in-law left for you. She said it in Polish and I can't remember what the word was, but I think it's cherry-flavoured vodka.'

Nell gave a little moan of pleasure. 'Now we're talking. Her home-made brew is legendary. Top me up, Woody, and pour another one for yourself. Let's get this party started.'

Within twenty minutes, the shop floor was pastry-crumb and mulled wine-spills free, and Woody and Nell had retired to the flat upstairs with the rest of the cherry vodka.

'Oh knickers,' she said, patting her pockets. 'I've left my phone downstairs in my coat.'

'And it can stay there,' said Woody. 'Give yourself a break and relax for a while.'

'I'll try,' she said, kneeling in front of the log burner. 'But I'm going to have to let Olek know where I am. And then there's Merry. I need to speak to her.'

Poor Merry. Goodness knows what was going on with her dad, but it hadn't sounded good.

'Far be it for me to interfere between you two, but maybe it's best to give each other some space tonight.'

Nell pondered on that; Woody might be right. They'd both said hurtful things to each other. Nell regretted hers and Merry was probably feeling the same. 'I will fetch my phone soon, but the thought of turning the world off for a while and giving my brain a rest sounds amazing.'

'You're such a tonic, Nell.' Woody stretched out on the sofa and plumped up a cushion for behind his head. 'I was feeling very down when I arrived in Wetherley, but spending time with you has done me the power of good.'

'Me? Bloody hell, you must be desperate.' Nell built a wigwam of kindling over some scrunched-up newspaper and set a match to it. 'I'm more miserable than Eeyore at the moment.'

'Oh, darling, that is sad. Tell your Uncle Woody what's wrong,' he said kindly, 'A problem shared and all that.'

Nell gave him a sideways glance, weighing up whether to confide in him or not. She'd already dropped hints to Merry, and divulged far too much to Yvonna, but she still hadn't told anyone the whole truth. Could she tell Woody? It would feel good to confess to someone, and then at least she could get another opinion. Plus, the benefit of telling Woody was that not only was he neutral, but he was only here for a short time, so less chance of him having the opportunity to tell anyone. 'Do you know what,' she said, feeling a rush of relief already. 'I think you might be right. So how about I tell you my story if you tell me yours?'

'My story? I'm not sure what you mean.' He gave a brittle laugh and poured them both a shot of Irena's vodka.

She raised an eyebrow. 'Oh come on. You've taken an impromptu solo break just before Christmas, leaving your husband home alone, but you nip back and make dinner for him while he's out. You've left a job which you apparently enjoyed and by your own admission you were feeling down when you arrived. If that isn't the basis for a good story, I don't know what is.'

He laughed. A proper laugh this time. 'OK, Sherlock, I submit to your powers of detection. I do have a story.'

'So, deal?' The fire was burning nicely in the log burner; Nell added a couple more logs for good measure and closed the door.

He nodded. 'It'll be like show-and-tell at school, except ours is the depression edition.'

'Never let it be said that we don't know how to have fun.' She let out a snort and crawled on her knees from the fire to the table, where the two shots of vodka were waiting for them both. She held hers up and waited for Woody to do the same. 'If we each share our problems, does that mean they get halved or doubled?'

'Maybe it just means that, for tonight, we put them aside altogether and get drunk,' said Woody.

'Good plan, Woody, I'm in.' Nell giggled and tapped her glass against his before knocking it back. 'Whoah. Gosh, that was good!'

Woody's eyes watered and he spluttered. 'Wowzers! No wonder your mother-in-law had a smile on her face if this is what she keeps in her handbag.'

'Oh God.' Nell groaned at the thought of Irena and Gienek, and how devastated they'd be if the truth of Max's parentage ever came out. 'OK, I'm just going to tell you the whole thing. It's about babies, so I apologise if this is not your thing.'

'Oh, darling.' Woody let out such a big breath that his body visibly slumped. 'I'm so sorry to hear that, but babies are my thing.'

He understood, thought Nell, and at once she knew she had made the right decision to talk.

'Come here.' Woody held out a hand to pull Nell onto the sofa beside him. 'Do you want to go first or second?'

'Um.' Nell's throat felt so tight with the effort of holding in her sobs that she couldn't have gone first if she'd wanted to. She sat down, tucked her feet beneath her and held out her glass for Woody to top up. 'Second please.'

'OK, so the reason I'm staying in an Airbnb and working for free in your shop is that Spencer and I have had the most traumatic of years and I needed a time-out from him. I thought our relationship was strong enough to withstand anything, but now I know I was wrong.'

Nell nodded. 'Sounds familiar.'

She'd always thought the same about her and Olek, but like Woody, she was having her doubts.

'We deliberated for the longest time about starting a family,' Woody continued. 'He was mad keen from the get-go, desperate to be a dad; I was more cautious. I love our life as it is, we're social butterflies, we go away at the drop of a hat and please ourselves. Both of us work long hours, mine being especially unsociable, running events all over the country. Anyway, we decided to go for it. I was primed to go through the adoption route. But Spencer flat refused. He wanted the child to be biologically ours and found someone who was prepared to be our surrogate. I had so many questions, so many reservations, but long story short, for Spencer's sake I went along to meet Jenny, and credit where it's due, she was lovely.'

Nell listened intently, completely in awe of how this couple had approached parenthood, determined to overcome any obstacles to have a family. Such a contrast to her own attitude of burying her head in the sand.

'It seemed too good to be true, especially as only a couple of months after us investigating the legal side of it all, Jenny was pregnant and expecting our baby. A few weeks in and the three of us attended her first scan. And that was it.' Woody smiled at Nell, his eyes starry with love. 'From the moment I saw that little chap waving his arms on the screen, and noticed the giant head which Spencer teased was the same shape as mine, I was in love. All my doubts about surrogacy evaporated. There in Jenny's tummy was the future of our family. Spencer and I had never been so happy. We were in our element, thinking of names, decorating the nursery, immersing ourselves in a brand-new world of buggies and cots and a wardrobe full of adorable clothes. And then—' Woody's chin wobbled.

Nell felt tears prick at her eyes.

'At twenty-eight weeks . . .' He covered his eyes with his hand. 'You know what I'm going to say.'

'She lost the baby?' Nell said softly.

He nodded. 'No warning, no reason, just . . . I still can't talk about it, and this happened in September.'

'Of course it's still raw and fresh in your mind. I'm so sorry, Woody.' She reached for his hand and held it tight.

'Our first concern was Jenny. It was terrible for her, physically and mentally. It was her first experience with surrogacy. She's vowed never to do it again.'

'Poor Jenny, she would have felt the weight of your grief on top of her own.'

He smiled sadly. 'We did everything we could to avoid that, but it was inevitable.'

'And since then,' Nell probed. 'What are your thoughts now? Or is it too soon?'

'This is where the problems began.' Woody pulled a face. 'I think we need a break from it, but Spencer was straight back on the case looking for another potential surrogate. His way of coping is to move on and try again. But not me. I feel the same as Jenny. Surrogacy was great until it wasn't, and meanwhile there are hundreds of children on adoption lists hoping for a better life than the one they've had so far. And Spencer and I can offer that, Nell. Yes,

I know the adoption process is rigorous, but it would be worth it. We'd be getting our family, and making a life-changing difference to a child who needs a loving home.'

Nell's heart ached for him. She knew the pain of longing for a baby, but what Woody and Spencer had been through was in another league. To have seen your living, breathing baby on the screen of a scanning machine only to lose it must have been unbearable.

'So if Spencer wants to go with surrogacy and you want to adopt, where does that leave you?' She nudged him gently to continue, even though it was clear now why they were having some time apart.

'When we were pregnant, he and I were united in our family plans. Now our dreams have diverged, we're on different paths and we can't find our way back to each other. I'd given up my job, ready to look after the baby full-time. My boss is hoping to have me back, but how can I return to work, knowing that everyone feels sorry for me, knowing that I should be on parental leave? Spencer is adamant that he wants a child to be biologically ours, but there are so many more important aspects to parenthood than sharing DNA. I'm ready to take on a nurturing role, I want to give a child a home; Spencer wants to procreate. So I'm here to figure out what I want my future to look like and to get some perspective on our marriage, decide what's most important. With Jenny, we thought we were out of the danger zone for miscarrying; next time around I'd never be able to relax for a moment. But because I love Spencer so much, the only way I can see this ending is if I'm the one to compromise.'

'Relationships only work if there's an element of compromise on both sides,' Nell began. 'Maybe you need to be honest with him . . . Oh.' She stopped mid-sentence, realising that honesty was something she hadn't afforded her own marriage.

'Wow.' Woody peeled away from her, and looked deep in thought. 'Maybe you're right, I think I've been too scared to voice my truth, not wanting to drive a deeper wedge between us. I just need to come up with a way of broaching it.'

'Honesty should be easy, shouldn't it?' said Nell in a small voice. 'But sometimes it's the hardest option.'

Woody picked up on her tone and eyed her curiously. 'So what about you? You said your story was about babies too. Are you ready to talk?'

She nibbled her lip, nervous suddenly. Woody's problems were not of his making, whereas she'd got herself into this mess.

'A problem shared, remember,' he prompted.

'I haven't been honest with Olek,' she blurted out in a rush. 'It started a year ago when I was secretly trying to conceive without telling him. I told myself it didn't matter, he'd be happy if I got pregnant, but I should still have been open about it. Then, when nothing happened, we were both tested . . .'

She shouldn't have told a virtual stranger things she hadn't been able to tell even her closest friend, but it felt so liberating to hear herself speak about the matters which had been churning away like acid in her system for the past few weeks. And Woody, bless him, listened with nothing but compassion and kindness in his eyes.

'I know there are much worse things happening to other people in the world,' she said, wiping tears from her eyes. 'I know I'm lucky in so many ways, but I always assumed that one day I'd have a family of my own, and now that it turns out that I can't, I can't focus on anything else.

I'm trying to be happy for Merry, but it's so hard when she seems, at best, so blasé about it, and, at worst, grumpy and ungrateful. I'd imagined us both having babies at the same time, and them growing up together. Instead, she's entering this new phase of life and I'm being left behind.'

The booze was taking effect on her, smoothing the sharp edges off the day, and she was feeling nicely fuzzy. She sipped her vodka, savouring the cherry sweetness before the hit of alcohol.

'I'm just so sad,' she said.

'Of course you are. That's the most heartbreaking thing I've ever heard.' Woody reached for the tissue box on the table and took one for each of them. 'And I know how much pressure this sort of thing puts on a couple. I hope you and Olek can support each other through this tricky patch?'

She mopped her eyes. 'We can't because I can't talk about it. And I can't talk about it because I told him a lie, the lie has snowballed out of control and now I don't know what to do about it.'

Woody chewed his lip. 'As you just said, honesty is usually the best policy.'

Nell pressed a hand to her forehead; it was getting more difficult to focus now, she was quite tipsy. 'I was trying to do the kindest thing. There's no obvious reason why I can't conceive, I'm healthy in every way. It's Olek who's infertile. The doctor said it was unlikely that he'd ever have been fertile, and I panicked.'

'But I thought Max was Olek's son.' Woody's jaw dropped.

Nell nodded gravely before letting out a loud hiccup. 'Olek thought so. Olek *thinks so*. Now I'm not convinced he can be. But I do know that he must never find out.'

'Poor Olek.'

'It's a shame I can't just use your sperm and—'

Woody spat out his vodka. 'What!'

Nell giggled. 'Well, I could, couldn't I? You could get me pregnant. No one would ever suspect.'

Woody went pink. 'Um, Nell . . .'

She waved a hand at him and laughed. 'Don't worry, I'm only—'

Downstairs, a door slammed. Nell and Woody jumped out of their skins.

'What was that?' Nell hissed.

'We're being broken in to.' Woody set his glass down on the coffee table with a trembling hand. 'We're in the middle of a robbery.'

They clutched at each other and strained to listen. Nell held her breath; her heart was pounding so loudly in her ears, she couldn't hear a thing.

There was silence from downstairs. Which might mean that whoever it was wasn't on their way in but on their way out.

She ran to the window and peered down to the car parking space behind the shop and her heart almost burst out of her chest as she watched with horror the lights of Olek's van come on and the van accelerate away into the darkness.

'Oh shit. It wasn't a burglar, it was my husband.' She squeezed her eyes shut as a wave of nausea rose to her throat. *Oh, darling, I'm so, so sorry*, she murmured under her breath.

'Ooh, shall I go and let him in?' Woody rubbed his hands together.

Nell shook her head. 'He's already gone. He must have heard what I just said. Oh god, this is a disaster.'

But how much had he heard? That she'd lied to him, or just the joke about using Woody's sperm? Her heart thudded as she ran downstairs to fetch her phone. She had to call him, get him to come back, at least let her try to explain that she'd only lied because she loved him.

Where was her phone? She frantically searched both pockets in her coat, tipped out the contents of her handbag to try to locate it, but it wasn't there. She'd thought that today couldn't get any worse; turned out she was wrong. And this time she couldn't see how to make it right. How was she going to get out of this one?

Chapter 22

Merry

It was late evening when Merry knocked on Olek and Nell's door. She was physically exhausted and wrung out from all her crying. But despite being desperate to collapse into bed, she couldn't go straight home from Springwood House without calling in on Nell to tell her the news of Ray's passing. Every time she'd called her number this evening, it had gone to voicemail. Merry didn't blame Nell for not wanting to take her call, not after the way she'd yelled at her in the shop earlier. She'd thought about sending her a message, but letting her best friend know that her dad had died was far too important to convey by text; besides, what she really needed from Nell was a hug, so here she was to deliver the news in person.

No one came to the door, and now Merry looked through the glass panel, she noticed that there were no lights on inside. She checked the time; it was only 9 p.m., too early for bed. She knocked again a little louder and waited.

After saying a final goodbye to her dad, she and Cole had spent an hour at Springwood House dealing with the immediate affairs which followed a death. It was a new experience for her, never having had close relatives until recently. For Cole, it was a reminder of the hours and days following his mother's death several years ago. It wasn't a pleasant experience for either of them, but Merry had never been more grateful that he'd been there to support her. Emily had been joined by Will during the last few minutes of their FaceTime call, and the four of them had discussed funeral arrangements. Emily wasn't going to rush straight over now, there wasn't much point, but she and Will were going to come over as soon as they'd fixed a date for the service and stay with Emily's parents right through until the New Year.

Merry was about to give up and drive off when the door opened, and Olek appeared.

'Sorry,' he muttered, running a hand distractedly across his stubbly jaw. 'I wasn't going to come to the door at all until I realised it was you.'

'Is everything OK?' she asked.

He looked as bad as she felt and if she didn't know him better, she'd guess he'd been crying. Olek never cried.

'Why wouldn't it be?' His blue eyes were trained on hers as if she'd asked him a trick question. Perhaps Nell had already told him how badly she'd behaved earlier in the shop. Her cheeks flamed with shame.

'I can't speak for you,' she swallowed, attempting to blink away the image of her dad's final breaths. 'But it's been a tough day. Is Nell in?'

He shook his head. 'Still at work. It was your shopping event, wasn't it? I guess she's clearing up after that.'

'Oh, bless her.' Merry felt a bolt of love for her best friend.

Even though Nell had been so fed up with Merry that she'd resigned from the business on the spot, there she was, still working at this time of night. 'It's just that she's not answering her phone and I need to talk to her.'

'She hasn't got her phone with her.' He pulled Nell's mobile out of his pocket. 'She dropped it on Yvonna's drive when she dropped Max home. I've been over to fetch it. She won't have heard any of your messages.'

'I haven't left messages,' said Merry. 'There's something I need to say to her, face to face.'

She let out a ragged breath. She was getting to the stage in the evening where if she didn't sit down soon, she was going to collapse.

'Are you feeling all right?' Olek asked. 'I guess that's a silly question. Do you want to come in, sit down?'

She shook her head. 'I'd better not, Cole is expecting me home. I . . . My dad has passed away, it happened this evening. I wanted to let Nell know.'

'I'm so sorry.' He gently put his arms around her, kissing the top of her head. 'Dear Merry, you are having quite a difficult time of it.'

'I am. I feel like I can't catch a break, so much is happening. Too much for me to process.' She rested her head on his shoulder, content to take advantage of his strength for a moment. She'd always liked Olek, he was like the brother she'd never had, and he was such a good match for Nell.

'It must be overwhelming,' he murmured.

'First me being admitted into hospital, then Dad getting ill. And now, suddenly, he's gone for good. But, hey, you're not having an easy time of it either. Nell told me about your test results. I'm so sorry to hear that. I hope it works out for you. You'll make such brilliant parents together and there are other ways to—'

'She's talked to you?' Olek stiffened and held her away from him. 'What did she say?'

Merry bit her lip, wondering if she'd spoken out of turn. After all, Nell had said she didn't want to talk about it. 'Not much, only that you couldn't conceive and that you were working it out between you.'

Olek stared at her so intensely that she felt herself shrinking back from him. 'So she actually admitted to you that it is *me* who's infertile?' He shook his head, bewildered. 'I don't believe this. Am I the only one who didn't know the truth?'

Olek was the one with the issue? She tried not to hide her surprise. Nell had been so adamant that it would be her that it hadn't occurred to Merry that it wasn't. 'No, no! That's not what I mean. When I said "you", I was referring to both you and Nell.'

'I see.' Olek looked dubious.

'But I am sorry this has happened now,' Merry rushed on, eager to steer the conversation to safer waters. 'Particularly as neither of you have had problems in the past.'

His eyes narrowed. 'What do you mean by that?'

'Nothing!' She recoiled from the anger in his tone. 'Only that with you having Max, and Nell having had a previous pregnancy, I assumed—'

'Nell?' Olek stared at her open-mouthed. 'What are you talking about?'

Merry was confused, thinking that it was obvious. 'The fact that she managed to get pregnant before, by accident, should imply that she wouldn't have any issue conceiving – unless there's a new issue, of course. I mean, that was a long time ago.'

'She was pregnant before?' Olek's eyes widened with shock.

Merry could have bitten her own tongue out for being so indiscreet. 'Oh my God. You didn't know. I assumed… it was never a secret, she was open about it at the time.'

'Not to me she wasn't.' A muscle in his jaw flexed.

'I'm sure she didn't mean to keep it from you.' She wracked her brains, trying to remember if Nell had ever mentioned not wanting to tell him, but nothing came to mind. She'd never have broken Nell's confidence if she'd known. 'It was a long time ago, before she knew you.'

'How reassuring.' He gave a harsh laugh. 'You know, until tonight I thought my wife and I didn't have *any* secrets from each other. Now I'm not sure if I know her at all.'

'It must be a misunderstanding,' Merry said hurriedly. 'She loves you, she'd never deliberately lie, or do anything to mislead you.'

'Oh really?' Olek said bitterly. 'I'm afraid you're wrong, because I've just heard her suggest to another man that she'd have sex with him to get pregnant and that no one would ever know.'

'What?' She inhaled sharply. 'Which other man? Nell would never do that. Never.'

'She just has. To the guy in your Airbnb. She was upstairs with him when I called in to give her the phone back. Once I'd heard her say that, I had to get out of there in case I did anything I'd regret.'

'Woody?' Merry breathed a sigh of relief. 'Those two are as thick as thieves, but I don't think she's his type. He's got a husband of his own.'

'That's not the point, Merry. The point is that she told him that I'm . . . that I can't . . .' He stared down at his feet and shook his head. 'Never mind. I'm sorry, this isn't your problem. And you have bigger things on your mind. You have my sincere condolences for the loss of your father, may he rest in peace.'

'Thank you. I'd better get home.' She turned to go. 'I'm sorry if I've spoken out of turn. You'll tell Nell for me, won't you, about my dad?'

Olek seemed to deliberate over his next words. 'If I see her before you, then yes, of course. Goodbye, Merry. Take good care of that baby of yours.'

'I will.' There was something so melancholy in his tone that she lingered on the path, unsure as to whether to probe further, but he smiled sadly and closed the door.

Merry wished now that she hadn't come and had gone straight home with Cole. She had a feeling that she might have just made things worse for the couple, and not better.

So much damage could be done simply by not telling the one you love how you felt, she mused. And she was just as guilty of that as Nell. She thought about all the things she'd been keeping locked up inside her over the past few weeks: her lack of confidence about becoming a mother, her anxiety about losing her sense of self once the baby arrived. Cole needed to know or else how could he support her? Now, with a funeral to organise and a baby only weeks away from arriving, it was time to loosen her grip on all the reins and let someone else in.

She took out her own phone and sent Cole a quick message before setting off.

When I get home, can we talk?

Gladly. Candlelit bath for two?

Yes please, but don't you mean three?

Of course, yes!! All three of us! X x (The big kiss is for you and the little one for the baby)

I'm on my way, I love you xxx

Chapter 23

Merry

In the bathroom at Holly Cottage, Merry slipped her robe off her shoulders and Cole hung it on the heated towel rail.

'So it will be nice and warm for you after your bath.' He tested the temperature of the water with his hand and turned on the hot tap.

'You think of everything.' She stepped as close to him as she could before her tummy got in the way.

He'd already helped her out of her dress and socks and into the robe. Normally, she'd insist on managing by herself, but tonight she didn't have the energy.

'I'm thinking of you, darling.' His gaze was solemn. 'Despite what you might think, and despite the fact I'm sometimes terrible at showing it, I always think of you. And I'm sorry for making you think that I'm only concerned about the baby.'

'Oh, Cole.' She rested her head on his chest. 'I'm so embarrassed about losing my temper in the shop. I'm sorry for what I said about the baby.' She stroked her bump gently. 'And I apologise to you too, little one, for calling you the bloody baby. I didn't mean it. I love you.'

'No need to apologise for anything. It's easy for me to give orders and remind you not to do too much. But if it was the other way around, I'd find it impossible to put my feet up. You know what a terrible patient I am.'

Cole had been properly ill only once since she'd known him, and he'd morphed into a cross between an overtired child and a starving bear. He'd injured his knee skiing and for an active man, that had been akin to a stint in solitary confinement.

'It'll be even harder to take it easier now that Dad . . .' A lump formed in her throat. She was going to miss having a parent in her life, especially now that she was about to be one herself. She'd gone from being the younger generation to about to become the oldest and it was quite a tough lesson in mortality. 'I'm so sad about my dad.'

'I know, darling, I know.' Cole stroked her hair and caressed the back of her neck. 'But you were there for him in his last moments and your presence is the best gift you can ever give someone you love.'

She nodded, swallowing her tears. 'And Emily was there too, even if she was only on a screen. I'm sure he'll have been able to hear her voice.'

'He was a lucky man to have two such wonderful daughters.'

They stayed like that for a few more moments, Merry relishing the comfort and steadiness of his body against hers, until her back started to ache from holding herself still.

The steam from the bath was mixing with the aroma from a Merry and Bright candle and the entire bathroom smelled amazing.

'Rose and Peony, I notice?' Merry inclined her head, impressed. 'Nice choice. I'd have thought you'd have gone for Mistletoe Kiss.'

He slid his arms around her waist, resting his hands on her bottom. 'I do have a soft spot for that one, seeing as I was your muse.'

She smiled, remembering how she'd tried to recreate the scent of his aftershave just after they'd met. She'd been dying to ask what he was wearing so she could google it and break down the essential oils, but to have done so, she'd have had to admit to liking how he smelled. In those early days, she wasn't even ready to admit to herself how much she thought about him, let alone alert him. Nell had seen the sparks between them straight away and had teased her constantly about how often Merry brought his name into their conversation. Their first kiss had been under the mistletoe outside Merry and Bright, and so Mistletoe Kiss had been the obvious name for the candle which smelled as delicious as her husband.

'However.' He bent his head and whispered in her ear, his warm breath sending shivers of pleasure down her spine. 'This is the candle you were burning in Holly Cottage the first time we met.'

'I'm amazed you remember that,' she murmured, tilting her head to one side as he traced a line of kisses from her ear to her collarbone.

'How could I forget, you made a big impression on me. Whenever I smell this candle, I think of that day and how pretty you were.'

'Were?' she repeated.

'*Are*, darling.'

Merry laughed. 'Good recovery, Mr Robinson.'

'I'm learning,' he said with a grin. 'Right, are you ready for a relaxing bath?'

'Absolutely.' Not only had he lit candles, but gentle classical music was playing from a speaker, the bathwater had been sprinkled with pink rose petals and a bottle of fizz and two glasses poked out from a bucket of ice. 'You're spoiling me.'

He touched a finger to her lips tenderly. 'Impossible. You deserve it.'

Merry didn't think she did, not after the way she'd behaved recently, but she said nothing, not wanting to ruin the mood. She'd tell him later about Nell's resignation and how she may well have just made things worse between Nell and Olek. For now, she needed this moment of romance with her husband. They needed to clear the air between them and reconnect, remind each other what made their relationship so special. Because it was, she thought, blinking away the tears which threatened to spill any moment.

'Allow me, my lady.' Cole held her hand to steady her as she climbed into the bath.

She sighed with pleasure as she sank lower into the warmth until only the baby bump was above the water. Her body began to unwind, and her legs, which had ached all day, suddenly felt weightless.

'Bliss,' she breathed, closing her eyes.

She listened to the sound of a cork being gently eased from a bottle and the fizz of liquid being poured into a champagne flute.

'A glass of *Nosecco* for Madam?'

She opened her eyes and accepted the alcohol-free glass of bubbles she'd taken to drinking.

The first cold sip slid down her throat, a delicious contrast to the hot water surrounding her. While he poured one for himself, it struck her that he'd stopped drinking alcohol recently. She knew why; if they needed to go to hospital, he would want to be able to get them there without worrying whether he was over the limit or not. The fact that he'd simply made this decision without even mentioning it was so 'him', and made her love him even more.

'Sit forward a bit.' Cole gingerly lowered himself in to sit behind her. 'Now lean back against me. Remember when you said this bath was too big and we'd never fill it,' he said, squeezing his legs outside hers.

She giggled and laid her head back on his chest. 'I do. I was wrong, you were right.'

'Pardon?' He pretended to be shocked. 'Did you just admit you were wrong about something? Are you feeling OK?'

She let out a deep breath. 'Not really. Everything is . . . well, life is a lot at the moment.'

He rested his glass on the end of the bath and encircled her with his arms, his hands resting lightly on her tummy. 'I get it. I do, and . . . Listen, I'm going to make a suggestion and, knowing you as I do, I expect you to say no to it, but hear me out.'

She smiled at his tentative tone. 'I'm all ears.'

'Let me organise the funeral.' He scooped warm water onto the baby bump and rose petals clung to her skin. 'I know, I know, you want to be in control of everything but—'

'OK,' she replied quietly. She'd been mentally constructing a to-do list ever since leaving Springwood House earlier and had had to stop because it had begun to overwhelm her. Would she like to manage it herself? Yes. Did she already have an alarming number of things that she wanted to accomplish prior to Christmas? Also yes. And it would go against every natural inclination she had to let anybody help her, but with her induction date only a couple of weeks away and Christmas even closer, even she had to accept that she was never going to manage everything by herself.

'At least let me deal with the funeral directors and do the running around, like registering the death, booking the wake and so on.'

'OK,' she said again.

'I don't mind checking in with you for sign-off, but it'll be easier for me to . . .' He stopped, realising what she'd just said. 'Did you just agree?'

'I did. There's no one in the world I'd trust more than you. I'd love your help.'

He hugged her gently. 'Thank you. You don't know how happy it makes me to hear that.'

'I . . .' She took her time, feeling her emotions thicken her throat. 'I need help with a lot of things.'

'Name them,' he encouraged her. 'Anything I can do to make your life easier, I'll willingly do.'

She looked at his hands and linked her fingers between his. What had she done to deserve this man? There were so many things she wanted to say, about how letting others in made her vulnerable, how losing control of her life, her body, her freedom was freaking her out. How already she'd alienated Nell and ruined not only their working relationship but their friendship too. But there was one worry above all others that she knew she had to share with him: her fear that she wouldn't be a good mother.

She shook her head, feeling embarrassed and glad that he was behind her and couldn't see her face. 'Cole? I'm scared.'

'Oh, darling, that makes me sad to hear.' He pressed his cheek against hers. 'Why? Tell me.'

She swallowed. 'I can't. I want to, but I just can't.'

He didn't push her any further, just held her close. 'When you're ready, I'll be there to listen. I'll always be there, and whatever you're scared of, we'll face together. We're a team, OK, you and me?'

'And baby makes three.'

'Hey, how about we talk about names?' he said.

‘I’d like that.’ She smiled happily. They’d broached the subject several times. Cole had even suggested creating a spreadsheet at one stage, but she’d managed to persuade him against it. Choosing a name for their child should be a creative task, not one with columns and rows and tick boxes.

‘OK.’ He picked up his glass and took a sip. ‘I thought Robin. Works for a boy or a girl.’

‘What!’ She propelled herself up to sitting, sending a tidal wave of water over the edge of the bath. ‘Robin Robinson? Are you kidding me?’

From behind her came a low rumbling laugh. ‘I was kidding, yes, and it was totally worth it to see that reaction.’

‘You tease!’ Merry peered over the edge of the bath and snorted with laughter. ‘You might be changing your mind when you have to put on wet pyjamas.’

Cole pushed himself forward, sending an even bigger tsunami onto the bathroom floor.

‘Cole!’ she squealed. ‘What are you doing?’

‘Making you laugh,’ he said, burying his face into her neck and covering her with kisses, ‘because it’s the best sound in the world and I love it. And I love you. Far more than dry pyjamas.’

‘I love you too,’ Merry said. ‘Far more than anything.’

She leaned back into his embrace and felt the steady beat of his heart. She’d be fine, she told herself, she might not have much confidence in herself, but he had enough for both of them.

Chapter 24

Nell

'Thank you.' Nell swung first one leg and then the other out of the taxi, took a deep breath and heaved herself out onto the street.

She was going to die, she was sure of it. And if by some fluke she survived, she was never drinking again. Never. Her hangover wasn't just in her head, it was in her stomach, her scalp, her toes – in fact, every cell in her body was hovering at the point of permanent failure.

'A cold can of Coke will do the trick.' The driver grinned as she handed him her fare, plus a generous tip for agreeing not to speak or play loud music. 'Works every time. Oh, and peanut butter on toast.'

Nell thought about how a layer of peanut butter would feel stuck to the roof of her mouth and tried not to gag. She shut the taxi door as softly as she could and weaved her way up the path to her front door. Her head felt as if someone inside it was trying to hammer tent pegs into concrete; the slightest noise was torture.

Olek's van wasn't parked in the drive. This shouldn't be a massive surprise given that it was almost 10 a.m. and he always left for work without fail at 8 a.m. sharp. But under the circumstances, she'd expected him to be waiting for her when she got home, either concerned about her or angry with her. Her stomach flip-flopped with nerves.

She'd never stayed out all night, at least not without letting him know where she was; there had never been a night when her preferred place to be wasn't in her own bed with her husband. If he'd done this to her, she'd have been worried to death.

Her hands fumbled with the keys as she let herself in through the front door, aware of the urgent upward pressure on her oesophagus. She dashed into the cloakroom, flung up the lid of the toilet and just made it in time before throwing up. She stayed still for a couple of minutes, waiting for the trembling to subside and thinking that she'd never liked herself less. Finally, she stood to wash her hands and face in cold water, caught sight of her own reflection in the mirror above the basin and shuddered in horror: murky complexion, bloodshot eyes and her hair, usually her crowning glory of auburn waves, hung in matted, dull clumps.

She couldn't remember much about how last night ended. She remembered not being able to find her phone and using that as an excuse not to call Olek. That was unforgivable and cowardly; she knew his number. She could have called if she'd wanted to.

Waking up this morning in the bedroom above the shop, snuggling up to Woody, had taken some unpacking. But she took comfort in the fact that neither of them had removed any clothes. What she did remember with absolute clarity was the sound of the shop door slamming and the revving of Olek's engine as he accelerated away from her. And the sick feeling in the pit of her stomach that her Jenga tower of lies was about to come crashing down.

If her husband had heard what she thought he had, she was going to have a lot of difficult questions to answer today. But maybe, maybe, he hadn't heard a word of their discussion. There was a chance that he'd come in as far as the bottom of the stairs, heard her having a good time and decided to leave her to it.

Wishful thinking, she thought as she dragged herself through to the kitchen. He'd never have slammed the door if that had been the case. No, there had been anger in that slam.

Nell put the kettle on, even though the thought of tea made her feel sick. She sank down at the kitchen table and dropped her head in her hands.

What a bloody mess.

A loud, shrill sound jolted her head from the table. She rubbed her eyes awake and wiped the drool from her chin; she must have fallen asleep. Damn. She had loads to do this morning: track down her phone, speak to Olek, check on Merry . . . She forced herself to focus on the noise. It was the phone in the hall. No one ever rang the landline except dodgy salespeople and her mother. She wasn't in the mood for either and decided to let the answerphone deal with it. But as soon as the caller began to leave a message, she jumped to her feet and ran to the hall.

'Hey, Dad and Nell. This is Max. Has something happened to your phones? I can't get through to either of you. Dad, can you call me please, it's about football practice tonight. I've texted you, but it doesn't look like you've read it. I'm really sorry, but I need a lift to Derby. Hope that's OK. You're the best. I'll try you—'

'Max!' Nell grabbed the phone quickly before he hung up and sat on the bottom step of the staircase, dizzy with the sudden movement. 'Sorry, I was . . .' She stopped short of telling him she'd been asleep, slumped at the table. 'Outside.'

'No worries. Is Dad there?'

'He's at work, love.' She supposed. 'But I'm sure he won't mind giving you a lift later. He's probably on an emergency job and can't answer the phone.'

'Hmm.' Max sounded sceptical. 'I left him a message late last night too, after you dropped me off, and he hasn't responded to that either.'

'Oh dear.' Nell felt a dart of fear. It was unheard of for Olek not to return his calls, especially one from Max. Was he out at work? Could he have had an accident or . . . She shuddered at the thought and then chastised herself for being dramatic, it was her hangover making her paranoid. Olek would have a perfectly sensible explanation.

'Nell?' Max's worried voice broke into her thoughts. 'Is everything OK?'

She straightened up and forced some lightness into her voice. Max wasn't stupid, he'd quickly pick up on an atmosphere. 'Everything's fine. Just busy.'

'OK, well . . .' he hesitated, obviously not totally convinced.

'Look, if all else fails, I can give you a lift tonight, how about that? I know it's not as good as Dad, but at least you can stop worrying about how you'll get there.'

He let out a sigh of relief. 'Phew. It's just Viktor and Mum have decided to go to the cinema now and they were going to drop me off.'

Nell managed not to tut with disapproval. 'Never mind, you can rely on us.'

'Yeah, what would I do without you and Dad in my life, eh?' he said with a smile in his voice.

She felt her chest contract with love; he'd always been a sweet boy and he was turning into a lovely young man. Olek had had a part in that, regardless of whether they were related by blood or not. 'That's something you'll never need to worry about, love.'

'Thanks, see you later, then. Oh, how's Merry's dad, have you heard?'

Her face flushed with embarrassment; what a terrible person she was for not finding out. Even Max had enquired before she had. 'I'm waiting to hear; I'll keep you posted.'

She ended the call and replaced the phone in its cradle. Next to it was a folded piece of paper. She picked it up and found her mobile hiding underneath. Thank goodness, mystery solved. She unfolded the page and registered Olek's handwriting. As her brain absorbed the words, her hands started to tremble.

'No! I don't believe it.' She pressed a hand to her mouth and sank to the floor. 'He's left. Olek has left me.'

Chapter 25

Nell

Nell,

I'm just letting you know that I'm going to stay somewhere else for a while. I need some space to get my thoughts in order and I can't be around you while I do that. My head is in a mess, and I don't know what to think. I found out tonight that you've been lying to me. And also learned that you don't think that Max is my son. I don't think it is possible for me to be any more hurt and confused right now.

I'm leaving your phone by this note. You dropped it on Yvonna's driveway, so I went to collect it once I'd finished on that emergency job where the house had been broken into. All five of them in the family, the parents and three kids, stood in the door to wave me off. I had been feeling so sorry for them, all their valuables stolen, all their Christmas presents taken from beneath the tree. But now I think they are the lucky ones. They have each other to lean on, the rock-solid support of the family unit. Possessions are nothing compared to the riches of family. Families come in all sorts of forms, Nell. You, me and Max are a family. I thought that was an unshakeable fact.

After I left Yvonna's, I drove to Merry and Bright to deliver your phone to you, I knew you'd be lost without it and worried about where it was. I wish I hadn't. My life would be so much less complicated and depressing than it is now.

The main lights in the shop were off, but I could see the flat was still bright upstairs. When I reached the bottom of the stairs, I heard you talking to the Airbnb guy. I still can't work out whether I am glad I heard what you said or not. Ignorance is bliss, right?

Wrong. It turns out that I've been kept ignorant of the facts for the last few weeks, and it's been anything but bliss. I have been so cut up about it. You let me think that you were the one with fertility problems. You even suggested as a joke that I should trade you in for a better model, one with fully working parts. All along it has been me with the problem and now I wonder, is that what you are considering doing: trading me in for someone else?

Knowing how much you want to be a mother to our child, knowing that Merry has managed to do the one thing that you can't (or so I thought) has torn me apart with grief for the kids we might never have. Ever since we got those results – results which I now know you lied about – I've thought of nothing but you, of what I can do to make things better. It confused me why you didn't want to go back to see Dr Bajek, we must have been offered a follow-up appointment? There are many routes to becoming parents and I was willing to explore all of those. But you made that decision on behalf of us both, that we weren't going to take this journey any further.

I assumed you and I were rock-solid like that family, but a family whose foundations are not built on trust eventually crumbles and that is where we are now.

Because Merry told me about your termination. You have been pregnant before and never once thought to tell your husband about it.

And because I heard you, Nell, with the Airbnb guy. I heard you joke about having sex with another man to get pregnant and that no one would ever know. Is that really how unimportant I am in this marriage? To you?

But none of this compares to what I heard you tell him about Max, about my boy, I've never even met the bright star in my sky. I can't believe you'd stoop so low as to suggest to someone I've never even met that Max isn't my son.

So now do you see why I have to go? I can't be around you, Nell. Not at the moment. I'm too angry, disappointed and confused.

Please do not try to call me, I have no wish to talk to you. If you have any remaining respect for me, you'll let me have this time alone to work through these feelings.

Yours,

Olek

Chapter 26

Merry

Cole helped Merry onto the couch in the antenatal room while they waited for the midwife to join them.

'Comfy?' he asked, after lifting her feet up onto the bed.

'Comfort is all relative at the moment,' Merry puffed, tugging down the waistband of her jogging bottoms. 'As is my fashion sense.'

'You look gorgeous.' He pulled up a stool and kissed her tummy. 'You have never looked more beautiful to me, and I mean that, darling.'

'In that case, I . . .' She stopped herself from saying that she must have looked horrendous on her wedding day if this was her most beautiful moment. *Let people compliment you*, she recalled Astrid saying once, *learn to accept praise with grace*. 'Thank you, darling, that's very sweet.'

Cole, unused to her replying without a witty comeback, looked surprised. 'You're welcome. Weirdly, it's quite an ego boost for a man, you know, to see his wife so big and . . .' He made a ball shape with his hands.

She snorted with laughter. 'You should have stopped at "beautiful."'

'Whoops.' He smiled sheepishly. 'Thanks for suggesting I come with you today. It's nice to be involved and I can't wait to hear the baby's heartbeat.'

'I'm glad you're here.' She stroked his hair. She rarely asked him to attended regular check-up appointments with her. She didn't need accompanying and knew he was busy so didn't want to disrupt his day. Last night during their heart-to-heart, he'd admitted that sometimes he felt as if his presence wasn't welcome and that she wanted her privacy. She'd felt awful about that and reassured him that wasn't the case and there was no one she wanted with her more. She'd then gone on to tell him all about her row with Nell. Cole had asked her what she was going to do about the shop if Nell was serious about not coming back. She'd admitted that her maternity plans had always been fluid and that without her friend to take the reins, running the business was going to be a nightmare. With that, she had started to cry again. She still needed to tell him how worried she was about becoming a mum, but she'd made progress last night and it felt good; today their bond was tighter than it had been for weeks.

'Later on I'll go and fetch the kids and do something with them,' he said, scratching his jaw thoughtfully. 'I suggested a visit to Santa, but they both looked at me as if I was mad. Even Freya.'

The schools were closed due to teacher strikes. Their mum was at home with them this morning but had asked Cole to help while she went to a meeting.

Merry shook her head in dismay. 'That's sad, she begged me to take her last year. She's growing up fast.'

'They all do,' said Cole, pressing his lips to her bump. 'So we have to treasure each day.'

'I need to go into the shop straight after this appointment, but we could take them to Meadow View later,' Merry suggested slyly. 'They might like to have a look at the progress on their rooms.'

'We?' he said with a grin. 'You mean *you* want to look at progress.'

She gave him an innocent shrug. 'Maybe.'

'Let's see if you get a good report from the midwife first.'

'I'm fine! And if you're driving, what's the worst that can happen?' Admittedly, she had been working more than was ideal and had a row while up a ladder yesterday, and her blood pressure wasn't perfect, but as her father had passed away last night, that was to be expected. Which reminded her: Olek must have told Nell the sad news by now. 'Odd that Nell hasn't been in touch to say she's sorry to hear about Dad.' She checked her phone for the umpteenth time. She couldn't help but feel hurt about the radio silence.

'There'll be a valid reason,' said Cole. 'Are you sure Olek will have told her?'

'He said he'd tell her if he saw her first and he will have done by now.' Merry's stomach flipped with an awful thought. 'Maybe she's resigned from being my bestie as well as my business partner. It was a bad row yesterday. I've never seen her so angry.'

Presumably Nell hadn't gone in to work this morning. She wondered if Nell had asked Woody to work in the shop on his own, or whether she was so annoyed she hadn't bothered to do anything. Merry had no way of contacting Woody because Nell had handled his Airbnb booking. It felt very odd to be so removed from the business that she wasn't even sure whether they were open or not.

She couldn't imagine working at Merry and Bright without Nell anymore. And she certainly didn't want to imagine life without Nell outside of work; she needed her more than ever. Nell made everything fun, she took the stress out of situations and even though she hadn't been there when Max was a baby, she had always been confident in her role in his life. Merry needed to borrow a bit of that confidence in the coming weeks. She loved Emily of course, but no one could replace Nell. She'd been her closest friend for more than half of her life.

'She'd never do that,' Cole said. 'You two are as tight as family; it'll take more than one argument to break up the dream team. Perhaps she's just got a hangover.'

'Possibly.' She wasn't so sure; he hadn't seen the look of contempt on Nell's face last night.

'Call her,' said Cole gently. 'Just call her.'

Merry pressed her lips together and said nothing. She couldn't bring herself to call Nell. She knew she was being stubborn, but if the situation was reversed and something happened to one of Nell's family, Merry would put her own sensitivities on hold to be there for her closest friend. Nell should be the one to call and check up on her.

'Good morning.' Pip entered the room, shut the door and washed her hands. 'How are we?'

'Not bad,' said Cole, stretching his arms above his head. 'It's always busy in December, of course, everyone wanting to move in to their new home for the New Year.'

'Your own wife included.' Merry gave him a stern look.

'Whoops,' he muttered, 'touchy subject.'

One of Pip's eyebrows hitched up a fraction and she locked her gaze onto Cole. The last time she'd done that was when Cole had declared that the fathers should be given gas and air to help them cope with the stress of seeing their partners in pain.

'I meant,' said Pip, pointedly, 'how are Merry and baby? How Dad's doing is beyond my remit.'

'Of course.' He scratched his head and moved quickly out of the midwife's way so she could pop the baby heart rate monitor onto Merry's stomach.

'I'm going to say this quickly and I don't want to talk about it. My dad passed away yesterday,' Merry blurted out.

Pip paused from wrapping the cuff of the blood pressure monitor around her arm. 'Message received. And you've got people around to support you, as well as rushed-off-their-feet builders?'

'I have.' Merry swallowed. 'My sister is coming over to help.'

'Good.'

For the next couple of minutes, Merry relaxed and let Pip do her work.

'Baby's heart rate is fine,' she said, packing away the heart rate monitor. 'Your blood pressure is high but not worryingly so. Baby growth has slowed up, I'm going to watch that. You can sit up now.'

'Thanks.' Merry was supremely grateful for Pip's no-nonsense manner; anything too cuddly and she'd have dissolved in tears.

Cole and Pip both hooked an arm under hers and helped her to sit up and she swung her legs over the side of the bed.

'I can't stress this enough,' Pip said, helping her down. 'Delegate, delegate, delegate. Understood?'

Merry nodded. Although whether she still had someone to delegate to at Merry and Bright was another matter altogether. Leaving her business in the care of an Airbnb guest seemed a bit flaky, even for her.

As Cole went to bring the car up to the porch of the clinic, Merry's phone buzzed. She grabbed it and her heart bounced when she saw Nell's name flash up. She'd sent a voice note. Thank goodness. Her relief, however, was short-lived.

Olek has left me and it's down to you. How could you have told him about my termination? It's not enough that you're having a baby when I can't and that you're constantly moaning about it, now you've come between Olek and me too. You and I are done, Merry. So just to confirm, I'm resigning from Merry and Bright and the way I feel at the moment, I'd rather not hear from you for a while.

Bile rose in her throat as Nell's words sank in. No condolences, no checking up to see how she was or whether she could do anything to help. What sort of friend did that? Merry was numb with shock. She had been so looking forward to this Christmas, but, suddenly, the festive season had never looked so bleak.

Chapter 27

Merry

It was late morning by the time Cole drove into Wetherley to drop off Merry. The town was buzzy and busy, with plenty of shoppers milling round, and the traffic was heavy in the pre-lunchtime rush. Merry was glad to be back, despite the problems which lay ahead. Merry and Bright was her happy place, where she felt in control and confident, and even though she'd only be here for a few hours, it was a chance to be that person again.

'I love Christmas decorations,' said Freya with a sigh from the back seat. 'Everywhere looks like it's ready for a party.'

'So does that mean you'd like to visit Santa after all?' Cole's voice was tinged with hope.

'No,' chorused both his children.

'Never mind, darling.' Merry rubbed a hand over her bump. 'We can take this one when it's old enough.'

Cole grinned. 'I'd like that.'

'Me too!' Freya piped up.

They reached Wetherley marketplace and Cole pulled into a parking space. The Christmas tree dominated, of course, but the Christmas decorations around the square and in every shop window lent colour and sparkle that even the grey wintry sky couldn't dim. Merry's stomach plummeted when she noticed the one store which remained in darkness. At Merry and Bright, the windows were devoid of their usual fairy lights, the 'closed' sign was displayed in the door and a sheaf of leaflets hung from the letter flap.

She slid her feet into her Birkenstocks and unclipped the seat belt with a sense of foreboding. 'Looks like Nell meant what she said,' she remarked to Cole.

The fury in Nell's voice note earlier was unmistakable, but even so, a little part of Merry had hoped to see her friend behind the counter, a big smile on her face, ready for anyone who walked in through the door.

'Call me if you need anything.' Cole leaned across the gearstick and kissed her, tucking a lock of hair behind her ear. 'Be careful. I love you.'

'Hurry up, Dad, I'm starving,' said Harley.

Merry and Harley had a good relationship, but two years in, he would still rather not witness affection between her and his dad.

She waved them off and let herself in.

The shop had always filled her with joy. Tinkering around in the studio with new aromas, chatting to customers about her products, even spending time alone pouring molten wax into waiting candle jars had provided her with happy moments of calm. But today as she walked into the space, she felt nothing but dread and sadness. The sense of pride she used to feel had been replaced with shame; over the past few weeks, and culminating in yesterday, she'd let her customers and Nell and, worst of all, herself down.

'Cooee?' Woody called as he tripped down the stairs. 'Thank goodness you're here.' Merry couldn't help smiling at him. He was wearing an Elf onesie with matching green slippers. 'There have been customers knocking on the door all morning! I've only been given a key for back-door entry, and I didn't know what to do.' He fanned his face. 'In the end, I stayed upstairs and watched *Christmas at the Castle* on the Hallmark channel.'

'I'm sorry you've been put in this position,' she said, heading to the studio, putting a herbal teabag in a mug and picking up the kettle.

'I called Nell, but no reply, and I didn't have your number,' he said, following her. He took the kettle out of her hand and waved her to a seat. 'I'll do that, I need some black coffee anyway.'

She caught a whiff of booze on his breath as she sat down. His complexion was a bit yellow too. 'Hangover?'

'Oh yes,' he confirmed, lifting her feet up one at a time and resting them on a second chair. 'On a scale of one to ten, with ten being in need of a six-week detox, I'm guessing Nell's at the stage of googling non-alcoholic beverages to enjoy this Christmas.'

'Thanks,' she sighed gratefully and leaned back to get comfortable. 'But I meant you.'

'Is it that obvious?' He pulled a dramatic face and moaned. 'Nell was far worse than me; she didn't even make it home last night, she passed out in the bedroom.'

'Crikey.' Merry raised her eyebrows, recalling the conversation Olek had overheard about Nell having sex with him. He'd been closer to the truth than she'd realised. 'So she stayed the night, in your bed?'

Woody gave her such an indignant look that she almost laughed. 'Nothing improper happened, we just talked. And slept.'

'And drank, by the sound of it.' She believed him. Nell was in love with Olek, a man who oozed testosterone from every pore. Drunk or not, she couldn't see her friend ever trying to seduce a gay man in a fleecy onesie.

He nodded gravely. 'Alcohol has a lot to answer for, but in this case, I think it helped her lose her inhibitions enough to share what's on her mind. And it transpired that she and I share some issues; we had a lot to talk about.'

'I haven't been there for her recently when she needed me, and now I've really upset her.' Merry felt dreadful. Nell hadn't felt able to confide in her best friend and yet had opened up to a relative stranger. Nell's message this morning was very final, but Merry wasn't going to let their friendship go without a fight, it was too important to her.

'It's not *just* you.' Woody set a mug of tea in front of her. 'But I think it will be a while before she's ready to come back to work with you.'

The prospect of running the business on her own with a new baby sent a surge of anxiety through her. 'I was hoping we'd get past this blip in our friendship. Especially as I'll take some time away from work when the baby comes. Does she really mean what she said, do you think?'

'For Nell, and for me, the only thing we can focus on is wanting a family. It's a need so all-consuming that it feels like a physical pain. When I see a baby, I'm drawn to it, I want to ask the parent how the baby is doing, are they sleeping at night, have they smiled yet. And while I'm asking these questions, and observing the love on the parent's face for their child, it's like a series of stabs to my heart. It hurts, but it's a hurt I can't resist exposing myself to.'

Merry's mind went back to the first time she met Woody and how strong his reaction had been to her baby bump. He was such a bright and effervescent character, she could never have foreseen the emotions bubbling away inside him.

'I'm so sorry you're going through this.' She reached for his hand and squeezed it.

'Me too.' He smiled grimly. 'Especially as it's caused a rift between myself and my husband. Hence me booking this place last minute to give myself some headspace. Although . . .' He let out a soft laugh. 'I've inadvertently landed waist deep in a quagmire of other people's baby woes.'

'Oh dear,' Merry winced. 'And you've ended up being our only member of staff. I feel as if you're due a refund.'

'The distraction has been good for me; it's struck me that everyone has something going on in their lives; Spencer and I don't have the monopoly on problems.'

'Do you want to talk?' she offered. 'A problem shared is a problem halved.'

He chuckled. 'That's how Nell and I got so drunk last night, by telling each other what was going on. So I'll save it for now, but thank you.'

'Of course, the person we should really talk to is the person most affected by the same problem. Spencer in your case, Olek in Nell's.' And Cole in her own. She wished she was brave enough to explain to him that motherhood terrified her and that she'd convinced herself she was going to fail at it. 'Why is that always the most difficult conversation?'

'Because of love.' Woody gazed into his coffee cup. 'The one we love is also the one we have the most power to hurt.'

'That's true.' She'd already hurt Nell and she'd hurt Cole if she told him the truth. He was already on edge about her physically since her waters had broken, if he knew how fragile she was mentally, he'd be worried to death. 'And now you've had some time away from him, are you ready to have the difficult conversation?'

He exhaled. 'Spencer finishes for the holidays next week. He'd booked some time off so we could enjoy a long

Christmas break together. Instead we're apart and each locked in our own bubble of sadness.'

'Ring him,' Merry suggested. 'Invite him over for dinner, get the log fire roaring, dim the lights, have something delicious to drink. Perhaps the neutral territory will encourage both of you to talk.'

He eyed her thoughtfully. 'I just might do that. And you should do the same.'

'Cole and I never seem to have the time at the moment, and now that my dad—' She stopped mid-sentence, the lump in her throat proving too much of an obstacle.

'I meant you and Nell,' said Woody. 'Her pain is more acute than mine because . . . well.' He paused and gave her a sideways glance. 'You're pregnant and there's no getting away from that.'

Merry's eyes felt hot with the effort of not giving in to tears. Poor Nell. Not only were she and Olek having problems, but her best friend was only days from giving birth and behaving like a spoiled brat. And, to top it all, Merry had revealed to Olek about Nell's previous pregnancy. No wonder Nell had no wish to be around her anymore, it must seem to her that Merry had the perfect life, with everything Nell couldn't have, and yet still Merry was moaning about it. If only Merry had been honest and expressed how scared she was about bringing a child into the world, this rift between them might have been avoided. And Nell might have been able to confide in Merry.

The baby, her dad's funeral, the new house, her best friend, the business . . . everything swirled around in her head like a cyclone, and she couldn't think straight, couldn't even deal with one of those issues while the others all demanded attention.

'I don't know where to start.' She sipped her lemon and ginger tea and Woody patted her arm. For a moment, neither of them spoke until the silence was interrupted by a loud banging on the front door; they both gasped with shock.

'See what I mean?' Woody clutched his chest. 'That's what I've had to put up with all day.'

'I should open up,' she whispered, as if anyone outside had a chance of hearing them through the thick walls of the old Tudor building. 'But I'm not sure if I'm up to it today.'

'Then don't,' he said, 'you're the boss.'

Merry and Woody sat as still as statues sniggering to each other and barely breathing until whoever it was had gone.

'I can make a sign if you like, saying closed due to personal reasons.'

'That would be sensible, thank you.'

It only took him a few seconds to draw up a makeshift sign, which he embellished with illustrations of holly leaves and candles and pinned to the door. 'Sorted. Next problem?'

'Good question. I don't know which fire to put out first,' she said shakily. 'I need to make it up to Nell, and I need to sort out some staff to run the shop. I should get over to Dad's care home at some point and then there's baby stuff still to organise. I'm going to have to come in to work tomorrow, although I'm not even supposed to be working at all.'

Woody pulled a face. 'I'm exhausted just listening to that lot. Listen, my maths is terrible, I've had more than a few clumsy moments so far and I absolutely can't start work before 10 a.m., but give me a key to the front door and I'll work in the shop for a few days. It'll buy you some time to make a more permanent plan.'

Merry could have kissed him. 'By yourself? You wouldn't mind?'

He lifted a casual shoulder. 'I'm a social animal, I'd rather be in a shop chatting to people than upstairs on my own. And think of all the Christmas sales you're losing while the doors are shut.'

'Wow. That's very generous of you, thank you.' Tears popped into her eyes. She hardly knew him, and it was obvious he was going through a tricky time himself, yet here he was offering to help her out.

'You're welcome, on one condition: you take some time for yourself while you can.' He gestured towards her stomach. 'You'll be busy looking after baby soon enough.'

She nodded. He was right. She had been busy enough before her dad passed away; now she was in danger of being snowed under. Ordinarily, she wouldn't have entertained letting a relative stranger run her business, but these weren't ordinary times. She had no choice other than to delegate. She would cancel the candle-making workshops, he couldn't handle those, and stocks might run low on some of their candles, but at least if the shop remained open, the turnover wouldn't be as dire as it would otherwise be. She thought back to those few moments when she'd walked in, how she'd not wanted to be there, how the comfort she'd once got from Merry and Bright seemed to have disappeared. She wrapped both hands around her stomach and wondered what it would be like to put Woody in charge for a couple of days. A break from it would do her good. Just then, the baby shifted, sending an undulation across the surface of her belly and forcing a sharp intake of breath.

'I think that's the baby's way of reminding me what's important.' She held her hand out for Woody's and, with his permission, laid it on the bump.

'Oh my word.' He fell silent for a few moments as the baby carried on kicking and moving as if it was frolicking in the bath and his eyes glittered with tears. 'That's life in there, that's your future, treasure it. Hold on to every second. Thank you for sharing.'

'And thank you for your offer of help,' she replied. 'And I accept gratefully. Because it's not just the baby I should be treasuring, it's all the people in my life; the business can't hold a candle to them.'

'A *candle*. Oh she's good,' grinned Woody, 'she's good.'

Merry pulled a face, thinking that she hadn't been very good at all, but it was never too late to make a change. From today, she could do better, she *would* do better. She was going to do everything in her power to make this Christmas the best ever, in spite of the circumstances.

Chapter 28

Nell

'I'll show you where the other parents hang out,' Max told Nell once they'd parked in the Derby training ground car park. 'Some of them are really nice. A couple of the dads get a bit extra, overriding the coach, but they're not allowed into training, so you won't see them shouting their mouths off tonight.'

He'd become more animated the closer they'd got; seeing his enthusiasm for running about in the dark and cold, practising his favourite game on a school night, was almost enough to pull Nell from her funk.

'Lovely offer, Max, but I'll stay in the car, thanks.'

'Training is two hours long.' Max was worried about her. 'Won't you get bored by yourself?'

'I don't mind, honestly,' Nell insisted, tucking a blanket over her knees and pushing her seat back to stretch out. 'I've got my Kindle and a juicy thriller about a family who get snowed in at Christmas and someone ends up dead.'

'Cheery.' Max hesitated by the door. 'There's a place inside where you can get drinks and stuff, if you get cold, or if you scare yourself to death.'

'Will do.' Nell had no desire to bump into any of the other parents. Normally, she'd be the first in there, making friends and proudly trading stories about her stepson, but tonight she didn't want to talk at all and the idea of two hours of enforced solitude was a relief.

Max got out of the car and opened the rear door to get his kitbag. 'I'm not a kid, you know. If there's something going on, you'd say, wouldn't you?'

His perceptive comment unbalanced her; she'd done her best to hide her emotional state, but he'd picked up on something anyway.

'If I had anything to tell you, I would. Promise.' She was grateful for the cover of darkness to hide the guilt on her face. 'Dad sends his love and says to listen to what the coach says, because even though you might not agree with him, he's been on the pitch longer than you.'

Only a slight bend of the truth; Olek had said this to her after watching him play last week, commenting that Max hadn't liked receiving feedback.

Max grunted. 'I'll try.'

'Go on.' She gave him a double thumbs up. 'Show those Derby boys that famous Dowmunt footwork.'

'OK.' He laughed and waved as he walked across the floodlit car park and into the training ground.

The smile drained from her face as soon as he was out of sight. She didn't know if she was coming or going today. Her hangover had evaporated, thankfully, but her head was pounding, and her heart hadn't stopped racing all day.

Everything had gone horribly wrong. She'd fallen out with her best friend, lied to her husband, and now lied to her stepson too about the whereabouts of his father (who was unlikely to actually be his father), and her husband had disappeared to goodness knows where.

She picked up her phone and dialled Olek's number again, waiting for the voicemail to kick in.

'I'm at football training because Max needed a lift. You let him down today. Even if you're too busy, you could have sent him a message to let him know. Come on, Olek. You can do better than that.' She hadn't intended to let herself get angry, but now she'd started, it was difficult to stop.

'It's fine to be pissed off with me, I get it. I lied to you, and you expected honesty from me. I have my reasons for that and I'd very much like the chance to explain. You and Yvonna . . .' she paused. 'That's not really any of my business, but I can appreciate you'll want some answers from her. But taking it out on Max isn't OK, Olek. He's hurt and confused. Whatever the truth is, you've been there for him his entire life in a way that no other man has. Even if you ignore this message, like you've ignored all the others I've sent you, please don't ignore Max, your son.' She was about to end the call when another thought struck her. 'If you've had a car accident or something and you didn't mean to ignore me at all, then I'm sorry, and I love you.'

She hung up and then redialled.

'I love you anyway, not just if you've had an accident. Just thought I should make that clear. Bye.'

She waited, phone in hand, for a full five minutes for a response, but none came. Could he have had a serious accident? No, if he had, his name and phone number were on the side of his van, it would be a moment's work for the police to track down his next of kin. He'd simply gone somewhere to lick his wounds, as he'd told her in his letter. He'd be back soon; she'd just have to be patient.

For the next half an hour, she tried to lose herself in the novel on her Kindle, but her mind wouldn't let her relax into the story. Giving up, she scrolled through her phone to her WhatsApp chat with Merry. The last message was her voice note from earlier this morning, ending their friendship. She played it again and recoiled at the bitterness behind her own words. No wonder Merry hadn't dignified it with a response. Nell toyed with the idea of sending a follow-up message but decided against it. She didn't want a conversation with anyone right now; there'd be time tomorrow to speak to Merry. For now, she just wanted to wallow in her own thoughts.

She opened up the photos on her phone and found the ones from last December. There were some of her final few days on her market stall Nell's Nuts, some of Olek, her and Max putting up the Christmas tree at home, pictures of the girls on Merry's hen night, hundreds of Merry's wedding on Christmas Eve and a lovely selfie of her and Olek looking in love on New Year's Day. In every picture, Nell looked happy, her eyes bright, her face animated and smiling. The contrast to today couldn't have been greater.

And she thought she knew why; it was this time last year when the desire to have a baby had kicked in. Before then, she hadn't been in the least broody. Babies were something other people thought about. Olek had Max, and she had Olek, it had felt as if their family was complete. She remembered overhearing two women talking about their relief when they'd found out they were pregnant and being bemused by how fixated on conceiving they'd admitted to being. And then suddenly, almost overnight, she joined their club. She couldn't remember why; although she'd had a niggle of sadness that she was losing Merry to Emily. Until then, Nell had been sister, best friend and as good as next of kin to Merry; there'd been no one else. She was delighted that Merry had found her real family. But at some deep, unknowable level, perhaps that had triggered a need to create a family of her own.

Over the course of the last year, she had carried on with life as normal, but the urge to start a family with Olek had gradually become louder and louder. Until eventually it had consumed her.

She scrolled back even further through her photos to the summer before last: the holiday she and Olek had taken to Croatia. Her freckles had come out in the sun, and she'd gone make-up-free for the entire week. They'd swum and explored and eaten seafood in harbourside restaurants and slept late . . . it had been one of the best holidays ever.

They'd had fun, they'd even, she remembered, privately congratulated themselves on being one of the few couples without young children in tow, able to do their own thing, in their own time.

Nell's eyes lingered on a picture taken by a waiter of the two of them on the last night of the trip. She had been wrapped in Olek's arms, their cheeks pressed together, both of them relaxed and happy. No one looking at that picture could fail to see that they were deeply in love. That was what was important, she thought, that was where she wanted to be again. Nothing else mattered; not her ego, not work, not money . . . not even a baby.

Forty-five minutes later, Nell was starting to seize up with the cold. She'd been switching on the engine every few minutes to inject some heat into the car, but she'd reached the point where her toes and nose had turned to ice cubes. The thought of a hot drink from the machine was almost enough to drag her from the car park and risk having to make polite conversation with the other adults. She dug in her purse for some coins for the machine and had just found enough when another car pulled up right alongside hers.

Why did people do that? she grumbled to herself. There were loads of spaces, why park next to her and risk scratching the paintwork on either of their cars? She was just in the mood to give the driver of the other car a thunderous look when she realised she was staring straight at Yvonna.

She groaned inwardly. She could do without this tonight; Olek's ex-wife having another go at her for daring to ask when her affair with Viktor had started. Mind you, on the plus side, Yvonna's appearance to collect her son meant that Nell's presence was no longer required. She could simply start her car and drive off, that way she wouldn't even have to talk to her at all. She quickly whipped the blanket off her lap and adjusted her seat and was about to wave and leave, but Yvonna was already getting out the car and heading her way.

Nell wound down the window, just as she'd done last night.

Yvonna bent down to speak to her, rubbing her arms to generate warmth.

'Mind if I get in your car for a minute? It's freezing out here.'

Yes, she did mind, thought Nell, but gestured towards the passenger side politely.

'Max says that his dad hasn't returned any of his texts or calls.' Yvonna shut the door and pulled the sleeves of her jumper down over her hands.

'He's very busy at the moment; he's hardly got time to sleep, let alone look at his phone.'

'It's not like Olek,' his ex-wife continued as if Nell hadn't spoken. 'I don't think I've ever known him ignore his son. He might not be the most dynamic of men, but as far as Max goes, I can't complain. Usually.'

Nell's hackles rose automatically, Olek had never put a foot wrong in his relationship with Yvonna, either during the marriage or after, but she never missed an opportunity for a little dig at him. Regardless of what was going on between them, Nell had every intention of defending her husband. 'I don't know what else you want me to say, Yvonna.'

Yvonna stared out of the window before turning to Nell. 'It just feels like a coincidence, that's all.'

Nell shrugged. 'You've lost me.'

Yvonna loosened her scarf a little. 'One minute you're asking very personal questions about Olek's relationship to Max. And the next thing I know, Olek goes incommunicado on his son.'

'You're right, it is a coincidence.' Nell's heart thumped against her ribs; she turned to face the other woman. She had to play this carefully, extract information without causing offence. 'Perhaps it just hit a nerve with you.'

Yvonna held her gaze, she was biting the inside of her cheek as if weighing up what, or how much, to say. Nell stared back, willing the other woman to tell her the truth, but also scared that if she did, Nell would be the keeper of even more secrets.

Yvonna examined her own nails. They were long and painted red; one was chipped, and she picked absentmindedly at the edge of it. 'I always wondered if Olek suspected anything.'

The air was so tense that Nell felt as if she couldn't breathe. 'About you and Viktor, or about Max being his?'

'Me and Viktor. I don't think it ever crossed his mind that Max wasn't his son.'

'So there is a possibility?' she demanded.

'I can't believe I'm telling you this. You of all people.' Yvonna blew out a shaky breath. 'Olek and I never used birth control; we decided that what was meant to be would be. But nothing ever did happen until I had a fling with

Viktor. Two months later, I was pregnant. I ended it with Viktor and focused on the pregnancy. It was only when Max was a toddler that Viktor came back on the scene.'

'And you didn't think you should mention it to either of the men?'

Yvonna's eyes filled with tears. 'I know it was bad of me, but I decided to keep quiet. I didn't know for certain, and Olek was ecstatic about the prospect of being a dad. Whereas Viktor acted like he'd had a lucky escape. The only way to prove it would have been a DNA test – I didn't want to put anyone through that. It was bad enough when Olek found out about Viktor and me, to then add, "oh and by the way, Max might belong to Viktor too," seemed too cruel.'

'So you let Olek bring up a baby as his own son even though you had your doubts,' said Nell, struggling to keep the disbelief out of her voice.

Yvonna covered her face with her hands. 'I shouldn't have done it, but I'm glad for Max's sake that I did. I love Viktor dearly, but Olek has made a better father than he ever would have done.'

'He had mumps as a teenager,' Nell told her. 'And it's rare, but I found out recently that it can cause infertility in men. I think this is what happened to Olek, which means he's been unable to father children ever since.'

'So Viktor must be Max's dad.' Yvonna swore under her breath. 'I knew about him having mumps, didn't know about the problems it can cause.'

Nell's heart ached for her husband; all those years building their close father-and-son relationship, all the proud moments, the happy memories, the shared hobbies . . . Rightly or wrongly, Yvonna had preserved those for Olek by keeping her suspicions to herself. Nell was the one who'd jeopardised Olek and Max's relationship. Never had the saying 'let sleeping dogs lie' felt more apt. If only she hadn't gone poking her nose in, all of this could have been avoided. 'Are you going to tell them? All three of them?'

Yvonna's face froze in horror. 'I . . . I don't want to. It'll cause so much upset. And they'll all be angry with me. I guess you're going to tell Olek?'

Nell shook her head. 'It should come from you, not me.'

Yvonna pressed herself back against the car seat and exhaled. 'Shit. This is a nightmare.'

'Finally, we agree on something.'

Nell needed Merry tonight more than she ever had done in her life. Under other circumstances, she'd have rung her and asked if the two of them could get together to set the world to rights, but that wasn't an option anymore. But there was somewhere else she could go, somewhere she was guaranteed to be pampered and cosseted and treated like a child for a while. In fact, she'd go straight there now, no need to even go home first.

'I think you and I have finished for tonight,' Nell told Yvonna. 'I'm driving to my parents' house now. So if you wouldn't mind getting out, I'll be on my way.'

A few days in her childhood bedroom, a chance to revert to a time before her life got so complicated . . .? Bring it on.

Chapter 29

Merry

Merry gripped Cole's arm tightly as he guided her from the kitchen at Meadow View out into the dark garden. She was pretty sure that being led blindfolded wasn't what the midwife had in mind when she'd advocated delegating chores.

'I've never been more nervous in my life,' she said, her voice muffled under the scarf Freya had tied over her face.

Cole was very strong, and she trusted him, but the ground was slippy underfoot and there was probably a frost.

'I've got you,' Cole assured her. 'I won't let you fall.'

'Keep your eyes closed,' Freya chimed in front of her. 'No peeping.'

'I can't see anything with your scarf over my eyes. I promise!'

She felt the hard surface of the terrace beneath her feet.

Cole stopped and tucked an arm around her waist. 'OK, you can look.'

'Surprise!' yelled Harley and Freya together as she pulled down the scarf.

'You guys!' Merry beamed. 'This is amazing!'

The back garden at Meadow View had been given a full-on Christmas makeover: the beech hedge twinkled with lights, a fir tree had been fully decorated with lights too, as well as baubles and even an angel on top. There was a picnic table set with a flask and mugs, marshmallows and biscuits. And as she took in the circle of deckchairs around a glowing firepit, Harley turned on the Christmas music and 'Last Christmas' by Wham! blasted out across the terrace.

'This is a lovely surprise, thanks, you three, I'm really touched.'

'We wanted to do something to cheer you up because your dad has died and you're probably sad,' Freya said earnestly.

Cole's arm tightened around Merry. 'Yes, well, we probably didn't need to bring that up, but thank you, Freya.'

'I'd be sad if you died, Dad,' she said innocently. 'I'm only saying.'

'It's very sweet of you and has definitely cheered me up.' Merry hugged Harley and Freya and reached up to kiss Cole's cheek.

'We haven't finished yet,' said Harley, wiping his cheek, even though Merry had kissed his father not him. 'This is only the first part.'

'Yes, there's s'mores. Get it?' Cole nudged Harley. 'Get it? There's more, except I said there's s'mores.'

'That's such a dad joke,' Harley groaned, trying not to laugh.

'We're lucky to have a dad,' Freya piped up. 'Merry—'

'Why don't you get the marshmallows, Freya?' Cole interrupted, sending a look of apology to Merry.

'I don't mind us talking about my dad,' said Merry. 'In a weird way, it helps to get used to it. When I was talking to Woody earlier, the words got stuck in my throat. I don't think I even got around to telling him in the end. And you're right, Freya, you are lucky to have your dad.' She smiled at Cole, who gave her a squeeze. 'And so am I.'

For the next few minutes, Cole organised his children into finding long sticks in the garden and preparing the marshmallows for roasting. Merry was given strict instructions to do nothing at all.

Cole had turned up with the kids to collect her from Merry and Bright, promising her a nice surprise. When they'd pulled up outside Meadow View, for one happy moment, she did think that he'd worked miracles and the house was ready for them to move into. But even she had to admit that there was still so much to be done before it was habitable, and now that there was Ray's funeral to arrange, her priorities had changed.

'This was one of your better ideas, darling,' Merry sighed as Cole tucked a blanket around her knees.

'It was forecast to be a clear night and I thought it would be romantic to sit under the stars beside the warmth of a fire,' he said, brushing his cold lips against hers. 'You've had a tough few days, I wanted to do something special to show you I care.'

Her heart swelled with love for him. 'I love you.'

'Er, this hot chocolate smells of sick,' said Harley, pouring some into a cup. 'I'm going to have Coke instead.'

Merry and Cole exchanged smiles.

'OK, maybe not that romantic,' he added.

She caught hold of his hand. 'It's family time, and it's just what I need to distract me.'

For so many years, she hadn't had any family. Astrid had been as close to a mother figure as she'd had, and Nell, her gorgeous, funny, kind-hearted Nell, had been like a sister. The rift between them was huge and hurtful and she wasn't quite sure how to heal it. But they would soon enough, she was sure: as soon as Olek told her that her dad had passed away, she'd turn up with hugs and flowers and they'd make up and it would all go back to normal.

And, in the meantime, thanks to Cole, she did have family. She had a wonderful husband, a whole bunch of in-laws, two stepchildren and a baby on the way. And courtesy of Emily's detective work, she had a half-sister and a father too. Or, rather, had had a father.

Her mind went back to last night at the home and the trauma of watching him fade out of this life and onto the next, whatever and wherever that might be. She looked up at the velvet of the night sky and gazed into the stars, thinking once again of the first night Emily had introduced them, and how they'd danced around his room to Fleetwood Mac. Merry didn't have many memories of him, but the ones she did have were all the more precious for that.

'OK?' Cole looked at her, concerned.

She nodded. 'More than OK.'

The night air was bitingly cold and the garden at Meadow View was unmistakably still a building site. But by the time Merry had been handed a mug of hot chocolate and fed a toasted marshmallow squished between two biscuits, she was perfectly able to see past the piles of bricks and the cement mixer and churned-up lawn and imagine how lovely this place would look next summer.

'I love it here,' said Freya, wriggling her bottom onto the chair beside Merry, as if reading her thoughts. She had a paper plate with two s'mores on it in one hand, her hot chocolate in the other, and a wide smile adorning her little face. 'You picked a cool house, Merry and Dad.'

'Thank you.' Merry felt her eyes prick with tears and tried to blink them away quickly. This time last year, she remembered feeling daunted about the prospect of becoming a stepmother to these kids. It had been a steep learning curve, with some bumps on the way, like the time Freya had told Santa that what she wanted for Christmas was for her parents to get back together. But a year on, with her stepdaughter beside her paying her compliments and her stepson proving to be a reliable member of staff at weekends, i.e. choosing to spend his Saturdays with her, she reckoned she hadn't done such a bad job.

'Let's have s'mores on Christmas Day,' said Harley, through a mouthful of marshmallow. 'This is way better than Christmas pudding.'

'Can we?' Freya joined in. 'I hate Christmas pudding.'

'Fine by me,' said Merry. 'Your dad is cooking Christmas dinner this year.'

'That's right.' Cole puffed his chest out. 'Soggy sprouts and lumpy gravy all right for everyone?'

'Hey, Dad, can we have Christmas dinner here?' Harley asked.

'Yes!' Freya bounced in her chair. 'It'll be cool.'

'I'd love that,' said Merry, 'but the house isn't quite ready yet. We'll be here next year, definitely.'

Freya sighed. 'But next Christmas Day we'll be at Mum's. And you'll be with the new baby without us.'

They took it in turns, with Cole and his ex-wife Lydia sorting out the child-sharing between them. Merry didn't get involved, but it was heart-warming to hear Freya speak so fondly about the baby already.

'I'm not sure whether Father Christmas will find you here,' said Cole slyly.

Freya gave him a knowing look. 'I'm not worried about that, Dad. I think you'll find us wherever we are.'

'That's the magic of Christmas,' said Merry, smiling to herself at the disappointed look on Cole's face. 'Santa will always find the good boys and girls.'

'Better make sure you're not naughty then,' Cole murmured in her ear when the children weren't looking.

'Define naughty,' she said, touching the tip of her tongue to his lips as she kissed him.

'Oh gosh,' said Cole, clearing his throat. 'It might be time to take the kids back home.'

'Shooting star!' Harley yelled, pointing up into the night sky.

'Wow! You're right, son,' said Cole, bending down to Freya's level to show her where it was. 'Everyone make a wish.'

'I wish we could have Christmas Day at Meadow View,' said Freya, looking beseechingly at her dad.

'I wish we could have Christmas Day here *and* we get loads of snow,' said Harley.

'I wish you two would stop ganging up on me,' Cole grumbled good-naturedly. 'And I'm sorry, but I'm wishing for a non-white Christmas this year, just in case the baby comes and I have to drive through snowdrifts to get to the hospital.'

Merry was thinking about that last message from Nell. Every time she remembered their argument, her stomach would churn. How had it come to this? Her favourite Christmas tradition was that they would speak on the phone on Christmas morning, and they'd wish each other a happy Christmas. Even last year, the day after her wedding, they'd chatted first thing, Merry blissfully in love and Nell over the moon for her. And the year before, when she'd woken up on Christmas morning at an airport hotel so that Cole could catch his early-morning flight to see his kids. And every Christmas morning before that in all the years they'd been friends.

'And I wish that you all get what you want for Christmas,' Merry said, mustering up a smile.

But what she really wanted was to get her best friend back, because Christmas simply wouldn't be Christmas without Nell.

Chapter 30

Nell

Nell woke up and yawned. She was warm and comfortable under the covers of her bed and, stretching her legs, she blinked herself awake.

A spilt second later, she remembered she was in her old teenage bedroom at her parents' house, and her contentment was quickly replaced by queasiness.

'Oh God,' she groaned.

Olek had left her and wasn't replying to her messages, she'd fallen out with the best friend she'd ever had, she'd run away from home and walked away from the job she'd loved. She was thirty-seven years old, and her life was a shambles.

She reached for her phone on the nightstand. It was five o'clock in the afternoon; she'd had a two-hour nap. Two hours! She despised herself for her laziness. What had happened to Nell the doer, full of energy and ideas and a new project on the go? She had probably spent more time asleep than awake since being here. Shutting the world out was the only respite she had from the car crash of her life.

Thank goodness for her parents, who had been a source of solace this last week.

When Nell had turned up unannounced, her dad had opened the door, taken one look at his daughter, muttered, 'Good Lord' and shouted for his wife to come running.

Ten minutes later, she'd been ensconced between them in front of the fire, nursing one of her father's legendary hot toddies and sobbing onto her mother's shoulder.

'Your face, your posture, your entire demeanour screamed total and utter defeat, Eleanor,' her father had later told her, calling her by her full name as usual. 'Something I've never seen from you in all your thirty-odd years.' He could never remember her exact age, and the older she got, the more grateful she was for his poor memory.

Now, Nell snapped on her bedside lamp and checked her phone for messages. There was one from Max, but that was it.

Where are you, Olek?

Surely he would want to speak to her again soon? Her heart ached at the thought of him hurting, wherever he was. It had been more than a week since she'd found that note; they had never gone this long without talking. Even in the early days of dating, they'd quickly got into the habit of calling or texting each other multiple times a day. She'd let Olek know where she was on the night she arrived at her parents' and had received a brief 'OK' in response, but nothing since. She missed him so much, but there were only so many times she could tell him that in a text or voice note.

And then there was Merry. Their WhatsApp chat had remained inactive since she'd sent Merry the voice note declaring herself done with their friendship. Nell had misgivings about that; she'd replayed her own vitriol-laden message over and over, and now felt ashamed of it. She would say sorry, but only once Merry had said it first. She was the one in the wrong, after all. But Merry hadn't even been in touch to say sorry for her part in Olek's departure, and her lack of response had hurt a lot.

Nell dropped her phone again, feeling morose and lonely, and tuned into the noises of the house instead. Her parents' house had five bedrooms, so plenty of spare rooms to accommodate guests without having to encroach on Nell's. It hadn't been decorated since the nineties. Her mother had wanted to give it a fresh look, but despite not having lived with her parents for almost twenty years, Nell had begged them to keep it as it was so she could return to the simple days of her youth whenever she came home.

Downstairs, the front doorbell chimed.

This happened all day, every day. Sometimes deliveries of food, flowers or dresses for her mother to take on their upcoming Christmas cruise around the Caribbean. Or often friends dropped in for coffee, or a game of cards, a pre-dinner G and T, or supper. Nell had had no idea that her parents' social life was so full. But for her, this regular occurrence sent her cortisol level sky high, because every time someone came to the door, Nell couldn't help thinking that this time it would be Olek.

Now, at the sound of her father's footsteps heading to open the door, she froze, her body tense, hoping that this time it would be him. She missed his voice, gruff and gentle at the same time, made totally unique by the subtle accent still evident years after leaving his native Poland. She missed the simple, happy life that they'd shared before they'd embarked on a quest to start a family. *Her* quest, she acknowledged sadly. She did want a baby, but not at any price; sometimes she wished she'd never caught the broodiness bug at all.

At the sound of her father's formal, 'thank you, goodbye,' she sighed, her body sagging with disappointment; it was another delivery.

She picked her phone back up, remembering that she had a message from Max.

Hey Nell, I know you said Dad is busy, but it's over a week now and I haven't had a single message off him. Have I upset him? If I've done something, please tell me. It feels weird not talking to him. In case he's interested, football training is going really well. Not long now until that final game at the Liverpool ground. I've still got him a ticket for that. I managed to get another one, so you can come too if you want. If neither of you can make it, it's cool. Max

Tears pricked at her eyes. Poor kid. Right in the middle of a serious situation and he didn't even know. She needed to tell him something, not the whole truth, but something. This was awful. For Olek not to contact his own son . . . or, rather, the boy who he'd always assumed was his son . . . She groaned. What a mess. She totally got why Olek was struggling to come to terms with the likelihood that he had never fathered a child, that Max wasn't his, but still, it wasn't Max's fault. He shouldn't be the one to bear the brunt of this fiasco.

She typed out a reply and pressed send.

Hey Max, please don't worry about Dad, you haven't done anything. I'm sorry he hasn't been in touch. He and I have had a bit of a silly row and he's gone away for a couple of days. Nothing serious. And as for your football match, THANK YOU! I'd love to come, and your dad wouldn't miss it for the world. You're a star x

She dried her eyes, made a screenshot of Max's message and sent it to Olek.

Darling, I'm worried about you, and I'm worried about us. Max thinks he might have upset you and that feels wrong. He needs to know that you still care about him. And let's talk soon, I miss you. X

She put her mobile down beside her on the bed. He'd read it, but if her other messages were anything to go by, he wouldn't reply. But this time, to her surprise, after only a few seconds, the screen lit up with a response.

I'm still angry, Nell. I don't know what to think, I don't know what to do and I don't even know what to say to you. I've been lied to by the people I trusted most and who I loved most. I need more time to work through all this stuff. Max should give the football tickets to someone else. I'm not sure I'm the right person anymore.

Nell had to read it twice to believe it and now there was a lump in her throat the size of a golf ball. One phrase stood out: 'who I loved most'. He had used the past tense. Had his love for her really come to an end? She'd never known him this low before. He couldn't be giving up on Max, surely? And there was no indication that he was missing her, no loving words, just anger.

Her first instinct was to dial his number and let it ring and ring until he couldn't ignore her anymore. But no, that wouldn't do, she couldn't trust herself not to say something she might regret, she was far too emotional at the moment. Instead, she took a few moments to compose a reply.

I understand, and I'll respect your wish to stay away for the time being. Tell me what I can do that would make things better between us. If there's anything that will help, I'll do it. I'm not giving up on us, Olek, I love you too much for that xxx

Three dots appeared beside his name, telling her that he was typing a reply. Her heart raced. This was the closest she'd got to having a conversation with him for days and days. She meant what she'd said, she really would do anything to get their lives back on track.

> The only thing you can do for us is to give me more time. I'm sorry I can't give you more than that.

She bit her lip, disappointed.

> OK xx

He replied again.

> But if you wouldn't mind posting a couple of envelopes for me? They're on my desk already sealed, just need stamps. Thanks

Ordinarily, she'd make a joke about being his secretary, but now she couldn't even bring herself to do that. All he wanted from her was to post his letters; it was unbearably sad.

> Sure. Although I'm still at Mum and Dad's, so it won't be for a few days.

> OK, thanks. I assumed you'd be home by now for the funeral.

Nell's blood ran cold.

> What funeral?

Merry's dad. Isn't it today?

Ray was dead?

No, no, no . . . Oh my God. Nell buried her head in her hands. Time seemed to stand still as she processed this information. Her heart beating so rapidly that she could feel the blood whooshing in her ears.

I didn't even know Ray had died!

She typed the message and then deleted it, too ashamed to admit to her husband that something so awful had happened to her best friend and she hadn't even known about it.

Poor Merry, she'd be devastated, and with the baby due any time too – and oh, the shop! How on earth would Merry be coping with everything? She'd had so much on her plate and Nell had deserted her over some silly row and was lying in bed wallowing in self-pity.

Nell thought about the unopened messages from Merry on her phone and felt sick with guilt. How could she ever make up for being such a terrible person? Merry would never want anything to do with her again and Nell couldn't blame her one bit.

Chapter 31

Merry

Before Merry knew it, Ray's funeral at Wetherley crematorium was upon them. The week since her dad had died had passed by in a blur of tears and tiredness, appointments and arrangements. Merry was vaguely aware of a muted vibration in her handbag, signalling an incoming message. She ignored it, hoping that nobody else had heard it. She should have turned her phone off completely, but her number was the contact for deliveries to the shop and it was inexorably easier to accept the call than sort out a redelivery at a later date.

'And now we say our final goodbyes to Ray as we listen to one of his favourite pieces of music.' Barbara, the celebrant, bowed in respect in the direction of the coffin, stepped down from the podium and off to the side of the chapel.

From the speakers came the sound of Frank Sinatra singing 'Fly Me To The Moon' and Cole tightened his arm around Merry's waist. Silently, the curtains glided on their rails across the front of the room, until her father's coffin was no longer visible.

Goodbye, Dad. May you play among the stars.

She let out a long shuddering breath. It felt as if she'd been holding that breath ever since she'd climbed out of the funeral limousine an hour ago. Beside her, Emily was crying softly, her hand tightly in Will's. Merry allowed her head to rest against Cole's shoulder. She was so grateful for his presence, as steadfast and strong as ever. She couldn't have wished for a more supportive partner since Ray had passed away. Cole had been her rock and although it was against her nature to lean on anyone, she'd found herself doing it easily recently.

'OK?' he murmured softly against her ear.

She nodded. 'Thank you, darling.'

Merry didn't know how Cole had managed it, but somehow, he'd persuaded the crematorium to open later this evening to accommodate them to hold the funeral as soon as possible. The nearest other date had been the twenty-eighth of December which was already circled in red in the calendar as Merry's induction date. She was still nervous about that, but at least she knew that she'd only have one major life event to deal with when the time came.

The chapel was by no means full, but seeing the crowd of people who'd come to pay their respects to Ray had filled her with joy. Emily's mum, Tina, and her husband, Ian, were here, staff from Springwood House, Ray's old landlady, plus one or two others neither she nor Emily recognised. But the largest contingent was her own family, or, rather, the family she'd married into almost a year ago. Freya was still a bit young, but Harley was here, Fred and Astrid, Hester and Paul newly returned from their holiday and, of course, Emily, now her next of kin.

She felt a wave of love for this tight-knit unit of hers, the unexpected family which she now couldn't imagine ever being without. The circle of life, she mused, as the baby shifted position, nudging her bladder dangerously.

We are born, we live, we pass away.

She had lost her father too soon, but at least they'd had a year together.

There was one couple absent whom Merry missed terribly. Only a couple of weeks ago, the idea of Nell and Olek not being here would have been unthinkable.

The funeral director appeared at the front of the chapel. She was dressed in a top hat and dress coat and extended her gloved hand towards the exit, while another member of her team opened the double doors leading to the remembrance gardens.

'That's the hardest part done.' Cole hugged her gently as they and the rest of the family led the congregation outside. 'You were amazing. You're always amazing, but today I'm especially proud of you.'

She nodded her acknowledgement, words strangled in her throat.

This was the first funeral she'd ever been to for a family member; she hadn't gone to her mother's for some reason. Maybe she hadn't been asked, or perhaps she had, and had declined. Sometimes she was grateful for the way her brain had blocked out painful memories; at other times it frustrated her that some of the important details of her life with her mum were gone forever.

'He'd have loved that,' Emily turned around to whisper to her, dabbing her eyes with a tissue. 'Dad liked a good singalong.'

Merry smiled at her younger sister. 'You did really well,' she managed to say.

Emily had helped Cole with the organising, consulting Merry only on minor details, and the service had been a true celebration of his life. Barbara, who'd officiated at her and Cole's wedding last December, had read a touching and funny eulogy, recounting the scary moment when Ray had interrupted the ceremony to hand Merry a gift. It had added a personal touch and had given everyone a giggle in the process.

It was pitch-black outside and everyone's breath was visible in the cold night air. There was a covered walkway from the chapel to a clearing where floral tributes had been arranged for everyone to admire and read the messages, and Cole and Will left Merry and Emily at the head of the walkway, to receive words of condolence from people.

'No word from Nell?' Emily whispered, pulling up Merry's collar and checking her scarf was blocking out draughts. 'Sorry, I can't help fussing over you.'

'I'm fine, honestly. Nothing from Nell.' Merry's stomach flipped at the mention of her best friend's name; she thought briefly of the buzz of her phone earlier. Could that have been her? Even if it was, it was a bit late now. Nell had chosen not to attend the funeral. It was her biggest sadness, to have fallen out with Nell so irretrievably that such an old friend felt she couldn't be here for her on the most difficult of days. 'She hasn't even acknowledged Dad's death.'

Emily frowned. 'And she definitely knows?'

'I've sent multiple messages, and Olek knows.' A flicker of doubt passed through Merry's head. If Olek had left her, there was a chance that he hadn't told her. She brushed away the thought. Even if that was the case, Merry had told her everything in her voice note. Besides, Olek wouldn't have left her for very long; those two were like swans: mates for life. They might have had a temporary blip, but they'd be back together by now.

Emily's mum, Tina, and stepfather, Ian, were among the first to give them both hugs, although Ian didn't linger once he'd done his duty.

'It was a super tribute to him.' Tina had always had a soft spot for her ex.

'Emily did most of it,' Merry told her.

'Ian hasn't got much to say,' Tina whispered, once he was out of earshot. 'Never had much time for him when he was alive. Now he's passed on, even less. But we know, don't we, girls?'

'We do,' Merry agreed, as Emily nodded and blew her nose.

'He was one of a kind, but the Ray I knew was long gone,' said Tina. 'Alzheimer's is a cruel disease, takes you from those you love piece by piece. And from yourself. We used to dance, him and me. Cheek to cheek, and he'd sing in my ear, all soft and quiet. I could forgive him anything when we danced together like that.'

Emily's eyes grew misty with tears. 'I remember. I used to love watching you dance.'

A fleeting image popped into Merry's head. Her own mum and Ray dancing around their flat, sometimes lifting her up to join in. Mum's girlish giggle, the contagious feeling of euphoria Merry had caught from her mother when Ray was around. He had been a special man, who had brought happiness to the people he loved.

'He and I had our differences,' Tina continued. 'But we had good times too. Plenty of them. Cling on to the nice memories, girls, and your father will always be with you. In your hearts. And he'll have loved getting to know you,' she added to Merry. Which was very charitable of her, considering it wasn't totally clear whether he'd been in love with Sam and Tina simultaneously.

Merry and Emily hugged her once again and she moved off to find Ian. Next in line were Fred and Astrid.

'*Mein Liebling.*' Astrid kissed both of her cheeks. 'I know today is hard for you. But your father was loved right until the end of his life. You gave him your time, you made him feel safe and part of your family.'

'And that's all anyone can ask of another,' Fred added, pressing his cold cheek to Merry's once Astrid had peeled herself away. 'To feel important to someone else.'

'Thank you.' Merry looked from Astrid to Fred, feeling as if they were talking to each other and not to her and that this was part of a much wider conversation.

'And you are important to me, *mein Schatz*,' Astrid murmured, linking her arm through Fred's as they walked towards the floral tributes.

'And I'll follow you to the ends of the earth, darling,' he replied. 'Even Germany.'

Merry frowned. If there hadn't been someone else approaching them, she'd tap Astrid's shoulder and ask for the context of this conversation, but as it was, Emily had already extended her hand.

'Thanks so much for coming,' her sister said, greeting an elderly man. He had a long whiskery beard and a silver hoop through his nose.

'Sad business,' said the man, shaking his head. 'My condolences to the both of you.'

He moved to Merry, and grasped her hand between his.

'I'm sorry,' she said, 'I'm afraid I didn't meet many of Dad's acquaintances.'

'Dave Rutt,' said the man. 'Although when he knew me, most people knew me as Rutty. And I *was* in a rut, too. We both were. He and I met on the streets. We lost touch years ago. I've done all right since. Looks like he did too.'

'We're his daughters,' said Emily. 'Life wasn't easy for him recently, but yes, I think he did OK.'

'A couple of crackers,' said Dave, with a wobble evident in his voice. 'I bet he was very proud. Is your mum here? I'd love to know who he finally settled down with.'

Merry's heart ached. She hoped that he'd been proud of her, but how much had he really taken in of her existence as his dementia took a greater and greater hold this year?

'My mum is over there,' Emily pointed out Tina to him.

'And my mum passed away; we're half-sisters,' Merry explained.

'So you knew our dad well?' Emily asked. 'In that case, I'm really sorry not to have met you before. When did you last see him?'

'Bit embarrassing.' He tugged his beard. 'We fell out, years ago. I accused him of stealing money off me. He denied it. We lost touch after that. I later found out that the thief was someone else. I've had that hanging over me for years. Always regretted the way I treated him. Then I saw the notice in the newspaper with funeral details. I thought, now's my chance to make amends. So here I am.'

'We're glad you came,' said Merry, preparing for him to move off. There were still other people waiting to speak to the sisters and Merry was ready for a sit-down.

'Funny, isn't it. I didn't make time to speak to my old friend. I put off apologising, too proud to admit my mistakes. Yet now he's died, I made the time to pay my respects. Ridiculous really. We should make time for the living while we still can. Friendship is a gift. We could have had fun in our old age, Ray and me. And now he's gone.' He pulled a hanky from his pocket. 'Sorry, girls.'

'That's all right.' Merry rubbed his arm gently. 'No need to apologise. We all do things we regret.'

The similarity between his story and her friendship with Nell was excruciating.

His eyes cleared and he looked at her curiously. 'Who did you say your mum was?'

'Her name was Sam Shaw.'

'Bloody hell.' Dave whistled under his breath. 'Now there's a name I haven't heard for a long time.'

'You knew her?' Merry gasped.

'Oh yeah. Stunning girl. There's a look of her about you, now you mention it.' He shook his head in disbelief. 'Ray was madly in love with her, but I didn't realise they'd had a kid together.'

'Here I am, living proof,' Merry could barely contain her excitement at meeting someone else who had known her mother. 'Sadly, she's no longer with us. She suffered from—'

'Depression. I know. I heard she topped herself.' Dave inhaled sharply. 'Terrible business. I can't understand how anyone could abandon their kid like that. Still, not everyone is cut out to be a parent, are they? And it looks like you turned out all right.'

Merry was so taken aback, she couldn't speak.

'Best of luck to you with that baby.'

'How did he know?' asked Emily innocently, as Dave walked off.

'It's a mystery,' Merry replied.

Both of them looked down at Merry's ginormous belly and smiled.

Merry groaned. 'Not everyone is cut out to be a parent, that's what he just said. What if I'm not?'

Emily pulled a face. 'You can't compare your situation with your mum's. This baby was planned and very much wanted. Your mum was young, vulnerable and alone. Besides, why would you listen to a man you've just met? Trust your own instincts.'

'Hmm.' Merry watched as Dave climbed into a waiting taxi. If only her instincts had more self-belief. She gave herself a shake and pushed the thoughts from her mind. But while Emily greeted Ray's previous landlady, she reflected on Dave's words about friendship. And Nell. And how they'd allowed a silly argument to grow and fester rather than sort it out. She had made several attempts to contact Nell to check how she was and to let her know when the funeral was, and so far, Nell hadn't responded. The ball was in Nell's court and up until now, Merry had decided to leave it there. But what if she was wrong to have given up trying? After all, she loved Nell, and deep down, Nell probably still loved her too. At some point, they'd make up, they'd have to; The alternative was to be like Ray and Dave and leave it too late. She couldn't allow that to happen. All it would take was one more message from Merry, to show Nell that she still cared.

She was going to do it; she'd send a few words to say how the funeral had gone and how much Nell was missed. She opened her bag, took out her phone and stared at the screen with joy. Because on it were the words she'd longed to see: missed call from Nell.

Thank heavens. Thank heavens for that.

Chapter 32

Merry

Merry stepped into her father's room at Springwood House and shivered as memories of her last moments with him flooded back. The air smelled of disinfectant, which was better than the musty stale aroma there'd been the last time she was here, but it felt as if her dad's physical presence had already been scrubbed out. 'I don't like this.'

'Me neither,' Emily whispered. 'There's such a sad aura in here.'

Gail had requested that they empty Ray's room as soon as possible.

'I'm sorry and I know it seems mercenary to ask,' she'd said. 'But space here is at a premium, and we have a waiting list of people desperate for help with their loved ones.'

The sisters understood how those families must be feeling, which was why, two days after Ray's funeral, they were packing up his personal belongings. Will and Cole would be coming along later to load up Cole's van.

'Let's cheer it up.' Merry turned on the twinkly lights on the small Christmas tree she'd bought him, and the ones wrapped around the headboard of the bed, now stripped and bare of any trace of her father. She cracked open a window to let in some wintry fresh air while Emily tuned the radio into Smooth FM. Elton John soon had them singing along with 'Step In to Christmas' and once Emily had made them a hot mint tea, they felt a bit brighter.

'Donate to charity, throw away, keep,' said Emily, pointing at the three cardboard boxes she'd put on Ray's bed.

'Great,' said Merry, tying her hair up off her face with a scrunchie. 'Where shall I start?'

'There.' Emily pointed to the armchair. 'With your feet up, sipping tea. I'll hold things up and you can decide what we do with them.'

Merry hesitated. Ray was a man who hadn't owned much, but there was still plenty to deal with. Her default position was always to argue, and prove herself fit and capable of doing anything, but today she was happy to capitulate. 'Sounds like a plan.'

'That was easy.' Emily raised a surprised eyebrow. 'You OK?'

She sank wearily into the chair. 'Still tired after the funeral.'

Her sister opened Ray's underwear drawer and tipped the contents into the box marked 'throw away'. No need to debate that one. 'I know what you mean. Will said I was asleep before my head hit the pillow after the wake.'

'It's stress,' said Merry, trying to get comfy, which wasn't at all easy now. The baby was pressing at the underside of her ribs, forcing her to take short sharp breaths. 'It tires you out. I don't think I'll ever not be tired again and that's before I've got to deal with night feeds.'

'What's worrying you the most?' Emily buried her nose in one of their dad's jumpers before folding it into the charity box.

Where to start, thought Merry, stifling a yawn. 'The shop being understaffed worries me. Not being installed in Meadow View for Christmas makes me stressed. Having to go to hospital for tests and check-ups twice a week is stressful. Living each minute worried about . . .' She stopped mid-sentence. About being a useless mother, she'd been about to say. And she didn't want to say that out loud. She had to start believing in herself or this would become a self-perpetuating belief.

'About?' Emily prompted. She inspected the soles of Ray's shoes and, after discovering they had holes in, threw them away.

'Um . . . giving birth,' Merry said, hurriedly. No one could blame her for that.

Her sister gave her a thoughtful look 'You know what you need to do? Find a way to relax.'

'Relax?' Merry scoffed. 'I haven't relaxed since—'

'Frankie went to Hollywood,' Emily finished for her with a giggle. 'That always reminds me of Dad, he used to say that!'

Merry shook her head in amazement. 'I remember! Gosh, I remember it *so* clearly!'

The thought warmed her; that there might be latent memories of him still to be unearthed, things which might suddenly crop up and take her by surprise.

'Oh gosh,' Emily gasped, turning up the radio. 'I heard this song the other day. It's called "Dance with My Father", by Luther Vandross. Listen to the lyrics, it's about remembering the happy times he spent with his dad, especially how he and his mum would dance together. It's so beautiful and perfect for today.'

Even before the first chorus, Merry was in tears. 'The first time I met Dad here we all danced together – you, me and him.'

'There were so many things he couldn't remember, but he knew every word of the lyrics. That was such a special night.'

'One of the best days of my life,' said Emily.

Merry opened her arms. 'Come here.'

Emily knelt and laid her head on Merry's knee. Together the sisters listened to the rest of the song. It was a celebration of love between a child and father, and between mother and father too. The message was that when you lost someone you love, you'd give anything to share one more happy moment with them.

'He loved music,' Emily recalled. 'The one thing he wanted to bring with him, when he moved in here, was his vinyl collection. Used to carry an album around with him sometimes.'

'You must keep his records,' Merry said. 'He'd like that.'

There was a box of them at the bottom of his wardrobe. One of the things she and her dad had done together on her visits to Springwood House was to choose an album and take it downstairs to play on the record player in the lounge. Sometimes he'd simply sit and listen, at other times he'd tell her things, memories associated with the band or the song, like the time he'd hitchhiked to London to see the Rolling Stones perform at a pub called the Windsor Castle. She never knew how much of it was made up, but she didn't mind, she loved hearing his stories regardless.

'I'd like that,' said Emily. 'I can still picture him at Christmas choosing which track to play. People stay the same, don't they? Even when parts of them start to disappear, intrinsically, the person is still there. He took me to my first music festival when I was sixteen. Glastonbury. Another of the best days of my life.'

'I'd have loved to have gone to Glastonbury.' Merry's arm's tightened around her sister. 'I'm glad you got to go.'

Merry couldn't help comparing her childhood to her sister's; when she was sixteen, she'd spent as much time as she could babysitting. It hadn't been just about the money. She relished the chance to be in a real family home for a few hours rather than sit in her room in the children's home. And she hadn't had anyone to take her to festivals. But once she was friends with Nell, she'd been scooped up into the Thornbury family and spent a lot of her free time at their house. They weren't fans of festivals, but she'd had several holidays with them. So many happy times. Two decades of friendship, she thought with a pang, but those days were gone.

Emily chewed her lip. 'I must sound so thoughtless. I used to resent Dad for the times when he disappeared and just bowed out of my life for months on end. Now I realise I'm still the lucky one. He was *our* dad, not just mine, and I'm the one with most of the memories.'

'Which I'm always happy to listen to,' Merry replied. 'I mean it, Em. Even listening to your stories teaches me little things about him that I didn't know.'

'In that case,' Emily said with a giggle, 'let me tell you about that Glastonbury trip. Dad told me he had a fantastic idea, and I should just follow him and go with it. I agreed, obviously. So we fought our way through crowds and over muddy fields until we found the VIP area. Whereupon Dad tried to convince security that he was Robbie Williams' dad and he'd left his VIP pass in Robbie's trailer.'

Merry cringed. 'I'm guessing no one believed him?'

'The security guard looked at me, hiding behind Dad, and said, "So you're Robbie's sister?" At which point I crumbled and muttered no. "God might love a trier," said the guard, with a face like thunder "at first, I don't. Off you go." And so off we went. I was mortified but Dad laughed it off and so I did too, even though we had to walk past a crowd of people sniggering at us.'

'Dad sounded like fun,' Merry said wistfully.

'He was, but he wasn't perfect. After that, we went to see a band I'd never heard of, and he bumped into an old friend. Somehow, I got separated from them in the crush. Lost each other for most of the day. Mum would have gone barmy if she'd found out.'

'Sixteen and all on your own,' Merry marvelled, shaking her head. 'I would have panicked.'

Emily grinned. 'I bumped into the most handsome boy, who had a tent all to himself. Had a great time.'

'OK, in that case I'll stop feeling sorry for you.'

'When I said it was one of the best days of my life, I was *not* referring to getting Nicole Appleton from All Saints' autograph,' she said with a smirk. 'Although that was a highlight. Or watching Dad dance to the Shire Horses, which most certainly wasn't.'

'I remember him dancing with my mum.' Merry scrunched up her brow. 'And with me.'

'He danced with my mum and me too. She'd pretend not to want to and bat him away, but I could see she was loving being in his arms,' said Emily. 'Is that weird?'

'That Dad liked to dance with both of our mums?' Merry asked. 'No, I'd like to think that he did that because he loved them both.'

Emily sighed. 'He did. Even though he managed to keep you and Sam a secret for most of his life. I miss him. You don't realise how many tiny little things you do because you caught the habit from someone else. Like the way he always folded his napkin into a triangle and made a boat out of it.'

'Yes!' Merry exclaimed. 'I found myself doing that at the funeral.'

'And the way he used to say, "right then" about five times when he was psyching himself up to go to bed.'

'Or get up from his armchair.'

'Talking of which,' said Emily, getting to her feet. 'I'd better get on with what we came for.'

For the next thirty minutes, Emily packed his belongings into relevant boxes and black sacks and Merry helped her to set aside anything they wanted to keep. And as Mariah Carey sang about what she wanted for Christmas, Merry remembered the Christmas wish she'd made in the garden at Meadow View: to get her best friend back.

Her heart sank, remembering the message that Nell had sent her on the day of the funeral. She'd been so thrilled to see a missed call and a voicemail message from Nell. After the service, they'd gone back to Holly Cottage for refreshments, so it had been a while before she had a spare moment to listen to it. But when she did, the tone of Nell's message had left her reeling. There had been a lack of empathy and emotion, so different from the Nell she'd always loved. Nell could have been leaving a message for an ex-colleague whom she hadn't seen for a decade, instead of the woman whose life she had been a part of for over two.

'What's up?' Emily said, noticing Merry had gone quiet.

Merry shrugged. 'Just Nell. I don't understand how our friendship can have just evaporated like this. The last voicemail I had from her seems so cold.'

'Have you still got it?' Emily asked.

Merry got out her phone and played it for her.

Hi Merry, I've just heard that your dad has passed away. I'm so sorry for your loss. I know how important it was to have found him and I imagine you'll be very sad that he'll never get to meet the baby. I hope these last couple of weeks haven't been too stressful for you and that you're keeping well. Take care, Nell.

'Keeping well,' Merry repeated. 'It's the sort of thing you'd say to an elderly aunt, not your best friend.'

'She doesn't sound herself at all,' Emily agreed. 'Do you think she's OK?'

'I don't know what to think,' she sighed. 'But if either of her parents had died, I wouldn't have missed the funeral for the world. Nell chose not to be there for me, and she can never undo that now. So that's that.'

There was a moment's silence and Emily seemed to understand that Merry didn't want to talk about Nell.

'What shall we do with Dad's ashes?' she asked.

'Good question. Did he have a favourite place? We could do it there,' Merry suggested.

Emily grinned. 'You might freak out at this, but how about taking him to Glastonbury next year?'

'Dad's ashes?' Merry frowned. 'I'm not sure . . .'

'You just said you'd never been; this would be a once-in-a-lifetime opportunity for us to all go together.'

'I'm not sure you can use "lifetime" when you're referring to someone in an urn.'

'At least he won't need a ticket,' Emily sniggered. 'He'd have loved that.'

'But what about the baby?'

'He or she won't need a ticket either,' she teased.

'That wasn't what I meant.' Merry gave her a playful shove. 'I was thinking of changing nappies and making up bottles in a tent, et cetera.'

'Don't worry about that, there'll be enough of us to help with the baby,' Emily said dismissively. 'Will and me, you and Cole, and I bet Harley and Freya will want to come too. We can make it a real family occasion.'

That was enough to grab Merry's interest; anything family oriented, a chance to make new memories and traditions, and she was there. 'We could sneak up to the VIP area and sprinkle the ashes through the wire fence.'

'Ray Meadows finally makes it in with the celebs,' Emily gave a snort. 'It's perfect. Bloody perfect.'

'Knock, knock!' came a voice from the door, and in walked Cole and Will.

'We're going to Glastonbury next year,' Merry announced, as Cole stooped to press his cold cheek to hers.

'Are we?' he retorted. 'What about the baby?'

'It won't need a ticket,' Merry replied swiftly.

She and Emily fell about laughing and Cole and Will exchanged bemused looks.

'I'm up for it,' said Will.

'Correct answer.' Emily beamed at him. 'Because Merry wants you to be in charge of nappy changing.'

'Happily,' said Will, whose expression said the exact opposite.

'He's a keeper.' Merry got to her feet and gave him a hug. Her sister had chosen well.

'How are you getting on?' Gail had come to check on them.

'Almost done,' said Emily, unwinding the lights from the bed frame.

'Excellent,' said Gail, 'Now, in terms of post and whatnot . . .'

While Gail explained that they'd forward any remaining mail on to her address, out of the corner of her eye, Merry saw Emily pull Cole to one side and whisper something in his ear.

'Thank you,' Merry murmured distractedly, trying to listen in on Emily's conversation.

'What's going on?' she demanded once Gail had left. She stuffed the mail in her handbag.

‘A surprise,’ said Emily, tapping her nose.

‘Cole?’ she demanded. ‘What sort of surprise?’

He scooped his wife into his arms and kissed the place on her neck guaranteed to make her forget everything else but the pleasurable sensations rippling through her.

‘If I told you that, it wouldn’t be a surprise, would it?’ His breath was warm against her ear.

‘Will I like it as much as this?’ She closed her eyes. ‘Because if so, surprise away.’

‘Get a room, you two,’ snorted Emily.

‘I hope so,’ said Cole, answering her question.

There was something in Cole’s tone which made her eyes fly open. She didn’t really like surprises unless she was in charge of them. But it was about time she learned to trust him implicitly. He would only ever have her best interests at heart, wouldn’t he?

Chapter 33

Nell

'*Kochanie*, I was passing, and I saw the light on.' Irena didn't wait to be asked in, but kissed both Nell's cheeks and bustled past her.

'What a nice surprise,' Nell replied, pressing herself against the wall, out of her mother-in-law's way.

She'd barely even unpacked the car and Irena had already appeared on the doorstep. Her ability to gauge when she and Olek were in was uncanny. It was often the way when they returned from a trip; no sooner was the first load of post-holiday washing in the machine than she would turn up with milk, a home-made cake and an update on any local goings-on that they might have missed. Nell sometimes wondered if Irena had hidden cameras set up somewhere and monitored their every move.

If Olek were here, they'd be exchanging amused looks. But he wasn't, and the house felt echoey and sad without him. Secretly, she was glad that her mother-in-law had, quite by chance, been in the neighbourhood.

'Bruhhhh!' Irena set down her handbag and some foliage wrapped in newspaper, peeled off her coat and rubbed her arms. 'This house is like my grandmother's farm in the country: dark and cold. Why is the heating not on, or the Christmas lights?'

Nell had shivered just like that only a few moments earlier. Was this going to be her future, coming home to a dark, cold house, night after night? Although, as she didn't have a job anymore, technically, there'd be no evening return from anywhere. *Every cloud* . . . she thought wryly.

'I only arrived from my parents' twenty minutes ago.' Nell closed the front door and followed Irena into the kitchen. She stretched and rubbed the small of her back, which ached after the car journey.

Irena touched the kettle with the back of her hand. 'Cold. You must need tea. You sit down, I make it.'

Nell had phoned her in-laws and let them know she'd gone home to spend time with her own parents, as they were going to be away for the Christmas season. But she still didn't know what Olek had told them about his whereabouts.

Nell gladly took a seat at the kitchen island. Walking into the empty house had shaken her. It wasn't just about the temperature, or the Christmas decorations; the very heart of the home was missing. And that, she thought, clamping her bottom lip between her teeth to stop it wobbling, was the love and laughter between her and Olek. And the sad fact was that things had been strained between them for longer than Nell cared to admit. She could pinpoint the moment exactly: the day they'd decided to seek help with their fertility journey.

Irena clattered spoons and mugs and jolted Nell out of her thoughts.

'So, it's lovely to see you. To what do I owe the pleasure?' Nell asked.

'I need to know how many for dinner on Christmas Eve,' Irena said with a pout. 'I've asked Olek, but he still hasn't said. Huh, boys.'

Christmas Eve at Nell's in-laws was taken very seriously and followed Polish traditions. It was raucous and fun, with mountains of delicious food, always served with plenty of booze. No matter how insistent Nell was that she be allowed to contribute something for the table, the answer was always no.

'The recipes are from our families in Poland,' Gienek had told her once. 'My mother's, my grandmother's, and so on. Same for Irena. Britain has been a wonderful home to us, but our hearts will always belong to Poland,' adding with a pat to his lean stomach, 'and our bellies!'

'Boys indeed,' Nell replied faintly. If only Irena knew.

'Gienek has ordered the fish already.' Irena rolled her eyes. 'We will have to hope it is big enough. I will not have my family going hungry at Christmas.'

'I doubt that would ever happen in your house,' Nell said, glad that the noise of the kettle was giving her an excuse not to answer Irena's question for a moment.

'So?' Irena poured water into two mugs and stirred vigorously. 'Are you and Olek trying to tell me that you won't be with us this Christmas, is that it?'

'No, no,' Nell protested. 'That's not it at all. I just . . . Olek's been so busy that we haven't had time to talk about it, that's all. And you know that Max has his football match in Liverpool on Christmas Eve, so by the time they are back, it will be late.'

Irena waved her concerns away. 'We can wait.' She set down mugs of tea on the table and climbed onto the stool beside Nell with a grunt. 'We always eat after coming back from Mass anyway.'

'True.' Nell cast her mind back to the first Christmas she'd spent with Olek and his family. So different to her own family's Christmas, which generally arrived in a hamper from Fortnum & Mason and was designed to have maximum wow factor and minimum effort. She'd been bewildered but beguiled by the Dowmunts and had escaped to the bathroom to message Merry about how much she loved it as soon as the chance had arisen. 'I'm looking forward to your *pierogi*, *kochanie*.'

She'd learned a few words of Polish but was usually too nervous to use them. *Kochanie* was a term of endearment which could mean anything from sweetie to darling, and Irena loved it when she used it.

'Ahh, *córunia*. I'm glad.' The older woman cupped a hand around Nell's face and studied her. 'The smile has gone from your eyes. I am worried about you.'

Córunia meant daughter. Nell swallowed hard. She couldn't bear to lose these people from her life. She just couldn't. She'd already lost Merry, who'd listened to the voicemail she'd left on the day of Ray's funeral but not acknowledged it.

'You know what my mum is like,' she joked, 'I love her, but I always come home exhausted from . . .' The excuse was so weak that she couldn't even conjure up the end of the sentence and Irena saw straight through her.

'Nell, where is Olek?' her mother-in-law asked.

Nell willed her cheeks not to flush. 'He's taken a few days off. He needed a break.'

Irena narrowed her eyes. 'Without you?'

'Hard to believe, I know,' she replied, attempting a smile.

'What is hard to believe is that you were not at the funeral for Merry's father. Astrid told me.'

'It's complicated.' Nell buried her head in her hands, willing her phone to ring, or carol singers to come to the door, anything to get her out of this conversation.

'Okey-dokey.' Irena's tone changed; she was clearly about to get tough. She folded her arms. 'Enough of the fairy tales. You at your parents, Olek away by himself. Neither of you going to the funeral. What has happened?'

'Nothing much,' Nell protested weakly.

'You are like a daughter to me. I care about you as much as Olek.' Irena patted her arm, then paused. 'Well, almost as much. If you were to split up, I would have to be on his side. I hope you understand, but family is family. He will always be my son.'

'I understand.' On any other occasion, Nell would be struggling to hold back a snigger at that point. But now, with the very real possibility that Olek had left her for good, her words felt too prophetic to hold any humour.

'Is this . . . Could this be about . . .' Irena faltered and rubbed her neck awkwardly.

In all the years Nell had known her, she'd never seen her mother-in-law stuck for words. 'What?' she prompted.

'Mumps?' Irena looked at her from under her lashes. 'Is this something to do with Olek having mumps when he was a boy? And babies?'

There was a pounding in Nell's chest. Now what was she going to do? She couldn't betray Olek's confidence; she'd already let him down in so many ways. 'You've lost me,' she said, attempting a laugh.

Irena gave her a stern look and Nell felt her face heat up. She wasn't going to get away with bluffing, she could tell.

'Olek is a proud man, but with his mama, he is sometimes still the little boy who sat on my knee for a cuddle when his English friends laughed at his accent, and who cried in my arms when he found out Yvonna had cheated on him. And . . .' Irena stared into her mug. 'And who confided in me that you and he wanted to have a baby, but that it wasn't working, so you needed to see a doctor.'

'He told you?' Nell stared at her, processing this, not knowing how to respond, or how much to say. He hadn't told her that, but it made her love him more, knowing that it was important enough to him to want to share with his mother.

Irena gently reached for Nell's hand. 'He did. I'd hoped that you'd be able to tell me too, but I respect that we are all different. And I'm sorry you are going through this, I really am.'

Nell swallowed a lump in her throat. 'Me too. It has been very difficult to stay positive, especially when Merry got pregnant.'

'In your shop that night, when someone said that mumps could lead to infertility, I was watching you,' said Irena softly. 'You looked as if someone had knocked the wind from your lungs. When I asked Olek about your results, he wouldn't tell me. But that evening, it all fitted together.'

'That was the night I fell out with Merry too. I was so angry with her for not keeping her baby safe. Climbing up that stupid ladder when she was supposed to be taking it easy.'

Nell's arms slid forward onto the kitchen island, and she let her head drop again. She was so weary, so heavy with emotion.

'Merry does not have a mother to talk to about having a baby.' Irena began to stroke Nell's hair. It was very comforting and soon Nell felt the tension melt from her shoulders. 'That, I think, is at the root of her fears. You have a mother and a mother-in-law who love you. And I am here if you want to talk.'

Nell lifted her head. Irena's gaze was soft, her eyes misty with unshed tears. She was lucky to have this woman in her life. Perhaps if she told Olek's mother the truth, between them they'd be able to get Olek to come home?

'I always thought that I would be the one to have fertility issues,' she began, 'especially as Olek already had Max . . .'

For the next ten minutes, she found herself confiding in her mother-in-law, expressing her worst fears about their marriage and confessing her regret about her friendship with Merry. 'It feels as if my entire life has derailed. Merry doesn't want to know me, and I don't know where my husband is.' She shook her head in disbelief. 'These last few weeks have shown me how quickly life can pivot from dream to nightmare. Everything I was looking forward to: watching Max succeed at football, seeing Merry bring her baby into the shop, and then Olek and I welcoming a child of our own into the world . . . it's all gone.'

Irena shook her head. 'It hasn't gone. But it will take a little effort from you and those around you.'

She smiled sadly. 'People only make an effort if they think it's worth it. Merry isn't speaking to me and Olek . . .' She sighed. 'He still hasn't forgiven me. I wish I knew where he was, then I could go to him and tell him how much I love him and want him home.'

'Take heart, *kochanie*, you are worth it.' Olek's mother took Nell's hand in hers. 'Tell me to mind my own business, but I might be able to make him come home. He might listen to me.'

Nell smiled weakly. 'Please try.'

'OK, first I call him.'

Irena pulled out her phone and dialled. Once his voicemail kicked in, she let rip with a torrent of Polish that Nell didn't need to be able to translate to understand; his mother was giving him a piece of her mind and Nell couldn't help but be in awe of her.

‘Give him twenty-four hours and he will be back,’ said his mother smugly. ‘His uncle has a cabin in Scotland. Olek used to love it there. I think that’s where he’ll be.’

‘I hope so,’ said Nell meekly. She had missed out a few vital details about the reason Olek had been so angry with her; she was only human, after all, and didn’t want Irena to think too badly of her.

‘And when he does, talk to him.’ Irena gave her a pointed look. ‘Men are simple creatures; they like straightforward information. Tell him what you feel about having a family.’

‘But what if I don’t know myself?’ Nell shrugged.

Irena’s face softened. ‘You know. You just haven’t allowed yourself to think about it properly yet.’

‘Thank you.’ Nell squeezed Olek’s mum’s hand. She wasn’t quite sure what Irena had meant, but she hoped it would become clear.

‘I’d better go home, Gienek will be waiting to eat dinner.’

‘Have you got to cook it first?’

Irena smirked. ‘He is cooking. We got the rules sorted early on. One night a week is date night, and nobody cooks. Then one night a week, plus one day at the weekend, he’s in the kitchen – it has worked for more than forty years.’

‘You two have got life sussed.’ Nell smiled. ‘And what do I do about Merry?’

‘Do you want to go for the rest of your life without being friends again, eh?’ Irena chided.

‘No, definitely not!’ She shuddered at the thought. ‘Not if I can help it.’

‘In that case.’ Irena regarded her for a long moment. ‘You do whatever it takes, Nell. Whatever.’

‘Good advice, thank you.’ Nell helped her on with her coat.

'Oh, you take this.' Irena handed her the foliage wrapped in newspaper she'd arrived with. 'Mistletoe. A big bunch. You will enjoy it more than Gienek and I will.'

'Thank you. Fingers crossed I get to kiss Olek under it.'

Irena kissed her cheek. 'You will – trust me, you will.'

Nell waved her off from the front door and turned to go back inside. Her mother-in-law was right, the house was looking dark and unloved. She'd ignore her unpacking for now and put her energy into turbocharging her Christmas decorations, starting with hanging mistletoe with red ribbon in every room.

Within thirty minutes, she was finished, and the house was transformed. She stood back and admired the bunch of mistletoe above their bed. Providing Irena's words did the trick and brought him home, she and Olek were in for a lot of fun.

Tomorrow, while she waited for him to return, she'd go shopping for Merry and the baby. And then, armed with a peace offering, she'd visit her best friend and grovel like crazy until they were on speaking terms again. Because it was already December the twenty-second and Christmas without Merry didn't feel like Christmas at all.

Chapter 34

Merry

Merry hadn't yet opened her eyes, but she could hear noises downstairs. Cole's side of the bed was already cold; he must have been up for a while. The last time she'd checked, it was only six-thirty. Perhaps she'd drifted off and had another two hours' sleep. She hoped so. It was Saturday, Woody was working at the shop, assisted by Harley, and neither she nor Cole had to be anywhere or do anything.

Tomorrow was Christmas Eve. The presents were wrapped, the house was decorated, and the last bits of food shopping were all done. The children would arrive tomorrow and then their last Christmas as a family of four would begin properly. And next week Cole would take her in to hospital for her induction appointment. Her hospital bag was packed with her clothing and toiletries, plus an even larger pile for the baby. Impossibly tiny nappies, the cutest vests with envelope shoulder poppers, and a few pastel-coloured babygros in the softest jersey imaginable. As she'd folded them into a pile, she'd had to pinch herself. These things were for her child, her baby.

She'd go into hospital as a pregnant woman and come out carrying her own baby in her arms. A mother, a parent to a tiny human who'd be entirely dependent on her. She felt a tightening across her chest and forced herself to relax. The baby was going to be born, come what may, there was no use worrying about it.

Relaxing was easier said than done. She formed a huge mound under the duvet now and had to sleep with a pillow underneath her knees to prevent her back from aching. Last night while she was in the bath, Cole had reminisced about the time he and his sister had seen a dead whale washed up on a beach. He'd sworn blind that it was pure coincidence that that particular memory had popped into his head. She wasn't so sure. Anyway, not long now. Her stomach felt as tight as a drum.

'But don't come out today, please, baby,' she murmured. 'Hang on until after Christmas.'

Through the open bedroom door, she heard Cole whistling and slow and steady footsteps coming up the stairs. She hitched herself up the bed, hoping he was bringing tea with him.

Cole entered their bedroom with two mugs and set them on the nightstand beside her. 'Your morning tea, madam.'

'And that is why I married you,' she replied, picking up one of the mugs and sipping it. 'Ah, perfect.'

He was wearing his coat and when he perched on the edge of the bed next to her, she felt the cold radiating off him. He'd brought the smell of the outdoors in with him: fresh cold air and wood smoke.

He kissed her, cold lips and warm breath against her mouth, and she lifted her hand to his face, enjoying the roughness of his morning stubble.

'And that,' he said, parroting her tone, 'is just the start of today's many treats. You need to get up as soon as you've drunk your tea. We've got somewhere to be, and it's been snowing, so the roads will be slippy.'

Merry beamed. 'Snow! Is there a lot? Enough for sledging?'

He almost choked on his tea. 'If you think I'm going to let you get the sledge out, you must be barmy.'

She laughed. 'Darling, even I would draw the line at flying downhill in this state. I was thinking about the kids.'

'I never know with you.' He grinned. 'And that's why I married you. There isn't much snow yet, but enough to slow down the traffic, which means we need to get moving.'

He opened the curtains so she could see the snow on the window frames, and she clambered out of bed for a better look.

'So pretty,' she said, leaning against him.

Hedges were hidden under white blankets, lamp posts had snowy hats and trees wore wintry layers on their branches. Spirals of smoke billowed from the chimney pots of neighbouring cottages and if it weren't for the cars on driveways, Merry could be looking at a scene from the Victorian age.

The driveway to Holly Cottage was the only one which had been cleared and both of their vehicles were snow-free too. Cole had clearly been busy while she'd been lazing in bed.

'More like pretty annoying,' he replied. 'The gritters never do the smaller lanes that really need it; if the temperature drops too much, the roads will be thick with ice. Scotland has had it really bad, some of the roads are closed completely.'

She gave him a bemused look. He was slightly obsessed with the weather, always kept an eye on it. His favourite was the shipping forecast; he'd memorised all the regions around the UK and tuned in religiously to the BBC to listen. 'Why the interest in Scotland, we're not going there, are we?'

He wrapped an arm around her waist. 'Not likely. No, our destination is much closer to home, but it's you who's going somewhere, I'm just your chauffeur. Emily suggested that I booked you a day at the Enchanted Spa to help you relax. So that's what I've done.'

'No way! Oh, darling, that's so sweet of you.' Merry was touched, remembering her conversation with Emily about Frankie Goes to Hollywood and discovering the shared memory they had of Dad. 'I've always wanted to go there. Nell and I have talked about spending a day there . . .' She sighed. 'Anyway, it'll still be lovely. Ooh, perhaps Emily is free to join me.'

Her younger sister deserved a treat as much as her and it would be good to spend some quality time together.

'Emily's busy today with Will,' said Cole. 'I'd already suggested it.'

'Oh.' She wracked her brains trying to remember if Emily had said she was doing something; she'd only seen her yesterday. 'I'll text her to thank her then.'

'Good plan.' Cole kissed her cheek. 'Do it from the car later. Emily also told me to book you a special pregnancy massage, which I've done. And there is a sleep room and plenty of sofas to curl up and relax on.'

Merry sighed with pleasure. 'This sounds absolutely blissful. Thank you, darling.'

'You're welcome,' he smiled smugly. 'Oh and I nearly forgot, slide your hand under my pillow, there's something for you.'

She gave him a mischievous look. 'This isn't one of your special surprises, is it?'

When they'd first got together, she'd told him how much she loved cherries and the next night he'd hidden a bottle of cherry-scented massage oil under her pillow and, once she'd found it, proceeded to massage her with it. Since then, hidden-under-the-pillow had become a part of their love lexicon, ranging from new pyjamas to edible bras and chocolate body butter.

'I'm saying nothing.' Cole grinned. 'Except that you look very sexy when you do that smile.'

She bent over the bed, steadying herself with one hand and sliding her other hand underneath his pillow. 'You did this on purpose, didn't you, so you could peer up my nightie?'

'I'm not complaining, that's for sure. Shame looking is the only thing on the menu since your waters broke. Especially as, according to our antenatal lady, sex is one of the things you can do to bring on labour.'

'I'd rather not bring on labour today, thank you very much. Not now I've got a massage booked.' She pulled out a package from under his pillow. Inside was a pair of white slippers as soft as clouds. 'Oh how gorgeous! I'll be floating on air in these.'

'Like a dainty little fairy,' said Cole. 'And not at all like a whale.'

She gave him a look that silenced him instantly.

'Whoops. I should have stopped at fairy, shouldn't I?' He slapped a hand to his forehead so comically that she couldn't help but laugh.

'Correct.' She put her hospital bag on the bed and unzipped it.

'What are you doing?' Her husband looked horrified. 'It took me ages to get you to pack that.'

'Don't panic, I'll take the things out and put them back in tonight.' Merry started to empty it. 'All I need today is a few toiletries and a snack or two, maybe my book.'

'It's a luxury spa. The place will be full of free toiletries and there's a café for snacks. Please, Merry, do not unpack your bag, I won't be able to relax all day,' he pleaded.

'Just stuff your book and a spare pair of knickers in your handbag. That's all you need.'

She suppressed a smile at his earnest expression, quite touched by how nervous he seemed despite being far more experienced at childbirth than she was. She leaned forward until her tummy was touching his, and kissed him. 'Fine. If it makes you happy, I'll survive without my holdall.'

He blew out a breath. 'Thank you. Now . . .' He checked the time. 'All I've got to do is get you there by nine. So get your skates on. To clarify, that's a turn of phrase, not an order.'

'Spoilsport. Can I have some Marmite on toast to eat in the car please?'

'Coming up.' He gave her one last squeeze before leaving the bedroom and jogging down the stairs.

Merry sighed. A day to laze around, relax and not to have to talk to a soul. After the stress of losing her dad and then attending the funeral, this was just what she needed. Absolute bliss.

Chapter 35

Nell

Nell made her third strong coffee of the morning; it wasn't even half past eight. Probably not a good idea, given that she was jumpy enough without the help of caffeine. But she'd been ready for ages, and it gave her something to do. The simple act of waiting for the machine to pour the espresso into her warmed mug, then frothing milk, served as a distraction. She looked at the time again. Only three minutes had elapsed since she'd last looked. She removed her mug from the coffee machine and walked through to the front room, where she could keep an eye on the drive. Her stomach was in knots. She hadn't been this nervous since her first date with Olek years ago.

She flicked on the Christmas tree lights and while she sipped her coffee, she allowed her mind to wander back to the last first date she'd ever had. Olek had picked her up from her flat and taken her to the cinema to see a James Bond film. They'd arrived a bit early, so he'd bought her a drink in the bar before the film. She'd asked for Prosecco and then worried that he'd think she was being extravagant. He'd returned with their drinks, choosing a cola for himself, as he was driving. She'd reached for hers, but nerves had made her clumsy and she had managed to knock the whole thing over onto her skirt and his jeans. The glass smashed and they'd both got soaked. She'd jumped up to buy herself another, apologising profusely, only to catch his cola with the cuff of her jacket, and knocking that over too. She'd been mortified. There had been so much liquid and broken glass that they'd had to abandon their table altogether while scowling staff stomped over to clean up. After that, there hadn't been enough time to buy more drinks, so after dabbing their wet clothes with napkins, they'd chosen snacks – salty popcorn for him, chocolate-covered peanuts for her – and gone straight into the theatre.

'These were the only free seats together,' he'd told her sheepishly, ushering her into the back row.

Would he try to kiss her during the film? she'd wondered; she hoped so. The thought had made her fluttery with anticipation, so much so that she'd opened her chocolate a little too vigorously, sending a shower of small chocolate balls into the air and clattering down under the row in front of them. 'I'm not normally this clumsy,' she'd said with a squeak, sinking deep into her seat with embarrassment.

By comparison, Olek had seemed completely calm and composed, he'd simply assured her it was no problem and risen from his seat. She wouldn't have blamed him if he'd done a disappearing act at that point, but he'd returned moments later with another bag. No hint of first-date nerves there. Daniel Craig, playing James Bond, and whom both Merry and Nell had massive crushes on, didn't come anywhere close to Olek. He was so handsome. She'd kept sneaking glances at him, and afterwards couldn't remember any of the film. She did remember wondering how difficult it would be to learn Polish to impress him (*very* difficult, it transpired; her vocabulary was still pitifully small). *A real man*, she remembered describing him as to Merry the next day. Ten years her senior and already with a son he adored and an ex-wife he tolerated, but for her that only added to his maturity. He was a proper adult, looking for a proper relationship.

'Makes a change,' Merry had quipped, not unreasonably. Nell's taste up until that point was men with boyish looks and immature behaviour to match. Merry's least favourite was the irrefutably pretty Jez, who spoke in a baby voice and liked to snuggle with his head in Nell's lap.

'You need a man, not a cat,' Merry had said about him. Right as ever.

Invariably, the men she dated couldn't drive either, so Nell would be the designated driver. Olek, on the other hand, had a car *and* a van, and had insisted on picking her up for their dates, seeing her home safely and even opening the car door for her. Even now, he would always offer to pick her up from wherever she was. He'd always cared, she thought, he'd always been so thoughtful.

And soon, his van – a different one these days – would be pulling up onto the drive of their home. Still thoughtful, still caring about her despite the tricky last few weeks.

She checked again; only five minutes to go before he was due. She should have one last nervous wee. The last thing she wanted was for their reunion to be marred by her bladder. She darted back to the kitchen to deposit her mug and ran upstairs to the bathroom.

Goodness knows what Irena had said to Olek yesterday, but it had worked. No more than an hour after her mother-in-law had left, she'd received a message from him inviting her to go to a spa with him. An invitation which had sent her spirits soaring; she'd accepted straight away, naturally.

She couldn't wait to see him. She was never, ever going to let them spend this much time apart again. She'd taken their relationship for granted, she saw that now. Well, no more. Olek Dowmunt wasn't going to know what had hit him. She caught sight of herself in the bathroom mirror and smiled at her reflection. For the first time in almost a month, her eyes were bright, her skin flushed, and her cheeks were almost aching from smiling in anticipation of his arrival.

Last night, she'd slept better than she had in almost two weeks. And now she was up early. She'd washed her hair and scrunch-dried it gently, so it was extra wavy. He'd never been able to resist her auburn curls. And she was wearing a bit of make-up. The truth was that she hadn't loved herself enough recently to bother paying any attention to her appearance. Today, she wanted Olek to take one look at her and fall in love with her all over again. A scruffy bun and a blotchy face wouldn't cut it.

Nell washed her hands, pulled out her phone and checked Olek's text message from yesterday one more time.

> Spa day booked for tomorrow at the Enchanted Spa, be ready to be picked up at 8:30. Make sure you take a swimsuit and a book, although you might not need that. This is a day for relaxation and chatting.

Relaxation and chatting; precisely what they needed.

Just reading the message again made her stomach do a loop-the-loop. It didn't sound like the sort of thing he'd normally say, but perhaps he'd copied and pasted it from an email. She'd replied to thank him and that she couldn't wait. He hadn't messaged again, but she didn't mind; the fact that he'd organised this for them both was more than enough.

She sighed happily and went through to their bedroom. She'd always wanted to go to the Enchanted Spa. She and Merry had talked about it, but as they worked together, it was difficult to both have time off. Now, though, she'd be able to enjoy it for the first time with the man she loved.

A whole day together in luxurious, beautiful surroundings. So much better than being at home. They'd be able to talk about everything that had gone wrong between them. She'd tell him why she hadn't told him the truth about the test results and how much she loved him and that nothing else mattered other than for them to be together. And that from now on, she'd never keep anything from him.

She checked her bag: swimsuit, toiletries, outfit for an exercise class (unlikely she'd do any exercise, but if he fancied going to the gym, she might be tempted), and good bra and knickers. He might not get to see them while they were there, but he would when they got home. She looked up at the bunch of mistletoe above their bed and grinned. She'd nearly put her back out hanging that up. At least it looked like the effort had been worth it. He was going to love it. Despite being a big burly man, he was a softie at heart and very romantic. This bed hadn't seen much romance recently; she'd been too sad about not being able to have a baby with him, too worried about harbouring secrets. Still, she thought, today was a fresh start. By the time they came back tonight, she was confident that things would be back to normal. And she couldn't wait.

At exactly half past eight, she heard the rumble of an engine pull up onto the drive. She pressed a hand to her chest. It was just as fluttery as it had been on that first date.

He was here.

Of course he was. Olek was always punctual, always reliable. He'd never once let her down in all the years they'd been together. He was still the man she'd married: loving, handsome, caring. She'd bruised his heart these past few weeks, and now he was giving her the chance to repair the damage. She could almost weep with relief. She couldn't wait to hold him, feel his arms around her, press her face against his.

With fluttering fingers, she put on her coat, picked up her bag and flung open the front door, a sob already bubbling up in her throat.

But what she saw completely threw her. Olek's van wasn't on the drive. Instead, there was a car parked there. And sitting at the wheel wasn't the man she'd longed to see, but Emily, looking rosy-cheeked and nervous.

Nell's first thought was for Merry. She blinked away her tears of disappointment and dashed to the car as Emily climbed out, wearing jeans and a hoodie with paint splatters on the front of it. It looked as if she'd got dressed in a hurry. 'What's happened? Is Merry all right?'

'Merry is fine.' Emily said calmly. 'Don't worry. I'm here to pick you up, that's all.'

'What for?' Nell shook her head, confused.

'For your spa day,' said Emily, frowning. 'Didn't Olek tell you?'

'Yes, but . . .' Nell stared at her. But Olek had said . . . No, this couldn't be right.

She fumbled for her phone and read the message to herself. She felt her face flame with embarrassment. He hadn't actually said he was coming. She felt like such a fool. She'd been so looking forward to spending the day with him that she'd read what she wanted to read.

'Come on, hop in. All will be revealed,' said Emily brightly.

Bewildered, Nell did as she was told. What on earth was going on? Where was Olek? If this was someone's idea of a joke, she wasn't finding it very funny.

Chapter 36

Olek

Olek used the sleeve of his shirt to wipe condensation from the window of his uncle's cabin and stared outside at the snow, his heart sinking. Bloody hell. The branches of the tree sagged under the weight of last night's snowfall, and there must be at least a foot of fresh snow on the van roof. The plan had been to start the journey south last night. He'd cleared the snow away from the van and sprinkled salt around the wheels to keep it from freezing, but when he'd checked the traffic news, there'd been so many delays and road closures that he'd decided to wait until this morning.

Now he wasn't sure if he'd made the right decision. His mum was going to kill him if he didn't get home. He gave a bark of laughter; forty-seven years old and still worried about what his mother was going to say.

He checked his phone again: no signal. The mobile mast must still be down. Shit. The last message he'd had was from Nell yesterday, about the day out Cole and Emily had organised. It was obvious she'd got the wrong end of the stick and thought he would be going with her. It was his fault entirely; he should have been clearer. But it had felt awkward messaging her with frivolous details of a spa day after not speaking to her about the major issues they were going through. The trouble was that he didn't know what Nell had told people about the state of their marriage, and didn't want to create any problems for her. So when Emily had asked him to make sure Nell would be prepped and ready by eight-thirty, he hadn't wanted to admit that two days before Christmas Eve he wasn't even at home with his wife. Which was where he wanted to be. Very much.

God, he missed her. He missed the way she felt in his arms, her head fitting just so underneath his chin. He hated waking up without her, he missed the little noises she made as she came to in the morning. He even missed having to make her first coffee of the day, just the right strength in just the right mug. He missed being in his own home, his own bed, and very much wanted their old life back. The one before all this baby stuff came along and turned everything upside down. Nell was his best friend. Even after years of marriage, she was still the person he wanted to hang out with more than anyone else. People talked about wanting to grow old with someone, but he loved the way he felt like a teenager when he was with her. They had fun, they laughed all the time, he could count the times they'd argued on one hand, and they had shared everything. Or so he'd thought.

He didn't understand why she hadn't just come out with the truth on the day Dr Bajek gave her the results. What had she achieved by pretending that it was her with the fertility problem? And then there was her termination. That had come out of the blue. She had been pregnant before, and in all their time together, she had not once thought it would be a good idea to tell him. But both of these things paled in importance when compared to the bigger issue. And that was Max. He would have got over the other things by now if he hadn't heard her tell Woody that she didn't think Max could be his son.

Olek felt sick to his stomach every time he remembered

hearing Nell's voice as he'd climbed the stairs to the Airbnb above the shop.

He must never find out.

Maybe he was unusual and other men would be fine with it, but he couldn't bear the shame of people knowing he was infertile. The pity on their faces when they put two and two together and realised that all these years, he'd been bringing up a boy who wasn't his.

He hated his own weakness. He hated his body for letting him down and all because of getting mumps as a kid. Mumps was a joke. It puffed your face up and made you feel like hell for a week or so. It wasn't supposed to ruin your life. But the thing Olek hated most of all was that he'd always had his suspicions about whether Max was his. He had managed to keep them at bay, never to examine them too closely. But now he couldn't avoid it any longer.

For years, Yvonna hadn't conceived, then one day she had changed, she had a new energy about her, a sparkiness to her behaviour, a reluctance to spend time alone with him. When she'd found out she was pregnant, it had healed their relationship for a time, and he'd pushed any niggling concerns to the back of his mind. Right up until he'd found her with Viktor, and it all came flooding back. He'd been humiliated and lost his confidence for a while, until he met Nell. Nell had made everything right in his world.

These last couple of weeks had brought those feelings of weakness into sharp focus again. But he knew what he needed to do.

Olek put the fire out, spreading the last few embers which still retained a glow from last night. He stuffed his remaining things into his bag, checked he hadn't left anything in the bathroom, and turned out the lights.

It was time to go home and face the music.

Chapter 37

Merry

When Cole turned down the long tree-lined driveway to the Enchanted Spa, Merry drew in an excited breath. It was snowing harder now, but ahead of them she could see the most beautiful country house, which, dusted with snow, looked absolutely magical.

'This is going to be wonderful,' she said, smiling at Cole. Even more wonderful had she had company, but it was understandable, Emily was bound to have other things to do so close to Christmas Day.

'I hope so, darling,' Cole replied, slowing down to manoeuvre the truck into a parking space right by the door.

A car passed by behind them as Merry opened the passenger door. She did a double take and then laughed. 'Gosh, I'm seeing things, I could have sworn that was Emily driving into the car park.'

She craned her neck for another look, but the car had turned the corner.

'Whoah, stay right there,' Cole yelled, running around to her side. His boots skidded in the snow, and he almost slid into her. 'Don't go anywhere by yourself, it's dangerous.'

'All right, keep your hair on,' she said with a giggle. 'Although I'd like to point out you just nearly knocked us both over.'

He grabbed her handbag from the footwell, slung it over his shoulder and then held her hand tight. 'I panicked. I'm under a lot of pressure today.'

She gave him a sceptical look. 'Care to elaborate on that?'

'Just you,' he spluttered. 'Dealing with my heavily pregnant wife in these conditions.'

'Fine,' she retorted, letting him lead her towards the revolving door. 'But less of the "heavily" please, I'm beginning to get a complex.'

'And I'm beginning to think I prefer you when you haven't had a good night's sleep; I can't keep up with you today.'

'Wowzers,' Merry breathed, turning a full circle as they stepped through the doors. The foyer of the spa oozed glamour and luxury, from the twinkling crystal chandeliers to the sparklingly clean marble floor. 'This is very fancy.'

'Glad you approve. Reception desk straight ahead,' said Cole, steering her forward.

There were already several other women checking in; Merry took a seat while Cole waited in the queue for her.

The Christmas decorations were the most extravagant Merry remembered ever seeing. Enormous festive floral arrangements adorned each end of the reception desk. Sprigs of spruce, trailing ivy, winter berries and velvety red roses spilled from vases and everywhere she looked, she saw red and silver bows woven through evergreen swags, wreaths and garlands, all plump with holly, mistletoe and eucalyptus. From hidden speakers came the gentle sound of Christmas music played on a harp. The whole effect was just as magical as the exterior.

The revolving doors started to turn again as someone else arrived and Merry suddenly found herself on her feet, her heart thumping with shock at the sight of her best friend. She glanced over at Cole and then back at Nell. This couldn't be a coincidence.

For a moment, she stood speechless, watching as Nell spun around exactly as she had, admiring her surroundings. It was so good to see her; if her limbs didn't feel quite so leaden, she'd have wanted to run to her and hug her tight. To hell with their argument, she just wanted her friend back.

Finally, Nell turned in her direction and noticed her.

'Merry!' she gasped, pressing a hand to her mouth. 'What the hell? What is going on?'

Merry took a step back, that wasn't quite the warm greeting she'd been expecting. 'I was about to ask you the same question.'

'Emily brought me,' Nell said, folding her arms. 'Have I been set up?'

Merry frowned; so it had been her sister she'd seen in the car park. She looked over at Cole, who appeared to be filling in a form and avoiding her eye.

'If you have, so have I,' Merry retorted, not knowing whether to be insulted or not.

Nell pinched the bridge of her nose and shook her head. 'Sorry, sorry. It's just today has not gone as planned.' Her voice broke. 'And I feel terrible.'

Merry's eyes welled up with tears. 'I feel terrible too. But at least you look amazing.' Nell looked very put together, hair falling in perfect soft waves, eyes framed with long lashes, cheeks pink and mouth glossy with nude lipstick.

Nell rubbed the back of her neck. 'Thanks. I thought I was meeting Olek, and I wanted to look my best, but hey ho. And so do you. I suppose you don't want a size-related compliment, but you look pretty amazing too. You look . . .' Nell's voice wavered. 'Ready to pop actually.'

'Let's hope I don't pop today.' Merry's hand went automatically to her stomach. She was so looking forward to her massage, mostly so she could legitimately lie down and escape from the world for an hour. Her earlier burst of energy was disappearing, and her back was really starting to ache. 'Because that would be extremely inconvenient.'

'I guess so,' said Nell, looking down at her feet.

The two of them smiled awkwardly and Nell cleared her throat.

This was awful, thought Merry. Normally, their chatter flowed as fast as a river into the sea after heavy rainfall, with both of them speaking so rapidly that one topic tumbled into another. But today, conversation was as dry as the desert. 'This is so weird, you and me struggling to know what to say.'

'Really weird,' Nell agreed, shoving her hands into the pouch pocket of her hoodie. It was her best Sweaty Betty one that Merry had bought for her last birthday. Nell loved it and had said it was almost too good to exercise in and she wanted to save it for best.

'Nell.' Merry swallowed a lump in her throat. The last couple of weeks had been hellish without her best friend. 'I've missed you.'

Nell nodded. 'I've missed you too and I'm so sorry about your dad.' She blinked tears from her eyes. Merry wanted to reach out and hug her, but Nell lowered her head, severing eye contact.

'Yes, me too,' Merry mumbled.

'At least we're agreeing on things today.' Nell gave a half-hearted laugh.

'Like we always used to.' Merry tried to match Nell's attempt at humour, but it felt false.

'I'm sorry,' they both blurted out at once.

They looked at each other and laughed in surprise.

Merry's heart lifted; it felt good to be with Nell. Perhaps they were going to be OK, she thought. As long as they could laugh again together, all might be well.

'This feels like the bit in Christmas movies when it starts to snow and the girl and the guy make up and he sweeps her off her feet,' Merry said.

'Don't expect *me* to sweep you off your feet,' replied Nell, 'I'll put my back out.'

'Rude.' Merry laughed.

'Give us a hug then,' said Nell, stepping forward and holding her arms out.

Merry stifled a sob. 'I've missed your hugs.'

'It's no easy task these days,' Nell groaned, trying to get close enough to get her arms around her.

'Again, rude!' said Merry with a snort, turning sideways to help her out.

'Oh, darling.' Nell pressed her cheek against Merry's. 'I feel so ashamed that I didn't know your dad had passed away for so long.'

'I sent you several messages.' Merry frowned; remembering how the WhatsApp messages had definitely been delivered. The notifications had said that they hadn't been read, but Merry had assumed that was wrong.

'I was so angry, I didn't open them. I . . .' Nell's chest heaved as if she was trying to hold back her tears. 'I'm a terrible friend, I know.'

Merry couldn't help but feel hurt. She didn't think she'd be able to ignore messages from Nell, regardless of how things had been left between them. Merry could have been ill, or could have given birth. How could Nell have not wanted to read them?

She opened her mouth to say this to her but thought better of it; their relationship was fragile enough right now. 'Let's talk about it later,' she said instead. 'We'll have plenty of time.'

Just then, Cole joined them, a sheaf of paperwork in his hands. He kissed Nell's cheek. 'Glad you could make it.'

'So you are behind this?' Merry's eyes widened. 'Why didn't you say?'

Cole put his arm around both of their shoulders. 'Emily and I concocted it between us. You two need to talk and where better than a spa?'

'It's a kind offer,' Nell gave him a thin smile, 'but I need to get hold of Olek and find out where he is. I'm not in the right frame of mind for this place today. Sorry.'

'Please stay, Nell,' Merry begged. 'It's been so long, and the baby will be here soon. I might not get another chance.'

Nell's face closed down completely and Merry realised her mistake.

'You stay and enjoy.' Nell wriggled out from under Cole's arm, taking her phone out of her bag. 'I'll call a cab.'

'You know what I want most for Christmas?' said Cole, catching hold of Nell's hand. 'I want the Merry and Nell show back in my life. I miss you. You two go together like . . . cheese and pickle, or Marmite and toast, apple pie and cream.'

'Someone didn't have enough breakfast,' Merry quipped. Nell conceded a tiny smile.

'Don't change the subject,' said Cole, steering them both towards the reception desk. 'The point is that it's unthinkable to separate classic double acts. And I don't think either of you really want to stay apart for ever. So why don't you both collect your gowns and your complimentary flip-flops and spend today together. Nell? What do you say?'

‘OK,’ she replied with a weary sigh. ‘I’ll stay.’

‘Well done, darling,’ Merry whispered in his ear.

‘You’re welcome,’ he replied, giving her a swift kiss. ‘Now have fun and try not to get into any trouble.’

‘I’ll try,’ she murmured, watching Nell out of the corner of her eye, who was typing furiously on her phone and brushing tears away with the back of her hand.

Poor Nell. Merry knew she had to find out what was going on between her and Olek and help put it right before Christmas Day and she only had a few hours to do it in.

You’ll have to wait, kiddo, she thought, caressing her bump as the baby flexed against her stomach muscles. For now, Nell was the priority; she didn’t have time to give birth.

Chapter 38

Nell

Nell was conflicted. it was good to be with Merry again. and she was grateful to Cole and Emily for giving them the chance to get their friendship back on track. But she hadn't gotten over the disappointment of not seeing Olek yet. And, on top of that, the Snow was getting quite thick and having the responsibility for a pregnant woman, this close to Christmas, was not one to be underestimated.

'Hello, ladies, welcome to the Enchanted Spa,' said the woman behind the desk. Her name badge identified her as Bernice. She offered them a drink from a tray of steaming glass mugs. 'Non-alcoholic festive punch.'

They both accepted one and Nell sipped hers straight away, wishing that there was an alcoholic version.

She had messaged Olek from Emily's car, letting him know that she'd misunderstood him and that she was sad he hadn't come home to see her. Should she have kept her thoughts to herself? Would he think she was nagging him? She let out a sigh; too late now. And besides, not telling him the truth had got her in this mess in the first place; surely it made sense to start being honest?

She checked her phone again in case he'd replied to her messages since she'd last looked, but she didn't seem to have any signal. She clenched her teeth; so much for a day of relaxation, she was going to be on tenterhooks until he replied.

Merry sniffed her drink. 'This smells of mulled wine.'

They pulled a face at each other, as memories of bygone Christmases and terrible hangovers came to mind.

'Not for me this year,' said Merry.

'Nor me,' agreed Nell, who'd only just recovered from the night of the festive shopping event with Woody. Thinking of him, she made a mental note to send him a text to see how he and Spencer were getting on.

'You're already checked in,' said Bernice. 'Day guests, only, yes? You're not staying overnight?'

'It's my first wedding anniversary tomorrow, I think my husband might want me to come home,' Merry replied.

'Whereas my husband doesn't seem to be coming home for Christmas,' said Nell, her voice a little higher than normal, 'so I might be tempted.'

Bernice blinked nervously. 'Just let one of the team know if you'd like to reserve a room later.'

Merry laid a hand on Nell's arm. 'We're going to have a lovely day, OK? We're going to relax and stuff our faces with cake and – *oof* . . .' Her face contorted with pain and her fingers tightened around Nell's arm.

'You've gone into labour, haven't you?' she murmured. 'Trust you to wait until Cole drove off.'

'No!' Merry insisted firmly. 'They are Braxton Hicks. I just need a sit-down and a cuppa. Honestly!' she added, looking at Bernice, who seemed to have lost her serene smile all of a sudden.

'In that case, I recommend the cinnamon buns from our café,' said Bernice, clearly not entirely comfortable with the way Merry was leaning on her desk for support. 'But save room for your lunch at one o'clock. Any questions?'

'Is there a code for the Wi-Fi, for my friend?' Merry asked.

Nell stopped waving her phone around in search of an extra bar of signal to listen.

Bernice shook her head. 'We actively encourage you to switch off your phones while you're here. It allows you to be more present and it's more relaxing for our other guests without the sound of phones ringing. Leave the busy world behind for a few hours, it'll still be there when you go home, I promise.'

'I don't want to leave the world behind.' No Wi-Fi? Nell stared at her in dismay. What if Olek was trying to get hold of her? Or Max? And she still hadn't been able to let Irena know how many there would be for dinner tomorrow. Although if Olek didn't show up, there was no way she was going to his family home without him. Even if that meant staying at home on her own, at Christmas . . . She couldn't even turn up at her parents' house last minute, they had already left for their cruise. She could cry; this had the makings of the worst Christmas of her entire life.

'I do,' said Merry, with feeling. 'For a few hours, I want to be the old me. The one that people look in the eye instead of in the stomach, swiftly followed by a raft of personal questions, starting with "boy or girl?" and ending with "can I touch it?" No, love. No, you can't.'

Nell noticed the tight set of Merry's jaw. It looked like both of them needed to chill out today.

'Great. Well, the Enchanted Spa will offer you the privacy you deserve.' Bernice attempted a nervous smile.

'But what about emergencies?' Nell asked, still worried about her lack of signal.

Bernice looked over her shoulder and lowered her voice. 'If you head up right to the top of the car park, near the smokers' shelter, you might get a stronger reception.'

Nell looked outside. The snow was coming down heavily now, big fat flakes floating lazily onto the shrubs, lawn and statues in the landscaped garden in front of the building, and already her footsteps on the path were no longer visible. Cole drove a truck, Nell reminded herself; whatever happened, no matter how heavily it snowed, he would be able to get through. If Merry should go into labour, she would not be giving birth at the Enchanted Spa. Olek's van would be able to get through the snow too, she thought. There was still time for him to come home. She bit back a sob.

Oh, darling, please come home, wherever you are, please come home.

'I won't be going out there,' said Merry, 'emergency or not.'

'I'll have to,' Nell replied. 'I'll just have to hope it stops.'

'Forecast says this is in for the day,' said a man pushing a cart stacked high with fluffy towels.

'Freya and Harley will be thrilled; they've both wished for a white Christmas,' said Merry, her eyes sparkling.

'I'm just wishing I'll wake up with Olek beside me,' Nell said morosely.

'Of course.' Merry chewed her lip. 'We've got so much to catch up on.'

Nell gave her a brave smile. 'We have.'

'I'm sorry I haven't been there for you.' Merry touched her arm.

'There's no need to apologise,' she countered. 'I've been selfish, so wrapped up in my own problems that I neglected you when you needed a best friend.'

Bernice cleared her throat. 'Follow me, ladies, and we'll get your spa day started.'

She glided down the corridor ahead of them like a swan, thought Nell, taking Merry's bag and gown from her. Merry waddled and huffed, and Nell . . . well, she dragged herself along with the weight of the world on her shoulders. She should book in for a massage too, see if someone could remove the knots of tension from along her spine.

Merry leaned closer to her. 'Do you think if I had the baby here, they'd give me a free membership for life?' she whispered.

'I'd rather not find out, if it's all the same to you,' she replied.

'I could wallow in the jacuzzi and have a water birth,' Merry mused.

'I think you'd be more likely to get a bill for steam cleaning the pool than a life membership if you did that.'

Merry gave a snort.

'Hey. I've missed you very much,' said Nell.

'Same,' Merry smiled sadly. 'But we're here now.'

Nell squeezed her friend's hand. 'We are. Let's try to enjoy ourselves.'

'We should see who supplies their candles,' whispered Merry, sniffing a lit three-wick candle as they walked by one on a display table. 'The perfume of these are not a patch on ours.'

Nell winced; that was something else they needed to address. Did she really want to leave Merry and Bright for good? Would Merry even want her back? She'd abandoned Merry right before her baby was due, on the day that her father had died, and she'd only been back to the shop once to see Woody and flick through the post for anything important. She really was the worst of business partners, let alone friends.

'Mine, I mean.' Merry caught her eye. 'Sorry, I forgot for a moment.'

'Don't apologise,' Nell muttered, feeling wretched. 'It's me who should be doing that.'

Bernice showed them into the changing rooms and left them to enjoy their day.

While Merry disappeared off to the loo, Nell found them a free locker each and began to undress, smiling at two women who looked as if they'd just arrived too.

'I love Christmas,' said one. 'I put my tree up straight after Bonfire Night and leave it up until the end of January, I think we need a bit of sparkle after Christmas, cheer us all up on the dark nights when we're too poor to go out.'

'I know what cheers Paul up after Christmas,' said the other with a snigger. 'It's no coincidence that both of our kids were born in the ninth month of the year.'

'Guess what.' Her friend beamed. 'We're going to start trying in spring. So this time next year, I could be a mum.'

'Amazing!' said the other. 'I'm so happy for you. And if you hurry up, yours won't be much younger than my Milly.'

'How cool would that be!'

Both women squealed and threw arms around each other in celebration. Nell couldn't bear it. She picked up her things and moved to the other end of the changing room. This time last year, she'd thought she might be a mum by now too. But as it was, she wasn't even sure if she was still a wife.

She thought again about how happy she and Olek had been last year, and how quickly it had all gone wrong.

She couldn't do this. She couldn't keep up her brave face any longer. She sank down onto one of the wooden benches lining the changing room and started to cry.

'Come on,' said Merry softly, holding out Nell's gown for her to slip her arms into. 'Time to find those cinnamon buns. And if you're ready to talk, I'm ready to listen.'

*

Ten minutes later, they'd found a cosy sofa and were sitting toe to toe, sipping tea. And while they demolished pastries as large as their heads, Nell told Merry everything.

'So not only are we dealing with the disappointment of not being able to have children together, but Olek is having to reframe his relationship with the boy he'd always thought was his son. He adores Max and Max idolises his dad.' Nell dabbed at her tears. 'Olek, I mean. Yvonna has admitted that she was having an affair with Viktor when Max was conceived.'

Merry groaned. 'And I made it worse by blabbing to Olek about your termination.'

Nell lifted one shoulder. 'That was just one lie among many. I'm not sure he'll ever forgive me.'

'He will,' Merry promised. 'He's hurting right now, but he loves you. Give him time.'

Nell looked at her friend through eyes full of tears. 'I'm not so sure. I'd been so looking forward to Christmas. Max has got his big football game in Liverpool tomorrow, Irena and Gienek will be preparing their Christmas Eve feast. Olek and I should have been hanging our stockings by the fireplace and then trying to fill each other's without being spotted. Christmas was supposed to have been all about family and traditions, and spending quality time with the ones I love the most. And now . . . goodness knows what's going to happen. No baby, no family and possibly no Olek.'

'It will all work out,' said Merry, firmly. 'I really believe that. For you, for Olek, for Max . . . You've got a lot of love in your family and love is stronger than anything.'

'Do you think?' Nell blew her nose on her napkin and scrunched it up on her plate.

'I do. And . . .' She paused, chewing her lip. 'This might not be the right time to say this, but I think, given my circumstances—'

'Because you're pregnant?' Nell did her best to hide her envy, but obviously didn't quite manage it.

A waitress swooped by discreetly and took their empty plates.

'No,' said Merry, pointedly, 'because I was once in this position myself. What I was going to say was that there are many ways to be a parent other than simply giving birth. Olek is Max's dad, always has been. There's no reason for their relationship to change. There are many types of family unit, and there are thousands of children in this world who'd love the opportunity to call you and Olek "Mum and Dad".'

'Adoption, you mean?'

'It's a consideration, that's all I'm saying.' Merry held her hands up. 'Your consultant has talked through all the options with you, I'm sure.'

Nell pulled a face. 'Dr Bajek has offered, but how could I make an appointment for us when I'd told Olek it was me with the issues?'

'Then there's something positive to come out of all of this,' Merry pointed out. 'At least now the truth is out, you can move forward.'

'Moving forward.' Nell squeezed her eyes shut. 'Sounds so easy when you say it quickly. I'm not sure Olek is ready to move forward with me at all.'

'Oh, darling,' Merry tutted with sympathy. 'He will. I've never known a man love his wife as much as he does. He's got a lot to think about, but he'll be working his way back to you, I know it.'

Nell's eyes started to leak tears again and she put her hand into her bag and pulled out a packet of tissues.

Merry pointed at the carpet. 'You've dropped something.'

Nell reached down to retrieve what had fallen out of her bag. 'Oh yes, 'I picked up a few bits of post addressed to you last time I was in the shop. I meant to drop them round, but I shoved them in my bag and forgot all about them.' She put the envelopes in Merry's lap. 'Here you go.'

One envelope was handwritten. 'A Christmas card, by the look of it,' said Merry, tearing it open.

Nell took out a tissue and carefully dabbed under her eyes, so as not to smudge her mascara. Beside her, Merry's eyes grew wider and wider, her face paler and paler and her hands began to shake uncontrollably.

'Merry,' Nell sat forward, 'what is it?'

'I don't believe it,' Merry stared at her. 'I've got a letter from my mum.'

Chapter 39

Hilary

Dearest Merry,

In case you don't recall, I am a friend of Bernard's and you and I spent a few minutes talking in the ladies, bathrooms at Springwood House recently. I was very sorry to hear of your father's passing and send my condolences. It is a long time since I lost my own father, but I can vividly remember that for months afterwards I was aware that the space that he'd left in my life would never be refilled and I'd never again get to hear his laughter.

Apologies, one's supposed to fill these sorts of communications with uplifting and stirring advice, isn't one? Such as he will always be with you in your heart, et cetera. But wouldn't it be nice if we simply spoke our minds for once? For example, what I really want to say is that it's a damn pity that you're going through a bereavement when, judging by the number of damp tissues you'd amassed, you clearly had plenty on your plate already. Life, as someone more erudite than I said, is a bitch and then you die. Hey ho.

Now down to brass tacks, Merry.

I mentioned to you that I had worked in social services during my career. There were reams and reams of paperwork; every case for every individual filed in manila folders and ring binders, piles and piles of it, literally mountains of paper. Generally speaking, records were well maintained, although every system has its faults, we're only human after all. Therefore, every so often, one could come across a stray piece of paper with no evident home, and then it was the Devil's own job to track down its correct folder.

All sorts of cases went under my nose. Unspeakable sadness and unfathomable behaviour. So much so that I'm ashamed to admit that one had to become a little impervious to the hardship of others to do one's job, sleep at night and return refreshed the following morning to do one's job again. But, occasionally, I'd come across a document that permeated my tough outer shell and I couldn't shake from my mind. Something you said during our conversation jolted a memory from the past of one such document which reached in and touched my heart.

When I was heading up the computerisation of the council's records, I was tasked with tying up each case and sending each as a whole to be scanned. I was not supposed to leave stray papers loose and uncategorised. However, I came across a handwritten letter with no notes attached, and no way of identifying the author or intended recipient. All I could deduce was that it was written by a mother to her child, whom she referred to by her initial, 'M,'. It was a letter brimming with such love that at the time it brought me to tears. When you expressed your sadness at your mother not leaving you a note before taking her own life, the details of that letter and what I did with it came flooding back.

Since our meeting, I've been like a dog with a bone trying to locate the whereabouts of that letter, if indeed it still existed. I'm quite proud to say that I used somewhat dubious methods in my quest, so confident was I that it would be worth it. And, Merry, I am delighted to tell you that I found that letter. And not only that, but using your mother's name, and yours of course, I was able to track down the file that it should have been in all along. This meant that (by pulling a few strings – luckily, my young assistant is now very senior) the handwriting in the letter could be matched with a sample of Samantha Shaw's handwriting. Social services will be in touch with you through official channels in due course, but I felt that after all this time you deserved to see the letter as soon as humanly possible.

My dear Merry, please find enclosed a letter from your mother, I hope with all my heart that it brings you the peace you've been searching for.

Kind regards,
Hilary Burgess (Ms.)

December 1996

Dear M,

I don't know whether you'll see this when I'm gone or not. I hope so. Maybe you'll get it when you're eighteen. I don't know how these things work. That's me all over – I never know the answers.

And that's how I feel now – that I've run out of answers. I don't know how to be your mum; I only know that I love you and want the best for you. I've decided that the best is not with me.

My own mother hardly ever looked at me, did you know that? She had no interest in me at all; I'm not even sure if she loved me. I had four nannies at one point, each of them competing with me for her attention. I know I'll never be able to steer you safely through life. I haven't even managed to do that for myself. I'd have no chance doing it for someone else.

But I do love you, you must believe that. I'm not like my mum, I can hardly take my eyes off you. I look at you and my heart wants to burst, knowing that you're mine. Against all the odds, I made the most beautiful child and, whatever happens next for you, please know that I loved you with every cell of my body.

I'm sorry for everything. I am so sorry you ended up with me as your mother. You deserve better. Without me around to mess things up, I hope that's what you'll get. I hope you remember me with love, even though I've let you down. But I wouldn't blame you if you don't. Will you miss me? I wonder. The selfish part of me hopes you will, but I know that's not fair. Above all else, I want your life to be full of light and happiness.

I've hurt everyone who ever loved me, including your father, Ray. Remember Ray? He used to visit sometimes when you were little. But not anymore. I sent him away when I found out he had another family, another daughter. I hope he manages to make a go of it with them. He's a nice man. A bit flaky, but then who am I to talk?

My darling girl, I spoke to you on the phone last night. You were full of stories about the foster carers you're with. About the snake and feeding it with frozen chicks. The massive Christmas tree in the living room. It sounds so much better than here with me. You're having fun, part of a big family, living with a woman who is so good at being a mum that she looks after other people's kids too. I envy her. But I'm grateful to her too.

I'm getting sleepy now, M, so I'll say goodnight. Always remember how much I loved you, you'll carry a piece of my heart with you wherever you go.

Your loving mum xxxx

Chapter 40

Merry

'"I look at you and my heart wants to burst." That's what she said.' Merry had read the letter twice and her tears were coming so thick and fast she could barely see.

These words were never going to leave her. She already knew that by the end of today she'd be able to recite the entire letter from memory.

Her mum had written to her. She had thought of her. Merry had been on her mind in her final hours.

The more she processed this fact, the more she was able to unpick her own thoughts, about herself, her lovability, her self-doubts about her place in the world and about their mother-daughter bond. She wasn't quite sure why this letter held such power, such magic, but it did.

'That's so beautiful,' said Nell, a wobbly smile on her own face. 'I'm so happy for you.'

Nell moved seats so that she was next to Merry, who leaned into her friend, resting her head on Nell's shoulder, both letters still on her lap.

'She did love me. Nell, she *did* love me. Right up until the end. I thought she didn't love me enough to stay alive for me. This changes everything. She was a good mum, wasn't she?'

'She was.' Nell kissed the top of Merry's head. 'She was ill and didn't get proper help, that's all. It was never about whether she loved you or not.'

'I'm so sad that she felt I'd be better off without her in my life. How could I possibly have had a happier life without my mum?' Precious memories flashed in and out of her head of the good times the two of them had spent together: her mum reading to her in bed, dancing around their flat to ABBA, sipping hot chocolate on Christmas morning while she opened her presents. It was little things like these which filled her with joy, both then and now. She wished she could have told Sam that. 'No parent is perfect, no human is perfect. Maybe if I hadn't been away in foster care when she'd been so low that killing herself seemed the only option, maybe then she'd have felt responsible for me and she'd have stayed alive.'

Nell was quiet for a moment. 'As tempting as it is to go over these scenarios, I think it's better not to torture yourself with what might have been. It sounds like she had a rough time with her own mum, and didn't receive love. Despite that, she knew how to love you, with every cell of her body, she says. And she passed on that ability to love to you.'

Merry nodded. 'You're right, I know. Let's focus on the important things. Like my dad. She confirms that Ray is definitely my dad. That's . . .' She sighed happily. 'Such good news. Emily and I never wanted to take any tests, we were just happy to have found each other. We decided to be sisters regardless of genetics. But now it's really true, and Emily will be pleased. That's a lovely thing to discover. And it means this baby will have a proper auntie on my side of the family.'

Nell laughed softly. 'Does that mean I'm an improper auntie?'

'Of course.' Merry grinned. 'Everyone needs an improper auntie in their lives.'

'I'll always be there.' Nell squeezed Merry's shoulders. 'For this child of yours, and for you.'

'I know. We've been idiots. I'll be there for you too.' She looked down at the letter again. 'Oh, Mum, of course I love you, I have always remembered you with love. And there isn't a day goes by when I don't miss you.'

'I think she'd be so happy to see the sort of life you've got. And very proud. She'd love Cole, she'd have boasted to everyone about Merry and Bright and how smart her daughter is.'

Merry made a noise somewhere between a laugh and a sob. 'I remember feeding frozen baby chicks to that hideous snake. I used to have dreams that it would escape from its tank and get me. And she was right about the big Christmas tree, I was very envious. We'd only ever had a tiny one in our flat. But I hadn't met you then, I had no idea how posh Christmas decorations could be. The first time I saw your house at Christmas, I thought I was visiting the royal family.'

Nell cringed. 'I blame the TV documentary Mum watched once about Chatsworth House, she modelled herself on the Duchess from then on. And our annual photo shoot in front of the Christmas tree, in Christmas jumpers, remember those? Always when I had a big spot on my chin.'

'I do.' Merry looked at her friend fondly. 'I'm so glad that it's you here with me right now. No one else would understand how much finding this letter means to me. You've always been there. For all the big things in my life.'

'I'm honoured to be here, and this really is big. When we were at college together and you used to talk about your home life, I used to feel so guilty for moaning about my parents when you didn't have any. You were always so cheerful and brave, I was in awe of you.'

Merry raised her eyebrows. 'Of me? I was the one in awe of you, so confident and outgoing and sure of your place in the world.'

Nell snorted. 'You've got me all wrong. Remember that first day when we met in the cafeteria?'

'You bought far too much food and wanted me to share it?' Merry laughed.

'And you would only agree if I shared your banana.'

Merry shrugged. 'I hated any sort of charity; it made me feel inferior.'

Nell pulled a face. 'You could never be inferior. I'll let you into a secret: I only bought all that food as an excuse to come and talk to you.'

'What? Really?'

'Really.' Nell bit her lip, sheepishly. 'I had a bit of a girl crush on you; it was the only way I could think of to get to know you. I even agreed to eat a slice of your banana and I hated bananas with a passion.'

Merry gasped. 'No way! You hid it well.'

'I was happy that my plan had worked, eating one slice of banana was a small price to pay.'

'You are funny.' Merry regarded her for a long moment. 'It's been really tough for you watching my pregnancy develop, hasn't it?'

'The toughest thing ever,' Nell admitted. 'I was so happy for you but couldn't help thinking it was unfair that it wasn't happening for me too. Especially as you got pregnant as soon as you started trying. And I'd been secretly trying for ages. Don't tell Olek.'

Merry felt a pang of sadness that Nell hadn't told her any of this before. But they were here now, and if Nell wanted her to keep secrets, it was the least she could do. 'I'm so sorry about that. I kept on . . .' She hesitated, not knowing whether what she was about to say would make things better or worse for Nell. 'Nothing, it doesn't matter.'

'No, go on, because it obviously does matter,' Nell urged her. 'Today's the day we start being honest with each other again, get it all out in the open.'

'I kept wishing that you'd get pregnant too, so that we could both be going through the same thing.'

Nell sighed wistfully. 'One of the hardest things has been hearing you not being happy to be pregnant. Sometimes I've felt you've been a bit . . .'

'Go on. Honesty, remember?' Merry had a feeling she knew where this was going and already she felt the shame creeping in.

'OK, I'll say it.' Nell turned to face her properly. 'I have sometimes got the impression that you felt resentful towards Cole and even sometimes towards the baby.'

Merry thought carefully before speaking. She wanted to finally tell someone her fears, though she was scared that once she verbalised them, she could never take them back. But this was her chance to come clean, to tell the person she trusted implicitly.

'It came across as resentment, but, really, it was fear. I've been too scared to think about being a mum. What happens when the hospital says that I can go, leave the sanctuary of the ward with the experts at hand to tell me what to do? I'd been worried that if my mum hadn't loved me, then maybe I wouldn't love this baby either, that history would repeat itself. I started thinking that I was a terrible woman who didn't possess any maternal instincts. And the awful thing was I couldn't tell you because I knew how much you wanted to be a mum. I couldn't tell Cole because he'd probably freak out and wonder what sort of woman he'd married. So I let it fester.'

'Oh, darling.' Nell held out her arms and Merry sank into them. I wish I'd known. I wish I could have helped.'

Merry let out more tears. Ones which she'd been holding on to for months and months. Acknowledging her worst fears about herself had kept her from fully connecting with the baby she was carrying, and yet now she had, she felt a lightness in her chest, a feeling of joy that she'd been missing.

'You know what, Merry?'

She sat up straight and accepted a tissue to dry her eyes. 'What?'

'I think your mum's letter has found you at exactly the right time. It means more to you reading it now, when you're on the cusp of motherhood, than it ever would have done in the past.'

Merry nodded. 'Thank you, that is a brilliant thought. It's the confidence boost I need.'

'If she was here in person, that's exactly what she'd be doing: building you up and telling you that you'll be a fantastic mum.'

'She didn't have a good role model to learn her parenting skills from, but actually I did. So I'm the lucky one.' Merry winced. 'And talking about being lucky, I didn't appreciate how lucky I was to have you at Merry and Bright until it was too late.'

Nell's eyes glittered with tears. 'I was the lucky one. I loved working with you – well, until . . .'

'Until I turned into a Momzilla, as Freya called me?' Merry finished for her.

Nell sniggered. 'Possibly a bit.'

'Is it too late?' Merry held her breath. 'Because I'd really love you to come back.'

'Um.' Nell touched her finger to her lips and waggled her head from side to side, considering her offer. 'I've had another thought. Woody. He's between jobs at the moment, and he's been a real star at Merry and Bright.'

Merry's spirits sank; so she had left it too late. 'True. Yes, of course, he'd be a good replacement.'

'Not a replacement for me!' Nell gave a hoot of laughter. 'Maternity cover for *you*. The business needs two people, and before you jump down my throat and tell me that you'll be bringing the baby in with you and that maternity leave is for wimps—'

'So just back up a bit,' Merry held up a hand. 'Does this mean you're coming back?'

'Yes please.' Nell gave her a sheepish smile. 'I regret resigning. I acted impulsively and would really love to come back.'

'Thank God.' Merry groaned. 'Because I don't want to do this without you.'

'And Woody?'

'I've been a bit blinkered where maternity leave is concerned, worried what would happen in my absence. But when you left, and Dad died, I had no choice but to step away, and surprise, surprise, Woody has coped just fine without either of us.'

Nell grinned. 'Hallelujah! She's seen the light.'

Merry laughed. 'And more than that, I think I owe it to the baby and to myself to focus on being a mum when this little one finally arrives. So, if it's all right with you, I'll definitely be taking some time off.'

'Phew.' Nell flopped back on the sofa, pretending to faint, making Merry laugh again. 'Let's try to find some signal and call him before you change your mind.'

'OK, as long as we don't have to go out there,' said Merry, glancing outside at the gardens through the window. The snow hadn't let up and everything as far as the eye could see was covered in a white layer.

'Agreed, it doesn't look very pregnancy friendly.'

'I don't even fancy crossing the car park when we leave.'

'I've got an idea.' Nell's eyes narrowed mischievously.

Merry shook her head fondly. 'When haven't you? Can I just say that us being friends again was my Christmas wish.' She took hold of Nell's hand. 'So I've already got all I wanted and it's only Christmas Eve Eve. Thank you for making it come true.'

Nell wrapped her arms around her. 'Friends forever?'

'You bet.' Merry closed her eyes and savoured the moment. Husbands were great, but there was simply nothing like a hug from your best friend.

Chapter 41

Merry

It was just Braxton Hicks.

Merry breathed through the pain the way she'd been shown in antenatal class, trying to distract herself with thoughts of food. She was starving and breakfast couldn't come soon enough. She was going to have Greek yoghurt and berries and then possibly pancakes. The fluffy American ones with crispy bacon and maple syrup. If she had room – she wouldn't, she knew that – but if she did, she'd have smoked salmon and cream cheese on a bagel. She was eating for two, so it was allowed. She wouldn't be able to get away with that line for much longer, so it was important to make the most of it.

In the bed beside her, Nell's breathing was soft and light, interrupted every so often with a snore which roused her momentarily and occasionally a little noise which sounded like a giggle.

Merry smiled to herself. It was Christmas Eve. Her first wedding anniversary. Instead of waking up with her husband, she was with her best friend in a Superior King room at the Enchanted Spa.

The idea Nell had had was to book a room. They'd gone to reception together to check the availability. The snow had been coming down fast at the time and although it had stopped before they went to bed, Merry had been quite relieved to stay cosy and snug at the spa. There hadn't been any twin-bed rooms left, but it hadn't mattered. They'd shared a bed many a time over the years and the size of Merry now had made her think that she might have rolled out of a single bed anyway. She'd called Cole to make sure he didn't mind her extending her stay.

'Not at all!' He'd said it with such gusto that she wasn't sure whether to be a bit offended. 'That's a great idea and it'll give me time to, er . . .'

She'd gasped. 'Cole! You hadn't forgotten it was our anniversary by any chance, had you?'

She'd heard a hoot of laughter in the background which Cole had tried to muffle with coughing, which made her even more suspicious.

'I'm glad you and Nell are having a good time, and you're obviously relaxing, that's all,' he'd said. She'd heard his breathing and footsteps accelerate as if he was striding away from whoever was laughing. There was more than one voice, and she could hear music playing too. 'And how could anyone ever forget the day they married a gorgeous woman like you?'

'Are you having a party while I'm out?' she'd asked, not fooled by his distraction techniques.

'A party?' he'd exclaimed. 'I wish! I'm on site, trying to get this job finished for Christmas.'

It was on the tip of her tongue to say 'lucky them' to whoever the client was, but given that he was working while she was swanning around at a spa, she'd thought better of it. They had arranged that he'd come and pick them up in the morning and once he'd established that she could obtain any emergency toiletries she needed from the spa shop, he'd rung off.

She and Nell had booked a table for dinner in the restaurant last night and it had turned a lovely day into a very special treat. They'd relaxed and reminisced and talked and talked and talked until they'd fallen asleep sometime after midnight.

She'd slept soundly until this Braxton Hicks contraction had woken her up. Although she was uncomfortable now, the thought that she and Nell were back on track was a nice one.

Her pregnancy and Nell's disappointment at not becoming pregnant this year had driven a tiny wedge between them, creating the slightest fracture. She hadn't been aware of it at the time, but looking back, it was obvious. Over time, without looking after their relationship, the fracture had widened and deepened to the point where they'd lost sight of each other and almost reached breaking point. From the moment she'd discovered that she was pregnant, Merry had been conscious that she had to be sensitive to Nell's situation. She thought she'd done her best not to talk too much about the impending birth, or to moan about the morning sickness she'd suffered in the first trimester, knowing how Nell would have happily endured a bit of nausea if it meant having a baby at the end of it. But it had been this last trimester which had been the most damaging to their friendship.

It was clear to her now that she and Nell had both held back their innermost thoughts and true feelings about the things which mattered most to them. She had felt unable to confide in Nell that she was convinced she'd be a terrible mother, for fear of being thought badly of, or her secret making its way back to Cole. Nell had kept her test results secret from her because she was scared of it getting back to Olek. On top of all that, because Merry had been so used to guarding her independence, she'd struggled to accept help on all fronts, including the business. No wonder Nell had finally resigned and no wonder their friendship had been so badly damaged.

Merry closed her eyes and exhaled. At least that conundrum had been resolved and Nell had decided to stay after all.

All along, they'd had the power to mend the rift themselves. And yesterday they'd done it. Just words, simple words spoken with kindness and listened to with care, and miraculously the underlying love they had for each other had come shining through. Thank goodness. And so, for now, being here and sharing these few hours with her best friend was exactly where she wanted to be.

It had been a sort of date night for friends, this little break. They'd eaten delicious food cooked by someone else, then taken herbal tea to bed and watched a film chosen by Nell. A Richard Curtis film called *About Time*. A romcom at heart, like all their favourites. But the message of this one was to live every day with wonder, respect and curiosity. To treat each day, each person you love, as a gift. Do the good stuff now, rather than rush through life never taking time to savour it or spending time with those whose sheer existence lights up our world.

That includes you. Merry touched her bump, tracing the outline of a currently resting baby, with the palm of her hand. She thought about how she'd been reluctant to schedule in maternity leave and how now that Woody had agreed to stay on, she and Nell actually had a sensible plan that everyone could work with. Cole was going to be impressed; he loved a plan.

She smiled to herself, thinking how Cole had done his best (as had Fred, her father-in-law) to introduce her to spreadsheets and planning tools for her business. Merry, at heart, was a moment-to-moment sort of girl. Do today what made your heart happy was the way she ran her life. Now that the shop was taken care of, this wouldn't be a totally terrible way to approach motherhood. Perhaps being true to herself, trusting her own intuition, was the way to go. She could let her own moral compass be her guide.

And her own mum? What a gift that letter had been, what an incredible treasure. She would be indebted to Hilary Burgess for the rest of her life. Her mum, Sam, had been thinking of her, loving her, caring what happened to her, right until the end. Pure unconditional love. How lucky Merry had been to experience that, for however long her mother had been able to give it.

Merry felt her eyes grow heavy, she was drifting off to sleep again. Later, Cole would collect her from the spa and take her home to finally celebrate their anniversary.

She was grateful that he hadn't minded waking up alone this morning. It wouldn't have been the way he'd planned to spend their anniversary – if he'd planned anything at all, she mused, remembering his odd behaviour yesterday evening. Still, she didn't need an anniversary present to know that he also loved her unconditionally, as she loved him.

And I already love you too, little one, Merry thought, resting her hands on her tummy. Another hour and she'd get up for breakfast, but for now . . . Merry's face softened into a smile as sleep finally claimed her.

Chapter 42

Nell

'I don't think I've ever seen you eat as much food as you just put away at breakfast,' said Nell, dropping both her bag and Merry's in front of the reception desk. 'I feel as if I let the side down.'

'Eating for two, aren't I?' said Merry, puffing slightly. 'And I won't be able to get away with saying that for much longer.'

Nell shot her a look. She'd stopped asking if she was having contractions because Merry was so adamant that her pains were simply Braxton Hicks, that she knew the difference and that Nell should stop panicking, but it wasn't easy to relax when your best friend was obviously uncomfortable. She'd had a lovely time at the Enchanted Spa, but even so, she was quite relieved that she'd be handing responsibility for Merry's well-being over to Cole any moment.

It was only 9 a.m., but Merry had insisted on them being in the restaurant for breakfast as soon as it opened at seven-thirty. Now they were checking out and she could see Cole's truck pulled up right outside the doors so that Merry wouldn't have to walk across the snowy car park.

She'd made that trek herself last night to check her phone for messages. Nothing from Olek, but there had been a voicemail from Irena to say that she'd see them for Christmas Eve dinner and wishing them both a happy day. Nell hoped that her mother-in-law got what she wanted. She'd also had a message from Cole, which had been absolutely lovely and that she'd replied to instantly. He really was a catch, she was so pleased for Merry, and from what he had told her last night, Merry was going to be very pleased with her husband.

'Where's my gorgeous wife?' Cole asked now, striding across the foyer towards them. 'I need to wish her happy anniversary immediately.'

'Here!' Merry held her arms out to him and they hugged. 'Happy anniversary to you too.'

He dipped his mouth to hers and whispered something Nell didn't catch before kissing her.

'It's like Narnia out there in Wetherley,' said Cole. 'Mind you, so is the rest of the country. The north has had a real hit of snow.'

'Oh no!' Merry's eyes widened. 'Are the roads bad?'

'No. Not bad enough to keep me from the love of my life. And my truck will get us through anything. So have you two had a good time?' he asked, kissing Nell's cheek.

'The best,' Merry replied. 'Very relaxing.'

'And fun,' Nell agreed.

She hugged her best friend's husband, holding on to him for a long moment, at least ten seconds, but if Cole thought it had gone on too long, he was too polite to say so. Those ten seconds were filled with snapshots of Merry and Cole together, and Nell thought how fortunate she was to have had a front-row seat watching their love for each other unfold. Cole was perfect for Merry, just perfect. And he'd be the steadying presence she needed to help her navigate this new phase of life.

Nell released him and thought of Olek, the man who'd been the rock in her own life. She wasn't going to let this be the end, she was going to fight for their love with everything she had.

She blinked back the inevitable tears and smiled stoically. 'Get everything done?'

Cole nodded. 'Everything.'

Merry looked from Nell to Cole. 'What were you doing?'

'Wrapping your presents,' he said, stifling a yawn. 'A new vacuum cleaner and an ironing board takes a lot of paper, you know. Luckily, I think sleep is overrated.'

His wife grinned. 'Very funny. And let's hope you're still happy not to sleep when I make you share the night feeds.'

He took her hand and kissed it. 'Foot rubs, cups of tea, cuddles, you name it, I'll accept all of them.'

'You tease.' Merry gave him a playful nudge before pulling a face. 'Oof. Shall we go home? I've got something amazing to tell you.'

'Intriguing. And a very good plan.' Cole picked up her bag and kissed Nell's cheek again. 'Merry Christmas.'

Nell felt a flutter of panic; she didn't want to put the Robinsons to any trouble, but she did need a lift home. 'Erm . . . I don't suppose you'd be able to drop me off en route?'

'Of course we can!' Merry rolled her eyes at Cole.

Cole's gaze flicked to somewhere over Nell's shoulder so fleetingly that she almost missed it. But a sixth sense made her turn around. Sitting in an armchair, hidden behind a copy of *The Times* newspaper was a man. Her heart started to thud and, for a moment, time stood still as she drank him in.

She'd recognise those legs, those jeans and boots anywhere. The newspaper lowered and there he was, her handsome, wonderful man, his broad shoulders almost filling the armchair. He was wearing his down puffer jacket and the blue striped scarf Max had given him last Christmas. His face not giving anything away, but his eyes . . . Oh, how she'd missed looking into those beautiful blue eyes. He set aside the newspaper and got to his feet.

'Olek!' she gasped. 'What are you doing here, how did you . . .?'

Her feet took her towards him, and he stepped forward to meet her, standing so close she could smell his cologne, feel the warmth of his breath and the cold radiating from his jacket.

'Nell.' His eyes locked on her as if she was the only person in the world. 'Sorry I didn't reply to your messages, I've been stuck in the snow, and I didn't have any signal, then my phone ran out of charge.' He batted a hand dismissively. 'Long story.'

'It's so good to see you.' Was she allowed to touch him? Kiss him? How did he feel about her? She wished he'd say something.

'You too,' he murmured.

She felt something inside her shift, a flame of hope ignite, a determination to not waste this moment, to be honest and true.

'I'm glad, and I'm so, so sorry for everything.' She swallowed the lump in her throat. 'For lying to you about the test results, and not telling you that I'd had a termination when I was younger.'

Mostly, she wanted to tell him how much she loved him, but did he still love her, *could* he still love her after what she'd done? Her pulse raced erratically as she watched him digest her words, willing him to forgive her.

'I thought we didn't have secrets from each other,' he replied, as he shoved his hands in his pockets, and she heard the jingle of his car keys. 'I thought that was something other couples did. Not us. You really hurt me, Nell.'

'I know, I know.' Tears streamed down her face, but she didn't have the energy to wipe them away. Her arms hung loosely by her sides; they'd never felt so empty. She had to hold herself back from burying her face in his neck. 'I have so many regrets.'

'Don't cry.' Olek touched her face, wiping her tears with his thumb. 'I've missed you.'

Thank you, thank you, thank you. 'And I've missed you,' she replied.

He wrapped his arms around her, holding her close, and she felt his body against hers. The cold fabric of his coat was a sharp contrast to the warmth of her hoodie. She slid her arms under his jacket, resting her cheek against his chest, and closed her eyes.

'I'm sorry,' he whispered, his breath warm in her ear. 'For walking out on us and for not keeping in touch. Not staying to work it out. But I had a lot to process and needed to work out how I felt about the whole situation first. And come to terms with this new version of the last sixteen years.'

'It's all right, I understand.' She smiled nervously up at him, willing him to understand her side in return, why she'd done what she had.

She held on to him and felt his embrace strengthen to match hers, his body soften. Their hug felt affirming and hopeful, and she didn't want it to end.

'Sorry to interrupt. We're going to go.' Merry's face looked pinched.

'You OK?' Nell asked her.

'Always OK. Good luck.' Merry kissed Olek, and Cole shook his hand.

'Thank you,' said Nell, 'and thanks for a lovely time. Speak tomorrow?'

'On Christmas Day? Of course!' Merry replied.

Nell and Olek waved the Robinsons off and then kissed each other.

Nell heard a few gasps and 'ahhhs' around them. Quite honestly, their kissing was probably a little too much for the foyer of the Enchanted Spa, but it was Christmas Eve perhaps everyone was feeling a bit festive and happy to watch something so clearly romantic.

They kissed again, both of them hungry for each other, making up for the days and nights they'd been apart. And when Olek finished their kiss by lifting her off the ground and twirling her around, everyone whistled and clapped.

'And now I would very much like to go home with you,' he said, lowering her back down.

The thought of being together again, in their own house, with no secrets between them, filled Nell with joy. 'I'd like that too.'

'Then let's go home, baby.' He scooped up her bag and held out his hand to her.

Together they walked out of the spa and headed into the white Christmas which greeted them. Nell knew they still had a lot of talking to do, they still had to clear the air and sort a lot of things out, but, for now, this moment on Christmas Eve was perfect. Absolutely perfect.

Chapter 43

Merry

As Cole had predicted, the roads around the Enchanted Spa were perfectly passable and soon they had left the Derbyshire countryside behind and were approaching Wetherley again. Merry had spent the journey alternating between gripping the handle of the passenger door to help her breathe through her pains and bringing him up to speed with the last twenty-four hours. First, her joyous reunion with Nell, which would have been news enough, but also the incredible letter that Hilary had found from her mother.

'It's made me feel more confident about becoming a mum,' Merry explained, folding the letter from her mother back up into the envelope. 'I'm not sure whether maternal instincts are genetic or not, but if they are, the fact that Mum really loved me is a good thing. Perhaps I'll be a better mother than I thought I'd be.'

'Oh, darling.' Cole pulled over into a layby, put on the brake and leaned across the gearstick to cup her face in his warm hands. 'This is fantastic news, although I already had full confidence that you'll be a wonderful mother.'

'These are happy tears, in case you were wondering,' she said with a sniff. 'Last year on our wedding day, Dad gave me a ring which should have belonged to her, and now I've got this letter in her handwriting. I feel, I feel . . .' She broke off to breathe, because it was quite difficult to distil her emotions into a single sentence at the best of times and also because she could feel another Braxton Hicks contraction on its way.

'There are so many things I want to say to you.' His brown eyes shone with love. 'I hardly know where to start. I'm happy that your mum wrote to you, and I'm extremely happy that her letter has finally found its way into your hands. But the rest of it, you doubting yourself, that has blown my mind. I can't believe that's how you felt.'

She gave him a sheepish look. 'I should have told you a long time ago how worried I was, but you've always seemed so sure of yourself where parenting is concerned. I didn't want you to think you'd made a bad choice when it came to life partners. You've been here before, you know what to expect, and, on top of that, your childhood was textbook perfect. I have felt terribly lacking on all fronts.'

He nodded. 'Life was relatively trauma-free growing up, and I had two loving parents. You grew up without those guiding forces in your life and yet you're still one of the most loving, kind and thoughtful people I know. Plus, you're the toughest cookie I've ever met. Which is why I know you will be an incredible role model and mother for our child, and, in fact, you already are for your stepchildren.'

'Thank—' She was interrupted by her stomach tensing and puffed her cheeks out. One hand still holding the letter, the other one gripping the door handle, her feet braced against the floor of the truck. 'That was a tough one.'

'Bloody hell.' Cole's eyes widened. 'Should we be heading to the hospital?'

'No need,' Merry said through gritted teeth. 'I've been timing them, they're just Braxton Hicks.'

'O-K.' He didn't sound convinced, but checked the traffic was clear and rejoined the road.

Soon, she was clear of pain and able to focus again. She tuned into their location just as they zipped past the junction they usually headed off at to get to Holly Cottage. 'Shouldn't we have turned left there?'

'Hmm.' Cole stared ahead. 'I just need to call in at the new house, I'm not sure the electricians will have locked up properly yesterday.'

'All right.' Merry bit her lip. She may have not been entirely truthful with him. That last one felt more intense; it could be that she was now in labour. She tried to remember what she'd learned in the antenatal class, but all she could think about was that she'd unpacked her hospital bag before the spa day and was worried that she wouldn't have time to repack it. But no need to panic, it would be fine. Cole could check the door, get back in the truck and they'd be on their way again in minutes. The main thing was to stay calm.

'It'll be worth the detour, I promise.'

Her heart lifted as soon as Meadow View came into sight. 'Oh, I do love this road, and our house is so pretty.'

Cole grinned. 'I have to say it, darling. I'm glad you made me take so long to settle on the right property. You were right to be so fussy.'

'I prefer to think of myself as having high standards . . . Oh—' She stared at their new home, something was different about it. 'Cole? What's going on?'

There were Christmas lights at every window. And in the front room – a Christmas tree? And cars on the drive, cars she recognised.

He stopped the engine, jumped out and came around to her side to open her door. 'Shall we go in and see?'

'Me? But—' she stuttered, highly confused as the front door flew open and Freya burst out, running down the drive to greet them, Harley sauntering behind her.

'Finally!' Freya yelled, waving her arms above her head. 'We've been waiting for ages.'

'This is a nice surprise!' Merry called, swivelling herself around in preparation for climbing out of the van. 'What are you doing here?'

The little girl looked as if she was about to burst with news. 'We—

Harley sneaked up behind his sister and put a hand quickly over her mouth. 'It's a surprise.'

'I see,' said Merry, who didn't at all.

While Cole helped her out of the truck, a crowd of familiar people appeared in the front-room window beside the Christmas tree. Will and Emily, Astrid and Fred, even Hester and Paul, who she'd thought were still in Australia, all with faces wreathed in smiles and waving enthusiastically.

'Everyone's here!' she gasped. 'I thought we were checking the house had been locked up?'

'I might have told a small untruth there. Welcome home, darling,' he murmured in her ear.

She looked at him bemused. Home? Did that mean . . . Had he . . .? She was awash with questions, but all that came out was, 'Oh.'

'It's not often you're stuck for words.' He kissed her, laughing as he led her up the path to the front door.

The driveway had been cleared of snow, but Merry was very wary of slipping on an icy patch and clung on to him with both arms.

'It's completely bamboozled,' she marvelled. 'And when you say home . . .?'

Freya's eyes were bright with excitement. 'Please hurry up, I can't bear it!'

'This snow is so cool.' Harley kicked his foot at a shrub weighed down under a covering of snow, sending a shower of icy flakes into the air. 'So, technically speaking, we got our Christmas wish a day early.'

'Except I asked for other stuff too,' said Freya. 'But this is still quite good.'

Cole helped Merry out of the snowy garden, up the front step and into the house. 'I'd carry you over the threshold, but I'm not sure that would be good for either of us.'

'Rude,' she replied and then sighed as a cosy waft of warmth enveloped her.

Merry thought her heart might explode with joy as she gazed down to the end of the hallway as far as the kitchen. The last time she'd been here it had still felt like a building site.

Now, under her feet was the rug she'd had rolled up in the spare room for ages. Familiar pictures hung on the walls where previously there'd been exposed wires. This was home. It looked like home, and it felt like home, and somewhere there must be some of her own Merry and Bright Winter Wonderland candles burning, because it even smelled like home too.

'Surprise!' Emily yelled, appearing from the front room. 'Come on through, everyone's waiting for you.'

'So you organised not only a spa day, but this too?' Merry looked from her sister to Cole, overwhelmed with love and gratitude.

'We wanted to get you moved in without you knowing,' said Emily, rushing forward to hug her.

'Thank you, thank you.' Merry kissed her cheek; her biological half-sister's cheek, she realised with a jolt. 'You're the best sister in the world.'

'Or without you needing to lift a finger, darling.' Cole edged her forward into the front room, their dining room.

'And in time for Christmas,' added Astrid, pouring tea out from a pot into several mugs. 'Happy anniversary, *Liebling*, and a happy Christmas too.'

Her sister-and brother-in-law, Hester and Paul, sporting antipodean tans, beamed at her. Freya was already halfway through a chocolate pastry. Harley was setting Christmas music to play on Alexa via his smartphone, while Fred and Will both tended the fire, with tongs and a poker respectively.

'Oh my goodness,' Merry exclaimed, dabbing tears from her eyes. 'You're all amazing.'

This room had been a cold and empty shell last time she was here. Now logs burned cheerily in the open fireplace and a table laden with pastries and tea and coffee pots formed the centrepiece to the space.

'G'day, girl,' said Hester, affecting a terrible accent. 'Betcha shocked to see us?'

'I am.' Merry ambled hazily towards them and kissed their cheeks. 'I'm shocked about everything right now.'

'Christmas in Oz just wasn't Christmas,' said Paul.

'Yeah, and who'd want to be surfing on Bondi Beach, when they could be here loading and unloading boxes in knee-deep snow, eh?' Cole slapped his brother-in-law on the back.

'We wanted to be here, with family,' said Hester softly. 'We missed you all.'

'Can we all have a sit-down now?' Fred said, pretending to mop his brow. 'It's been non-stop since yesterday morning.'

'I've done the Wi-Fi router and set up Alexa in all the rooms,' said Harley.

'I've made the bed myself in my room,' Freya chimed in.

'Thank you,' Merry's stomach tightened again, and she braced herself for another contraction. 'Excuse me a second. I'm a bit overcome.'

She hurried to the door, trying to get out of sight before the pain took hold, but Cole had decided to follow her.

'Happy?' he said, catching hold of her hand. 'I wanted to make our first anniversary extra special.'

'Thank you, darling.' Merry blinked at him, jaw clenched. 'It was always going to be special, but to be in our house for Christmas . . . it's more than I could have dreamed of.'

'Ready for one more surprise?' he asked, looking very pleased with himself.

'Absolutely,' she managed to squeak out.

'Then follow me upstairs, darling.' He waggled an eyebrow and held her hand up the stairs.

Once they were on the first floor, she expected him to open their bedroom door, but instead he led her along the landing and pushed open the door to the nursery.

'Oh, Cole.' Merry pressed a hand to her heart.

This was the room she had dreamed of for her baby. The last time she had seen the cot, it has still been in its flat-packed box. Now it was ready for their baby: with soft pastel sheets and blankets patterned with baby animals, and over it a mobile hung with rockets, planets and stars which sparkled when the light caught them. At the windows hung the roman blinds she had chosen, a bookcase displayed the set of Mr Men and Little Miss books she'd found at auction and there was a changing station, wardrobe and a set of drawers that she'd seen online but only mentioned in passing to Cole.

'Happy?' he murmured, standing behind her and encircling her in his arms.

'Darling, I couldn't be happier.' She turned to kiss him. 'This room is everything I imagined and more. I love you.'

'I love you too. I promised I'd have you in our new home before the baby came,' he grinned. 'And for a while I didn't think I'd make it.'

'Home,' she breathed. 'We're finally home. Did you hear that, baby? Mummy and Daddy are ready for you.'

He laughed. 'Technically, we are, but I'd rather—'

'Oof.' She gave him a crooked smile as another contraction hit. They were getting worse. This one felt as if she was being strapped into a steel corset. She was going to need pain relief imminently. 'Four minutes.'

Cole's jaw dropped and he pulled back to look at her. 'Not until the baby comes, surely?'

She giggled despite the pain. 'No, between contractions. Cole, I think this baby is as keen to see its new room as I was.'

'OK.' He ran a hand through his hair. 'Maternity hospital. In the snow. Right now. Bloody hell.'

She leaned her head on his chest. Her hands gripping his arms. She puffed out her cheeks and blew rapidly. Once the worst of it was over, he helped her navigate the stairs.

Freya bounded up to them, brushing pastry crumbs from her lips. 'My room is smaller than Harley's, but when he leaves home, can I swap?'

'Of course,' Merry panted.

'Cool. Harley?' To Merry's relief, she went off to tell her brother.

'Let's go.' Cole poked his head into the front room on the way past. 'Merry has gone into labour, we'll see you later.'

His announcement was met with noisy replies, and they all scampered out to the truck to wave them off.

Emily squealed. 'I'm about to be an auntie. On Christmas Eve.' She dashed forward clumsily to hug Merry. 'Dad would be so proud. I love you.'

'Love you too,' Merry grunted, 'but can you get off my toe.'

'Oops.'

'Righto,' Fred bellowed. 'Everyone keep calm! Do you need any cash, son? For the car park. Or a cup of tea. Course you don't. Best of luck with it, Merry.'

'Every time you see me, you need to be hospitalised,' Hester teased. 'I'm going to get a complex.'

'Good grief,' spluttered Will. 'I've heard of the expression new house, new baby, but this takes the biscuit.'

'Or the mince pie, in this case,' Fred chuckled.

'Be a girl!' Freya held up her crossed fingers and squeezed her eyes tightly shut. 'A girl!'

'Don't be as annoying as this girl,' Harley sniggered, copying his sister's body language and crossing his fingers.

'Breathwork,' Paul said earnestly. 'Stay in control of your body through the breath.'

Merry grimaced. 'Thanks, Paul, but I'll be taking all the drugs. Someone else can control this situation for a few hours.'

Astrid kissed both her cheeks. 'I can't wait to meet your baby, *mein Schatz*. And make sure you take lots of photos as soon as it's born.'

'Enough chatter,' said Cole, helping her into the truck. 'See you later, everyone.'

'My hospital bag!' Merry gasped, gripping his hand. 'I'm not giving birth without it.'

'Don't worry. It's already in the truck, behind the passenger seat,' he said with a hint of pride.

'Of course it is. And that is why I love you.'

'I'm a planner, remember. I was going to take it everywhere with us until your induction date.'

She leaned back hard against the seat, bracing herself with her hands. 'I'm not sure this baby of yours got the memo about waiting for induction day,' she panted. 'This one might have my more spontaneous attitude to life.'

As Cole started the engine and reversed off the drive, everyone in the house waved and shouted their goodbyes from the doorstep.

'If it puts your mind at rest,' said Cole, accelerating cautiously along the road, 'I've watched a YouTube video of a birth happening in the car on the way to the hospital. It worked out well and the father even managed to cut the umbilical cord.'

'Thank you.' Merry shuddered and laughed despite the rising panic. She crossed her legs with great difficulty. 'I think that image has effectively temporarily halted labour.'

He chuckled. 'I love you, Mrs Robinson.'

'I love you, Mr Robinson,' she replied, 'and I'll love you even more if you can get me to hospital without needing to rewatch that YouTube video.'

Chapter 44

Nell

Nell could hardly contain her excitement. It was Christmas Eve and everything in her world was suddenly looking so much brighter than it had twenty-four hours ago.

She wouldn't class herself as a football fan in the least, but despite there only being a couple of hundred people there (friends, family, coaches and scouts), the atmosphere at the Anfield ground in Liverpool was electric and seeing her stepson down there running up and down like a gazelle was very exciting. But even more thrilling than that was watching the expression of pure pride on Olek's face as he watched Max display his incredible talent on the pitch. She was holding Olek's hand, and his attention veered regularly from intense focus on his son to making sure she was warm and cosy under the blanket he'd brought for her knees. And as if this wasn't enough joy for Nell to contend with for one day, Merry and Cole were in the labour ward at Wetherley Maternity unit awaiting the arrival of their baby! She glanced at her phone again in case of updates. Nothing new.

'Look at my boy.' Olek squeezed her hand and whistled appreciatively. 'If he doesn't get man of the match, I'll be having words with the coach.'

Nell adjusted her new Derby County hat and shot him a stern look. 'You'll do no such thing; Max will be mortified. Tell your son how fabulously he played, that will be quite enough.'

It warmed her heart to hear him refer to Max as his boy. Of course he was his boy and always would be. Nothing could ever change the bond between them.

'You're right, of course,' he replied meekly. 'You're always right.'

She leaned her head against him. 'No I'm not, I've made some terrible mistakes these past few weeks.'

He gave her a kiss. 'So did I, baby, so did I.'

'We're going to be OK, though, aren't we?' She looked into the face of the only man she'd ever really loved.

'We are going to be much better than OK.' He wrapped his arm around her waist, and she settled into him, thinking that there was absolutely nowhere on the planet she'd rather be.

One of the Liverpool players was on the ground and the game stopped while he received some medical attention.

'Olek?' she murmured, kissing him on his neck where she knew it drove him wild. 'I lied because I love you, you know. Because I thought me being infertile would be easier on you. When Dr Bajek said that my results showed no issues and yours did, I panicked. My mind flew straight to Max. The tests were supposed to help us to move on with our future, the last thing I expected, or wanted, was for them to dig up the past. I was trying to protect you from all that.'

Love for her flared in his eyes. 'I understand that now, but at the time it was hard to accept. And then when I found out about the termination you had, the sum of the two things felt much worse. Merry said that you hadn't hidden it at the time and assumed that I knew about it, but you'd never mentioned it.'

She exhaled, letting her mind float back to those exciting days and weeks when their romance had just begun. She'd been obsessed with him, had hardly been able to eat or sleep for thinking about him. She'd had lots of boyfriends before meeting Olek, but compared with her exes, he had felt in a different league, a proper grown-up man. Someone she trusted and wanted to impress. 'When I met you, you seemed so worldly-wise and mature. You'd come out of a marriage; you were a father clearly besotted with his son. I was worried that I'd come across as immature and irresponsible if I told you the truth. I didn't want to give you any reasons not to like me. So I decided not to mention it, that was all.'

He lifted her hand to his lips and kissed it, his expression unreadable.

'Say something,' she whispered. 'Please.'

'I had a call with Dr Bajek a few days ago and I've had the results for myself.' He twisted her wedding ring around on her finger. 'My sperm count is zero, Nell. It has been such a shock to get my head around, but it was important that I knew. It's my body, I deserve the truth.'

'I'm so sorry,' she said hoarsely. 'I thought I was doing the right thing, I really did. And once I'd lied, I had to follow along with it.'

'I had a lot of anger inside me that needed to come out.' He gave her a cheeky smile. 'It's out now. At least the worst of it.'

'Where have you been since you left home?' Nell laced her fingers through his.

'My uncle Marek has a fishing cabin in Scotland. I spent the days walking up hills and yelling at trees.'

'Your mum thought you might be there.' She understood his need for solitude, but how sad that he'd felt he needed to work through it by himself. 'Sounds lonely.'

'It was. It snowed a lot and when it wasn't snowing, there was thick fog which froze my extremities. But, worst of all, you weren't there. Eventually, I realised that the only way I was going to be able to move through this is by doing it with you. By talking about it.'

'Agreed. I've avoided talking to you, scared that I'd blurt out the truth. I couldn't talk to Merry about it either in case she said anything to you. The only person I felt able to talk to was Woody.'

'The Airbnb man?' Olek's face darkened.

'Yes. He and I confided in each other on the night I didn't come home. He and his husband had been expecting a baby via a surrogate, but the mother miscarried at twenty-eight weeks. He's grieving not only his baby, but the life as a father he thought would soon be his.'

'I . . . I . . .' Olek coughed and shook his head. 'I can imagine how hard that must be.'

'When it's something we want so deeply, it hurts when it's taken away from us.' Nell's heart ached for him; her big gruff husband was tender and loving, but when it came to expressing his own emotions, words sometimes failed him. He'd be thinking of Max and reflecting on sixteen years of being a father to a boy who might not be his.

'And what about you, Nell? Having a baby means the world to you.'

She thought carefully before responding. 'It's something I became a bit obsessed with. The longer we didn't conceive, the more it occupied my mind, that's true. But it's not my world. It's you who are my world. Yes, I'd have liked us to have a baby, but being a family, being a Dowmunt, means even more to me.'

'For me too,' Olek whispered.

They kissed again, and Nell felt desire building in the pit of her stomach for this gorgeous man. She felt like a teenager again. She hooked her leg over his and shivered as he ran a hand down her spine.

After their mouths parted, Olek stroked her cheek. 'I spoke to Dr Bajek about our options. There are many ways of building family other than biologically.'

Her heart began to race; this was a conversation she'd thought would never happen. How foolish she'd been to think that Olek couldn't handle the truth. 'There are. But the most important thing is that both the parents are happy with their choices.'

'By not telling me the truth, you removed my chance to choose, but you also removed your own chance too.'

'Because to tell you the truth would have made you wonder about Max, and I know it's happened anyway, but at the time, that was what I cared about most.'

'And that is what I love about you, Nell. Throughout all of this, my hurt and anger and shock about you, our fertility investigation, Yvonna and Max, that thought has sustained me. The fact that you loved me enough to sacrifice your own happiness.'

'I do. When you're happy, I'm happy,' she said simply.

'Likewise.' He kissed her nose.

'How do you feel about Max?'

He let out a deep sigh. 'I've asked Yvonna to meet me next week. I want answers. But as far as I'm concerned, nothing needs to change. I'll always think of Max as my son. And as long as he wants me to be his father, I'll be proud to be so.'

'And I'm proud of you, darling.'

The crowd cheered and applauded as the ball was kicked back into play and the game continued.

Olek's attention was recaptured by the football match and for a moment, Nell just looked at her husband, suffused with love for him.

'Hey,' she whispered in his ear. 'There is an expression that says that anyone can be a father, but it takes someone special to be a dad.'

He grinned. 'I like that. And I think it applies to mothers too in a way. I know you love Max, but I also know how much more love you have to give.' He kissed her lips. 'And so do I. So if it was something you might like to consider, I was wondering whether adoption might be an option for us.'

A lump formed in her throat so that she couldn't speak. She nodded instead, aware that warm tears were trickling down her cold face. As Woody had said, there were so many children looking for a family to belong to. She and Olek could be that family, could share their love, their home, with a child who needed it.

Finally, she found her voice. 'When I got our test results, I assumed it was the end of our dream of having a family together.'

'Absolutely not, Nellie,' he said, pulling her close. 'This is just the start.'

'I love you, Olek Dowmunt.'

'Love you too.'

They kissed again, not caring that the men behind them were laughing about the two of them being lovebirds. Suddenly, Nell became aware that her phone was ringing.

She gasped, seeing Cole's name on the screen, and answered it with shaky hands. 'Cole! How's things, what's happened?'

'Everything's brilliant!' he cried. 'Fantastic, in fact. The baby has arrived and Merry was incredible. We've had a little—'

'Goal!' Beside her, Olek leapt to his feet, shouting at the top of his voice, drowning out Cole's news. 'Max has scored. Oh my Lord. My son, everyone! My son has scored a goal! He'll be playing for England in five years' time, you watch.'

Nell laughed, pressed the phone to her ear tightly and blocked her other ear with her hand. 'I'm delighted for you, I really am. Kiss them both from me and we'll see you soon.'

She ended the call, happy tears streaming down her face. This was the absolute best Christmas ever.

A Letter From Mummy

Dearest darling child,

And so you're here. And I feel like the luckiest mummy in the world. You are perfect. From those tiny fingers which already have a very assertive grip (good for you!) to your delicious little toes – so delicious in fact that your daddy has pretended to munch them on more than one occasion. Your face is so beautiful that this morning an hour slipped by with me and Daddy just holding you and marvelling at how we managed to create such a perfect little cherub between us. Your tiny rosebud lips, and your little bottom, even the midwives have commented on how cute you are!

I recognised you straight away as mine, you know. That thick shock of blonde hair which has just a hint of your daddy's russet glow when it catches the light. And those blue eyes. I know all babies have blue eyes, but yours are so like mine, when you look at me still scrunched up and unfocused, it feels a little bit like mini me is looking back at me. I've spent months wondering about you and then as soon as you were born, I thought, oh yes, of course that's what you look like. It was as if I recognised you already.

Today we had our first bath together. (If you're fifteen and reading this, I apologise wholeheartedly, but right now, you're only two days old and you LOVED it!) I'd heard all the stories on the maternity ward about babies pooing in the bath and I must admit I was ready to leap out at the first sign of that. Fortunately, your bowels behaved – as did mine, you'll be relieved to know.

We brought you home this afternoon. It's Boxing Day and the lovely thing is that it's not only your first night at Meadow View, it's Mummy and Daddy's too! I'm so happy that you have a lovely place to call home. But it's not just about the house, it's about the love that lives here. I will do everything in my power to give you the very best childhood I can. I'll always be here for you, darling, always. You can wake me up in the middle of the night (like last night – not once, but four times), you can cry when I try to put you down and I'll probably give in and carry you around for the next two years. You will probably get away with anything because all I have to do is look at you and my heart melts.

We are going to have such fun together, and you will love your big sister and brother, who already adore you. And I hope you will always love your name as much as I do.

Rae Astrid Eleanor, welcome to the Robinson family, my darling girl.

Love, always,

Mummy xxxx

A Letter From Your Potential New Mum, Nell

Dear Felix,

I am so excited to meet you. You are the most beautiful boy I have ever seen. Possibly the most beautiful child in the world. So far, I have only seen your photograph, but already I love you with all my heart. What a journey you have been on in your little life already, my angel. And yet your smile shines like the sun. I will never know everything that you have experienced in the past four years, but now your journey will cross paths with ours and if it all works out, we will continue together as a family – you, me, Olek and Max, your big half-brother. You will never be alone again, you will be loved and cherished and I hope you will love us too.

The past few weeks have been agony, waiting to jump over all the hurdles, going to the meetings and approval panels, filling out endless forms, answering hundreds of questions, all the while knowing that there are other parents who have no doubt fallen in love with you too. But I know that as soon as I get to hold you in my arms for the first time, all of that will disappear and it will have been worth it.

I'm staying calm at the moment, not wanting to get too excited in case something goes wrong. Soon, we'll be introduced in real life and then the panic will start. Will you like us, will something go wrong, maybe you aren't meant to be ours after all?

But, darling boy, all I know now is that when I look at your picture, and I see your dark-brown curls and those startling blue eyes, it feels as if my heart has been waiting to love you and that it is only a matter of time before you come home with us and I'll be your mum. Until then, my sweet boy, I'm thinking of you, and when you go to sleep at night, I'll be wishing you sweet dreams.

Lots of love,

Your new (potential) Mum xxx

Acknowledgements

The Thank Yous!

It's hard to believe it but A Merry Little Christmas is the seventeenth novel of mine to be published and, as ever I couldn't have done it without an enormous amount of help. Some very special people have assisted with this book's storylines: Olivia Atkinson for teaching me about football, Issy Bourton who helped me with Merry's pregnancy story, Joe Deane, and Bobsie and Dickie Hallam for their amusing incidents involving escaped birds, Alex Brown and Nikki Morris who kindly gave me their insight into the adoption process. And finally my thanks to Gina Bajek for her medical advice regarding mumps and infertility. Thank you to all of you for your time and help. Mistakes, inaccuracies and artistic licence are all mine.

To my agent, Sheila Crowley, you are such a source of strength and wisdom, I'm very grateful to have you on my team. Thank you for all that you do for me. And talking of teams, I am eminently thankful to be published by a wonderfully talented bunch of professionals at Orion. Thank you to my indomitable editor, Sam Eades for your boundless enthusiasm and for always making me feel special. To Anna Valentine for championing my publishing and for your much valued friendship. To Frankie Banks, Sian Baldwin and Sandra Taylor for top-notch publicity, Sister

Paul for your audiobook expertise, Victoria Laws for your consistently amazing selling skills, Lindsay Terrell and Hennah Sandhu for your creative marketing campaigns, Snigdha Koirala and Sanah Ahmed for your editorial support and Rachael Lancaster for designing this beautiful cover.

Two very important people who deserve a special mention: Jon who has brought so much fun and love into my life, thank you. I've got a feeling that you might recognise some of your own words on the pages of this book; and Broom, thank you for everything, from boosting morale, and keeping me on track to brainstorming plot ideas, I'm glad you're my work wife. I love you both.

And finally, a big thank you to my readers who have been following Merry since The Merry Christmas Project and the booksellers and book reviewers who help my books to reach their audience. Without you, there wouldn't have been a second or a third book in the series, I really don't take your support for granted. Thank you so much for sticking with me!

With love and best wishes

Cathy xxx

Credits

Cathy Bramley and Orion Fiction would like to thank everyone at Orion who worked on the publication of A Merry Litte Christmas in the UK.

Editorial
Sam Eades
Snigdha Koirala
Brittany Golob

Copy editor
Sally Partington

Proof reader
Jade Craddock

Audio
Paul Stark
Louise Richardson

Contracts
Dan Herron
Ellie Bowker
Oliver Chacón

Design
Rachael Lancaster

Editorial Management
Charlie Panayiotou
Jane Hughes
Bartley Shaw

Finance
Jasdip Nandra
Nick Gibson
Sue Baker

Marketing
Hennah Sandhu
Lindsay Terrell

Production
Ruth Sharvell

Publicity
Sarah Lundy
Sian Baldwin

Sales
Catherine Worsley
Esther Waters
Victoria Laws
Toluwalope Ayo-Ajala
Rachael Hum
Ellie Kyrke-Smith
Frances Doyle
Georgina Cutler

Operations
Jo Jacobs

If you loved *A Merry Little Christmas*, then don't miss more Christmas cheer from Cathy Bramley!

Christmas has always meant something special to Merry – even without a family of her own. This year, her heart might be broken but her new candle business is booming. The last thing she needs is another project – but when her hometown's annual event needs some fresh festive inspiration, Merry can't resist.

Cole loves a project too – though it's usually of the bricks and mortar variety. As a single dad, his Christmas wish is to see his kids again, so getting the new house finished for when they're all together is the perfect distraction.

But this Christmas, magic is in the air for these two strangers. Will it bring them all the joy they planned for . . . and take their hearts by surprise too?

After all, anything can happen at Christmas . . .

ORDER NOW

In picturesque town in Derbyshire, Merry has always wanted a family to spend Christmas with, and this year her dream comes true as she says 'I do' to father-of-two Cole. But as she juggles worries about her business, last-minute wedding planning and the two new children in her life, Merry is stretched to breaking point.

Meanwhile, only a few miles away, Emily is desperately waiting for the New Year to begin. Her father Ray's dementia is worsening, and she's struggling to care for him alone while holding down a job. When Ray moves into a residential home, she discovers a photograph in his belongings that has the potential to change everything .

As shocking secrets from Ray's past finally come to light, will this Christmas make or break Emily and Merry?

ORDER NOW